THE
THIRD
FRIDAY

ALSO BY George Bellak
Come, Jericho

THE THIRD FRIDAY

a novel of suspense

George Bellak

William Morrow and Company, Inc.
New York

Library of Congress Cataloging-in-Publication Data

Bellak, George (George J.)
    The third Friday : a novel of suspense / George Bellak.
        p.   cm.
    ISBN 0-688-04399-2
    I. Title.
    PS3552.E5317T47   1988
    813'.54—dc19   87-31251
                                                             CIP

Printed in the United States of America

First Edition

1 2 3 4 5 6 7 8 9 10

BOOK DESIGN BY CATHY AISON

This book is for SWB,
who survived its making with grace,
and for PG,
who always believed it.

THE
THIRD
FRIDAY

1

As he fell, the man's body, hurtling down, tumbled clumsily through the heavy summer air. Its arms flailed helplessly, and the hands reached out to clutch at the nothingness surrounding them. For one long moment, he was on his back, looking up with rage and panic toward the terrace and the shattered railing above. Suddenly, the head jerked back with the force of the fall and the legs kicked wildly. Then, abruptly, the body ceased its struggle. Everything seemed to stop, the wind, his motion, the whooshing sound. The mouth opened in a final silent incantation. The eyes closed to blackness. The hands unclenched. Three seconds later, on this third Friday in July, he hit the pavement.

Max was sleeping when the phone beeped its electronic tune. It was an old dream, the one where he had the ancient quarrel with his mother. Adeline was in her Miami condo kitchen in her usual sundress with the Murray Space Shoes of yesteryear—God, those old, solid plastic clunkers that made her feet appear as though she were walking in molded mud. Did anyone wear those anymore except seventy-year-old, unreconstructed anarchist-socialist mothers from the ancient lefty Bronx co-op apartments that everyone called simply "the coops"?

"So," she was saying for the hundredth time, "what did I do so wrong that my only child becomes a Wall Street bloodsucker? It's like God is giving me some kind of punishment and I don't even believe there *is* a God!" She was coming toward him, in slow dream motion, putting the iced tea on the Danish teakwood table, a plump figure with gray hair defiantly long and tied with a red ribbon at the back, her once-burning eyes now only a little dulled by the decades. "Max, tell me what I did?"

In the cloud of his dream, Max squirmed in his chair, as always. His eyes, not unlike hers except for the intensity, rolled in his head and his right hand went instinctively to his hair, swiping across it in frustration and love. "Give me a break," he pleaded. "I don't suck anyone's blood. I'm part of mainstream America."

"Stop talking like *Time* magazine," his mother was shouting, when he heard the song as though from another world. He groped, found the instrument, and rasped, "Hello."

"I'm sorry to wake you this time of the morning," a male voice, calm and reasonable, said. "Are you Max Roberts?"

"Yes." He came totally awake suddenly and only later did he realize he had had a premonition.

"You related to a Cy Bannerman?"

"I'm not related, no. Why?"

"Are you his lawyer?"

"I'm his partner, business partner. What is this?"

"I'm sorry to have to tell you this but Mr. Bannerman's dead."

"What?" It didn't register because it was impossible.

"We found your name in a 'notify in case of accident' policy in his desk."

"What did you say?"

"Mr. Roberts." The voice was patient, experienced. "Your partner fell from his terrace about an hour ago. This is Detective Shamski, thirty-third precinct. The doorman called us."

Max sat up and a slight sweat broke out on his forehead despite the air-conditioned chill. Was this some dumb joke?

"Why would he fall?"

"We don't know, Mr. Roberts."

"He's a great athlete, he doesn't fall," Max said, his voice rising, "and he almost never goes out on that goddamn terrace, never—so why should he fall from there?"

"Mr. Roberts." The detective's voice remained calm. "We don't know."

Max took the phone away from his mouth, away from his ear. He looked across the rose-walled bedroom to the mirror over the hand-hewn oak bureau. Reflected back he saw himself, naked to the waist, tanned, smooth, the face well proportioned, interestingly planed with a sweep of brown bristly hair. He raised his right hand. The figure did likewise. It was he. No dream. Adeline had been a dream. He heard sounds from the earpiece, brought it back.

". . . there? Hello?"

"I'm here," Max said, dull-voiced. "I'll be right over."

On the sidewalk in front of the East Side apartment building, all windows and terraces, setbacks and potted plants, there was a police barrier guarding an ugly stain. Around the stain was chalked a crude outline of a body, hands and feet outstretched. Max looked away, hurried past and into the building. Janos, the Yugoslav immigrant, one of the two alternating night doormen, looked at him, wide-eyed, his face still ashen, and shook his head. Max went right up to the thirty-second floor.

The apartment, usually so familiar in its sleek yet tasteful modernity, seemed unfamiliar with the uniformed men eyeing all the built-ins, the Danish console that controlled the VCR, the remote Mitsubishi rear-projection television, the laser-disc stereo, the speakers in all the rooms, the slave TVs in the bathrooms, all of the technical toys with which Cy had eagerly surrounded himself once the money had started to roll in. A compact man in a well-cut gray suit moved toward Max. He had steady blue eyes in a somewhat pudgy face and exuded an unnerving calmness, staring out with an appraising look that inspired instant guilt and malaise. He proved to be the caller, Detective Shamski.

"Sorry about this," Shamski said. "Could you go down to the morgue and make positive official identification?"

Max nodded.

"We're looking the place over. Seems in order. No evidence of any violence, fights, robbery stuff. Matter of fact, the TV was still on when we got here."

And would be, Max thought bitterly, even when he slept.

"But he had a couple of visitors tonight. One was a young black guy who's been here before, according to the doorman . . . a messenger maybe. He came in sometime after eight and left fifteen minutes later. We'll be looking for him. The other was a woman." Shamski led Max to the corner with the luscious Brazilian leather couch and the stainless-steel coffee table with "found" objects imbedded. A silver champagne bucket graced the steel. Within, half drowned in melted ice, was a bottle of Dom Perignon, '73. Beside it were two champagne glasses. On one Max could see a smudge at the rim.

"Some kind of lip stuff. We'll take samples and look for prints, of course. But I wanted you to see it as is in case you could tell us anything."

What could he tell him? That Cy loved women? That Cy had exquisite taste in that department? That Cy Bannerman was known for the quality ladies in his life, the high-tech glossies, the Kamali-Kenzo connective tissue running between them all? He told Shamski about Barbara. She was current, but as with all of them, impermanent. Shamski took notes in a precise hand, using, Max noticed, an old Waterman fountain pen with real ink.

"Maybe she was here," he said, distracted, confused, trying to accept that Cy was really dead, actually gone, never to appear again in all his glowing vitality, his sharp intelligence. "I don't know."

"We'll check," Shamski assured him.

Max looked past the small Modigliani, which had been Cy's opening art purchase, bought with the first big hit, out to the terrace doors, open now to the almost unused table and chairs, the lush plantings. The latticework barrier, over waist height and topped by two wooden railings, was broken through. It took violence to do that, to hurl a hundred and sixty-five pounds against those constraints, and smash them.

"Would you come with me, please?"

Shamski moved to the Art Deco bedroom around the little bend in the hallway. The bed had been used. Three white cartons of half-eaten Chinese food, their flaps open like wings, decorated the lacquered right end table.

"Moo shoo pork, shrimp lo mein, and dumplings . . . fried dumplings," Max said. "Cy often had Chinese food in."

Shamski continued. "This woman comes in with your part-

14

ner sometime between six and seven o'clock. The doorman says he hardly noticed her. He doesn't remember her leaving either, so either she left through a side door—there are two downstairs that open only from the inside—or through the front while the doorman wasn't paying attention."

"Janos," Max said, "is on down there. Janos is crazy about TV. He loves the night shift because he gets to see all the reruns."

"Anyway, your partner and whoever she is have a little party in here and then go out to finish up with the champagne. It's all easy. He gets a little high, goes out to the terrace, and accidentally . . ."

"No," Max said. "Never."

"There was no struggle here," Shamski said. "There's no sign of a struggle, none at all."

"He never went out there voluntarily." Max pointed a quivering finger at the terrace. Cy had a fear of heights. He liked to be inside if he was above the second floor. It would take a derrick to get him to lean against that railing.

Shamski looked at him reflectively.

"What kind of business are you in, Mr. Roberts?"

"We're in the market, we're traders. Commodities, options, things like that."

"Wall Street. Uh-huh." Shamski's eyes swept the room. "Lot of money in Wall Street, they tell me."

"Sometimes," Max admitted uncomfortably.

"You and your partner do well, though, I can see."

"I said sometimes," Max repeated irritably. "What has that got to do with . . . what happened?"

"They jumped out of windows and balconies in the crash of twenty-nine," Shamski said. "They say they had to sweep them off the street."

"This isn't twenty-nine, this is now. Cy had no reason to do what you think he did. It happened some other way."

Shamski looked at him reflectively. "All right—who'd want to kill him?"

Max looked blankly at the detective.

"This is your partner, right?" Shamski picked up two five-by-seven color photos and exhibited them. Max stared at Cy pumping iron, sweat pouring down his torso. He remembered the dumb pictures, remembered the gym in the village, remembered Cy sweet-talking him there to try it out that cold winter day, remembered his muscles aching and his back locking.

15

"Yes."

"You think he could be muscled over the edge by this girl drinking champagne with him?"

"Maybe not."

Shamski replaced the photo. "You two get along all right. I mean, sometimes partners . . . you know."

Max was about to say they were like brothers but couldn't, could not bring himself to try to explain to a stranger what their relationship was . . . had been . . . older brother, mentor, guide, provider of entrée to the world of money, of risk-taking, success. If it had not been for Cy, then what? And had it been only seven years, just seven years ago they had met? It seemed to him that he had known Cy Bannerman all his life, grown up with him, played stickball together. But no, only seven years. He remembered the first time they had met at the Akeman and Collins ad agency. He had been a minor television time buyer, Cy had been writing copy for an automobile account, and they had gone out for a quick lunch together. Cy was only two years older than Max's twenty-eight but he seemed to have had a lifetime more experience, to have come from some other planet, with his vitality and midwestern good looks, seemed to have discovered some secret for living that no one else possessed—and a mind that operated at ten times the speed of that of anyone he knew.

"Listen," Cy had opened, "this is a fateful generation, Vietnam, Nixon, Reagan, all of it. We owe it to history to be clear-eyed."

"Meaning what?"

"I'm talking about realities, our obligation to see the sham all around us, to take advantage of it, somehow—make it work to our advantage, and still know who we are."

He had been flatteringly confidential, told of his days in San Francisco during the sixties.

"I ran there, Max. I flew as fast as I could when the word filtered out about what was happening—love, peace—all of it."

"My mother said it was capitalism eating its own children," Max had remembered. "I was about sixteen and wished I could be eaten too."

"Crazy—absolutely, wonderfully insane," Cy had ruefully recalled. "We blew dope smoke rings at the faces of the police. We fucked anything that moved. We believed the power of our love could raise the Pentagon from its foundation and knock it all to hell. It was terrific. I was at San Francisco State supposedly, and that got me a deferment from the war."

Something had happened at that first lunch. With anyone else, it would have been inconceivable for Max to have talked about his own life, his own dreams, at a first meeting. And yet he had reached in and peeled parts of himself bare. When that single lunch was over a bond had been forged that never developed a flaw, a bond that produced a life successful beyond any fantasy Max might have had.

"Max, we have it all inside us, see. The trick is to get it out, mine it—let it blossom. There's no limit to what we can do, then we can have it all."

Those words, pronounced in Cy's characteristically intense way, rang in Max's ears still. But that voice, that life, was extinguished, blown out. By whom? For what? This detective didn't know what he was talking about. Someone had done this, someone had done it very cleverly, and for what reason Max did not begin to know.

Shamski held out his card with an address he had written on the back. The city morgue.

"We'll talk again, if you don't mind, afterward."

In the bedroom, two uniforms were admiring the way Cy's computer was built into the wall. When they started discussing the merits of its operating system, Max felt his stomach begin to heave.

Back home on the west side of the park, he sat at his tenth-floor bedroom window and stared out over the broad avenue, now deserted.

The park at this time of night was a lush, dark mass, sparsely speckled with light. The moon, half full, hung over the reservoir like a guardian spreading its thin rays over the dead, calm water and creating mysterious shadows along the banks. Here and there Max thought he detected movement, but who would be out there at three in the morning? Insane lovers? Demented joggers?

He picked up the phone and punched Julian's number. It took five rings to wake him.

"Julian, it's Max."

"Jesus Christ, Max, it's the middle of the night."

"Julian, listen to me. The police called me over to Cy's place. Something terrible's happened there."

"Huh? Oh Jesus—what?" Julian Berns's voice was deep in his throat. Max told him what he had just been through and Julian gasped in disbelief. "Dead? Oh God—! How could it be? I mean, shit, why, how, how could it happen?"

"The detective says he, you know, jumped . . ."

"No," Berns exploded. "Not Cy—never!"

"I know," Max said. "Something is wrong, something is crazy."

"He was going on the show next week," Berns groaned. "We're doing a segment on options risks. I can't believe this."

"Believe it," Max shouted. "He's gone, Julie."

"Oh God."

"I'll meet you for breakfast, eight o'clock, the Regency, OK?"

"OK . . . Jesus."

They hung up then. Max continued to stare out the window. It stank. Something was wrong, very wrong. No matter. Whatever happened from now on, his life would be changed entirely.

The Xanax put him to sleep, finally, for three hours. He awoke in a haze and the early-morning Channel 4 news had it as a minor item. A self-made millionaire Wall Street speculator, they called him—a boy wonder of the commodity markets—a big player at the fashionable discos and restaurants—constant escort of glamorous women—intensive investigation is ongoing. All of the expected clichés served up for a slavering audience aching to believe that, yes, the rich and powerful are not as happy as everyone thinks. Max got out before the calls started to come in and started across the park.

There had been a respite from the thick, mind-killing heat and this early there seemed to be actual oxygen in the air, gift of the leaf-laden trees he walked past. Joggers, fresh at the start and heaving with tortured lungs at the finish, clogged the bridle path and the reservoir roadway. Cy had done four miles religiously three days a week, checking his heart rate with an electronic gadget he wore on his wrist. Once he had met a great-looking girl on the road who turned out to be a celebrated *Vogue* model. Three days in Saint Croix had ensued. Max's encounters were more prosaic and were likely to be with lady lawyers or girls getting their master's.

Max reached Park, and the clog of cabs going downtown was solid, as usual. He left the street, entering the cool comfort of the hotel. He nodded to the maître d' at the restaurant, who ushered him to the table near the wall, the one Cy used frequently, the one that enabled you to see everyone there and yet be private. Julie Berns was already there, an anxious figure in a wrinkled blue suit, his thinning hair combed down to the side, his sorrow-filled eyes slumping in their sockets. He rose as Max approached and extended his hand, gripping Max's strongly.

"How are you, Max, you OK?"

Max shrugged and sat. Berns put himself back into the chair. "What could have happened—what the hell could have happened?"

"Nobody knows." The waiter came. Max ordered coffee and a toasted bagel.

"You think it was some kind of robbery, some nut who heard about Cy and thought he kept, like, gold in the apartment, Krugerrands, something like that?"

"It's possible. There's no sign of it," Max said, "but that doesn't prove anything to me. As a matter of fact, just the opposite. It's all too clean, it's all too straight."

Berns sat up. "Who would want to do . . . something to Cy?"

"That's what Shamski asked, the detective. Cy never kept anything from me but"—Max shrugged—"who knows."

"You're right," Berns echoed. "Who knows?"

"Even that girl who was with him could have been a setup."

"For what?"

"I don't know," Max replied sharply. "I've got to think about all this, try to figure."

"After you called," Berns said, "I tried to think but none of it makes any sense." He shook his head and took a deep breath. "We go back almost twenty years. Twenty years. From the San Fran days. We grew up together. Whoever dreamed it would turn out like this? Whoever had a clue that any of it would have happened? Now this—"

His fingers trembled as he lifted his coffee cup. Max looked away from him and around the room, where every table was

19

occupied. Deal making. Somebody romancing somebody. Expensive haircuts, expensive suits, expense accounts. A usual Regency breakfast crowd.

Max looked back at Julie Berns, who stared at his buttered roll as though it were the *I Ching* oracle. Julie had been close to Cy in a way that Max had not. It was those early days in "San Fran," as Julie always called it. Cy had nursed Julie through a breakdown after his wife had left him. He would always be a failure, she had declared, and simply walked away. Shortly after that, when the public-TV network he worked for started thinking about a stock-market program, Julie had taken a crash course with Cy and invented a show. He had found an oddball of an irreverent financial writer and gone into partnership with him, Julian producing, the oddball hosting. The show had become phenomenally successful. The partner, brilliant, slightly mad-looking Lawrence Alloway, was pun-addicted, brash, an instinctive master psychologist. He and Julian had brought the hitherto obscure Wall Street operators to the TV screen, massaging their egos one moment, goading them the next. They created an entertaining hour that had come along at exactly the right time, synergistically locking into the current public wave, which expressed itself in a patriotic belief in the free-market system and the absolute duty of everyone to make some millions painlessly—by investing in the stock market. "San Fran" Julian now moved in sleek and powerful circles and almost everyone returned his telephone calls.

There had existed, Max recognized, a kind of minimal unspoken rivalry between Julian and himself for Cy's friendship. An uneasy distance had developed between them. But Julie had been the one he called first, and as he looked at the distraught man now, some of that gulf vanished. Both of them had loved Cy and both were experiencing the same grief.

"Julie," he said, "I know how you feel."

Berns nodded. "You speak to Barbara yet?"

"No, she knows by now of course, but there are so many things to do—"

"Max, is his father still alive? I don't even know."

"No, he died years ago."

"But his mother's still around?"

"Yup," Max said grimly, "in the institution. Totally gone."

"Imagine," Berns said, pursing his lips, "she'll get everything he has. Talk about ironies."

20

THE THIRD FRIDAY

From the time he was very young, Max knew, Cy had been aware that his mother was strange. She would disappear into the bathroom for hours on end. Eventually the door would open and she would stagger out. Max remembered Cy's retelling of his discovery, at age six, of the gin bottles hidden there.

"I never blamed her. Even as a kid, instinctively I knew what kind of hell she was going through with my old man. He'd get frustrated and just lash out at her, across the face, the chest; he'd kick her in the legs, I remember. This dumb Willy Loman, this incompetent insurance salesman, meek to the world, you know, white shirt and tie, all of it. He'd come home and not even drink, just sit and brood and if my mother said one wrong word, bang— Then later, oh, do I remember the sounds in their bedroom. He'd cry, beg her to forgive him, then the bedsprings would start. Meanwhile I'm just on the other side of the wall not knowing what was going on."

"Things are falling apart," Julie said nervously. "People are going crazy." He mopped his forehead. "Did you see the paper this morning? This back-office man was picked up by the SEC for illegal insider trading. He found out about some profit statement or other and acted on it. They were going to throw the book at him, make an example. On the way downtown in the car, right in the backseat, he pulls a gun and shoots himself. He's in critical condition. Craziness. Half the profits on the Street are made by getting information first, and now they're going to make examples. Those hypocritical bastards." He waited for a response from Max but getting none, took a deep breath and became reflective again. "That character, the one Barbara was going around with before Cy met her."

"Catalfo?"

"Right. Catalfo, the real estate operator. Didn't he threaten to get legs broken when she quit him for Cy?"

He remembered Catalfo, had seen him here and there, at restaurants and once at a freaky downtown club he frequented. Not yet forty, he was never without a cigar in his mouth or between his fingers. Heavyset, pink-eyed, he had sprung from the pavements like a weed, shooting from small-time Queens apartment-house owner to Manhattan developer with all the right political contacts in the space of two years. Undoubtedly, he had the proper bent-nose, flat-eared connections as well; for you couldn't rise so far in construction in this town without them. He seemed to be an eighth-grade dropout with a vocabulary that consisted mainly of "hey." Obtaining Barbara Stratton had been a crowning achievement. He had not lost her graciously. He had, yes, vowed to "take care of" Cy. But it was all too open, too blustery, too obvious. And yet—

When breakfast was over and the two men walked out together, Max felt less alone, more comforted. He took a cab to the office, three small rooms on Third Avenue, far away from the Street. After the first year of their partnership, Cy had decided it was best to stay away from the frenetic turbulence of the trading pits, and having an office downtown would only sweep them along in every rumor, every shade of gossip, every wave of speculation, even if they were at lunch. So the uptown offices insulated them while the telephones and the tape machine and the computer screens kept the umbilical cord intact.

He opened the door on which was emblazoned WHIZKIDS TRADING, and found Martha sitting at her desk, numbly staring at the front page of the *Daily News*. The photo had been taken from some distance so there was little clarity, merely a shadowy figure on the ground near a manhole cover, arms and legs akimbo. She turned to Max, her eyes red, her lipstick, hastily applied this morning, smeared off her top lip. She said nothing, just stared at him and pointed to the paper.

Max patted her on the back and told her to take it easy. It was Saturday, he pointed out, she need not have come in, but things would be messy and he was glad she did. Martha, at thirty-six, divorced and raising her son alone in Brooklyn Heights, had been with them since the child's birth three years ago. Fiercely loyal, somewhat in awe of Cy, more at ease with Max, she knew, of course, that tens of thousands, sometimes much more, rode on an order slip that she made out confirming a phone conversation, but the fact of actual *money* being involved somehow escaped her. Money was in the check she received twice a month. Money was in the cash she paid out for the soft drinks and the cookies and pretzels that she bought for the office closet. That was real money; the other, the numbers on slips, the numbers with all the zeros, that was like play, like some kind of game, Monopoly play that the bosses did seriously.

"What happened, Mr. Roberts, what happened? My God—"

Max soothed her. It might have been an accident, no one knew. The railing might have been weak. She shook her head.

He was uncomfortable with heights. She knew that Mr. Bannerman hardly ever went out on his terrace.

"He might have, Martha," Max said, hoping he was persuasive. "He just might have, you never know."

He left her still numb, unable to take her eyes from the front page. In the back room Jimmy Singh was hunched in a chair in a corner before his computers, but the Quotron was off and the direct-commodities screen empty of its usual clutter. Singh's working PC was on but the green screen held no figures, no calculations, no chart evaluations; it glowed but it was blank.

Short, delicately boned, a shock of straight dark hair falling across his walnut-colored forehead and spilling down over his horn-rimmed eyeglasses, which seemed too large for his heart-shaped face, Singh wore his habitual short-sleeved white Dacron shirt so porous in weave that the snowy V-necked undershirt he had on underneath seemed like a principal garment, while his also habitual black trousers and shoes only served to emphasize the whiteness on top. His smooth skin, with too-little beard for a man of forty, always seemed coated with shine, though, he claimed, he never sweated, the hottest climate feeling to him mild and pleasant.

Singh had been in the States for ten years. He came from the low end of a high-caste Amritsar Sikh family. Most of his relatives maintained their warrior traditions. Jimmy was peaceable. He had studied mathematics and, eventually, computer science at the university. When he'd immigrated, his gifts for programming had been recognized by Merrill Lynch, and it was there that his first name, unpronounceable to the Bobs and Franks and Harrys, had been anglicized to "Jimmy." When he had gone on to the Bank of New York, that name became official.

Cy had met him by accident one day as he bought a peach at the farmer's market incongruously set up in front of the World Trade Center. He seemed very knowledgeable and meticulous about the peach he picked and Cy, fascinated, questioned him. Singh responded with typical Indian courtesy. Within minutes Cy had asked him to come to work for Whizkids. Within minutes he had accepted. Neither had reason for any regrets. Singh's ability to make a program to track whatever Cy wished and to operate it was masterful. Unlike Martha, he knew very well that the zeros on the slips were real. He had great respect for Cy's judgment and risk-taking. He had respect, too, for Max's role at Whizkids, for the second-thinking and holding back that Max represented, which often proved to be the correct assessment. Above all, he had, from the first, been impressed with the closeness of the two men—"like a family, like brothers," he had been fond of observing and then adding with a quick smile, "we Indian people are very much for families, you know."

Jimmy Singh sat and his eyes blinked behind the lenses as his hands kneaded each other.

"Such Karma," he murmured, "and the road to end like this, smashed on the stone—"

"Jimmy," Max said softly, "just try not to think about it."

"How could I do that?"

"It's Saturday," Max said, softly admonishing. "You should have stayed home."

"I went to the temple this morning," Singh said reflectively. "It is only six blocks from my house. I said a prayer for him." Suddenly Singh's reflection changed to deep agitation. "It's horrendous, inconceivable. What are we going to do, Mr. Max?"

"We'll just . . . go on, carry on." Max had rarely seen Singh become emotional.

"Yes, but there are things . . ."

He stopped, blinked, and the thin mist on his cheeks had turned to actual sweat. ". . . things that only Mr. Cy could deal with. No offense."

"I realize that, Jimmy, but we'll do the best we can."

"I would like to go home after all, Mr. Max, please."

Max thought, So would I like to be home.

At eleven he met Shamski at the Bellevue morgue.

"It's just for the paperwork," the detective apologized.

As the attendant pulled out the cold slab drawer, Max's stomach tightened in anticipation. The roller creaked and became stuck halfway. The attendant yanked and the drawer shot open. The sheet covering the body slipped, revealing blackened toes. Max stepped back, swallowing hard. Shamski, in a practiced move, whipped the sheet off the top part of the broken thing on the slab. Max stared at the features swollen almost out of all recognition, at the purple bruises, the blotches, the dried-blood ooze on the forehead.

"Oh, Jesus. . . ."

24

Shamski moved the sheet and the attendant shoved the slab back.

"Let's get out of here." Shamski took him by the arm and marched him out of the building.

"The organ autopsy's a little inconclusive. He had a couple of drinks in him, though, that's for sure."

"He had champagne," Max protested. "He had a few glasses of champagne. That's what he did, that was his limit."

"I said it was inconclusive," Shamski backtracked. "And they can't tell anything about the railing break. It could have been weak there."

"Oh sure," Max said derisively. "Cy had all these drinks, see, and he comes staggering out on the terrace and goes right to that weak spot, leans over to vomit, and breaks through. Case closed."

"No one's trying to close a case," Shamski said, not offended. "We're going at it but right now it's classified as an accident—if you can show us more, OK."

As they walked, Shamski told him they had been back to the apartment and had checked once again, very carefully, for prints and other things. The apartment had been released from any surveillance and Max was free to make his arrangements for it, since he was, Shamski understood, Bannerman's executor, the alternate being Julian Berns.

"It's worth a bundle, I guess," Shamski said. "You Wall Street guys . . ." He shook his head in wonder.

"What about the lipstick?"

"It's being analyzed. We'll have that by this afternoon. And they found two fingerprints, not Bannerman's, on one of the glasses, but they're smudged. The guys say they're useless. I'll want a list of the women he knew for us to talk to, though."

That would keep a squad busy for a while, Max thought. The past women, the models, the TV-news anchorwoman, the designer, the political press attaché . . . and they were simply the serious ones, the ones he acknowledged. And it wasn't as though he had sought any of them out; in some fashion they had all fastened on him, on that body in the morgue, that poor broken thing.

Back in his office, Max found there had been calls from reporters, traders, Julian, and an urgent message from an organ-transplant foundation wanting whatever of Cy's that was available—and operative. When he got back to Berns, Julian was excited.

"Max, I had to call you. I just got a call from the coast. Roy Herbert is at the Beverly Hills Hotel. He took the red-eye out last night. It was sudden. Not even his office knew he was going. I checked. He arrived high as a kite on his nose candy, I'm told. Does that sound funny to you, the suddenness of it?"

Max thought about it. William Roy Herbert, the son of a bitch's son of a bitch, was the offspring of the founder of a power-packed Wall Street firm, and a VP as a result. Roy Herbert's dislike was sometimes enough to make decent traders become Maalox junkies, Valium fiends, aspirin heads. He had, it was rumored, given more than one enemy a case of early Alzheimer's, watching their disintegration with satisfaction. The major pursuit of his life, an open secret, was to bed any female actress available. He would stop at nothing if star quality was involved. And he had hated Cy, hated him not passively, but actively—with volcano heat. It was as though from the moment they met, Herbert had recognized that he and Cy were natural enemies. He had attempted to triumph by seducing Cy into his orbit. When that failed, ending in an open, bitter confrontation, Herbert had developed a smoldering grudge, which, Max had known, was potentially dangerous.

"I hadn't thought of him—but he's crazy enough to do anything."

"Just keep it in mind, Max. How did it go this morning?"

"I'm trying to forget it." He frowned. "I'm going to have to see Barbara later."

"Be careful with her."

"What do you mean?"

"I'm just saying. She's not the most sterling character in the world either."

"I know what she is. I've got to go, Julie."

"I'm going to do a couple of minutes of memorial on the show this week, for Cy, Max. Would you come?"

Max groaned.

"I know, I know. It was Alloway's idea. I'll let you know when we're taping. But come by, please. I'll need the company."

"I'll see."

He made one more call—to Barbara. They made a drink date at her place. He went through the rest of the horrifying routine in a daze, lawyers, the undertaker, the newspaper notice—"in lieu of flowers, contributions can be made to the Bannerman Foundation for Child Care." There would be no service, none at all. Cy would have hated that.

Walking back aimlessly from a dreary meeting, trying to force his mind along organized paths, he found himself, as though moved by a magnet, near Cy's apartment building. The police markers had been removed. The stain on the pavement had been scrubbed. Nothing remained. From across the street, he looked up at the apartment. From this distance, the railing could not be seen, only the glare of the sun reflecting from the glass terrace doors. As he looked, that glare was momentarily interrupted. Max squinted hard. Again it was broken, and this time by something or someone moving behind the glass, flitting by. Max strained to see more. An illusion of light? It could easily be that at this distance. But once again something moved past the glass doors, hesitating long enough for Max to see, even at this remove, that it was a human figure.

Max leaped forward, racing across the street to where Connor, the day doorman, was talking into the intercom. Leaning into his startled face, he demanded, "Who's up in Mr. Bannerman's apartment?"

The doorman looked at him blankly.

"Who's there?" Max repeated. "Did you let someone in?"

"No, nobody up there. I don't let nobody in up there."

Max strode past him and into a waiting elevator. He pounded on the penthouse button and drummed his fingers on the walnut walls impatiently as the car rose. It had been no visual error—he had seen someone in the apartment. When the car stopped smoothly and the doors slid back, Max charged out to the carpeted, low-lit hallway, which, with its single elevator shaft, served the two penthouses on the floor. He moved swiftly to Cy's, stopping at the door to put his ear against it. He heard rustling sounds too vague to identify. Maybe his pulse, he decided, which was pounding. For a fleeting moment, he thought he should go back down and call Shamski. He dismissed that, and tested the door gently. Locked. As silently as possible, he took out his key ring, found the key Cy had given him two years ago when he had bought the place, inserted it into the lock, and turned gently. Grasping the doorknob at the same time, Max hesitated, then, with one sudden shove, pushed the door open. Blazing sunlight dazzled him. Momentarily blinded, he shielded his eyes, looking right and left, but saw no one in the living room, which led from the entrance foyer. Pulse pounding more than ever, he focused on the hall-closet door. With a grab at the knob, he jerked it open. The sunlight revealed only Cy's three raincoats, boots, umbrellas, hats. Leaving the front door open as a precaution, he padded toward the bedroom. No one there. He stared intently at the two huge closets for a long moment. Gingerly, he approached the one nearest the window and swung the door back. Only racks of clothing, shoes, suits, robes, confronted him. He went to the other. More clothing, a discarded rowing machine, a no-longer-used small telescope, a portable television set, two portable radios, an electronic chess set, a lap computer. Cy's toys.

He returned to the living room; whoever he had seen was not here now. But how did they get in and had anything been taken? He closed the front door and went back to the bedroom, eyeing the objects, the walls. It was all so familiar, the Rauschenberg painting, the silver-framed picture of Cy's mother taken when she was in her teens, the photo of himself and Cy at the ski lift, a blurry print of Cy at twenty, a ton of hair its most evident feature, and a fist raised in laughing defiance. All in order. Then he became aware of a small red glow in the corner—Cy's computer. It was on.

Max walked to it quickly. It had not been on only last night. Absolutely not. Would some police idiot have put it on and left it that way? Possible. The screen was dark. Max found the brightness control and brought it up. The pulsing cursor greeted him. Acquainted with computers, of necessity, at the office, he checked the drive slots. One held a game disk. Cy had long since grown bored with computer games, never played them anymore. He would never have a game disk in his machine. Who had inserted it, then? Max slid open the lower desk drawer. A dozen disks were there, but had there been more?

A telephone ring broke the stillness, startling him. It rang again. Eerily, Cy's voice, so warm and familiar, issued from the answering machine. "Hello. Sorry, but it's impossible to answer this. Would you leave your message? Thank you."

The caller was a woman. "Cy, it's Sonya. Are you there? What? Oh, Lord, I do hate your machine, and I'm not going to speak to it."

Max listened, riveted. The voice, low and throaty, was not one he had ever heard before. And never had he heard Cy mention any name like "Sonya." And she was speaking as though he were alive.

"I was waiting for you at ten, and if you aren't coming up at all, let me know. Call me. Good-bye, machine."

Max reached for the phone on the end table but it was too late, the woman had clicked off and the recorder beeped to a halt. Instantly, Max played the tape that had just been made. Sonya. Sonya who? Sonya what?

He went to the desk, pulled open the top drawer, where, he knew, Cy had kept a telephone-address book. He thumbed rapidly through but found no Sonya. He dropped the book back, thinking to himself with a groan that it would soon fall to him to pack up all these damn possessions and decide what to do with them. He would ring Julian in on that, let him share some of that onerous burden. He shut the computer off, and as he did he heard a muffled thump.

He charged quickly back to the living room, but nothing had changed, and he realized that the sound had come from beyond the apartment, out in the hall. He rushed out and saw instantly that the elevator door was closed and the indicator was blinking its digital message, recording descent. He shot a look at the other penthouse door. Had someone come out in the last minutes? Or had someone been hiding there, around that alcove, or behind that column, watching him go into Cy's and then, finding the chance, going down?

As he watched, tense and helpless, the lights spelled out ten, nine, eight, seven, six, five, four, three, two—and stopped. Max stared at the red glow. Two. Why would someone go from the penthouse to two? He jabbed savagely at the call button, stepped back to Cy's, slammed the door closed, and returned impatiently to watch the indicator record the rise. It seemed an eternity before the car reached him, and the door hissed open smoothly. He stepped inside, hit "two." The door closed again, making the soft slap he recognized as the sound he had heard.

He descended in a whirl of feelings, uncertainty tinged with a slight fear. When the door opened on the second floor, he stepped out warily to gray, velour carpeting and beige walls. Again, two apartments were on the floor, their doors facing him stolidly, no concealing columns here, and no windows. Max, perplexed, walked slowly toward the apartment to his right. It was then that he saw the service door in the center of the hall, and halted before it. Slowly, he opened it, to find a narrow

29

staircase. He descended cautiously to the landing below, to a door that he tried and found locked. He continued down the staircase. At the bottom another door faced him. He tugged at the knob until it gave. He stepped through and found he was in a dimly lit section of the basement. Sounds of machinery echoed from the concrete walls. He walked forward slowly in the gloom. He turned a corner, and as he did he heard the sound of footsteps some distance in front of him. He hugged the wall, peering, trying to pierce the darkness. The footsteps continued, hesitated, came closer, moved away, and then, in the light of a fifty-watt bulb, Max made out a man, squat and powerful-looking, carrying a small suitcase.

In his excitement, Max slipped. His heels slapped the basement floor, echoing down the hall. The squat man turned sharply. Max's first impulse was to run, but it was already too late, as his quarry doubled back, advancing upon him rapidly, looming up. Max straightened, tensing, and in seconds the man was upon him, eyes wide. For two seconds they stared at each other, then the squat man said in some Middle Eastern accent, "I am try to go to the C and the D apartments, but I always get losted down here."

"Oh," Max said, watching carefully.

"I take shortcut down here from the F and G but I make wrong turn. You know where is C and D?"

"No," Max said, alert, "I don't."

"I go up to lobby then and go all the way around." The man said nervously, "You carry all day, gets heavy." He shook the suitcase.

"What gets heavy?" Max asked.

"Demo. I make demo Eureka vacuum cleaners. Very good product, you know."

Max let out a long breath. "Vacuum cleaners?"

"Oh yes . . . filters, bags, belts. You got to carry much things."

Max examined him closely.

"You come to this building often?"

"Every three months, I come around. The doorman and me, we have understanding." The salesman grinned broadly. Max slumped momentarily, then straightened up.

"So you can go out to the lobby from here, then?"

"Oh sure." The salesman gestured. "You come out back. You go lobby?"

Max nodded.

"OK. You come with me."

He guided Max through another door and up another flight of steps. "You know," he laughed as they walked, "when I hear you behind me, I say oh boy, maybe I get mugged. I be scared."

He opened still another door and Max found himself in the rear of the ceramic-floored lobby. Some distance away, Connor, oblivious to them, talked on the lobby telephone. The salesman went toward another elevator shaft, waving. Max watched him go, then walked briskly to the concierge desk, passing behind Connor's back. Connor talked on. Max passed back into the lobby. The doorman did not miss a beat in his conversation. Angry, Max whirled about and shoved himself right into the doorman's face.

"Listen to me, Connor, listen."

The startled doorman hung up the phone.

"Who's come out of the building in the past ten minutes?"

"Who, what?" The doorman was rattled.

"Who's come out? I want to know who's come out."

"Oh—well." Connor grimaced. "The maid from Twelve G, the fat one. She comes out."

"What *man*, what *man*?"

"I don' see no man . . . I don' think."

"You didn't see me, did you? I walked right past and you didn't see me."

"It's the telephone," Connor accused promptly. "Six F. He's a old man an' he always wants me to do some damn thing for him. Drives me crazy."

"Is the door, the back door from the second floor to the basement, supposed to be unlocked?"

"Uh . . . not supposed to be open, that door."

"Connor, Connor." Max put a five-dollar bill in the doorman's hand. "I don't want a story."

"Uh—sometimes," the hapless Connor confessed, "one of the boys forgets to lock it, like, y'know what I mean? Like, he's in a hurry with garbage or somethin' and it, like, you know, goes out of his head. Because he's so busy here."

"Busy—" Max said bitterly. And so anyone might have gone to two, come out behind the doorman, and gone out, waiting his chance—anyone, including whoever had ended Cy's life.

"Make sure it's locked all the time. Will you make sure?"

31

He placed a twenty-dollar bill in the hand now, and the doorman stopped being hapless, became aggressively reassuring.

"You don' worry, Mr. Roberts, that door is gonna be locked day an' night an' in between. Believe me."

He held tightly to the bills. "I'm really sorry about Mr. Bannerman." He hesitated, then, "What do you think I oughta do about that Advanced Meecro, Micro—whatever it's called, that I bought two months ago? It's on the OTC. Mr. Bannerman said it was gonna go up, maybe do a two-for-one split. It did go up, but now I don' know if it's like a 'hold' or a 'sell.' "

"Call your broker," Max said over his shoulder, going out into the street. Outside, he crossed and looked up at the apartment window. It was in shadow now.

2

He called Shamski, who was out. Then he walked the nine blocks to Barbara's duplex, which occupied the top two floors of an old alabaster-stone town house on a quiet street. The property had been bought for her four years ago by the CEO of a good-size conglomerate, a man she had met at a cocktail party in East Hampton. She had rented a summer house in Georgica, on the pond, that year, specifically to meet someone new after an affair with the owner of a silk-importing company had gone sour. It was a fairly cold-blooded move, but Barbara thought of it as a practical matter, a conservation of energy; she went directly to where the possibilities were.

Barbara's field of possibilities was always limited to men who wielded power in one area or another, men who would advance her "particular life-style," as she called it. This was a style particularly suited to a twenty-eight-year-old, quite beautiful woman who had been offered professional modeling jobs time and time again. With a thick sprawl of tawny hair surrounding her exquisitely cheekboned face, with a complexion something between cream-tinged porcelain and light ivory, Barbara Stratton drew stares, even from women in the ladies' rooms of restaurants. Especially from women. She appeared tall but was not. Slender, she had what seemed to be traditional long and shapely American legs, which she used carefully as part of her sexual armament. She dressed in an expensive casual mode and never used taxis, there always being a stretch limo at her convenience to whisk her from one place to another.

Barbara's life, from the moment she left St. Louis and her middle-class family at seventeen, had proceeded in a series of steps, from cocktail-lounge waitress, to secretary for a TV producer who wanted to marry her despite his analyst's objections, to so-called research assistant at an avant-garde magazine run by a well-known devotee of S and M. Once she had perceived that, despite their station in life, their age or experience, men were flattered by the thought of a beautiful young woman lavishing attention on them, were thrilled by the possibility of going to bed with such a creature, and were astonished by the possibility of possessing her for a time, her steps led inexorably upward.

The CEO had been a fifty-five-year-old devoted husband and father. But Barbara was something else, an ornament in his life, a happening he had never imagined would occur in reality. His gratitude was large enough to encompass the down payment on the town house and arrangements for a low-interest mortgage. Seven months later, he suffered a severely enlarged prostate, which he took as a sign that the Almighty had taken a hand in his affairs. After undergoing the operation, he announced that he was curtailing his travel in favor of participating in more local civic events at the Minneapolis corporate headquarters. The liaison ended but the town house stood four stories tall and healthy.

Barbara held a nominal editorial job on a magazine devoted to fashion and literature. In every issue, sandwiched between the highest of high-fashion photo layouts and the ads for "full leg and bikini wax," there was always a story by Borges or an excerpt from Italo Calvino. In the mysterious ways of publishing, it was Barbara's task to choose and acquire this material, which meant dealing with literary· agents who were totally baffled by her. The fact was that it made practically no difference to the readers what Barbara chose to be published; they were primarily interested in how far they ought to go in waxing the "bikini area." The publisher knew his readers' passions very well and when Barbara wanted a legitimate post that would allow her to move freely in circles of her choosing, he rewarded her for the late-night suppers and the country weekends with the position of fiction editor.

Cy Bannerman was an anomaly in Barbara's life, for he was neither old nor married. Still, his free-spending style and the business he was successful at—money—fulfilled her requirements. Moreover, given his looks and his undeniable brains and charm, she had almost fallen under his spell—almost, because her practical side recognized the danger.

They had met at a fashionable downtown disco, fashionable meaning that the men and women patrons shared the same androgynously decorated toilet facilities, where, some said, the stalls were used for more than hygienic purposes, PCP and cocaine being prominent in the whispers. The place, called simply Space by the two ex–kosher delicatessen owners who started it, was cavernous, having once been a Presbyterian church and later a warehouse, but it never shed its religious look, compounded by soaring Gothic arches (where a score of television screens now belted out the latest rock videos) and heavenly skylights (now replaced by abstract images, in glass, of pop stars). This religious look became a natural attractant for those desiring to party away the night.

Cy and Max went to Space from time to time. It was, after all, a voyeur's paradise. The habitues came up from the underbelly of the city or descended from its top strata to exhibit themselves, to brush body parts, and to take part in the tableaux, an S-and-M scene complete with whips, chains, and a six-foot-four blond dominatrix one night, a transvestite-chorused, bare-rumped Busby Berkeleyish romp the next. The name of the game was outrage.

One night a party had been arranged at Space for an important Wall Street figure. Max and Cy had gone down. Barbara was there, an "upper," looking on it all with amusement. She had come with Catalfo, who had some connection with the place and to whom she had gone originally to solve certain real estate problems that had arisen with her town house. Catalfo, thick, tough, and effective, had been bowled over by her, encircled her, had her for the odd weekend in Jamaica or the quick trip to Paris with a shopping stopover in Rome. He was not Barbara's style but his insistence prevailed. There was something else as well, something that frightened Barbara for the first time in her life; Catalfo was explosively jealous, bullying and threatening whoever stood in his way. Though he had never acted in that fashion with Barbara, there was always a subtle, unspoken undercurrent. She would end up with him, he had a habit of saying through his cigar—and she ought to know that because he always got what he was after—always.

That night at Space, Cy had been introduced to her by a mutual friend. Even then, Max had noted the darkening look on Catalfo's face as Cy danced with her, she moving sinuously amid the shaking, quaking crowd and Cy matching her. Max, dancing nearby, had predicted trouble.

Max was right. Once it was established that Cy and Barbara had become lovers, Catalfo's response was rage. He accosted Barbara at the magazine office, causing a well-remembered scene. He vowed that she was his property, and that anyone crossing the line would find themselves in hot water. With Bobby Catalfo's connections, that was not impossible to imagine. More than one opponent had caved in after midnight visitations or simply because an odd-looking man was seen, every day for a week, staring in at the playground where the opponent's kids were playing.

Ringing the bell downstairs at Barbara's, Max decided to tell Shamski about all this as well. Buzzed in to the columned, gilded Regency-furnished lobby, Max took the brass elevator to Barbara's top-floor duplex. She opened the door wearing a floor-length dressing gown, a swirl of Chinese red. Her face, without makeup, was starkly stunning. Her eyes were wide and she said in a very tight voice, "Max, what happened to him?"

"We're . . . not sure," Max replied.

"I saw the newspaper picture. Max—"

In the next moment, she moved into the comfort of his arms, her own clutching his back. Max felt her softness, the spring of her hair and the outlines of her belly against his. She was not crying but saying things like "Why?" and "My God," and "How terrible."

Holding her this close, Max felt uncomfortable, and he moved her away from him gently.

"Easy, easy—it's OK, it's OK."

She nodded, broke from him, seemed in control again.

36

"When did you see Cy last, Barb?" Max tried to make it sound casual. "I mean at his place."

She poured them both some white wine. "We went to a backers' audition of this musical Wednesday. It was terrible. Then we went back there."

"So you weren't at his place last night?"

"No. . . ."

She wouldn't be lying, Max knew, because if she had been there, she'd have known about the champagne glasses and the possibility of fingerprints.

"That detective wants to see me," she said.

"He's OK," Max assured her. "Don't worry about it, just tell him the truth."

She nodded, sipped the wine. "You think he . . . did it?"

"No," Max said, "I don't."

She looked at him, eyes wide. Max nodded.

"Today's Saturday," Max said. "You saw him Wednesday. How did he seem to you—same as always?"

"I'm . . . not sure," she said.

"What do you mean?"

Barbara thought of how it had been that night. The huge bed had been a little rumpled, as always. His housekeeper made it up every day but there was something about these specially made, oversize designer sheets that creased just a little. It drove him crazy.

"Jesus," he had said to her, smoothing the hillocks with a palm, "is there anybody you know with good sheet Karma? This is intolerable."

She had felt the satiny thread under her back and wondered what he was talking about. Cy could be the princess in the princess-and-the-pea fable, she knew, but this was ridiculous. These sheets cost hundreds each; when they cost that much they had to be good.

"Screw it." He'd flopped down beside her, his face on her right breast. His lips had started to nuzzle her nipple, then stopped. He sat up again, reached over to the ice bucket, touched the champagne bottle, then stopped also. She watched him curiously. He was not usually that restless in bed. Otherwise, *restless* just began to describe him—coils of energy, constant movement. In bed, however, he was gentle, considerate. Not that she actually cared. She had never been crazy about any part of the sexual act. It was pleasant enough in a neutral way, but

37

all of the multiple orgasms and flashing lights and search for the G spot they were constantly writing about in *Vogue* and *Cosmo* eluded her. She did not feel deprived. She had long since learned how useful sex and so-called sexiness might be, however. It was something men wanted in a woman. It provided constant flirtation, titillation, a level of excitement that rippled in the background of every meeting. Cy had left the bed entirely, his muscular body reflecting bronze from the overhead track lighting. He reached for a drawer.

"Want some blow?"

She'd refused; she used no drugs at all, drank wine sparingly. The refusal had dampened his desire and he sat down on the edge of the bed, looking away from her moodily.

"Sometimes you don't know where it's going to come from."

She had not the slightest notion what he meant but had learned in her life to simply nod and look sympathetic.

"Phil Carmody says the one thing that's predictable is a degree of unpredictability. The trick is to predict even that, though—that's the real hat trick, that's where the really big hits are."

"Oh," she'd said, soothing syrup in her voice, "you do that."

"Sometimes. Not enough. It gets dangerous when unknown elements get involved."

"Umm." It was almost three.

"Deep water, Barbara, it's deep water."

"Cy, it's so late. I'm getting sleepy. And there's too much air conditioning in here—I'm getting cold." She pulled the covers up.

"Oh Jesus, you covered them up, honey, you covered them up—why'd you do that?" Gently he had removed the offending cotton and her breasts gleamed again.

"Cy, you're crazy, you know that? I said I was cold."

"I'll make you warm. I'll make you warm."

He had bent over her, his hands caressing her skin lightly.

"I know," he'd said. "I know you don't love this but it doesn't matter."

"Cy—"

"There are priorities."

"Do you want me to stay tonight?"

"I want to light candles, I want some masses said. I want some good luck to fall on my side of the line."

Then his hands had cupped her breasts with startling pressure.

"Ouch—Cy, you're hurting me."

He had clung.

"Cy—don't."

He'd put his eyes an inch from hers. "What do you think I mean?"

"I don't know. Cy, please."

"What do you think I mean? Tell me."

"I don't know. You'll give me cancer. Please, Cy."

"Take a guess. Give me a goddamned informed guess as to what might happen without novenas."

She had squirmed, and his hands lifted from her. "I'm sorry."

Her breasts bore red marks where his fingers had sought refuge. "Look what you did."

"I'm really sorry. It's an 'or else' thing, see."

"A what?"

"Or else, or else."

He had turned away from her then, and all the joy left his face, all the energy sapped. He looked older, suddenly, than he ever would be, and even his body, that body he tested and hardened and punished, sagged. She had never seen him like this and it frightened her.

Max listened with surprise. There had been no hint of a Cy so shaken, so worried about something; what did "or else" mean?

"I can't almost believe it," Barbara said.

Or else *what*?

"It's scary."

Or else *what*?

Max stayed another half hour. They talked of Cy mostly, but throughout the thirty minutes Max was conscious of a current passing between himself and Barbara. Her way of looking at him, her body language, suggested an intimacy that had never existed before, a closeness. He put it down to their shared memories, but when he rose to go and leaned over to give her the ritual kiss on the cheek, she clung to him as she had when he arrived. Her head moved so that his mouth met hers full. He felt her lips move under his ever so slightly and her hips sway.

When her eyes opened again, he patted her face clumsily and said, "I'll be in touch." She nodded, still looking at him, her eyes wide, lips parted.

In the lobby he shrugged off Barbara's kiss. Pure reaction. Had Julie Berns come to see her, she would have kissed him the same way—maybe.

He opened the front door and was about to step out into the sunlight when, directly across the street, he saw a dark-suited man, who was unmistakably peering up at Barbara's windows. Instinctively, Max stepped back and closed the door. He waited a tense minute, wondering if he was going paranoid. The man might be someone just killing time; he could be a bill collector, anything. He steadied his nerves and opened the door again. The man was gone.

Max walked down the front steps, berating himself for a fool. As his foot touched the pavement, a taxi swung by in front of him. Max caught a glimpse of a bulbous nose. It was the watcher, staring out at him!! For a moment their eyes met, the watcher's cool, Max's startled. Then the man pulled back from the window and the cab sped on.

Shamski's reaction to Max's recital was gently skeptical.

"I believe you. You really think you saw someone running around Bannerman's place, only he was a vacuum-cleaner salesman. And you really believe someone was watching that woman. Only nothing's missing from the apartment and this guy in the cab could be a hair-grower salesman. That's 'thinks,' not facts. Tell me something. Do you think somebody got your partner and now they're out to get you—you're next?"

"I don't know," Max faltered.

"Think about it."

"I have . . . a little."

"A lot?"

"I thought cops are suspicious of everybody, of every action, every motive. You just lay back."

"You've got points," Shamski said, unruffled. "Some cops do think that if you're not guilty of one thing, you're guilty of another. Me, I was trained by the Jesuits. I like to nit-pick, see what the nut inside the shell is like before I call it a pecan."

"Even when it has a pecan shell?"

"Even then."

It had become an affable exchange, almost impersonal. Max felt frustrated.

"What about the lipstick on the glasses?"

"It's not a lipstick exactly. It's a lip gloss, the shiny stuff. Been analyzed already. Something called Slickers." He winked. "You were going to give me a list of all his women."

Max produced the list with the twelve names he had been able to reconstruct. "There are probably others—not so important."

Shamski glanced at a pad before him. "Elizabeth Evers in there?"

Liz? Why would he ask about her? "Yes, she's there."

"Who is she?"

Liz Evers, he told Shamski, was someone whom Cy had gone around with for almost a whole year. She had her own ad agency, was a partner. Shamski tapped the pad impatiently. "I know all that; I mean *who is she*? What's her story?"

"They were very close for a time, saw each other a lot, went away on weekends."

"What happened after a year?"

"I don't know. It ended."

"End bad?"

Max tried to remember. Had it ended badly? There was some sort of tension toward the end that Cy did not speak of. But given the way men and women were—

"Tension about what?"

"I just told you that Cy didn't speak about it."

"Something—a guy tells his partner, his best friend, *something* when he breaks off with a woman."

What had Cy said about Liz? Not much. The relationship had been very intense, Max knew—but there had been something, yes—Max remembered feeling two strong forces meeting on some loving battlefield whenever Cy spoke about her.

"She has these strong opinions about everything," Cy had complained. "Comes from being overeducated, maybe—I don't know, Max. Set ideas. Hard to change."

Max had been amused. "What you mean is you can't get her to do something she plain doesn't want to do."

"What she wants to do," Cy had said then, "is wrong."

Max had laughed outright, knowing Cy. "By you."

41

Cy had not answered.

"Why Liz?" Max demanded. "I tell you about people snooping, following me, and you ask me about Liz Evers. Why don't you check out Roy Herbert?"

"Hey—you don't murder somebody just because you don't get along with them."

"It's a hell of a lot more than that. And what about Catalfo? You know damn well what he's capable of."

"Talk."

"Dammit." Max went into high gear. "It's your job to get into that kind of talk."

"OK," Shamski said, smiling, "I'll get the guy in and we'll smack him around a little and get the truth out of him."

"Not funny." Max had a sudden insight. "You won't touch Herbert, will you—because of who he is, who his father is, who the company is."

Shamski stopped the comedy. He thrust a finger into Max's face. "Hey—cool out!"

Max stood his ground. "Don't tell me the idea's new to you—I mean, looking the other way when it comes to Herbert and Company. Or even some hood real estate operator like Catalfo."

The detective's eyes narrowed. "And you never look the other way when it comes to making a buck or two down on Wall Street, do you?"

"I'm talking about a murder."

"You talk about murder as though it was spit. I know who Catalfo is. I know Herbert's a sleaze. You think we don't know how many callgirls he's beat up? He pays well. Nobody complains."

"He almost killed a girl once. If it hadn't been for Cy—"

"Yeah—well, all right. Good." Shamski was openly contemptuous. "Your buddy was at the same party, wasn't he? I mean everybody at that party were high rollers, weren't they? I mean it was money to burn, wasn't it? Money to buy any toy in the world, boys, girls, coke."

"That wasn't Cy," Max murmured. He had a vague suspicion that Shamski was right, though. They were high rollers. And some of them had the means to buy any toy in the world. But wasn't that the end goal of everyone? Didn't entire populations dream of being able to buy any house, any car, any boat? "I'm sorry," he managed to say. "I didn't mean to be insulting."

42

"That's OK. That's all right." Shamski became immediately accommodating. "You're upset. You and Bannerman were very close. I can understand that. I have three brothers myself."

I don't have any brothers, Max thought. Adeline didn't want to unbalance the population of the world. One child only. That way the rest of the world could be fed, the future could be planned.

"Listen"—Shamski went another mile—"don't think I'm ignoring what you say. I chalk it up. We'll see how it all fits." He hesitated. "You know, I don't give a good goddamn about Herbert and his company. Or Catalfo. I know how they're wired in, but I don't bother my head about that."

For the rest of that day the calls kept coming. Max ducked most of them, but could not avoid Marcus Rich, the *Journal*'s columnist, the financial Liz Smith. Persistent, prissy, impeccably turned out, his small frame always in nervous movement, Rich was read first by a sizable majority of the Street community on the train down. He had a miniature commanding presence and contrived the aura of knowing, for openers, more information than was being given him. As a result those he interviewed fell all over themselves giving up confidences, blurting out speculations, or revealing weaknesses, in all of which Rich reveled, as did his readers. Which he knew very well.

Max was tired and depressed when he saw Rich at the office as the daylight waned. The columnist, in a pinstriped suit and two-tone shirt with a Windsor collar, Gucci loafers burnished exquisitely, crossed his delicate legs and said, at first, that he simply wanted a statement from Max as Cy Bannerman's partner on what had happened. Max rubbed his eyes tiredly and said no one knew what had happened. All the police knew—

"I know what the police say, Max. I'm more interested in what you say."

"It's a shock."

"Umm, yes, we're all shocked. . . ." Rich had watery eyes and they seemed to drift off by themselves. "So you don't think it was an accident?"

Max became instantly alert. "Where'd you get that? I just told you no one knows what happened. Me included."

"But I understand you have . . . certain ideas."

That weasel, Max thought; already he has a pipeline to

Shamski's, already he smells scandal. He's sniffing the air the way a fox does smelling the barnyard near.

"I'm trying," Max said, "to make some sense out of it, that's all."

"And what conclusions do you come to?"

Max jumped up from his chair in irritation. "Cy died from the fall, that's my conclusion."

Rich uncrossed his legs, checked the crease in his trousers, and said, "He had a fear of heights. Why would he stand up against the railing?"

"Listen," Max said, "is this an inquest? What do you want me to say, Rich?"

"Max." Rich's alto voice was innocence. "Cy was a wunderkind. He was a flash across the trading-pit sky. He made it. He made it very large. My readers are interested. I owe them some insight."

Some dirt, Max thought, that's what you owe them, some juice—who's screwing whom, one way or another. Aloud he countered, "My partner's dead, Rich. I have to tell you that right now I don't give two hoots in hell about your readers. OK?"

Rich ignored that completely. "And there is nothing that you know of that's occurred in these last few weeks to indicate anything . . . unusual?"

"What do you mean by 'unusual'?"

"*Irregular* might be a better word."

"What do you mean by 'irregular'?"

"Out of the ordinary."

Rich stared straight at him now. Max stared back. What was this gambit?

"The market's always out of the ordinary," he chose to say.

Rich's mouth made a small disappointed moue. "So, you're telling me that Cy Bannerman met an accidental death, falling from his terrace through an over-waist-high railing, not having enough alcohol in his blood to classify him as drunk."

Already this weasel had the coroner's preliminary report, Max thought, half-admiringly. And he probably knew exactly what Max was thinking of too. But he was damned if he'd give him any fuel for some stinking column of innuendo.

"That's it."

"Umm."

Rich put his notebook away in an inner breast pocket. The

44

silver pen followed in a stately, ritualistic fashion. He rose. "OK."
He walked to the door, seemed gone, but turned back and said,
almost as an afterthought, "I've heard a few things I thought
you might have liked to talk about." He waited a split second.
Max did not pick up the cue. "See you later," Rich said and
closed the door behind him.

Max discounted the parting shot as another gambit, but
the encounter after the night and day left him miserable. He
went home, lay down on the sofa, and tried to nap. The phone
woke him. He was prepared to ignore it but it was Adeline,
from Florida. She had heard the news on the television only half
an hour ago. Was it true? She knew how the media lied all the
time, but such a thing—

"It's true," Max said heavily, the truth bearing in upon
him more and more. "Cy's dead, Adeline. He's gone."

He heard his mother let out a heavy breath at the other
end.

"He fell—like they say?"

"Somewhat, yeah."

"The poor boy," she whispered.

"Yeah."

"All the money, all that funny money . . . didn't help him."

"Mom, you're not going to start, are you?"

"I'm just saying . . ."

"I heard you."

"Maxie—are you all right?"

"I'm OK."

"What about the funeral? He doesn't have family. He told
me his mother was in an institution."

"She is."

"Should I come?"

Cy had charmed her, of course, the way he could charm
anyone he set out to capture. He had talked earnestly of his San
Francisco days, of his feelings for the working class. He had
whirled Adeline in the schottische at the folk-dance center. He
had brought her Mexican ceramic-bead necklaces. When she
talked about the rot of capitalism he had agreed. When she
expressed amazement that he was in Wall Street, that he dealt
in money undoubtedly somehow cheated from the workers, he
had taken pains to explain that it had nothing at all to do with
the workers. As a matter of fact it had nothing at all to do with
anything. The gains they made by buying whatever they bought

at a lower price than they sold meant nothing to anybody. It was all myth. Nothing ever changed hands except paper. It was all, to an extent, a simple gamble, but with foodstuffs or lumber or oil as the excuse. Funny money, she had declared. Cy had sprung to agree. Exactly. Funny money. And so many utterly respectable and powerful families had been founded on that base. Max had discovered them once, together in her kitchen, in that Bronx apartment on Cruger Avenue, drinking tea and laughing at the world. She had patted Cy on the cheek and Cy had kissed her nose. Max, standing in the doorway, thought he might be seeing two mismatched lovers. But Adeline was not captured entirely. Cy was a capitalist, like the rest of them. She would not forgive him that but liked him in spite of it, she declared.

"No, there's no need to come up," Max told her now.

"Maxie, are you going to go on with that money business?"

"Addie, please." He softened his voice. "How are you feeling?"

"Oh"—she was vague about herself, as always—"so-so. You know doctors. They always want you to come back. That's their training. What do they care. Medicare is paying. If there was real socialized medicine it would be different."

That meant her heart was acting up again. It became arrhythmic every so often and she dumped the medication down the toilet because it made her sleepy.

"Take care of yourself."

"Max—" Her voice was suddenly filled with apprehension. "You take care of yourself."

"Absolutely. I'll speak to you soon."

"Yes . . ." She was reluctant to end it but did. "Bye-bye, Maxie."

He spent the next two hours of that Saturday night sunk in a stupor in front of the television set, where the colors dazzled him and eventually put him to sleep. No dreams, no dreams at all.

3

Max spent most of the next week in a fog. He delayed discussions with Singh, who, shaken by Cy's death, smoked four packs a day of his unfiltered cigarettes rather than the usual three. He walked through the lunches, the meetings he could not avoid. He didn't read the mail. But in the crowded, narrow downtown streets he tensed at every jostling shoulder, at every stare.

At midnight, sitting in front of the cable-ready Sony, barely conscious of the 1953 grainy, black-and-white movie afflicting the twenty-five-inch screen, he wondered at the depth of his reactions. Other men had lost partners and friends. Other men had even lost fathers and brothers to violence. But not to know *why* was something else again. Why, he kept asking himself, why did Cy die?

He spoke to Barbara every day. Either she called or he called. She was certainly warmer than he had ever remembered her being. She invited him to accompany her to a funky fashion show but he declined. At a deli lunch he confided in Julie Berns that she seemed to need him, in a strange way—perhaps they

47

had underestimated her or her feelings for Cy. Julie was more hard-nosed. "I wouldn't trust her as far as I could throw her."

"She wasn't with Cy on the night. She talked to Shamski very openly. She was at a party in Soho. It all checked out. And she doesn't use lip gloss."

"Not now maybe," Berns growled. "What I'm saying is that she's a role-player. You can't trust her."

"Julie, Cy told Barbara that there was some kind of an 'or else' situation. What do you think that could mean?"

" 'Or else'?"

"That's what she remembers."

"That's crazy," Berns said vehemently. "I think she made it up."

"Why would she make it up?"

"I don't know—maybe just to show you how close they were." Berns leaned back in the plush chair. "Christ, who knows what Cy told that bitch." He shook his head. "Take my word, she's out for no good."

Max then related Shamski's interest in Liz Evers, and Julie became thoughtful.

"Something happened there, Max, something Cy didn't tell either of us, and Shamski's got a source."

Max stared at him. "What are you saying? That Liz had something to do with Cy's death? Come on, Julie."

"Listen," Berns said, putting his sandwich down. "I've been thinking about it. And I have the same gut feeling you do. Somebody pushed Cy over that railing. Somebody who wanted him dead. I'm not ruling anybody out." He stared at his plate morosely. "We go back so long. He was one in a million. A man. A mensch. After those crazy days, he pulled himself up. How many can say that? And he pulled some of us up along with him." He flushed with emotion. Max looked away.

"Julie, did Cy ever mention a woman named Sonya to you?"

Berns thought a moment. "I don't think so, no. Why?"

"She called him. It's on his tape. But I can't find her in his address book or the Rolodex."

"Who knows?" Julie went back to the brisket. "He had these one-night stands sometimes." He reached for the Diet Pepsi. "What about his estate?"

"The accountant's pulling the papers together."

That was another paradox. Cy had cared nothing about

the money itself, nothing at all. Other men hoarded. Other men haggled. Cy had spent. Almost as though getting rid of the money had been a sacred duty. The seventy-foot sailing yacht sold, impatiently. The small Lockheed propjet almost given away. The outlandish investments in start-up companies that never had a chance. The catalog went on and on. And the personal net worth went south. It didn't really matter, Cy had often stated, the markets were always there to provide more. And if things went to negative income every so often, why that was fine too. It was the way of America, it was the way of traders to use all the credit they could. That was the basis of the banking system, after all. And he was just being a good American boy and supporting the system.

"Keep a week from Friday open," Berns interrupted the reverie. "That's when we're taping the show and the tribute to Cy."

Max groaned.

"You promised," Julie reminded him.

Max nodded, resigned.

At the office, Max decided to plunge into tying up the loose ends. They had open option trades to follow, they had commodity positions, and anything could happen. Jimmy Singh had been working on a new information system. But cornering Singh in his computer-screened lair, Max found the Indian uncharacteristically unprepared for a full discussion of the company affairs.

"I have been lax," Singh confessed, puffing away and tapping at keys nervously. "I claim *mea culpa*. Data is missing, you see. Some supporting records have been mangled by a bad program—or maybe it was just the disk—I do not understand it. I am retrieving from the back files, but they were made on the old IBM we had. This new one is faster but doesn't read accurately for some reason. I am having an on-site repairman come for a look-see. We'll get at the problem then." Singh was so upset by his lack of performance, he who had always been so meticulous, so careful, so totally the master technician, that he had developed a small tick at the corner of his right eye.

"He's taking it very hard," Martha whispered to Max in the outer office. "I see him sometimes just staring at one of his screens, and I know he's not watching them. And sometimes he talks to himself—but in that Indian language so I don't know what he's saying."

Wholly sympathetic, Max understood that Jimmy's center had been Cy. It was Cy who had found him. It was Cy who had seen his potential. It was Cy who had enriched him enough so that the neat two-story house in Flushing had become possible, and the Chrysler that drove him to the Swami Ram Prebotha's retreat once a year to fast and concentrate on ethics. It was Cy who received the elaborate hand-printed and colored birthday cards from Singh's children, Sanjay Tommy and Indira Betty.

"Look," Max told him, "maybe you ought to take some time off."

"No, no," Singh replied hastily, his eye going, "I will not leave you alone, you see . . . Absolutely not. This firm is all that is left of Mr. Bannerman. For his memory, it must go on. The Swami, who does not care for earthly things, has mentioned him in his teaching."

Why not, Max thought irreverently; Cy had contributed heavily toward the construction of the retreat, including the giant hot tub that soothed the muscles of the faithful, opening their minds to the Swami's message.

"There are special men put upon this earth," Singh said in solemn tones, "to do special things, you see. I am not going to be sacrilegious and insist that Mr. Cy was one of them but I will go so far as to say that it is possible. And so we must be very loyal to his memory. Thus he achieves immortality, you see. Now," he added, handing Max a printout, "these are the current positions and the program's decisions. But, of course, Mr. Cy evaluated them all himself."

Max decided to clean things up, and ordered them all sold at market. There were also three open orders in gold, cocoa, and cotton. These were holdovers, remnants of the original feverish activity in commodities that had launched Whizkids into orbit. Since those days, Cy had reduced the pit trading to almost nothing in favor of options trading, where the leverage was good but the risk less than that in the commodity pits and the ulcer rate lower.

Max recalled Cy trying to explain to Adeline what leverage was all about. "Addie, it's simple. You put in a little bit and you make a lot. Isn't that intelligent?"

"And so who is being exploited?"

"Nobody."

"Cy, don't tell me fairy stories."

"It's economic theory . . . like Marx."

"Some theory. Look what Stalin did to Russia."

"Listen, it's called an 'option.' " Cy was determined to educate her. "It's the right to buy the stock of a company at a higher price than it's selling at, get it?"

Adeline was unbelieving. "That's smart—trying to buy something at a bigger price than it is?"

"Listen to me. The important thing is that you only pay a dollar, two, or three for that right while if you bought the stock itself you'd have to put up a lot more. Now, here's the move: When the stock goes up, so does the price of the option."

Adeline considered that carefully. Max interjected, "Cy, forget it."

"Am I a dummy?" Adeline demanded indignantly. "My own son thinks I'm a dummy. Never mind him, Cy. Go on."

"All right. Get this. While the stock price goes up maybe only a couple of dollars, the option price can double, triple, and more. You sell and you net a lot on a little. You have moved a big weight with a little stick. That, my sweet anti-Russki, is leverage."

"But what," Adeline asked, "if this company is bad and this stock price goes, instead of up—down?" She looked at Max in triumph then.

"You have just," Cy had responded, "put your finger on a basic problem."

At which they had all broken out into laughter, Max recalled, and Cy had hugged his mother, dancing her about the kitchen.

"You are sure we wish to close everything out?" Singh questioned.

Max said he was sure. In fact he found it difficult to concentrate on business. It hardly seemed to matter, seemed like a totally foreign process, empty of meaning.

Singh made his notes. "Things are so complicated," he muttered. "Oh, Mr. Cy, Mr. Cy." He smiled wanly at Max and left.

In the outer office, Martha was struggling with the phone, her forefinger rapping viciously on the pads.

Max held up. "Trouble?"

"Ugh," she said, exasperated, "a mess. Noise. Crossed wires. I'm calling ten blocks downtown and I can hardly hear them. "She made her connection. "Harriet? It's me. . . . Oh God, just listen to that."

Max listened intently. Staccato clicks. He hunched over the phone worriedly. He had heard those clicks before—or something very close to them. It was during his affair with the funny French girl when her idiot husband had a private detective put a tap on her phone. That damn fool. Those sounds were very much like these. But abruptly the line cleared. The clicks vanished and Harriet was asking where Martha had gone to.

"It's OK now," Max said. Martha resumed her conversation and Max left her alone. At the elevator he wondered if his imagination was overheating—the way Shamski claimed. Why would there be a tap on the office phone? Who would want to know what? What was there to know?

Leaving the building, Max walked uptown on Third. Still unnerved, he stopped for a gelato. As he munched the cone behind the store window, he became acutely aware of someone staring at him. It was a man in a seersucker suit and a rep tie eating his ice cream automatically. He had sandy hair blowing across his forehead and very round blue eyes. Square-faced, slightly built, in his thirties, a leather portfolio under his arm, he gazed away into space as Max started to move past him, but then muttered, "Got a minute?" Ignoring him, Max continued on. The man took a step with him. "Be good if we spoke, Mr. Roberts."

Startled at the use of his name, Max demanded, "What is this? What's the game?"

"Are we talking?" The man's round eyes bored into Max's.

"Who are you?" Max stared back.

"Call me Billy—how about that?"

"Listen," Max said angrily, "I don't know what kind of a scam you're trying to pull but . . ."

"I'm selling."

"Selling what?"

"Then we *are* talking."

Max said nothing. The second time today, he told himself. Things were coming apart. "Did you follow me here?"

"What I'm doing is dangerous," the Billy man said, "you

52

understand? There are people who wouldn't care for it at all."
He hunched closer to Max, his voice low. "It's better in a public
place like this right now."

"OK." Max decided to play along. "You tell me what this
is all about."

"You know."

"What do I know?"

"Mr. Roberts, you *know* what this is about. I'm prepared
to give you information that'll get you out of the trouble
you're in."

"What trouble am I in?" Max asked cautiously.

"Don't play dumb."

"You expect me to trust you—just like that?" Max was
hoping all the way. "How do I know what you're really after?"

"OK, all right"—the man seemed mollified—"but not here.
This was just a good contact point. I'll call you in a day or so
and we'll get down to it in a place I can trust."

"I'll wait," Max said.

"I'll be in touch. Billy. You wait a minute after I leave.
There's no point in taking chances. I'm taking enough talking
to you."

Abruptly he turned away from Max and made his way to
the door. Switching the portfolio to his other arm, he stepped
briskly out into the street. Max watched him go, bewildered.
What would Shamski say about this? In the cab to Cy's, he tried
puzzling out the encounter. What was he supposed to know?
He came up with nothing. In front of the building he stared,
almost hypnotized, at the remnant of the chalk marks. They
were all but invisible, yet to Max they jumped up off the asphalt.

Julio was already on and saluted him as he entered.

Max nodded.

" 'Scuse me, Mr. Roberts. I saw where there's gonna be a
secondary issue of that GCN company stock. You t'ink I oughta
get into it?"

"I have no idea," Max said. It never ends, he thought
gloomily.

When he opened the door to Cy's apartment, contrary to
what he had expected, Max experienced a sense of calm, of
relieving familiarity. After all, he told himself, he knew this place
as well as his own. As he looked around he remembered with
dismay that his own apartment was due for a painting, that

53

ultimate dislocating horror. It occurred to him that it might not be a bad idea to make an interim move here. Why not? It made sense. Better than a hotel, certainly.

Max removed his jacket and shoes and stretched out on the leather couch. On a table nearby, in a silver frame, was an eight-by-ten photo of Cy and Barbara on a beach. They were both on their backs in the sand, eyes closed against the Caribbean glare. Barbara was in a bikini, long legs glistening. Cy wore his cutoffs. Max lifted the picture to his eyes. Something about Cy—he realized what it was. In the morgue, Cy had looked like this—stretched to full length, eyes closed, unmoving. He felt the same stab he had experienced standing before the icy drawer. When the phone at his elbow rang he almost dropped the picture. Setting it back, he reached over. "Hello?"

A woman's voice, throaty and uncertain, came through. "Hello?" A hesitation. "This isn't Cy?"

"No."

"I must have dialed wrongly, I'm sorry."

"No, wait a minute. You dialed OK. Who is this, please?"

Silence. Max sensed that if he didn't speak she would be gone.

"I'm a friend of Cy Bannerman's." He waited for the reaction.

"Yes?"

"Can you tell me your name?"

"Would you just tell him that Sonya called, please?"

Max sat upright.

"You called last weekend."

"Yes."

"He never called you back, though."

"I don't think I want to continue this."

"Wait a minute. Listen, he didn't call you back because . . ." How to say it—how to say this thing? He cleared his throat. As he did, she asked,

"Are you Max?"

"Yes," he said, surprised, "I'm Max Roberts."

Who was she that Cy would speak to her about him?

"Sonya," he inquired cautiously, "how long have you and Cy known each other?"

"Why is that important for you to know?"

"Because . . . because Cy's dead, Sonya."

He heard the intake of her breath and a noise as the telephone hit something.

"You there? I'm really sorry to have to tell you like this."

Silence once more. But he knew she was there.

"No one is sure how it actually happened, I—"

Her voice shrank. "I have to go now. Thank you for telling me."

"Wait a minute."

"I have to go."

How close were they? She seemed remarkably contained at the news he'd sprung on her and yet—

"Listen, can I come to see you, talk to you?"

Silence.

"Maybe there are things you can tell me . . . or I can tell you."

"I think not."

"You'd be doing me a big favor, honestly—and for Cy's sake . . ."

He heard the deep sigh, then she said, "If you want to."

"That's very good of you, it really is."

"I don't live in New York, though. I live in Sky Mountain—that's the township—in Vermont."

"Vermont?" What was Cy doing with some woman in Vermont he never talked about? Quickly he said, "I don't know exactly when I could get up there, so could you give me a phone number or an address?"

She spoke a number, which he jotted down.

"And what about your last name?"

"Call, just call." And she hung up.

Sonya? Cy had never mentioned a Sonya. Cy, who talked all the time about the women he knew, who dissected their looks, their motives, their moves endlessly, Cy had kept this woman, whoever she was, a secret. For what reason? And did she use lip gloss? He was about to call Shamski and add her name to the list but decided, stubbornly, not to trust the police. In further defiance, he spent endless hours tracking down the phone numbers of women whose names he had, for one reason or another, neglected to include on Shamski's list. Some of them had disappeared into that abyss that holds the past years' fashion magazines' favorites. Some had not known of Cy's death and were shocked at this reminder of their own mortality. A few were wary of speaking to him. One, Max remembered, had never been without her little gold coke spoon, which came encased in its embossed Florentine leather case. In the three-year interim since Cy, she had married a congressman from the Sunbelt and become born again.

Max had resolved to check them all out but in every instance it was clear that any connection with Cy was long past and gone, and if Slickers had any significance at all, it was on the lips of someone Cy had been with on the night his life had ended. Max realized that he had embarked on this quest out of the need to do something on his own, but it was futile.

On the weekend, in preparation for the painters, he moved a suitcase filled with clothing to Cy's. On Sunday, sitting alone with the bulk of the Sunday *Times* scattered over Cy's couch, he contemplated the day. Sometimes on Sundays he and Cy would play ball with a group of admen whose turf was the northwest field of Central Park. Cy, a natural athlete, would play first base. Max would play centerfield. After the game they would watch the local action for a while, as the Latinos partied with hot food, beer coolers, and loud salsa on the boom boxes. Still later, there would be friends, crazy types who had latched themselves on to Cy, fashion people, movie people, weird musicians. Cy drew them like a magnet. They seemed perfectly cast for the nonstop play they performed. No more.

He sorted through the *Times* sections absentmindedly and flung them all to the floor. An endless Sunday loomed. How long, he thought, would it take to drive to Vermont? He called the number Sonya had given him. She answered on the second ring. The same throaty voice.

"Hello?"

"Good morning. Hi. It's Max Roberts. Is it a bad time?"

"Not—really."

"Good. Good. I was wondering if I might drive up to see you today?"

"Why?"

He was taken aback by her directness. "Well—about Cy."

"What about him?"

"Just—things."

"What kind of things?"

Why would she put up this kind of resistance? Two could play at the "direct" game. "Listen, it's obvious that you don't want to see me—"

"Not particularly."

"But why? I mean you had some kind of a relationship with Cy. I'm just . . . kind of trying to pull some things together. You might be able to help."

"I doubt that."

"Let me be the judge."

"Mr. Roberts." Her voice was firm and sure. "I live a simple life, uncomplicated. I like it that way. I don't want it disturbed."

But Cy was not simple and uncomplicated, Max thought instantly, and if she was telling the truth it would be the first time he had known Cy to be involved with anyone like that.

"I promise you, I have no intention of disturbing your life." Inspiration struck him. "I just want to check some things out with you that I don't think should be done over the telephone, Miss . . . Miss . . ."

"Koanis," she said, and the throaty quality was back, "my name is Koanis. All right, I'll see you. But not today."

Max tried to keep the elation from his voice. "When, then?"

"Oh—next week sometime."

Was she evading? "Why not sooner?"

"Next week. Say—Tuesday?"

"All right. Next Tuesday. What's the best route to take to Sky Mountain? That's the town, isn't it?"

He heard a slight relaxed laugh then. "You won't find it. Fly to Manchester. I'll meet you at the airport."

"Great. I'll call you again about the timetable."

"No," she said, "be on the two-ten." She hesitated. "That's the one Cy usually took."

"OK." Now he hesitated. "Will we have any trouble recognizing each other?"

"I know you," she said cryptically, "or what you look like. Good-bye."

Before he could say anything more, she had broken the connection. Max sat back. He would see her. He would discover what this was all about.

Churned and restless, he went out to the terrace. Two steps from the railing, he stopped dead still, suddenly conscious of where he was. His eyes focused on the new wood where the railing had been repaired, then he looked at the flooring. Shamski had said that there were no scuff marks, which a struggle would have produced. But the flooring was wooden planks,

57

raised from the roof below it to provide drainage for the plantings. Wood, rough redwood, would never show scuff marks.

He looked through the high bamboo fence to the other penthouse, with its much smaller terrace. He saw that it was almost flush up against the neighboring building. How easy it would have been to get up on that roof, step over to the terrace, and await the chance. Cy seldom opened the terrace doors—particularly in the summer with the air-conditioners going full blast. But if whoever had been with him had done so or asked Cy to, how simple it all would have been for anyone waiting to jump through, grab Cy, and hurl him over. Even if Cy had called out, who would have responded? Who would even have heard, with their own windows sealed shut in these high rises? And even if they had heard, who would pay attention? Who responded to cries in the night?

He was so engrossed that when the phone rang he almost missed the sound. It was Barbara, who wanted to know if it was true he was staying at Cy's and didn't he feel kind of spooked there? Max told her he did not and before he even realized he was saying it, asked if she was free for dinner.

"No," she answered, "but I've been thinking about you. I mean, you were so close to Cy, you have to be hurting."

"How about you?"

"Oh," she said, "you were *really* close to him." Then an idea struck her. "Listen, the magazine is giving a shindig tonight at Space. Late. Would you like to come?"

At the disco?

"Come on. It'll be fun. You need some getting out."

He hung up with a small thread of excitement creeping through him.

It was the usual crazy Space scene. They had turned the place into a mad parody of a fashion magazine. Editorial rooms with almost-nude "editors" hunched over layouts, crazily angled photo studios with models in session. A huge photo montage of a press room, complete with pressmen in newsprint hats, a gigantic light-encrusted front page. On the balcony, famous ads were brought to life, the Calvin Klein girl eternally pulling up her undershirt, the Jim Palmer figure staring out defiantly in his Jockey shorts, the Frederick's of Hollywood baby doll, in her bra with the nipple cutouts, licking her lips.

THE THIRD FRIDAY

Picking Barbara up had been an experience in itself. She had dressed herself in a short, sequined, skintight confection that had a spun-candy effect and ended in patterned silver legs coming down to black pointed boots. Her hair flowed up and down and around but stood up a bit on top in small spiky curls. Her eyes, large and lustrous, were made even more so by the deep dark shadow she wore. Her lips were carmine drenched. But not with Slickers; Shamski had already determined that. She greeted Max warmly and, in the cab, placed herself so close to him that their hips touched and her breast casually brushed against his arm. There had been no mention of Cy at all, surprising Max, but he found that he had no desire to talk about that either.

Inside the club, Barbara greeted people right and left, waving, blowing kisses, patting faces. Max hung back. But when, finally, the loudspeakers slamming sound at the mobbed dance floor, he and Barbara chanced it, Max was entranced at the sight of her movement, hips nonstop sinuous, arms waving like enhancing snakes, behind her back, over her head, in front of the slight curve of her shimmering belly. After an hour, he felt heady. He moved through the throng to get some wine, returning with two glasses. As he handed one to Barbara, she stopped in midsentence, and he saw that she had frozen with fear.

"Max." She swallowed hard, staring across the room.

"What is it?"

"He's here. Look. Over there." Max followed her glance to where the thickset man in a gray suit was lighting a cigar. His fleshy face and thinning hair were caught in the glare of a spotlight and his eyes searched the dance floor.

"Jesus Christ," Barbara whispered. Max felt her hand go clammy. "He's looking at us, isn't he?"

Max peered. Who was that? Finally he saw that it was Bobby Catalfo.

"God," Barbara shuddered, "he's going to come over, I know it."

"No," Max said, "he's going to stay far away from me. Watch."

They stood on the edge of the floor, feeling the bass beat through the soles of their feet, hand in hand, waiting. Across the room, Catalfo turned, like a radar seeking the target, until he faced them. And he saw them. Without doubt, Max knew.

His slash-thin lips and broad nose faced them directly, his pupils reflecting pinpoints of light even from this distance.

"Let's go." Barbara pulled at Max. "Let's get out of here."

"No," Max said, "come on, let's dance."

He slid around moving bodies onto the floor, Barbara, protesting, behind him. In a moment they were lost to view amidst the gyrating figures.

"Every time I see him," Barbara muttered, "I get this chill."

"Take it easy."

The music pounded for twenty minutes, the jock segueing from one beat to another. Then he broke, and Max led Barbara away. He looked for the real estate man and saw him in another corner now, glass in hand, two women near, listening attentively. He glanced over to Max, a casual glance, and turned back to his audience.

"It's OK," Max said. "He doesn't give two hoots about us."

"It's no fun anymore," Barbara complained. "I really want to get out of here."

"All right," Max agreed. "We'll leave."

They were out in minutes, forced to pass Catalfo on the way to the door. Barbara clutched Max's arm, looking resolutely at the floor. Max steadied himself for anything but there was nothing. Catalfo ignored them, his wide back stretching the fabric of his jacket as they went by. On the street the hulk-shouldered, skin-headed guardian of the gate was still being besieged by the shouting mob desperate to pass the portal to paradise. Max led Barbara past just as a taxi drove up, dropping three new hopefuls. He helped her in and closed the door.

"I'm sorry," Barbara said, sitting back. "I just got freaked when I saw him. Ugh . . ." She shuddered. "It reminded me."

The traffic was light and they moved uptown rapidly. Barbara said nothing. She sat back, her legs stretched out as much as possible, her hair now and again brushing Max's face. Her hands, in her lap, played with the small disco purse and she faced away from Max. Just once during the trip did her eyes moved toward him. The look, he thought, was an odd one—cool, yet with something more. When they arrived at her town house, Max asked the driver to wait and accompanied Barbara to the door as she searched for her keys.

"Thanks for asking me," he said. "It was a little crazy but I think I needed something a little crazy."

Barbara opened the door and turned back to him. Her face,

60

lit only by the streetlamp, was shadowed and exotic. "Do you really need the cab?" It took Max seconds to realize it was not a question.

"No," he said, "I guess . . . I can always get one." He had bills out before he reached the driver, and shoved them into his hand.

They pressed into the tiny town-house elevator, which rose in a slow and stately fashion. So close to Barbara he could feel the texture of her dress, Max said awkwardly, "You can't get out of here in a rush."

She patted his face, smiling. "You know, you don't resemble Cy at all, but sometimes when I look at you—and even the way you sound . . ."

The elevator stopped. She opened the door and led Max inside. Though he had been there only a week before, it seemed different to him now. The stainless-steel chairs, the huge pink couches forming a conversation pit, the Toulouse-Lautrec poster, an original, over a candelabra-laden oak-and-brass dining table, appeared as though through a haze.

"Would you like a drink?"

"Not really," Max said. "Not actually."

"Me neither." Barbara pulled at her waist. "This dress is too tight. I like it close, but . . ." She kicked off her boots and headed toward the bedroom. From where he was, Max saw the dress come flying off over her head. She wore no bra and her breasts, tanned and firm, sprang free. Catching his breath, Max turned away, turned back. Barbara was perfectly visible, removing the spangled pantyhose, seemingly oblivious of him. She stretched toward the ceiling, and the slight pink bikini she wore pulled tight across the hips. All of her was tan, not deeply so but with a golden glow suffusing her thighs and shoulders and buttocks. "Be right out," she called.

Max felt the blood rise in him and fill his body. He fought the feeling. Barbara pulled on a purple wrap and came to the doorway.

"This is better."

"Yes," Max said, stunned.

"Seeing that man . . ." Barbara shuddered. ". . . scary. If you hadn't been with me . . ."

"Forget it."

"You're comforting." Barbara moved closer to him. "Really nice."

What, Max asked himself, is going on; what is happening

here? This was Cy's preserve, all of it, yet . . . She had been stimulated by the excitement, he reasoned—it didn't mean anything. But Barbara's arms went around him and he could not keep his from going around her, could not keep his fingers from moving down the back he had seen, to her hips and thighs. He pressed forward against her, his lips eating at hers, giving up altogether, a mixture of reluctance and acceptance, of disgust and urgency.

At something after five in the morning, Max could see the first hints of morning light come in through the south garden window. At his right, an arm thrown up revealing the lightest part of her skin, Barbara slept. The light cotton cover had slipped down and a round small breast edged out. Max pulled the cover up over it. He looked around the room, at the outsize bed and at Barbara herself, beautiful and serene in slumber. He shook his head in incomprehension and secret delight. Not at the sexual aspect of the night, for, after all the display, Barbara had been surprisingly passive; rather, his wonder was at the simple fact of his *being there* at all, in Barbara's bed, experiencing everything that Cy had.

Barbara stirred. Her eyes blinked and opened. She looked at him for a long moment as though placing him in some mental pattern and said, "What time is it?"

"Early," Max told her. "Go back to sleep."

"I'm awake." She yawned, "God, I hate to be awake this early."

"I'll go and you can get back to sleep."

"Not yet—in a little bit."

She settled herself, one arm behind her head. She was terrific, Max thought, even in the morning, this way.

"For a minute," she said, "I thought you were Cy—isn't that kooks?"

"Sorry."

"I didn't mean it that way. I meant it just . . . seemed to me to be him."

"I understand."

"I really liked him." She pushed a strand of hair from her eyes. "You really think someone killed him?"

Max nodded. "I'd just like to know who—and why."

She was silent for a time, then said, "He was a funny guy.

He never really talked to me too much, but then all of a sudden he'd say some things. . . ."

"Like 'or else'?"

"Yes." She looked at Max speculatively. "What's going to happen with Cy's place on the Island?"

"I don't know." Max reached for her smooth round shoulder. "It'll be sold, I guess."

"We had some fun times there. Too bad."

Max wondered what his response was supposed to be, a lamentation, an invitation? "I suppose it could be used for weekends for a while," he said cautiously, "until Julie Berns and I work out the disposal details."

"Berns?"

"He's alternate executor."

"Ugh."

"You don't like Julie?"

"Not much."

Max looked at her attentively. She shrugged. "Oh—it's not important." Her eyes closed. She moved about restlessly, settled, and Max realized she was asleep again, breathing in a shallow rhythm, her knees drawn up fetally, her arms crossed overr her chest.

He rose slowly, retrieved his clothing, dressed, and left the apartment. In the elevator he couldn't repress a smile. He felt fine, strangely fine. He had never expected any of it to happen. Now that it had, he was filled with a sense of satisfied wonder, and he chuckled.

The street, just barely morning-lighted, held the only freshness the day would bring. Max breathed deeply and sauntered west. There would not be too many cabs at this hour but he would find one. He had taken only a few steps when he heard the sounds of rushing feet coming toward him. He stopped, whirled, and felt the first smash at his back as though a sledgehammer had hit him. He arched, staggered, and the second blow came at his stomach, jerking him straight again. In pain, instinctively, he lashed out with his fists, finding solid flesh.

There were two of them, two pounding, beating experts. No matter how he tried to evade them, they flung him to the wall, punishing his face and torturing his ribs. He flailed about, twisted, ducked, the pain vanishing temporarily with the shock. At one point, he managed to break away, and he ran down the street, where a car was parked with a driver at the wheel.

"Help!" he shouted thickly, "help me!" As he yelled, it flashed across his mind that Cy might have screamed those words out.

They caught him near the car. He staggered back to the wall. One held him by the arms. The other poked his face at Max, nose touching nose. And Max saw he was facing the bulbous nose.

"You got the message?" The voice was raspy, thick.

Max stared at him dumbly, conscious that blood was streaming from a cut on his cheek.

"You got it?"

Max felt himself being shaken like a mouse in a cage.

"You better believe."

He was hurled to the pavement. The two men raced away, fading into the dappled darkness. Max rose on one knee. The blue sedan was starting up. He tried to wave to the driver, who turned for a bare second, and Max saw Bobby Catalfo's face. In the next second the car shot away and Max looked after it, dazed and frightened.

4

"You're sure it was Catalfo you saw?"

Max touched his cheek where the dressing covered the bruise and glared at Shamski. "I'm sure, yes. And that gorilla was the one who saw me come out of Barbara's house before. You want videotapes?"

"Easy," Shamski soothed, "easy. It's not good to get riled up when your ribs are strapped." He leaned back into the deep down of Cy's couch with admiration. "It's really nice here."

"So—what are you going to do about him?" Max sat stiffly in the chair. If he moved too suddenly, the side felt as though it were coming apart, rib by rib. Boxers must feel this way after a bout, he thought irrelevantly.

"All right," Shamski said, "I'm going to believe that you saw that bum and made identification."

"Thanks."

"So, the next question is, are you prepared to swear out a complaint for assault and battery on him?"

"Damn right I am."

"OK."

But Max could see the hesitation. "What's the problem?"

Shamski frowned. "The problem is that he wasn't the guy who worked you over. It was two other guys . . . who you don't know."

"Come on," Max said. "He was behind it. Or else what was he doing there—out for a joyride?"

Shamski nodded. "I know it and you know it, but knowing isn't proving."

Max groaned. "Are you a detective or a lawyer?"

"You want to keep a guy when you collar him, you need solid proof, or else he's gone. Believe me."

"Terrific." Max pounded the chair in frustration. "I get beat up and you tell me I can't do anything about it."

"I didn't say that," Shamski corrected. "You can swear out the warrant and we can bring him in maybe, and his lawyer will laugh. You come out of a woman's apartment in the early A.M. and get mugged. Then you blame it on a man who you say you saw for only seconds at the wheel of a car down the street, a man who used to go with the girl."

"Exactly what happened."

"So Catalfo swears he was in bed asleep, counting sheep all night. Where does that leave us? Your word against his. And with egg on our faces, that's where. It's a bad collar. It'll never stick."

"Dammit," Max shouted. "If he could do this to me, he might have had those same goons murder Cy. Isn't that important? Doesn't that count for anything?"

"He's tough," Shamski agreed, "but crazed enough for murder? Still, you never know. There are guys who have to own women. And they can go pretty far."

"So what am I supposed to do now?"

Shamski thought a moment. "I think the best bet is to spread it around that you and I talked, that he was mentioned, and that we're putting it on hold for the time being. That'll let him know we're into it and he'd better watch himself."

So—nothing again, Max saw. People were killed, beaten —and it was uphill all the way to get even rudimentary justice.

"Does the Stratton woman know what happened?"

Max shook his head. He had not yet told her. She would be terrified if he did but if he didn't she would have no warning. And who knew what Catalfo might try next.

"She'll find out," Shamski said, "somehow."

Max agreed. He would have to tell her and that would probably end it. He was not altogether regretful. Cy's print was on her and he had been conscious of that even as he had lost himself in her.

"What do you make of that 'Billy' stuff?" he asked Shamski. "The guy who approached me?"

"Weird" was Shamski's response.

"You believe me on that? You don't think I'm making it up?"

"No," Shamski assured him, "but it's weird. What trouble would you be in that he's going to get you out of—for a price?"

"Market stuff? We're hooked on certain options." Max tried to reason it through. "Maybe he just knows something about those stocks. But why talk about how dangerous it is to talk to me? Unless it is."

Shamski considered that. "Well, if he calls you, make a meet and get to me. I'll put someone on him. We'll find out what his racket is." He prepared to leave but as he opened the door, Max called out, "Have you seen Liz Evers yet?"

Shamski turned back. "I talked to her. Quite a woman."

"Cy used to say she had a whim of iron. Does she use that lip gloss?"

"She says not the brand that was on the glass. Mostly she wears Estée Lauder lipstick. Tangerine." He reached into his jacket pocket and drew out a small silver tube. Pulling the cap off, like a magician producing the rabbit, he revealed the creamy head. "Slickers. Comes in flavors. This is pineapple. On the glass there was cantaloupe. It's manufactured by a company in Chicago." He smiled. "Some of the guys are getting worried about me."

"One more thing," Max said. "Do me a favor. Would you check to see if my office phones are being tapped?"

Shamski stowed the tube away and cocked his head skeptically.

"Just do me the favor," Max said.

"Take it easy on your ribs," Shamski replied and left.

By late afternoon, when some of the discomfort had vanished and Max was able to move about, he called Barbara. She was aghast at what had happened and said she had been right all along to be frightened. Max assured her the police had it in hand and nothing else would occur. She was not convinced. They did not make another date, neither of them bringing the subject up. Replacing the phone, Max conjured up for one last moment Barbara's bed, her body, and the feel of her skin. After that he called Julie Berns, told him what had happened, and how he could not then make an appearance on the Alloway TV show. "My God," Berns said, shocked, "I'm coming right over."

Max hung up, checked the strapping on his ribs, and felt —disconnected from things. He rummaged in the freezer, found a pizza, microwaved it, wandered about the apartment munching. Meandering in the bedroom, he sat down at Cy's PC. He knew that Cy had been totally taken with the computer, used it for every conceivable purpose. Max dropped a game disk in the drive and spent half an hour trying to land an airplane at O'Hare Airport. He crashed the plane four times and on the fifth try managed to overshoot the field. In disgust, he replaced the disk with an unmarked one from a stack and checked the directory as it came up on the screen. A series of stock tables. He tried another, letters that Cy had written, innocuous all of them, including one he had knocked out to Liz Evers. One passage, however, was cryptic.

. . . you know that we are both very strong-willed people and what you are asking, given the situation, could never work out. It would cause us all a lot of misery. Why can't you understand that?

As he tried to decipher that, the phone rang. It was Adeline, from Miami. Not now, Max said to himself despairingly, but there she was.

"Hi, Mom." He tried cheer.

"What's wrong?"

What a witch. "Nothing, absolutely nothing."

"Why aren't you in your own apartment?"

"You heard my tape. This is a temporary move while they're painting." He left the subject quickly. "How's the weather?"

"Max," Adeline admonished, "you know I hate to talk about the weather. That's all they do around here. The weather and what wonderful children they have, which I don't believe in the first place, and what people are coming out of whose rooms in the morning—with their walkers yet."

Max sensed labored breathing as she talked.

"Mom, are you all right?"

"Me? I'm a hundred percent. So, maybe not a hundred but ninety."

"Have you seen the doctor?"

"He gives me a pain, that doctor—one injection of whatever it is. Good-bye. Next. Sixty-five dollars from Medicare."

"Ma—you and your friends had how many demos for state medicine?"

"This," Adeline said with dismissal, "is a corruption. Like Russia."

A perfectly normal conversation.

"I want to speak to you, my son, about the future."

Max braced himself.

"It is my opinion now that Cy, he should rest in peace, is gone, that you should stop what you're doing."

"And do what—?"

"Something good—look at young Kennedy, not that he isn't a capitalist paragon—but he uses the corrupt money to start this oil business up in Boston which helps poor people. I read all about it in *People* magazine."

"Ma—you said that was a rag."

"So—even a rag can be useful. It can clean a window, sonny boy."

"Ma—these are the eighties, not the thirties—there's not even a May Day parade anymore."

"Because labor is big business now, that's why."

Sweet Adeline, Max thought. So long as she retained her anger at what she felt was history's betrayal of her ideals she would be fine. It was the engine that kept her moving forward.

"Mom," he said, "I'll think about it."

"Come down to see me sometime."

"Soon, Mom, I promise."

He hung up, remembering a small, slim woman, jet-black braids wrapped about her head, sandals on her feet, in dirndl skirts, coming home from work, rushing food to the table, and rushing herself to endless meetings. When she had taken him along, all he recalled was a loud babble, voice and countervoice. Nobody ever agreed on anything. Total anarchy. "That's the whole point," she had informed him. "No dictators." He had fled. Now she had breathing problems in Miami, where the others praised their good children.

An hour later, true to his word, Julian came by, listened to Max's somewhat expurgated version of the past evening's events, and pronounced, "That woman is bad news, I keep telling you."

"She doesn't exactly think you're tops in taps either, Julie."

"Oh yeah? What did she say now?"

"She didn't say anything—exactly. She implied."

"Implied what?" Before Max could respond, Julie added darkly, "I don't count that bitch out of this. And I'm a little surprised that you went out with her. I mean—" He didn't finish and Max wondered if he considered that Cy had been betrayed somehow.

After Julian left, Max called in for messages. There was one from Phil Carmody for him to drop by anytime. He had forgotten about Carmody, he realized. One did not do that, not to Phil Carmody. He called now and apologized, said he was on his way over, if Carmody had time for him. Carmody, courteous as always, said that of course he had time for Max; he would be waiting for him. Max rushed off.

The thirty-second floor of 43 Wall, by some miracle of builders' oversight, had an unobstructed view of the city. It was open to the west, where the twin boxes of the World Trade Center made dwarfs of the buildings below, and to the east, where the garbage-infested river flowed. The southern windows looked out toward the always brooding Ellis Island, and the northern vista reached to the arch of the George Washington Bridge and beyond to a glimpse of leafy Riverdale.

It was a power view, and Phil Carmody's office suite at the corner of the floor lived up to the responsibilities. The desk was rolltop, huge and solid American oak, made in Lincoln's time. The other furnishings were eclectic yet harmonious, providing a restful, latter-century feeling. The three telephones were state-of-the-art, however, for the phone was the umbilical, the line that connected this calm haven to the blood-gushing, head-bashing markets of the world just beyond the windows, and in fact, just a floor down, where some of the trading rooms of Carmody's old firm were situated.

Some say that when you live with a glorious view long enough, it becomes invisible. Yet Phil Carmody eyed his northern view, his island view, with a relish that never faded. He had been, by the fortune of circumstance, allowed through the privileged gates of this city to the place where great fortunes had been and would be made, where money was spun off money, where all that was required was brains, an opening stake, and an understanding of the anxiety and greed of the vast majority of the sprawl down there and in all the floors and rooms opposite. Others understood that as well, but Phil Carmody, they said, could gauge exactly how much pressure a particular market could sustain and thus know the exact time to make his move up or down, in or out, real or fake.

These days, Phillip Carmody traded very little for his own or any clients' accounts. At sixty-four, small and trim, conservatively clad in neat browns, grays, and blues, his calm, piercing eyes belying a swiftly advancing cataract, his hair thinning but still sandy, he counseled now, advised, appeared as an eminence on Alloway's program, and issued a newsletter six times a year. After a lifetime on the Street, it was enough.

Waiting to see Carmody in the anteroom, Max fidgeted on the leather sofa. If Cy had talked about something "or else" to Barbara, he would have spoken to Carmody, the godfather, about it for sure. For this is where it had all started—and only half a dozen years ago. It seemed incredible. Only six years ago, Cy Bannerman had been scrounging along, another intense figure in the cityscape.

At what Village party had he met Kristin Carmody? Max recalled, vaguely, Cy's telling him she was only twenty-two then, a long-haired art student. Fighting her father every inch of the way, smashing herself against the image of the Wall Street shark, the budding artist painting furiously in the loft he'd bought for her, living off the allowance he gave her, trying desperately to paint him and the city house and the country house and the shore house out of her mind, out of her life. Ah, but the old fox had been wily. He had given her all the rope she wanted. Morality, Cy had reported, wasn't the question. The old man knew all about human lusts. Her bouts with Cy were ignored. The long term was what interested Carmody—and so far as he was concerned, Cy Bannerman was a short-term investment, but one he chose to deal with since his daughter seemed intent on making it long term.

The door opened and Carmody welcomed him warmly, taking Max's outstretched hand in both of his own.

"I'm so glad you came."

Max stood for a moment, transfixed by the views; he had been here only twice before. Carmody's brow wrinkled. "Max, what happened to you?"

"I was mugged on the street. It's not serious."

Carmody nodded. "The price we pay."

"I meant to see you before but a lot's broken loose."

"What a waste." Carmody sighed, "What a terrible waste."

"Mr. Carmody," Max said, "it wasn't an accident."

Carmody cocked his head, eyes opening wide. "I read—"

"Wrong. No accident. No suicide. Not Cy. Somebody was there with him. He was pushed over." He saw Carmody's skeptical look and added, "I'm serious. There are scary things happening."

Carmody examined him intently. "You mean all this, don't you?"

"Someone was in his apartment after it happened. I saw him. And I'm not so sure my mugging isn't related to it all somehow."

"Max—my God." Carmody became agitated, started pacing. "What about the police?"

"Nitpicking. The detective in charge is a Jesuit."

"Let's look at this calmly," Carmody said. "Who . . . who in the world would want to do . . . what you say?"

"Have you seen Cy in the past couple of months, Mr. Carmody—has he talked to you about anything? Whenever we're in trouble he comes to you . . . came to you. Has he said anything about something that might happen to him?"

"I haven't seen him, no," Carmody said after taking a moment to remember. "As a matter of fact I was upset because I hadn't. I called two weeks ago and gave him a little brimstone. He promised we'd have dinner on Wednesday but he never called back. I said he can go to the devil, you know—and then I heard about it on the Channel 4 news." He sat heavily on a side chair. "I felt it . . . it was a mistake, some reporter made a mistake. I called the network and they confirmed."

They both fell silent and after a moment Carmody nodded at the doorway. "I remember when he first walked through there. I didn't know what to expect precisely. Kristin was so unstable then."

"How's her new little boy?"

"Wonderful. Just wonderful. That's the whole point, Max. I knew she'd be all right, with time."

They had faith, Max thought, those with the right background for openers, with the right bank accounts, they had faith in flings and futures.

"The point was that if I could convince this Bannerman fellow, you see, that it would not profit him in any way if he kept on seeing my daughter, I knew she'd come out of it and marry as she should."

72

He was off to the past, Max saw, frustrated.

"So," Carmody continued, "when the private detective tracked him down and gave him my message and he said he'd see me, I was convinced half the battle was won, you see."

"Yes," Max said dutifully.

That was the first time Carmody had ever seen the man whom he would come to regard as almost a surrogate son, and from the moment he had entered the office, he felt he knew him, felt it absolutely. For before even a word had been spoken, both men understood each other. Carmody had allowed no hint of rancor, almost no hint of anything personal to enter his slightly gravelly voice. They had talked around the subject, in generalities, as both sized each other up. It had been Carmody who approached the issue bluntly.

"Mr. Bannerman . . . you know, I feel quite peculiar addressing a man who has just come from my daughter's bed as 'mister,' so may I call you Cy?"

Cy had smiled. "What'll I call you?"

"Mr. Carmody, of course."

"OK." The smile turned into a laugh. "You probably have researched me to hell and gone."

"Oh yes."

"So, what's this meeting all about?"

"To talk about priorities. That's what everyone lives by when you get right down to it, wouldn't you say? Tell me, how do you feel about Kristin?"

"I'm very fond of her."

"I'm sure. But you didn't really talk to her about getting married, did you?"

"No, but *she* talked to me about it."

"You would never consider that, of course."

"I never took it seriously—till now. Mr. Carmody, I don't actually know why I'm here."

"I called you."

"I didn't have to show up."

"But you did."

"I know you're her father, and I respect that, but Kris is her own person and whatever goes on between us . . ."

"Cy, Cy"—this had been said with an edgy tone—"if I wanted to cut off this affair before, or punish you for it, I would have, and could have, believe me."

"I'm sure of that. So why this meeting?"

73

"Because I don't like crude methods—if I can avoid them."
He had returned then to affability. "You're a very personable
young man; I would say you have no trouble with the opposite
sex, no trouble at all."

Cy had shrugged and sat back into the plush veal of the
club chair. His eyes had roamed the office and Carmody had
known exactly what was taking place in him.

"Kristin has looks but she doesn't reason too well. She'll
be married in a year, two the most, if you're out of the way.
Don't you think so?"

Cy had grinned. Like a young boy, Carmody remembered
thinking, like a really nice young man. "You do know her, Mr.
Carmody."

"Oh, I do, I do. Yes."

"Sir," Cy had said then, "I don't really want to make any
family problems. She's a sweet person. You seem like a really
good guy—even with your reputation."

"Oh? What is my reputation?"

"You get things done that you want done. You know the
ins and outs. What buttons to press."

"You've researched me, I see." Carmody remembered fo-
cusing his failing eyes on this young man—how young? What
difference did it make; everyone looked young to him these days.
He had understood, the instant Bannerman stepped into the
office, why Kristin was attracted. It wasn't just the looks, though
the man was good-looking enough, with solid, regular features
and big brown eyes that, he supposed, spoke volumes to impres-
sionable postadolescents; no, there was something else—it was
some depth that swam in those eyes, some intelligent restless-
ness combined with the capacity to turn those eyes on you and
project absolute and genuine interest. And more—there was
sympathy in his face, and humor. At least his daughter wasn't
a total fool.

"You work at this agency, Cy. What do you do there?"

"Oh," Cy had answered disparagingly, "I've done a few
things. Right now, I sell ad space."

"And what did you do before that?"

Cy had ticked them off disparagingly. "Sold insurance,
worked in a PR outfit . . ."

"I mean," Carmody had probed, "what you had in mind
originally, as a boy."

"What I had in mind," Cy said, "was this notion of healing people, becoming a doctor."

"And?"

"I never followed through on it; other things got in the way. I did try to organize a farm cooperative, though." He laughed at the memory. "I was run out of town—by the farm union. I was cutting into their territory. It was hysterical."

"And what do you believe is important now?"

Cy had turned serious then. "Important—well, the truth as I see it, bottom line, is that just about everything except medicine, or science, or teaching in the jungles of Africa is some kind of a game, isn't it, Mr. Carmody?"

"Maybe," Carmody had conceded, "and so where does that leave you?"

"At the ad agency, I guess. There's some money there if I can make it work, go out on my own."

"Money? You want to make money?"

Cy had looked at him reflectively. "Maybe."

"Umm." Carmody had offered him one of his hand-rolled Cubanos from the humidor. Cy had refused and as Carmody clipped the end of the one he had chosen, he asked, "Do you take advice well?"

"Mostly not, I'm afraid."

He is, Carmody had thought, definitely unusual, no question.

"Would you like some?"

"From you, maybe."

"If you want money," Carmody said, exhaling the pale blue smoke happily, "stop selling things. And stop dreaming about going into your own ad-agency business."

Cy cocked his head to one side. "OK, and do what?"

"Don't try making widgets or buying widgets or selling widgets. That'll get you a profit margin, that's all, four-point-five, five-point-two. Peanuts. And you have to have a plant and a staff and long-term debt and short-term debt and worry about rejects." He puffed his cheeks out. "You say you want to make money?"

"I've been trying."

"Real money?"

"I said—"

"I want to hear it again."

"What do you mean?"

"I mean I want to hear you tell me about wanting to make money. Go on."

Obediently Cy had said, "I want to make real money. I really want to make real money. I don't want to have to ask the price of anything. I want to answer to no one and the only way you do that is to make real serious money, so that's what I want to do."

"Then listen," Carmody had said, "and listen carefully. If you want to make money, *you go where the money is*—where people deal in only that commodity, where everything revolves around cash and margin and nothing else, where nothing gets made or sold, where nothing is added to or subtracted from the economy, where the only product involved is money itself and the only aim is to make as much of it as possible. Do you understand what I'm saying?"

Carmody had seen, then, in Cy's eyes, the headlong rush of excitement as he leaned forward intently.

"What are you telling me?"

"The Street. Go to the Street—if you want to make money —is what I'm telling you. The gold is all there if you can dig it out. Never mind what the financial pages tell you about long-term investments and 'holding value' and 'the right time to sell.' It's all about digging gold out, about taking chances, about being right more than you're wrong."

"You mean stocks, bonds?"

"I mean anyplace and anywhere and any vehicle there is on Wall Street, Lord knows there are so many of them these days, anyplace you can buy from somebody at one price and sell to some other fool at a higher price—trading. Commodities. Options. Great risks, but greater rewards. That's where you want to go. Maybe." He had taken another puff and waited to see what the reaction would be to this declaration of faith. It was intense interest.

"Why are you telling me all this? I mean the situation here, the reason you called, the whole thing . . ."

"You seem like a reasonable man, Cy, an honest one. You didn't make any excuses or explanations—and you're making things easy, so . . ."

When Cy sat back and then thrust himself forward again, Carmody had asked, "What's the question?"

Cy blurted out, "How would I get started? What would I

do first? I mean how would I go about it? Who would help me?"

Carmody, sensing the epiphany he had created, had been pleased.

"Well, I might."

"Why would you do that?"

"I don't know," Carmody had said musingly, "but I might."

The look on Cy's face had been gratifying.

Carmody roused himself from the past. "Terrible, terrible. He had such promise." He sighed and put a firm hand on Max's shoulder. "I know how close you two were, but he's gone. Let him go, Max."

"He was killed, Mr. Carmody, murdered."

"I know you think that."

"I know that," Max said in anger.

"Max, be rational. Accidents do happen."

Why wasn't he more concerned? He had taken Cy under his wing, given him the keys to the kingdom.

"Max," Carmody said mournfully, "we have to face it. Cy is no longer with us. It's hard to deal with, but it's a fact that stares us in the face. The thing for all of us to do is get on with our lives. If you need any help putting things in order, call me."

Max looked out to the northern view, to the Queensboro Bridge, where a traffic jam was in progress. All this man could say was "get on with your life." He left Carmody's office feeling angry and unsettled.

In the days following, apart from Julian, who called constantly, Max felt alone. In the office, the depressed silence was thunderous. He checked out his apartment and found more silence as the two painters were in recess, nowhere to be found. Drop cloths were everywhere, creating a gloomy sea of gray. Max threw some clothes into a suitcase and fled back to Cy's.

Later that week, Max went downtown. On the eighth floor of the Trade Center building, where the Commodities Exchange boiled, he affixed his badge and moved toward the action. Here were the concentric rings of the trading pit loaded with standing, screaming, gesticulating men and women, their eyes on the the foot-high electronic tape moving around the wall. Max watched as the prices changed by the second, a fraction of a cent up or down depending on the last trade. Each fraction could spell thousands or hundreds of thousands of dollars for the trader who had bought or sold thousands of pounds of cotton that he would never see. So far as he was concerned, they were simply numbers on a board.

Cy Bannerman had found himself a home in the pits. There, he had discovered an ability to ambush a fake, smell fear, sense the slightest change in the conditioned air. There, above all, he found the courage to take the plunge his instincts ordered him to take, and face the consequences. "All you need," he had often proclaimed, "is to be right once out of every five times— but to be right at the right time."

On the floor, the assorted brokers nodded to Max, waved, winked, shook their heads in sympathy, never ceasing for a second their verbal outcries, for fear the moment would pass them by. Most were in their late twenties or early thirties. The forty-year-olds on the floor were respected veterans and the occasional gray head stood out like a beacon. Commodity trading was a young man's game. The tensions, anxieties, the sheer *stakes* of the pit, the staggering risks and rewards, provoked all ills, real and psychosomatic, ruthlessly burning out bodies and minds.

The voices heard carried the accents of the Bronx, of Brooklyn, roughened southern or midwestern tones. Most of their owners had come to the Exchange with little educational sheen. They came with the single-minded drive to make their fortunes here, where social contacts were unimportant, where degrees were superfluous, where the only criterion was the ability to risk—and to be rewarded.

Some of these hoarse-voiced, blue-jeaned men in short-sleeved shirts traded for the huge brokerage firms, usually moving up from telephone assistant to telephone order-taker, to pit assistant, and finally to pit trader. The process could take a surprisingly few years. And then the boy from Bensonhurst would become the man from Bache or Merrill Lynch, buying twenty contracts of coffee futures, or thirty contracts of sugar, or a hundred of gold for sophisticated clients. Others, looking exactly like the brokerage traders, the same blue jeans, the same intent faces, crying the same cries, were the elite, trading for themselves. Somehow, they had managed to find the money needed to buy a trading membership—one had just gone for over half a million dollars. More often they rented seats through private arrangements. Some had strange sources, some had relatives, some had patrons who saw in their eyes all the necessary tools to make millions and had subsidized them. They stood at their places in the pits alone, depending on their nerve, their calculator minds, their touch and feel. Always there was the dread of "going bust," of losing all that the good days had brought. When the bell rang for trading to cease, some were exhilarated, some had migraines, ulcers that perforated, psyches that crumbled. Traders, at the end of a day, had been known to dance hysterically. Others broke down in tears. Cy Bannerman had never done either. He had stood apart from the day, analyzed it carefully. Even as he traded with an acumen others envied, he did it with a degree of objectivity, standing aside, observing, interested and amused. The rationale for the trading markets was given as an attempt by huge companies using basic commodities in their manufacturing processes to "hedge" their buying needs against future price rises. Others admitted that the markets existed simply to harness human greed.

Max returned the nods, checked the prices, and entered his bids. His mind far away from where he was, his eyes idly roamed the pack on the ring. Here and there, scattered like flowers in a thistle field, a few women stood shoulder to shoulder with the men, gesticulating, jotting, calling out in shrill tones designed to compete with the baritone yawps all about them. They were outnumbered fifty to one, but their intensity matched the men's, their dedication to the trade equal.

Max noticed that one of the women was looking directly at him. Unlike the other women, who wore blue jeans or slacks, she had on a dark skirt buttoned down the front and a blazing red overblouse. Her legs wore the same red blaze. She was small-framed, with an oval face and oversize dark eyes made even darker by lavishly applied eye shadow. Her hair was chestnut, cropped short. From one ear, a long tear-drop pearl earring hung, emphasizing the nakedness of the other. For a moment, Max's eyes caught hers and then, uncomfortable, he shifted. When he looked back, she had broken the contact and was shouting out a bid in a firm treble. Max leaned over to Stanley, who traded for a house, who lived with his mother on Pelham Parkway, and who owned four computers, two espresso makers, and a matched set of Gucci luggage.

"Who's that?" Max nodded vaguely in the woman's direction.

"Her?" Stanley grinned.

"Come on," Max said.

"That's Carol."

The grin continued, a knowing, annoying grin.

"So what are you saying?"

"The word is she really likes to do it."

"With you, Stanley, with you, personally with you?"

Stanley backed off fumblingly. "No, but I wouldn't anyway, with disease and all." He turned away for a second to shout a bid, turned back. "We were talking about Cy yesterday at lunch."

Max grunted.

"He was a real trader, the real merchandise." Stanley was admiring. "I mean some guys are OK but Cy had the guts. We were trying to figure it."

"Stop trying," Max said sharply. "None of you know a goddamn thing."

"Hey, I'm sorry."

"OK."

Stanley tried to make it up. "Did you hear about that secret weather projection the Egyptian government just did?"

Max had not.

"Long range—into the nineties. Predictions on crops and everything."

Max sighed. Another rumor. He escaped quickly around a bank of TV sets. The din diminished slightly. Heading toward the phones, Max slowed and turned to look at the third ring again. The red blouse was gone. He checked prices once more and decided he'd had enough. He walked back out past the guard with the metal detector, took the elevator, and was in the lobby in minutes. He moved quickly to the telephone booths on the right side, found an empty one, slid in, and was searching for a quarter when a hand touched his shoulder from behind.

He jerked erect, almost cracking his head on the light fixture. He grabbed the hand and clutched it tight. A body loomed up in front of him and he squirmed back, ducking down to escape an arm coming down on him. Avoiding it, he pushed out of the booth, head first, stumbling into flesh with his skull. He heard the whoosh of expelled breath and then a choked voice called, "Let go, let go."

Before Max stood the seersuckered sandy-haired weirdo who had accosted him once before. He was breathing hard and gasped out, "Jesus what are you trying to do?"

Max wiped some spittle from his lips.

"What are *you* trying to do?" He looked beyond to the lobby.

"I'm alone," the Billy man said.

"Did you follow me?" Max demanded.

"I told you I'd call you, didn't I? I did. They told me you were coming down here." He rubbed his forearm. "Well—I suppose you've got a right to be edgy."

Max took a deep breath. "So now what?"

"You come with me and we'll go someplace safe and we'll . . ."

"No," Max exploded, "I'm not going anywhere with you. You have something to say, here's as good a place as any."

"You're crazy . . ." the Billy man said. He looked behind him nervously. "I told you how dangerous this is."

Max waited a moment. "Does this have something to do with my partner?"

"What do you think?"

"In what way?"

"You know damn well. Now you're playing games, Roberts—that's not going to get us anyplace."

"I don't know anything," Max insisted. "You're the only one who knows what the hell you're talking about."

The Billy man's voice turned sharp. "Why are you playing dumb?"

"I'm not playing anything."

The man's voice changed to a harsh whisper, the wispy lock across his forehead quivering. "I'm going to tell you one more time. You don't do business with me and you're in big trouble. You think you're going to get out of this by making believe you're a pussycat, you're making one big mistake."

"Just tell me . . ." Max started to say, but the man waved him away impatiently.

"You're running out of time, Roberts. And you can't hide. You'll be found. Now I have the information you want. Are we dealing or not?"

Max stared at him, perplexed. This was crazy. But it was all crazy.

"OK," Max said, "I'll deal."

"Of course you'll deal, you've got no choice."

"Just tell me what the deal is."

The Billy man hesitated. "Not here."

"Wherever you want," Max said, "all right."

"Follow me, but stay behind some."

He turned, adjusted his rumpled jacket, and started toward the street. Max followed, two yards behind him. They reached the center of the lobby this way, and there the man turned to Max, was about to say something, when his body froze in place. An equally frozen voice issued from him, slurred, terrified.

"They're here . . . Sweet Jesus, they followed me. Oh God . . ."

"Where?"

"There, there." The seersuckered body lurched to the right, stumbled, recovered, and, with surprising agility, bounced away, almost fell, clawed the air, caught balance, and ran, hopping, jumping around a kiosk.

Startled, Max moved to catch up, but already the man had vanished, racing around a tourload of Japanese whose leader held a small flag. Deciding to retreat, Max placed his back against the wall. He searched the crowd for who had triggered the flight, but it was impossible to tell. It was past noon and the lunchtime mob was surging in from the escalators and the whirling doors. Men and women of all shapes and sizes filled the maze. A tight-faced teenager in a leather jacket swung by, looking at Max. Max gave him room. Doing that edged him into a hard back. A stiletto-eyed twenty-year-old pushed at him in return. Max stepped aside hastily and as he did he saw red legs. Raising his eyes, he recognized the girl from the trading pit. She was looking at him with some amusement.

"Crowded down here at lunchtime."

"It is," Max said, "yes."

"I saw you upstairs," the girl said. "I know who you are."

"Did you know Cy?" Max asked directly.

She shook her head. "Uh-uh. I saw him a few times on the floor but we never spoke."

This close, Max saw that she was quite small but well made. She was not beautiful but there was a harmony about her features that gave her more than grace. Her complexion was almost a liquid almond. She had very full lips and the eyes he had seen from a distance were lustrous yet guarded. She appeared to be young but there was an overlay of experience about her. The pits, Max reflected, aged you quick.

"I'm Carol," she said and smiled. Max saw that when she did, the watchdog in her eyes vanished temporarily.

"Max Roberts."

"Yes."

Max watched her lips move with fascination.

"I'm going to have what's laughingly called lunch. How about you?" It was said simply and directly, catching Max off guard. He hesitated, the aftershock of the violent encounter ebbing slowly.

"I'm not dangerous," the girl said, smiling.

"OK," Max said. "Sure—why not?"

They went to a restaurant out of the building that looked to be turn-of-the-century, all dark beams, tile floor, and café curtains. In fact, only six months ago it had been a failed Chinese take-out place bought by two young brokers as a lark and converted. They called it The Pits, the double joke for the insiders; for the others, a smoldering barbecue pit in the open kitchen attested to the name.

Max discovered that Carol traded for a small brokerage firm.

"I do pretty well," she said, picking at her Caesar salad, "but I have this feeling I'm marking time."

"Till what?"

She shrugged and laughed. "That's the problem. I don't really know. How's the shrimp?"

"Fine." He was surprised how at ease he felt. He wondered if she felt the same or was putting on an experienced act.

"I saw you talking to Mr. Creep," she said.

"Stanley?"

"Oh yes, Stanley." She held a forkful of salad in the air and giggled. "There are an awful lot of overheated imaginations on that floor."

"Stanley has one of the best."

"I didn't want you to . . . believe all that junk."

"Why?" Max asked. "I mean we've never met each other before. And if we hadn't been in the lobby at the same time, what difference would it make?"

The smile disappeared. Serious this way, the whole quality of her face changed, Max thought. It became less sure of itself, more vulnerable.

They ate in silence for a while. Then, from nowhere, Carol said, "I'm really sorry about your partner. I heard how close you were."

"Yes, we were."

"He must have been very troubled to do . . . that."

83

"Do what?" Max's voice leaped in rebuke. "He was murdered. The papers don't tell you that but I'm telling you. Killed. Thrown off that damn balcony."

"I . . . I'm sorry," she said. "I didn't know."

"You couldn't," he told her. "How the hell could you?"

They finished in silence again. The mood had altered completely. As Max was signing the check, Carol said quietly, "Would you like my phone number?" Max pretended not to hear. Once again she said, "I'd like to give you my phone number—if you'd like to have it?"

"OK," Max mumbled.

She scribbled it swiftly on the back of an envelope and gave it to him. He nodded, took it, put it into a jacket pocket, still looking down at the check, not sure why he was doing this. When he looked up, she was sitting back quietly looking at him, and he felt an unaccountable wave of pleasure but it was tinged with wariness. She had sought him out, of that he was certain.

But why?

5

Any weekday, one P.M. finds The Four Seasons filled with lunch regulars. The noise level is low. The air is not charged but solid and certain as befits those who are not on their way but who have already arrived. Today Julie Berns waited at a corner table for his partner, Alloway, to show up. They had both, by a lucky roll of the television dice, been on the scene when money talk became not only respectable dinner conversation but a prime focus. Suddenly "The Fed," CDs, junior debt, senior debt, muni bonds, all entered the vocabulary. Suddenly the media had front-page stories about the fortunes to be made in penny stocks and the millions to be acquired by clever investment in start-up companies. Academics, heretofore lost in the clouds, rock musicians lost in angel dust, all came alert at the subject of "capital formation." Plumbers talked of "my broker." And everyone tuned in to Lawrence Alloway, with his collection of pundits. Julie Berns had risen with that tide.

As he waited, sipping the white wine, Marcus Rich, his white suit perfectly tailored, came up and dropped casually into the empty chair. "Well, hello, Julie—how are things?"

"Hey, Marcus," Berns replied, "good to see you."

Neighboring eyes turned furtively toward the table, straining to see who the object of Marcus Rich's attention might be.

"How's the show going?"

Berns put his thumb up. "Solid numbers."

"I've been meaning to call you. Nothing for the column, just to get your reaction."

"About what?"

The columnist purred in his confidential, hissing tone, "I have been told that Bannerman's old flame Liz Evers had some sort of a medical problem at the time she knew your partner."

"Medical problem?" Berns laughed genially. "You must have me confused with my brother-in-law. He's the surgeon in the family."

Rich smiled. "The medical problem had something to do with your old friend Cy, I'm told." The hiss became more pronounced. "What's your take on it?"

"I don't have one, Marcus, honestly."

Rich regarded Berns with doubt. "My information is that they broke up over it."

"He gave her the clap?" Berns chuckled again. "Is *The Wall Street Journal* giving medical advice now?"

"Just checking." A couple came by, catching Rich's alert gaze. "Roy," he called out cordially, "little lunch-lunch?"

The man was tall, self-assured, with a deep tan that extended across the top of his balding head. The woman with him was Barbara Stratton. She saw Berns at the same moment he saw her and both their faces clouded over. Her companion didn't seem to see Julie. He concentrated on Rich, bent toward him, extending a hand. "Hey, Marcus, what are you doing . . . ?" Then suddenly he became aware of Berns and the cordiality vanished. Tension leaped into his eyes behind the gold-rimmed glasses. "Catch you later." He took Barbara authoritatively by the arm and led her away. Berns stared after them, his lips tight. As they left, with absolute calculation, Rich said, "A dynamite combination, wouldn't you say?"

Max watched the Alloway show, a gin and tonic in hand, listening to the odd-looking, leonine-headed host mouth regrets at the "untimely passing of a brilliant market personality." Earlier, Max had called Brian Shamski and reported on the encounter in the Trade Center lobby. The detective had been no help. It would go down in the case file but if Max had no idea what it was all about, certainly he didn't.

Max zapped the TV power—what a crock. He reached for his jacket and irritably rummaged in a pocket for a cigarette. Clinging to the package was the envelope on which Carol had written her phone number. He contemplated it for ten seconds, then muttered, "The hell with it," and punched up the digits. When she answered, almost belligerently he said, "Hello, this is Max Roberts."

"Oh—hi." Carol did not seem surprised.

"Did you see the Alloway show?" It was a lame attempt to relate.

"Isn't it dumb?" She laughed. "But I'm hooked. It's like a soap."

"Friend of mine produces it."

"Really."

"Did you hear that dumb eulogy?"

"Yes. Talk about clichés . . ."

"He never liked Cy anyway. Cy was too cynical for him."

"I can imagine. Oh . . ." Carol took a moment. "That was a really pleasant lunch."

"Yes," Max said.

"I don't have lunch with guys from the Exchange usually."

"I'm special then."

"You're rarely there, so I haven't really broken my rule."

"I suppose," Max said, "you're on your way out right now someplace."

"Yes. Almost gone."

"I'm making this sociological survey, see."

She came back quickly. "Would you like to survey me tomorrow?"

"I may have some other subject. If I don't, maybe I'll call you."

"I might even call you," Carol said. "It's equality of opportunity, you know."

"I know," Max said. "My mother taught me all about it."

"Your mother?"

"That's another story. So—goodnight now."

"Goodnight."

When he hung up he wondered why he had called in the first place. Had she been free and had he seen her what would have happened? What did he want to happen? Sex? He would not admit that to himself but the tingle when he thought about it said otherwise. Then the phone rang and those thoughts were driven from his mind.

At three A.M. Barbara Stratton turned on her back in her darkened bedroom, then on her side, then her stomach. Usually she fell asleep within minutes of lying down but not tonight. She had come home at two, alone, undressed watching a late show on the tube, slipped between the D. Porthault sheets, watching the western from there. A half hour later, she shut off the set with the remote and snuggled into her spot on the right. But sleep eluded her. Fully awake behind her closed eyes, she was tempted to try a Seconal. She rarely used the pills, though she kept a vialful in a drawer. She sighed, opened her eyes, and stared at the ceiling. Soon she flipped the covers off and glided from the bed. Slivers of light coming in through the curtains played on her unclothed body. She opened the dresser drawer, reached for the vial, shoved the drawer shut again, and was turning back when she heard a scraping sound.

She looked up, startled, searching for the source, and heard the sound again. It was a foot scuffing on concrete. It scuffed again. And again. Barbara froze in place. Then she heard a squeaking on the glass terrace door. Summoning strength, she managed to turn in that direction. The door, too, was covered by the curtains, but as though imprinted on it, the dim, shadowy outline of a figure could be seen pushing something against the terrace glass, and once again she heard the spine-grating *chuff*.

A small cry escaped from Barbara's mouth. Her hands went slack and the pills dropped to the carpet. She backed away, stumbling over a chair, and screeched again, louder. At this, the figure on the terrace pressed close up to the glass and pounded on it. Barbara heard the door latch rattle, and a crack like a rifle shot split the night.

"Go away," Barbara screamed out. "My God—go away!"

A shard of broken glass slid softly into the curtain. Barbara could see the material billow as a hand thrust into it. She stood in the center of the room, her terrified screams following one another in crescendo, till the sound caromed off the walls.

The figure moved abruptly back until the shadow was no longer visible. The sounds of clambering feet and clanking metal retreated until only the whoosh of the air-conditioner could be heard. Barbara waited, then snatched up a robe from the chaise, and ran into the living room. She dashed to the phone, sobbing and whimpering as she pounded the buttons.

When Max arrived, eyes red, trousers barely zipped, Barbara had recovered somewhat but she still would not return to the bedroom. Max went into it, pulled the curtains, and saw that a pane of glass had been broken from the terrace door. Cautiously, he stepped out onto the terrace. A few gleaming bits had fallen there as well, and there were scuff marks on the concrete.

He looked at the drainpipe descending from the roof and saw that rust had been knocked away every few feet. Looking more closely, he saw dents and chips. He stepped back inside and locked the door again. Barbara was standing near the kitchen, eyes wide.

"It was horrible." Barbara sank into a chair. "So scary."

"Why didn't you call the police?"

"I tried. I dialed six-eleven three times . . ."

"It's nine-one-one."

"Oh."

She looked at Max, huddling into her wrap. "Should I call them now?"

"I'll do it." But he took no steps to the phone.

"I called Cy's number. It just came into my head." She shuddered. "He was so near. It was lucky I couldn't sleep."

"Why couldn't you sleep?" Max asked.

Barbara shrugged. "I don't know, I just couldn't."

Max came close, stood directly over her. "Conscience?" She looked up at him, puzzled. "If you have one, I mean," Max added brutally. "What were you doing having lunch with Roy Herbert?"

Barbara was startled. "He asked me."

"And you agreed? I can't believe it. You know all about his vendetta with Cy. You know he skipped out of town just after Cy was killed."

Barbara cried out, "Max, *I* could have been killed."

Max drove on, "Didn't you have any feelings for Cy, any real feelings?"

She looked at him, stunned. "I guess I . . . never should have called you."

"But you did. And I came."

"Max," Barbara said, exhausted, "Cy is dead. Someone asked me to lunch."

"He's not just someone."

"Max—please."

Max calmed himself. "I didn't even know that bastard was back."

"He came back from the coast yesterday."

"And calls you first shot out of the box, right?"

"You're too crazy," Barbara said, "from all this. I knew him before I knew Cy."

"You know how he almost killed that girl in the summer house he had, except for Cy stopping him . . . all that kink, with dogs."

Barbara tensed in the chair. "I don't want to talk about that now. A half hour ago, I could have been beaten, raped, anything."

"Yes," Max echoed, "anything."

Barbara glared at him. "I know who told you I had lunch with Roy—that creep Berns."

"Lunch and what?"

"I had lunch," Barbara shouted. "They don't have beds at The Four Seasons. And so far as Berns is concerned . . ." She stopped abruptly and her eyes went wide. "Max, do you think this has anything to do with what happened to Cy?"

"It could be," Max said.

Barbara started to weep. Her head bent and her hands went to her eyes. Her voice choked, "Roy said he would protect me from Catalfo. That's why I went to lunch with him, Max. You think I like him? I know all about that girl. I know more. But he said he'd protect me." She looked up. "This is too scary. I'm getting out. I'll just leave for a while. I'll go someplace quiet." Her cheeks were flushed and wet. The robe had fallen away and Max could see the curve of her belly and the deep cleavage above. Her hair was limp. Her makeup had run across the corners of her eyes and down her face. She looked very young and very frightened. Max reached over to pat her shoulder. She clutched at him, burying her head in his midriff.

"Oh Cy . . . ," she moaned, then she caught herself and looked up at Max apprehensively. "I mean . . ."

"It's all right," Max said, "It's OK."

Shamski's people snooped on Barbara's terrace, paced, measured, dusted glass, but the only conclusion they came to

90

was that someone had definitely shinnied down the drainpipe from the roof and tried to get in. This was a less-than-brilliant deduction, Max told Shamski.

"Sherlock Holmes," the detective retorted, "doesn't carry a badge in the NYPD. Could be a coincidence, could be more."

He queried Barbara about the incident but she could tell him nothing helpful. It was Max who mentioned Catalfo, but Barbara didn't want to discuss it.

"I just want to forget about it," she insisted.

Within forty-eight hours, Barbara had her terrace door boarded up, her front door triple-locked, and was gone. She told no one her destination and made no good-byes; she simply vanished. Trying to call her a day later, Max learned that the telephone had been disconnected.

"She's scared to death," he told Julie Berns as they sat around the Whizkids office.

"Listen, she runs with a lot of crazies," Julie observed. "Cy was only part of her life, remember. But if you buy her story that she was cozy with Roy Herbert just because he was going to protect her from Catalfo, you're getting to be Simple Simon." He looked up, annoyed, as Martha interrupted with a question, and resumed instantly when she left. "And this other crap that Rich dropped on me about Liz Evers's medical problem that had something to do with Cy and that's why they broke up, the fag is talking about it to other people, running Cy down—it really gets me."

"It's ridiculous," Max said. "What kind of medical problem would she have that might break them up?"

"Beats me." Berns clenched his hand into a fist. "I'd love to punch him out. What a shit. Where was he twenty years ago when Cy broke his balls in the street clinic with kids who were ODing, when he ran around scrounging day-old food for the hungry? Rich was little Lord Fauntleroy, Mama's little angel in a private school. His father was with Bache and his brother was with AT and T. Still is. I know all about that little bastard. He isn't worth a hair on Cy's head. I'll be damned if I let him get away with saying that."

To Berns's annoyance, Martha returned again, and this time Max had to confer for a few minutes. Julie wandered off to the computer room, where Singh stared at a changing screen. When Berns appeared, he turned to him, startled. "Ah—Mr. Berns."

"Don't let me interrupt you," Berns said. "How are you doing?"

"Things are . . . somewhat confused since Mr. Cy died." He lit a new cigarette, though the half-smoked one still burned in the ashtray.

"I'll bet," Berns said. "Which reminds me—my accountant tells me I need another copy of that trade Cy made for me in IBM last year." Singh wrinkled his brow. "Just bring up my account on the screen," Berns suggested, "and you'll see it."

"Oh"—Singh almost scorched himself on the burning match—"I cannot do that right now because the password is changed and I have not yet conformed those records to respond."

Berns stared at the edgy Singh speculatively. "But you do have my account records, right?"

"Oh yes," Singh assured him, "absolutely. I will send what you wish over tomorrow—or so."

"Thanks." Berns nodded and left. When he did, Singh closed the door behind him and stood for a long moment before seating himself again in front of the changing screen.

At five o'clock, walking past the kite fliers and the speakers blasting Latin rhythms, Max wandered through the park and returned to Cy's place feeling adrift. He contemplated calling Adeline but as he thought about it he smiled at the absurdity. He was trying to go back to some home, find the comforting center. He had begun to think about these things during his six months of analysis with Dr. Lochbreit but it all seemed to go nowhere. Uncomfortably so, he had to admit, and one day, he had simply quit the couch. Lochbreit had never got Adeline right, anyway. He was too serious a man to understand her jokes. Max had barely closed the door behind him when the phone rang and when he answered a female voice, vaguely familiar, said, "Hello."

Cautiously, he responded, "Hello."

A tinkly laugh then. "You don't know who this is. It's Carol Cooper. I told you I might call."

"Oh, right."

"Listen, I took off early today from the crazy house, and there's this great rib place near here. How would you like to spare-rib it tonight? Or we could eat take-in."

"I don't know," Max said, confused. Her tone was that of an old friend.

"You have a better offer?"

"No, just . . ."

"Well, then come on over . . . or I can come over there."

"No," Max said hastily, not wanting her here. "I'll come over to your place."

"See you in half an hour then. Bye."

What had happened? Railroaded toward ribs? He could have said no. Why had he agreed? And why had she called?

Carol lived in a new high rise on the West Side. The building was marbled on the outside and atriumed in. The desk man wore a sky-blue-and-gold uniform with a badge reading CON-CIERGE over his heart. In the elevator, a moving display indicated the approaching floor. When it reached the targeted nineteenth and the door slid back, letters formed themselves. HAVE A NICE DAY appeared.

Carol was already at the doorway of the apartment, a slim figure in a fuchsia jumpsuit. She welcomed him with grace and certainty.

"I'm glad you came."

"Why is that?" Max asked, uncomfortable.

"Sunday blues," she explained. "You know." And went to pour some wine.

"I'm sure," Max said, "that a lot of people would come if you called."

"A lot of people I might not want."

She returned with the wine and tucked her small body into the velour couch at the window facing south. Max sipped.

"Good wine."

"Isn't it? My father made it." She saw his unbelieving look. "He lives in northern California and has a small vineyard. He brought me six bottles on his last visit."

"You don't look like a California girl," Max said. She laughed and he saw her eyes burst into sparkle.

"Northern California and southern California are two different countries."

"How long have you been at the Exchange?"

"Training and trading? All together about four years."

"You like it?"

"It's exciting—and it pays. Oh, I ordered some food. It's just a corner rib place but it's not bad."

She takes charge, Max thought. Almost as though reading his mind, she asked, "Is that OK with you?"

"Oh, sure." He sipped again. "What made you get into the market?"

Carol snuggled into the cushions even further. "It just happened. I came to the city about five years ago, did a little of this and that. Then my health-nut uncle came to town on a visit. He carries his own food with him wherever he goes, preserved tofu, stuff like that. However, he also, I learned, had some contacts on the Street. Would you believe? He got me a job selling bonds at a small muni house but I had to quit because a manager had absolutely no control over his sex glands. I escaped, at first, because we had a secretary who thought she was the reincarnation of Marilyn Monroe, so his concentration was mostly on her. But when she left and he started vibrating when I was around, it became a little much and I shipped out. Some more wine?"

Max held out his glass. She filled it. "After that I worked at Dreyfus, then at Bache, and then where I am now. End of employment record. It's not gun-slinging independent, like you, of course." The intercom sounded. "That's our food." She went to the door.

Max sat in a Danish swivel chair opposite the couch. He swung a few degrees, looking at the place. It was undistinguished by any style, cluttered: more books than he would have expected, a laser-disc player and records on a light-wood cabinet, magazines in unruly piles; he made out the *National Review* and *Vogue*, a large-tube television staring nakedly out. Not a picture graced any wall—stark off-white in four directions. She returned in minutes with the cardboard boxes.

"Here we go." Setting the cartons down on a gate-legged table, Carol moved toward the small kitchen, announcing, "We're going to do this right. No just digging into greasy boxes."

"Need any help?"

"Glasses," she said. "You can carry glasses and the beer. Beer always goes with ribs, doesn't it?"

"Absolutely."

The kitchen was, surprisingly, packed with equipment, a small scale, Cuisinart, expensive-looking pots and pans suspended on a butcher's rack, two ovens, and a shelf crammed with cookbooks. Carol saw his surprise. "I like to cook. It's kind of therapy. I don't say I do it well, but I like it."

THE THIRD FRIDAY

They carried the settings back to the table. Carol swept up a small vase of blue flowers from over the TV set and set it down near the ribs, now nestling, black and shiny on a platter, between the rice and the green paste of the guacamole.

"Shall we?"

Max nodded.

"Then I declare this meal open." Carol reached over with the tongs and deposited three ribs on Max's plate and three on hers. "Grace," she said and, with expert fingers, attacked the meat.

Max felt himself surprisingly comfortable in her presence. But as they ate and drank the Dos Equis and talked with an easy flow, he found himself watching her for cues, searching her eyes for messages. At one point he thought he found one. It happened as he turned away from reaching for his third paper napkin. Turning back, he glanced into the small mirror on the opposite wall and caught sight of her eyes, taut with intensity, staring at him. By the time he was all the way around, the look had vanished.

The Coffeematic had already ground and brewed the beans. Carol poured two cups. "Let's have our coffee like elegant folks," she suggested, bringing the cups to the coffee table.

Max took the Danish chair again.

"No," Carol objected, "there's room for us both here." She indicated the couch and Max changed to it. "Would you like some music?"

"Not really," Max said. He stirred the coffee, looking down into it. When he looked up, Carol was looking down into hers.

"You asked me how I got started. I'm really curious about how you did but I know how hard on you these days must be and I don't want to give you any more pain." She looked up and her eyes were moist.

Unless she was a very good actress, Max decided, this particular look was genuine.

"We got started," Max remembered, "through my mother, who is an anarchist."

"A what?"

"An anarchist," Max repeated, "a disciple of Bakunin, whom you probably never heard of, a Russian from way back who believed in no government at all."

"Your mother?"

"Right. Sweet Adeline, whose real name was one of those Russki jawbreakers—Adelusha or something."

"Sounds pretty."

"You think so? How about Maxim for a kid growing up on the street and playing kick-the-can?"

"Who's that?"

"Me," Max confessed. "Adeline was so crazy about Bakunin, she was going to name me after him. He was—get ready for this—Mikhail Aleksandrovich. But she was also cuckoo about a writer named Maxim Gorky—which wasn't even his real name but never mind—Gorky won out, so I became Maxim. In two minutes on the block it turned into Max, thank God. Even Adeline gave up after a while. 'America,' she'd say, 'a powerful country—but no soul.' "

Carol listened, wide-eyed.

"Adeline marched before there were marches. She demonstrated before there were demonstrations. She picketed before they thought of that word. She is an archenemy of capitalism. She lives in Florida now, retired."

"Wait a minute." Carol put the coffee down. "What did she think of Cy Bannerman?"

"She loved him and he loved her."

Carol grasped his forearm. "Are you making this up?"

"Uh-uh." Max felt the warmth of her palm on his skin. "She started us, but she didn't know it, of course." Carol sat up, her hand still on Max's arm.

"Tell me."

"Do you know who Phil Carmody is?"

"I've heard about him, sure."

"All right. Carmody arranged for us, Cy and myself, to lease a seat on the Exchange and he would sponsor us. But there was no money for a trading account for that first day. So we went to Adeline and we asked her for ten thousand dollars."

"Your anarchist mother? Where did she get ten thousand dollars?"

Max laughed. "From a little capitalist gimmick called life insurance. On my father."

That day was burned into Max's memory. Adeline had looked at them not with suspicion, but with interest.

"So, what are you going to do with the money?"

"Adeline," Cy had sung, "sweet Adeline, this is a matter of faith. Either you have faith in Max and myself or you don't."

"I have faith, Cy—I have faith, but give me a hint. Come, we'll play twenty questions."

"It's for a business," Max had blurted out, only to be greeted by Adeline's outraged howl.

"I don't believe in business—it's exploiting the consumers."

"It's a special business," Cy had leaped in, "and you'll have to take my word that it's exploiting nobody, no one, not a soul."

"How do you make money in a business without exploiting someone? That's not capitalism, that's charity."

"Adeline, Adeline." Cy had been at his most persuasive. "I've read a little Marx and a little Engels and a lot of Che Guevara, and believe me, this is a business that even Bakunin would understand. There is no exploitation here."

She had come through. And twenty-four hours later, they were standing on the outermost ring of the Cotton Exchange, dazed by the action, deafened by the cacophony. For two solid hours they had watched the tape, Cy whispering, "Not yet, not yet."

Then, at minutes before the closing bell, Cy saw something in the selling pattern. His voice burst from his throat louder, Max remembered, than anyone else's. "Two and a half," Cy bawled, "two and a half." A hand, palm up, fanned the air, fingers beckoning, signifying his offer to buy two contracts of cotton, one hundred thousand pounds at sixty-two and a half cents a pound.

Max had blanched. Two contracts at one shot, the first time out.

In seconds the offer had been taken, deal slips passed. Then the closing bell.

"Cy," Max had moaned in the coffee shop later, "two contracts. Why didn't we do just one? We can't risk holding them for any kind of time and if it goes against us, even by fractions and we can't dump—my God, we've lost two thirds of Adeline's money in one day."

"Be cool," Cy had suggested, biting hard into his cheese Danish. "Somebody's selling too much, paying too much. It's a ploy. It'll break up, I know it will."

"And if it doesn't?"

"Max," Cy had declared, not missing a beat on his Danish, "we have just bought over sixty thousand dollars' worth of something . . ."

"Cotton." Max had been grim. "What do we know about cotton?"

"Cotton is just a word; it could be x. It could be y. Doesn't matter a damn. The point is we made a sixty-thousand-dollar investment and only had to put up six. Six, Max—we haven't found a business, we've discovered a gold mine . . . and it's going to be ours."

The next morning, on the sixth ring of the Exchange, as Max watched the tape in terror, Cy bought another contract. Max announced that he was about to be sick. But at ten fifty-five, a special murmur could be heard in the trading room. The sound took on a swelling urgency and became a roar. As Max watched, cotton prices began to rise, at first slowly, then steadily. Traders began to buy frantically before it rose further. Cy watched. Max had shoved him in the ribs.

"Cy, let's get out now—we're up a full two cents a pound, that's three hundred thousand cents, that's . . ." He had whipped out the calculator.

"Not yet."

"Cy, it can reverse in seconds."

"Not yet."

It did not reverse; it rose two more cents a pound, as a flood of rumors spread like ripples on a pond—a new political crisis in the Middle East—the boll weevil had come back in India stronger than ever—the Bass brothers were cornering long staple. It rose two and a half cents a pound; it rose four cents a pound; it rose further.

"Sell three, a half—sell three, a half."

Max jumped at the shout. It was Cy. He was selling at sixty-seven and a half. Nearby, a sweating trader fumbling at his pad answered the shout, buying the contracts.

Max breathed a sigh of relief, then elation swept through him. Adeline's money was safe. And they had made . . . what?

"Seventy-five hundred on our nine thousand dollars. On one trade. In a twenty-four-hour turnaround. I told you." Cy had wide excited eyes. "We've found the gold mine."

Only later had they both realized how unusual such a move had been. But then unusual things were always happening, Cy had declared. If they had been able to buy ten contracts, twenty . . . ? The fact was that if you wanted to get rich, you had to be where it was that people got rich, as Phil Carmody knew, wise Phil Carmody.

Carol listened with delight. Stories like that were the meat and drink of the Exchange, but, she said, she had never made a coup like that.

"He had it," she said admiringly. "No question about it."

"Yes," Max said. That had been the start. Seventy-five hundred dollars. Three contracts. When had they ever traded three contracts again? He could not remember. It had been five and ten and twenty after that. He remembered the laughter and the jokes after each coup, the shrugs and wry cracks after the miscalculations. A somber mood came over him. Carol, whose hand had never left Max's arm, increased the pressure.

"I'm sorry. I didn't mean to stir things up."

"Not your fault." Max moved away. "Well, thanks for the ribs."

Carol followed him with her eyes as he rose. "Why are you going? Is it something I said?"

"No."

"Then?"

Max pinned her with a look. "Why did you call me? I mean, really?"

Carol hesitated. Her voice was defiant. "Because as anyone at the Exchange can tell you, I just like to jump into bed with people."

"I told you I didn't believe that."

"I told you I had Sunday blues."

Max moved closer. "My partner gets killed; you bump into me accidentally . . . it looks like. You suggest lunch. Then you call me to come over."

"You called me first—remember?"

"Yes," Max fumbled, "I did, right."

She waited. He added lamely, "Just to say hello."

"Could I just like you and want to get to know you better?" Carol asked. "Is that a possibility?"

"I suppose it could be," Max conceded.

"Well, go home then and think about it." Carol stood and turned to the dishes. Max could see her lips tighten. He felt a skein of confusion.

"Wait a minute." He reached over to her shoulders, turning her toward him. She moved into his arms naturally and completely, her head nestling into his shoulder. He held her this way, becoming aware of his excitement as his hands moved over her back and her body arched against his. She looked up at him, her eyes wide, her lips parted. He kissed her then, giving up. If it was seduction, then the hell with it.

It was after one in the morning when he left. In the elevator Max felt oddly buoyant. Carol had been a very satisfying bed companion. The lovemaking had been good, the talk had been interesting, the future prospects left vague. He was convinced that her call to him had had nothing to do with Cy, that this encounter was . . . fortuitous. As a matter of fact, it was the kind of episode that Cy might easily have had. The thought came to him that he might be carrying on Cy's torch, and he laughed at the idea.

He emerged from the building, noting with pleasure the clear, starry sky. The soggy air had lifted, to be replaced by a light breeze. Max walked north on Central Park West, checking for cabs as he went. He saw one with its light on a block down the avenue and lengthened his stride, but before he could reach it, the taxi swung around and went away from him. Max looked down the street. A black limo with its windows ominously smoky made a U-turn to come gliding in his direction. He watched with growing apprehension as it rocked to a halt at the curb near him. When it stopped, the rear door opened and a thickset figure in a wrinkled poplin jacket hurled itself out, reaching Max in three steps. Max broke back but Bobby Catalfo spun into his field of vision like some dreadful apparition.

"Where is she?" Catalfo snarled. "Where'd she go?"

"What?" Max asked, shaken.

"Where, where?" Catalfo shouted.

Barbara, Max realized, the man was talking about Barbara Stratton. Quickly he said, "I have no idea where she went."

Catalfo placed a powerful hand against Max's chest. "Don't give me bullshit. I'm warning you. I know every move you make. You fucked her, you son of a bitch. You fucked my property. She told you where she was going."

"Get away from me," Max warned. "Not again. Shamski knows everything."

"Screw Shamski," Catalfo spat. "Who do you think you're talking to—some flea? I've got ten Shamskis on my payroll. If I want you, he couldn't help you in a million years. I operate in this town, and no one takes anything away from me—nothing."

The depth of Catalfo's rage was frightening. It was animal,

straight from the jungle, and powerful enough for anything. "Now, where'd she go?"

"I don't know," Max said. He threw a quick glance up the avenue. Not a soul. And the limo had a driver, probably the same horrifying thug who had beaten him before.

Catalfo glared, thrust his neck out, eyes only inches away from Max. "You think you're a real smart-ass, don't you? You and your partner both. But don't get as smart as he was. Believe it." He grasped a handful of Max's jacket and pulled him in forcibly. "Now you tell me where she went or . . ." Max slashed at the iron hand on his chest and tried to twist away. Catalfo pulled up again but Max had broken his grip. The crazed man jerked his knee up toward Max's groin. It missed, hitting Max's side instead. The stab of pain revived the ache in Max's ribs and he felt himself going down.

Abruptly Max became aware of another body present amidst a whirlwind of movement and noise. For a moment he thought the limo driver had raced over to complete the job, but when he looked up, to his astonishment he saw not the big-nosed thug he expected, but the man who had twice accosted him, the man who had called himself Billy, smashing away at Catalfo with his attaché case, catching him on the side of the head and bringing a yawp of pain. As Max pulled to his feet he wondered where the hell *he* had come from. Now the limo door burst open again and released the thug Max thought had already arrived. Shoulders heaving, he hurled himself forward, but Max managed to move away in time and the Billy man met the thug with a smash to the ribs from the blessed attaché case. The hoodlum gasped and held up. Attracted by the noise, a uniformed doorman in the next building peered out from behind locked doors. Instantly he pressed an alarm button, which triggered a grating siren and flashed a red light on the canopy. For good measure, he put a police whistle to his lips and blew long blasts. Catalfo retreated hastily back to the limo. His driver followed quickly, jumping into the front seat and kicking the engine to a dull roar. As the black car burned rubber, accelerating away from the curb, Max turned to his rescuer, but he was not there. Already the man was loping down the street. At the next corner, he skittered ninety degrees to his right and disappeared. Max, bewildered, could only stare after him as the ear-splitting alarm rang through the night, alarming no one.

6

Brian Shamski was used to lawyers, but this thin-haired, blank-eyed corporate type was particularly irritating. He had come in response to the call, but without Catalfo, who claimed to be busy at an important function—a fund-raiser for the mayor. Not too subtle, Shamski thought.

"Be serious, detective." It was a voice above the battle, calm, judicious, used to scoring points. "This complaint is ridiculous without at least one supporting witness so why are we wasting time?"

Max, in the corner, looked away in disgust, and Shamski countered, "We may have a witness, counselor, we're working on it."

Max fumed silently; working on it—what a joke—the doorman had done the usual, declined to involve himself, insisting he could not make out anyone clearly enough to identify.

"Mr. Catalfo was at home, a very late business meeting— we're prepared to give you the names of his associates who were with him, of course."

I'll bet you are, Max raged, and they'll swear to it up and down. Power is power in this town. And real estate is the most power.

"The fact is"—the lawyer let the barest possibility of a smile move his thin lips—"this complainant has been pursuing a young woman who prefers my client."

"What?" Max lost control.

The lawyer was unruffled. "We have some witnesses aware of that state of affairs who can so inform you, if you like. Oh, the complainant may have been involved in some street scuffle or other, but Mr. Catalfo can hardly be held responsible."

"This is the second time," Shamski said, "that Mr. Roberts was attacked."

"I suggest," the lawyer said mildly, "that he stay away from dangerous streets. Anything else?"

Shamski sighed in defeat. "No."

"Then good-bye, detective." The lawyer left the room, ignoring Max, just as he had upon entering.

As soon as the door closed, Max whirled on Shamski. "He tells lies with the straightest face I've ever seen."

"He's a lawyer," Shamski shrugged. "That's his job."

Max felt helpless, he confided to Julie Berns, and yes, scared. Catalfo had real power. Julie zeroed in on Max's savior. "Why would this bozo come barreling in to save your ass? He says he knows something, right? What could he know? What is he trying to sell?" Martha rang, breaking off Berns's questions. Could Jimmy Singh come in to see Max now?

"In a few minutes," Max told her, and he explained to Julie, "Singh isn't happy here. He wants to leave."

"Oh," Julie bristled, "I thought he had so much respect for Cy."

"He says his mind's not on his work anymore."

"Is that so?" Berns scoffed. "He worked all the programs. He knows all of Cy's little secrets. Wherever he goes, he takes that stuff with him. I don't like it." He grimaced. "Everything's so complicated now. You know what I'd like to do—take some time off, go back to San Francisco, see what's happened to all the places Cy and I knew so well." He looked off into some moody distance. "There was this one house we lived in, a big old Victorian right near Haight, twelve of us, all dropouts. Cy was the inspiration, a hundred ideas a day. He had the coolest clothes, the coolest girls. He was the best cook. He could make things out of day-old bread or week-old vegetables that were terrific. One day, two sets of parents turn up scared for their kids, really horrified by the way we lived. Cy got into it. He did a fantastic number on them about having to 'let go,' to allow their kids 'to grow.' When he finished, everybody hugged in a circle, the parents contributed to the food fund, and left happy. It was a great rap." He roused himself, regaining animation. "Listen, I've been checking out that medical business Rich told me, about Liz Evers. It turns out that she went into a wingding when it ended with Cy. She had a full-fledged breakdown."

"How did you find that out?"

Berns was smug. "From the girl who used to be her assistant. Evers made a million demands on her time, pushed her to the wall. The girl almost had a breakdown herself."

Max was puzzled. "How could she keep that so quiet?"

"Remember, she restructured her company—no one heard from her for a while? That was the cover. She went into deep treatment. I even have the name of her doctor."

"He won't tell you anything. And anyway what would that have to do with Cy's death?"

"Listen," Berns said, "we're talking about an unbalanced woman. Who knows what she'd do?"

These days Jimmy Singh looked uncomfortable whenever he saw Max, quickly lighting up one cigarette after another. As the remaining market positions began to close out, the question became, What next? Not facing Max in his office, Singh sighed, "I must be thinking about my family, you know."

Max's answer was that he needed more time to sort things out.

"Oh yes, oh, indeed yes, but perhaps it is best if I find another post," Singh said, gaze glued to a screen.

"Maybe," Max agreed, "but let's give it a little while."

Singh was clearly unhappy. "I am not doing good work here now, Mr. Max. For my work, extreme concentration is needed, you see, and my brain is not responding."

Singh should be a little more tolerant, a little more helpful, Max thought resentfully. But he was not; he was stubborn, almost eager to get out, the sinking-ship syndrome.

With only a few minor Commodities Exchange matters pending, Max might have made phone calls to finish them off but chose instead to go downtown. Once there, checking the price moves, he decided to hold longer, and was moving away from the ring when he spotted a familiar figure not ten steps away. He froze in his tracks. It was Roy Herbert, with half a dozen fawning men clustered about him. William Roy Herbert was in a position to throw many favors their way, spread the rich glow of joint commissions. It made for an easy journey, being the son and heir of a strong brokerage-firm founder; things just—came your way. Max observed him with loathing. Herbert's face was planes and angles, and his brown eyes twitched everywhere at once. He hauled away at his Sulka tie, at his red suspenders, at the lapels of his Italian suit. Unaware of Max's scrutiny, he was holding court as he always did. His usual repertoire concerned escapades with movie actresses, with porno queens, with sexual tricksters of every kind—all possibly true because it was common knowledge that Roy Herbert spent whatever he had to on the wild and dangerous pleasures that fed him. Max watched him and remembered Cy's account of one weekend morning at Herbert's house on the Island.

"She was a kid from Westchester trying to become a model. She'd come to the house that weekend because he had all these contacts. I was there and Barbara was there and about five others. At about three in the morning, I woke up, hearing these scuffling noises. I went out into the upstairs hallway and looked down that big staircase. Roy was at the bottom with her. He had his pajama bottoms on but she was stark naked. And he held her—God, it was awful—by a breast, just gripped her, pulling her around. She was crying and he smacked her across the face and kneed her in the stomach. He was high as a kite, manic—he'd been free-basing earlier. He screamed at her that she'd better listen to him or she wouldn't see the light come up. He wanted her to get into a scene with that Dianne, the porno actress he brought out. He got his kicks watching. The girl was in such pain she could hardly stand. And he was making such a racket I thought the whole house would wake up, but I was the only one who came out. I called out to him to cool it. He looked up and told me to mind my own business. Then he lifted the girl—just lifted her up to him like a rag doll and put his hands around her throat. He'd lost control entirely. The girl was gagging and choking. I came down the stairs and pulled him away from her. She fell down in a heap on the floor. He whirled on me then and went for my throat, but I pinned him and held

106

him and tried to talk sense into him. His eyes were rolling back in his head, though. He screamed that if I didn't get out of his face he'd get me. I didn't know what to do. There was the girl on the floor, out cold. I didn't know how badly she was hurt, so I simply let Herbert go and told him I'd put him away if he interfered with me. Then I called the hospital and told them to come over, emergency. When I hung up, the crazy bastard stared at me, just stared; he was ice. Then, without even one look at the girl, he went back to his room. The girl was out when the ambulance arrived. I went with her to Emergency. She was a mess. She told them she'd fallen down the stairs and pleaded for me to go along with her story. What a night! Not your expected summer weekend at the beach."

There was Herbert now, laughing and scratching. Untouched. And Cy was dead. Max walked a deep circle, left the trading room, passed the hallway, and entered the comparatively quiet, deeply carpeted foyer of the Exchange offices. He was approaching the semicircular desk on an account inquiry when a young black man in a green clerk's jacket emerged from a doorway. The young runner—his badge identified him as such—locked eyes with Max for a quick moment, looked away looked back, looked away once more. His face went taut, then, as though he had decided something, he came over to Max quickly and said, "You're Cy Bannerman's partner, right?"

"Right," Max said, surprised. "And you—?"

"Luther Robinson."

Max wondered if he had ever seen him on the floor. As only one of six black men there he would stand out. Robinson moved closer, his voice lowering.

"Listen, can I talk to you—private?"

Max sat down on one end of the banquette that ran around the room, now empty of anyone except the curly-headed girl behind the desk, who was deeply engaged on the telephone. Robinson sat close to him. "Mr. Bannerman was a good guy," he began. "He helped me a lot, gave me a lot of tips about what goes on here."

Max waited. Robinson cleared his throat.

"I didn't say nothing to anyone before but when I saw you at Wall, it kinda bothered me."

"Something about Cy?"

"About the night he bought it."

Max's heart jolted. Robinson's voice became even lower.

"I did some things for Mr. Bannerman, see—like I got him some things, time to time."

Max understood instantly. "Are you telling me you were his connection?"

Robinson wasn't happy with the characterization. "I wouldn't say it that way. I know some people, that's all. I can get some stuff from them anytime, you know what I'm saying? I used to get Mr. Bannerman some good grass and . . . like that, whenever he wanted."

"I understand," Max said, nodding. "What about that night?"

"That was Friday—and he asked me to get him a couple of ounces of good powder."

Max jumped. "It was you there."

"Wait a minute." Robinson hesitated. "I got to tell you that I do some favors for one or two other people around here, OK? Like, I mean—Mr. Herbert."

Max stared at Robinson intently. "Go on."

"Mr. Herbert wanted some stuff on Friday too. I told him I'd be late with it 'cause I had another delivery to make. When I told him who it was, I could see his wheels go, you know what I'm sayin'?"

"Go on." Max dug his nails tightly into the banquette's plush.

"Then he asks me what time I'm up there. I tell him 'bout nine. He asks me do I stand at the door or do I go in? I tell him I go in, but I'm in the foyer. He asks me if Mr. Bannerman leaves me there to go out by myself or does he stay to lock up after me? I tell him sometimes one way, sometimes the other. He says he'll give me a big bill to work it so I stay there after Mr. Bannerman goes back to the livin' room. Then I flip the doorlock buttons so the lock is off, understand me?"

"Jesus," Max said.

"He tells me he wants to play a practical joke on his buddy."

"Did you do that?" Max demanded. "Did you leave the door open?"

"No," Robinson said quickly, "I never did. I came and I went, that's all. I didn't think anything 'bout it till I heard what happened to Mr. Bannerman, then it worked on my mind."

Max studied Robinson's face, trying to judge whether he was being told the truth or fed an alibi. Did Robinson actually do as Herbert suggested, leave the door open, and was now covering himself? Or did he refuse, as he was saying now? Either way was possible. And even if Robinson had not left the door unlocked, what if Herbert's goons, set to do whatever he planned, found the door locked but also found another way in?

Robinson's worried tones intruded. "This be the truth, the way it happened. I got no reason to lie to you."

Maybe, Max thought, or maybe not.

"I'm not sayin' Mr. Herbert wasn't going to try some trick joke. He does that kind of stuff."

"Like what? What kind of trick would he try?" Max demanded.

"I don't know what was in his head." Robinson's face contorted with anxiety. "Man, I sure as hell don't want to get into the middle of this. I'll get squashed like a bug if I do, you know that. They don't like blacks around here for openers. I do them the favors and they say they grateful but first chance they get they knock me out. Hell, I do them the favors I can, just like anybody around here does the favors they can to make friends, but it don't work the same way."

Max wanted details. "Did you see anybody at Cy's when you got there?"

"I heard some woman. She was in the big room."

"High voice, low voice? What did she say?"

"I couldn't make out." Robinson was sweating now, small droplets forming on his temples. "Hey, I told you everything I know. I got it off my chest."

The woman and Herbert. Max saw a glimmer.

"Robinson, you've really got guts coming forward like this. Now here's what we're going to do. You and I are going to go see the detective working on the case . . ."

The runner threw up his hands. "Hey . . . no way, no cops, no."

"You've got to," Max urged. "That's the only way . . ."

Robinson shook his head with great agitation. "No way—no way, man. You want me to cut my throat altogether? This be my chance here at the Exchange. You expect me to blow it?"

"You won't. I'll stand behind you." Even as he said it, Max realized how ridiculous that was.

"Listen," Robinson said, "I'm just a guy tryin' to get along, you understand? It's no rap on you, but I gotta go. 'Scuse me." He jumped up and fled.

Max sat, stunned. The girl behind the desk hung up her

109

phone and looked inquiringly at him. He shook his head, rose slowly, and returned to the trading floor. Herbert was leaving his coterie. He waved a good-bye, tugged once more at his tie, and started to the exit, not seeing Max waiting there until he was about to pass. Pressing forward, Max spat out, "You son of a bitch."

Herbert stopped; he grimaced in mock sympathy. "Look who it is! Oh, you poor little bastard."

Max took another step toward him. Herbert stood his ground. "You take one more step and I call the guard. You want to make a scene, I'll make you one. I'll make you one that'll get you thrown out of here for good."

"I know what you did," Max said, trying to keep his voice from trembling.

"What I did? When? What? What did I do? Get out of here." Herbert's voice was loaded with scorn. "You're nothing without him—I know that and so does everybody else. Don't try to take it out on me."

"I know what you did," Max repeated. "You won't get away with it."

Herbert's voice rose. "What do you know? What is that, some kind of accusation? You be careful how you talk." His angered look changed to one of crafty amusement. He smiled, too-perfect tooth caps filling his mouth. "You must be talking about Barbara. Maybe you thought she'd go into some kind of mourning for that prick but that shows what you know. I'll fuck every part of her and dance on his grave."

Max made a move toward him but the security guard came over quickly.

"Gentlemen, gentlemen. Please." He seemed distressed that they were Exchange members. Exchange members did not get violent with one another; they were fraternity brothers. Outsiders were the ones you had to guard against.

Herbert threw one final contemptuous look and quickly walked away out to the elevator. Max tried to control the seething in his chest. When he had, he walked out also. Behind him the din continued; the Exchange had not missed a beat.

Max walked the floor of Cy's apartment, filled with what he had learned. What to do about it was another matter. He groaned in frustration, foreseeing another futile episode with Shamski and another whey-faced lawyer. He tried anyway. Out. He hung up. Bursting, he called Julian; out—leave your message

110

at the sound of the beep. Max slammed the phone down. There was no getting through—to anybody.

He spent the next hour stewing about his helplessness and pulling himself up short, decided he needed company for dinner. He called three women he knew in succession, none of whom were home. Then, with a slight twinge, he decided to call Carol. When her answering machine came on the line, he thought that was that, but before it could beep, Carol's breathless real voice intercepted. She had just come in. Max asked lamely whether she would be interested in dinner. She replied that she would be.

Carol arrived very promptly at the Mexican restaurant, looking like a small painter's palette in a hot-pink-and-orange dress, which, she claimed, was in honor of Mexico. The restaurant was cavernous, two-tiered, stark white, with cleverly placed spotlights simulating odd beams of sunlight dappling floor, table, and mahogany bar. Leotard-clad waitresses rushed about with enormous goblets of margaritas. As they ate their nachos, Max told Carol a little of what had happened in the past between Cy and Herbert. Carol had, of course, heard all sorts of stories about Herbert. As they went on to the tortillas and *chiles rellenos*, as the margarita juices worked their way down and then up into Max's brain, he told her about his encounter with Luther Robinson.

"Oh Lord," she responded, "that's spooky."

"A trick." Max found his tongue getting thick. "Some trick."

Carol shuddered. "You really think he'd go that far?"

"Cy told me things . . ."

He found it increasingly difficult to form words and realized he was getting rapidly drunk. Carol's image seemed to waver in front of his eyes. She went in and out of focus.

"That woman," he managed to mumble, "she's key. I know she is." He examined his glass. The huge tumbler was empty. Carol tactfully suggested he didn't really want another, did he? He guessed not.

"So, let's go then."

In the taxi, he tried to sit up but kept listing to the side. "I'll be all right," he managed to get out. "Where we going?" Then he slumped against her, his head falling to her shoulder.

She took him to her place, maneuvered him into her bed, removed his shoes, but couldn't do much else. He allowed her, feeling neutral about it all. Lying back, hands behind his head,

111

he floated. All the recent events seemed dim, shadowy, not to be concerned with.

Carol stood over him, smiling. "You do this often?"

"Uh-uh," Max giggled. "Adeline thinks . . . alcohol is . . . a . . . a capitalist plot . . . to keep the underclass down."

"How about vodka?"

"Ah—" Max laughed, "a Soviet plot . . . to keep control . . . over the betrayed . . . masses."

His laughter faded as his eyelids became impossible to control. Down they slid. Carol began to disappear, but before she vanished completely he saw a look of concern creep over her face as she looked down at him. What do you know about that, he told himself before it all went. She's worried about me.

When Max awoke, the sun was already baking the drapes. Carol was gone but she had left a note about coffee and grapefruit. He rose feeling surprisingly whole, no hangover, no dry mouth, but felt very alien to the silent apartment. He found his shoes, discovered his feet swollen and resistant to them, but managed. He scribbled some words of thanks on Carol's note and left.

In the street, as he marshaled his thoughts, he had a brooding sense of forgetting something. He tried to bring it forward but it would not come.

He went back to his own apartment to find one painter gone and the other eating a banana and watching a game show on television. His first reaction was one of fury, but he repressed it, knowing you never let out your true feelings to a house painter; he would either pack up and leave in a huff or, worse, take it out on your walls.

He returned to Cy's, showered, and was combing his hair when it came forward—Tuesday—the woman in Vermont. He hesitated. Was it a ridiculous chase—all the way up there? What could she tell him about what had been happening? Curiosity decided him. He called the airline, called Martha at the office and told her he'd be gone for the day. When he asked to speak to Singh, she informed him that Jimmy had gone home not feeling well—some kind of a flu thing. He had left early yesterday as well. Max called Singh at home, where his wife said he was sleeping and should not be awakened. But as she spoke, Max could hear Jimmy's unmistakable voice in the background whispering something. Max pressed with another question and her English broke down. "Sleeping," she burst out, obviously panicked. "Sleeps. Cannot speak now, you see. Bye-bye." Another job, Max immediately thought. Singh was arranging for another job and couldn't face him. Did it matter? Probably not.

He took the two-ten to Manchester. Strapped in his seat at twenty thousand feet with a cup of airline coffee and a sickly sweet pineapple tart, he realized Shamski had not returned his call. As he thought about that, he dozed off, had a dream in which he was sliding down a mountain without a rope, and awakened to see the "no smoking" sign lit, indicating an imminent landing.

He entered the small airport building and mounted the staircase to the main floor, wondering how he would recognize this Sonya. He found clusters of people in the usual airport wait mode and paused near a ticket counter to study them. Most were men, though a few women were seeded about. He looked over each of them. A very pretty blonde in leathers was possible but as he watched her, a man, also in leather, took her arm and led her off. Max swung his head in a radarlike arc, a very obvious search maneuver, but no one approached, though one seated woman in a floppy sun hat and dark glasses seemed to look at him. He focused on her. Her gaze still held. He made a move toward her, but as he did she picked up a suitcase and walked to another gate. Perplexed, Max watched most of the crowd melt away, until a lone woman was left, a short, blunt-nosed, cropped-haired androgynous figure in dungarees and work shoes. Max waited five minutes more. The woman stayed, lit a cigarette. What would Cy have been doing with someone like that? Still . . . He had decided to try her and was taking his first step when he heard a voice behind him call softly, "Max?"

He turned quickly, gratefully, toward the woman who had called his name. Willowy, in a floor-sweeping white cotton skirt and a colorful laced blouse, long auburn hair streaming down her back, she seemed out of another time and place. Her eyes were dark, deep-set over high cheekbones that caught the light and helped form a heart-shaped face. Her nose and full mouth seemed a perfect union in their conjunction and her skin glowed delicately amber. There was about her such an aura of radiance that Max blinked. "Max Roberts?" she asked again in the recognizable husky tones.

Max came to life. "Yes. Max. You're Sonya. Hello."

He extended his hand awkwardly. She shook it, smiling.

"Sonya Koanis, yes. I've got a car. Come on."

It was an ancient VW Beetle, once blue, now dust-blasted to an anonymous color. It coughed, chugged, but went. The interior was tidy but the time-ravaged upholstery sported cuts and bruises. Seated on dubious springs, jouncing along a small rutted road, Max was conscious of luxuriant green hills all about him but had eyes only for Sonya, leaning forward, competent hands on the steering wheel. He asked her how long she had known Cy.

"About six months."

She was, she explained, a weaver, a designer and maker of cloth on her own loom. She sold what she made locally but every so often she made a trip to New York to see buyers at a department store to show her wares. They seemed to like what she did and bought whatever she made.

"It's a city I feel very foreign in, though. It overwhelms me. I leave it as soon as I can."

She had met Cy in that department store. Leaving one day, she had paused at a handmade-jewelry counter. Quite suddenly, she became aware of this man watching her from a few steps away. It was Cy, staring at her, unabashed. Next, he had approached, apologizing for his boldness, but said he absolutely had to know her; he realized how rude this was, but insisted that he had no other choice. She had always shied away from this kind of an encounter but Cy had been persistent. And there was something, she admitted to Max, in the very openness of his appeal that spoke to her. She was an instinctive person, not a cerebral one, and so they had gone for a cup of tea together. Within a short time he was flying up to spend time with her.

They had been driving for almost an hour and now the road became somewhat better paved as they entered the main, and seemingly, only street of a small village. A few stores graced it, some substantial houses, a post office flying the flag.

"Sky Mountain," Sonya said. "Possibly the only community in Vermont that doesn't have a ski lift."

In minutes they were past it and made a right turn up a hill road. Shortly after that they came to a gorge over a deep-running river spanned by an old wooden bridge. Beyond the bridge and to the left was a log building. Max craned his neck.

"Is that an actual log cabin?"

"Actual," Sonya said, "and mine."

She had lived there for four years, she informed Max as they entered. It had been a dream of hers ever since she had

114

been a little girl growing up in Oregon, on the other side of the country.

It was a three-room cabin. The main room was surprisingly large, with bookcases flanking the stone fireplace. A deep couch, two old leather chairs, a rocker, a gleaming refectory table, and captain's chairs made it cozy. At one end, a kitchen with an old woodburning stove had been established, replete with hanging plants and a wrought-iron grill. At the other end of the house a doorless doorway led to the bedroom. It held a spooled-rail four-poster bed covered with a blazingly beautiful star-patterned quilt, a rocking chair, two handsomely wrought pine chests, a red velvet footstool, and more hanging plants in profusion. Another doorless doorway opened to the workshop. Here the old wooden loom reigned amid drawing table, work table, and curved, upholstered couch. Max sensed instantly the serene ambience of this house, its removal from the world outside. He was hypnotized, and watched, dazzled, as Sonya, her long hem sweeping the polished wide-plank floor, put some groceries away.

"So—now"—she turned to him—"would you like some cider?"

"Fine."

She poured the cider into two well-turned pottery mugs, and curled up on the wood-framed couch topped by huge down pillows, while Max chose the upholstered rocker. He heard odd noises outside and glanced at the window near him. A goat's whiskered face was there, and a donkey's sad long one.

"Don't mind them," Sonya said. "They want to come in. But I draw the line at that. The cats, of course—they must be out hunting a present for me."

She must be, Max thought, the most unlikely woman for Cy Bannerman to have had a relationship with.

"I know," Sonya said, "how close you were to Cy and how you must feel, but I don't know that I can help you in any way."

"The thing is," Max confessed, "I'm still in shock that he never said a word to me about you; he kept you a secret, totally."

"But I know about you—about your mother the anarchist, God bless her, about how you met, about the girl you almost married, about another close friend—Julie?"

He shook his head in wonderment. "Julie Berns, right. Tell me, did you ever see Cy in New York?"

"Two or three times . . ." She smiled. "But he was always worried about bumping into someone he knew."

Totally secret. His alone. What else had he shared with her?

As the afternoon passed and the sun's light changed, Max heard things that Cy told Sonya, things Cy had never told him, brutal scenes with his father when he was a child.

"He always hit him with this wide belt, he told me. One day Cy hid the belt. But his father was so enraged at that, he hurt him more than ever." Sonya shuddered at the memory. "My own father is a loving and gentle man; I found it hard to understand." She was so distressed that Max wished he could hold her, smother his face in her light-flecked hair.

"And that tragic mother. Once, he told me, he was visiting her in that place. She was in a restraining gown to keep from hurting herself. They were alone. She looked at him, he said, and told him to forget she was his mother, to save himself. It was an amazing moment. For that instant, Cy said, she was not someone who heard voices but someone totally sane—as though the insanity was a pretense. And when he tried to pursue it, she changed—before his eyes."

Max listened attentively. Cy had rarely talked to him about his mother, close as they were, but to this woman he seemed to have opened like a flower. Sonya, still wrapped in the memory, fell silent. Max asked about her parents. Her father was Greek—he should have known that from the name, but her mother was Romanian.

"Some combination."

Sonya laughed. "Temperament all around. I went to Oregon State, did one thing and another, and then decided it was all too hectic. The world was a little too much for me. So, here I am."

"Did Cy tell you about himself, what he did?"

"You mean that money business?" She laughed. "I couldn't take what he did seriously." She turned her dark eyes on Max momentarily. "Or you—if you'll forgive me. It just seems so far away from anything I know or care about . . ."

She had never met anyone, anyone at all, in Cy's world, knew absolutely nothing about it.

"What did you think of Cy?"

She looked at him as though it were a novel thought. "I've never met anyone like him. I think of him—thought of him . . . no, think of him . . . as some great curiosity. A millionaire? I'm thirty-two and the richest person I ever met in my life was a college professor who had tenure."

THE THIRD FRIDAY

There was darkness outside and Sonya lit an old lamp. The donkey brayed. Suddenly two calico cats appeared and padded toward their bowls in the kitchen. It was hard, here, to keep track of what was important.

"Can you remember Cy ever mentioning someone named Catalfo?"

"Doesn't sound familiar."

"Or Roy Herbert?"

"Uh-uh."

Why would he? That was one world, this was another. This woman and this world had become, Max thought, Cy's secret treasure.

"I told you," he continued, "that I know he was murdered."

She nodded.

"Did he say anything to you, anything at all, that could help me with that?"

"No." Her hair had come forward somewhat, falling down over her shoulders. "But he did say that he was thinking about giving everything up, getting out of that meaningless game you and he played."

That was a surprise. Cy had never mentioned quitting.

Sonya looked at her watch. "Oh Lord, it's after seven. We'll have to hurry to make the airport by eight-fifteen. That's the last flight out." She rose. "I'll just get a shawl."

She walked to the bedroom. Watching her go, Max felt his heart racing like a boy's, felt the impossibility of leaving. "Wait a minute," he called. "We don't have to rush. I'll stay over tonight. There's got to be an inn or a hotel or something, isn't there? I'll take a plane tomorrow."

Sonya turned back, framed in the doorway. "If you want to. You can sleep here if you like. On the couch. It's not bad."

"Great," Max said, smiling, ". . . but I didn't bring my toothbrush."

"There's an extra."

Cy's, Max thought, and felt strange but content.

The dinner was an earthy soup and a crusty loaf, both from Sonya's hand. She topped it off with Vermont apples and a cheese provided by the goat. Max told her stories about Adeline, whom she said she admired. He told her of meeting Cy and

117

their almost immediate friendship. He told her there were men in their world who hated Cy because of—one thing or another, omitting large parts of the truth. She told him that, for her, Cy Bannerman was like traveling a road she didn't know, an exploration that had ended too abruptly.

At eleven, Sonya provided sheets, pillow, and quilt. She said goodnight, went into the bedroom. Max turned his back on the doorless doorway and soon the bedside lamp went out.

Lying on the couch, Max had visions of Sonya's body on the high platform of the spool bed. Instant guilt assailed him, as it had before. He was the intruder. This territory was Cy's. But mingled with the guilt was the excitement of trespass. Gradually, the day overcame him; he relaxed and fell asleep.

He awoke suddenly in the night, sensing a presence. Inert, eyes half closed, he tried to locate the sounds. A rush of padded paws and a muffled meow told him, to his relief, it was only the cats, but sleep had gone. Wide awake, he glanced at his watch. Half past three. He sat up. The cool northern moon shone in through the window, spilling over the bookcases. He glanced over to the bedroom, where the light did not enter. He could make out the bed but not the form.

Still hours before daybreak. Restless, he rose, went softly to the kitchen, drank a glass of the clear, icy water. He had come hoping for one thing, he reflected, and found something entirely different. Now what? He walked, barefoot, over to the bookcases and tried to make out the titles. Biography—history, the history of crafts, Thomas Mann . . . Emily Dickinson, Thoreau. He had never actually read Thoreau. He reached in for the book and upset something resting there. Grabbing, he juggled, felt a large manila envelope, and managed to snare it before it fell to the floor. He was replacing it gently when, even in the half-light, he recognized the Whizkids Trading logo at the top. Surprised, he brought it closer and saw what appeared to be random numbers scrawled on the flap. The writing was instantly familiar—Cy's.

Wide awake and curious, Max opened the envelope to find a sheaf of computer printouts. He tried to make out what they were, angling the pages to catch the moonlight, but it was impossible. He went into the rustic bathroom with the cast-iron tub, closed the door, switched on the low-wattage bulb, and studied the envelope's contents. The printouts were odd—they recorded option trades but held no record of anything except price—no companies, no ownership, just trades. No names or dates. It was a chart of price swings, Max thought, on some stock and its options, but why would Cy chart something and not code the company name in? And why were they here? It was after four when Max fell asleep again, the manila envelope on the floor near the couch. Brayed awake by the snorting donkey making a racket, he staggered up, saw that it was seven o'clock, and collapsed back. Bleary-eyed, he saw Sonya outside, dressed in jeans and boots, cleaning up a small pen with a shovel, an activity that the animal was loudly objecting to.

Max took his clothes to the bathroom, dressed, washed, and by the time he returned, Sonya was there, her cheeks flushed, her eyes sparkling. Over steaming mugs of herb tea, Max produced the manila envelope. Sonya glanced at it briefly.

"Cy's. I guess he left it here."

"Would you remember when he brought it?"

Sonya could not. Sometimes Cy would come with his attaché case, she recalled, but he would rarely open it.

"He must have looked at this, though, since it was right there in the bookcase."

"Probably." Sonya slathered a whole-wheat muffin with her strawberry jam. "Is it important?"

"I don't know." Max glanced at the clips. "It's odd."

Sonya presented him with the muffin. "Your whole business sounds odd."

Max took his first bite of the savory muffin and leaned back in the captain's chair, contentedly contemplating the pastoral scene outside. Past the thick tangle of tomato plants and the low crimson strawberry patch, beyond the grazing donkey, he noticed a blue sedan on the road slow and stop under a huge maple tree that half obscured it. Ten minutes later, as Sonya was relating a Willie-the-goat story, the sedan was still there, doors and windows closed.

"Any of your neighbors have a blue sedan?" Max asked casually.

"My nearest neighbor is half a mile away and they have a Jeep," Sonya said. "Why?"

"There's a blue car there, under the tree. I just wondered."

Sonya peered out. "I never saw that car before. Maybe they're in trouble."

"Someone would be over here by now if it was trouble." Max rose and went to the window. "I just think it's peculiar."

119

Sonya rose to stand by his side. "They could be just admiring the tree."

"Why don't they come out to admire it?"

"Maybe they don't want to."

"They haven't even put a window down." Max saw no sign of movement in the car.

Sonya returned to her chair. "Are all city people paranoid?"

"Only those whose friends have been murdered." He saw her look. "I'm sorry. But a few things have happened to me and I've learned a few that make me . . . concerned."

Sonya was sober-faced. "You're serious, aren't you?"

Outside, the white plume from the exhaust told Max the car engine had started. In seconds it moved away down the road and disappeared around the bend.

"Why in God's name would anyone snoop around here?" Sonya asked.

"I don't know," Max said. "No reason at all. Forget it."

Sonya poured more tea and produced more muffins. Max stuffed himself.

On the drive back to the airport, little was said. Max sat close to Sonya, covertly observing the play of her features and her hair, which she had gathered up, securing it with an ivory comb so that it fell in loose waves. Max began to understand why Cy had kept her apart, in a corner of his life.

At the air terminal, Sonya waited for the twenty minutes before Max's flight was called. When it was announced, Max put out his hand awkwardly. "I feel like I've known you a long time."

"Yes," she agreed, "somehow."

"Listen." Max moved with the passenger line. "I have to see you again. Don't say no."

She laughed, leaned over, kissed him lightly on the cheek, and said, "All right, I won't say no."

She turned, waved, her smile radiant, and disappeared. Later, on the plane, settling into his seat, Max conjured Sonya up. She was a gift, he concluded, an absolute gift.

Slowly, with the miles, the otherworldliness began to fade and the ongoing reality of his life returned. He opened the manila envelope to examine the printouts again, looking for some further clue, but found none.

120

THE THIRD FRIDAY

The plane touched down at eleven. He phoned the office immediately, asking for Jimmy Singh. Jimmy was sick again, Martha informed him. Max hung up angrily, jumped into a cab, and sped to midtown. Miraculously, traffic was low, and before twelve, to Martha's surprise, he walked in. There was a call from Detective Shamski, she told him.

"First get me Jimmy."

She got Singh's wife again with tentative, breathy tones. Poor husband was not feeling so well; that virus was very strong; Indian people are not used to American viruses.

"Yes, but please put him on," Max ordered. "I won't be long."

"He is in the bathroom being very sick."

"I'll wait," Max said grimly, "but tell him he'd better be sick very quick."

He heard distressed conversation and then Singh's constricted voice came on the line. "Oh—Mr. Roberts, I am so sorry."

"You're really bad, eh?"

"Not so good, no."

"Jimmy, I have a set of printouts on some stock with no name at all, just prices. Did you make those for Cy?"

"Hard copy on prices with no name? That is not the drill. Oh no."

"Yes, but did you make them?"

"I do not think so." Singh's voice quavered and he apologized. "I am thinking I have fever, you see."

"Have you seen a doctor?"

Singh was contemptuous. "These doctors—they just take your money and give you aspirin. I will be all right soon."

"Jimmy, what's going on? Are you coming back to work here or not?"

Singh's voice began to fade. He coughed, gasped. "The virus. The American virus. We Indians . . ."

"Yes, your wife told me," Max said, "but I want you here tomorrow."

"I . . . will . . . see the . . . doctor on the next block today. He is Indian—from Delhi, and if he says . . ."

"Tomorrow," Max said. "Dammit." He hung up, opened the door. "Martha . . ."

Martha was having a hard time with a lanky messenger who tried to put a package into her hand.

"Hey—look, six twenty-two—that's you, right? So don't give me no hard time, lady, please."

Martha tossed the package back at him. "Don't you give me a hard time, buster. This says suite six twenty-two but we're six twenty-two *A*. Got it? Now get out of here."

The messenger, one of the hard-riding bike breed, retrieved his package, grumbling about "old women," and went next door. Martha retreated to her desk. "I'll old women him."

"What's going on with Jimmy?" Max demanded.

"Funny stuff," Martha said laconically. "Very funny."

He asked her to get him Shamski and retreated to his office. In a minute his intercom buzzed.

"Detective Shamski is on the line."

He picked up the phone. "Shamski, listen to this—"

He hunched over the phone and as he did an enormous roar erupted, blasting his eardrums. He felt himself being lifted from the chair and dropped to the floor. Before his astonished eyes, half of one wall collapsed, filling the room in seconds with blinding smoke and dust. From outside he heard shouts and calls, and a woman's piercing scream rose over it all, then cut off abruptly.

Managing to get to his feet, the blast still echoing in his head, Max kicked away the debris of his chair, stepped over broken plasterboard, fractured wood lathing, and half a contorted steel filing cabinet to get to the door, which had swung open at the shock.

Martha sat at her desk, stunned. A wall behind her had shivered with the explosion but shattered only partially, dumping wood, plaster, and powder on her head and face. As she saw Max, she jumped up, crying in fear. "Oh—my God. Am I cut? Am I cut?"

Max reached out for her in fear that the walls would collapse around them.

"Let's get out of here!"

He grabbed Martha's arm, pulling her out with him into the corridor. Here, the full shock awaited him—the office next door was twisted and wrecked. Desks, chairs, cabinets, had been flung about like matchstick furniture. A middle-aged man held his bloody right side, moaning in pain. A young woman sat dazed on the floor, her legs askew, a sweater almost completely torn from her body.

"Oh—oh," Martha moaned.

122

THE THIRD FRIDAY

There was a rush of feet behind Max as other tenants on the floor huddled close. A siren shrieked somewhere in the building. Max and two others struggled through into the exploded office. They went to the woman, raised her gently, moved her to the hallway, and set her down. Another woman tried to arrange her sweater to cover the exposed flesh. Max went back to the man.

"Can you walk to the hall? Let me help you."

With Max's help, the bleeding man limped to the hallway. There, two frightened men helped him sit down, back against the wall. In the destroyed office, smoke and dust still swirled. The front door, which had been holding by one piece of hinge, now toppled over and crashed. Everyone jumped and moved back. The unconscious young woman did not stir. The wounded man began to cry—a terrible, whimpering cry.

"Easy," Max said. "Try to take it easy. Help will be here soon."

The sobbing man turned uncomprehending eyes on him. "It . . . exploded," he said in a choked voice. "I took off the . . . the cord . . . and it . . . blew up."

He subsided into moans, closing his eyes.

Max bent over him, his own eyes closed as well.

7

"Tell me what happened—slowly." Shamski eyed the damage in the Whizkids office. With the smoke and dust gone, it seemed remarkably superficial. Martha searched through her desk drawers for another box of tissue. Max stood by, keeping his ideas to himself.

"I told it to the bomb-squad people ten times," Martha complained. "I've got it memorized by now. All right. This messenger comes in with this package. . . ."

"Small—large?"

"Medium—just a package in brown paper, tied up. I hardly took notice because I saw right away it wasn't for us—it was for next door, the diamond people. It happens sometimes."

"Then what?"

"I told him it was for them, not us, and the stupe argued with me. But he went next door. Then, in a few minutes— boom." She found the tissues and blew her nose.

"Do you remember where the messenger was from—the messenger service?"

Martha gave Shamski a disdainful glare. "I wasn't interested."

"But you're sure the package was for next door."

"I'm sure." Martha was annoyed. "I can read. I saw who
it was for."

"But it didn't have a name." Max spoke with quiet intensity. "It had our suite number except for one letter, an *A*."

"Meaning?" Shamski became interested.

"Meaning this." Max moved close to the detective. "It's
possible it was a mistake by whoever addressed the package.
It's possible it was meant for here, meant for us, for me."

Martha's eyes opened wide. "I never thought of that."

"It's possible," Shamski agreed. "Anything's possible."

"I told you about Roy Herbert. That son of a bitch is capable
of—"

"Hold it." Shamski tried reason. "According to you, maybe
Herbert put out a contract on Bannerman—OK?"

"OK."

"So why you? Why would he be crazy enough to send a
bomb to knock you off?"

"I don't know," Max said, "but if he was crazy enough to
ask Robinson to keep the door unlocked—"

"That's something we'll get into. But this—? We've got
some serious checking to do." Leaving Max and Martha, Shamski went next door to the C. & L. Importing Company, which
had taken the explosion.

Standing with a bomb-squad boss amidst the rubble, Shamski poked at a blackened men's shoe in a corner. The front
room of the two-room suite was a mess of twisted metal and
splintered wood. The blasted, broken walls bore jagged holes.
The floor had buckled and what was once a massive safe built
in near the rear room was now a yawning, cracked tangle of
steel dropped halfway down to the floor below. Shamski was
impressed.

"So—what was it, Keller?"

Keller, the bomb officer, a quiet ten-year veteran with a
slight limp acquired when he was a shade too careless during
a disposal, held a piece of deformed coil spring in his right hand,
which he was sniffing.

"Primitive is what it was. But you don't need more. When
that poor bastard opened the package, this spring uncoiled and

one end made contact with the battery terminal. That completed the circuit and the plastique inside went off. I'd say it was a very heavy charge too. Did a grand job."

Shamski grimaced. The man who had opened the package was critical at Bellevue. The woman with him had so much internal damage it was doubtful she would ever be whole again. They both worked for the diamond-importing firm, which had rented the suite for the past five years with no history of violence at all.

"This little number," Keller said, "is a professional job."

"Why would someone want to blow this place up?" Shamski gestured toward the safe. "If it was a plan to get hold of diamonds in there, that's dumb; they would have to know the whole thing would blow.

"You'd think so, but sometimes crooks do dumb things, just like the rest of us."

"What are the chances of finding out who sent the device?"

"Not much," Keller said. "We might dig out the messenger outfit—maybe—most of those people are fly-by-nights and like to keep away from trouble. But even then, all they have is an address to pick up from and an address to deliver to. The pickup address can be as phony as a three-dollar bill; they couldn't care less, so long as they get paid. And if you're going to send in a package bomb to somebody, you pay in advance—and that ends that."

"The man next door," Shamski said, "thinks the bomb may have been meant for him but was misaddressed. What would you think of that?"

Keller pocketed the spring. "I'd think he was lucky, that's what I'd think."

The next day a small AP story appeared on the wire about the bombing, noting that it had taken place next door to a company whose president had been found dead on the pavement less than a month ago. In Florida, Adeline Roberts, waiting to see her heart specialist, read the paragraph in the waiting room and left without making another appointment. She went directly home to call her son.

"Are you all right? Max, how do you get mixed up with bombs?"

"Adeline, as an old anarchist . . ."

"Don't joke. This isn't Russia."

"They bombed the office next door," Max explained, "and anyway, I'm all right."

"Does it have to do with Cy? Tell me the truth."

"No—no—it was next door, I just told you."

"The stock market, then—it has to do with your business?"

"How could it? Adeline, it was an accident."

"You swear you're all right?"

"I swear. Are you all right?"

"Come down sometime and see."

There were other calls as the word spread. Carol, concerned, wanted to see Max, was he really all right, what was going on? Max said he'd get back to her later. Phil Carmody telephoned, concerned as well. "Max, take care, for God's sake. Watch yourself. Why don't you close up shop for a few weeks and go away someplace?"

"Maybe I will."

"Remember," Carmody concluded," if I can help in any way, don't hesitate to call on me."

Julian Berns charged in, full of gloom. He had already heard through the grapevine that Marcus Rich, the bastard, was planning to do an in-depth piece about the bombing, linking it to Cy, most likely smearing him with his brand of innuendo-filled prose.

"Forget it," Max advised, "and listen to this." He told Julie about Luther Robinson. Julie was horrified.

"No way it was going to be some kind of joke. Never."

"But Robinson swears he left the place with the lock on."

"That's what he told *you*." Berns was all for getting Herbert worked over. "I know some people who would do that, you know," he said darkly.

"What good would that do?" Max countered. He produced the chart he had found in Sonya's cabin. "Look at this."

Berns studied the squiggles. "A stock movement chart?"

"Yes. Some company Cy was following. He left it with that woman I told you about, the one in Vermont."

Berns looked at him with disbelief. "What was it doing up there?"

"Cy might have been analyzing it."

"In Vermont?"

"It was in his attaché case, I guess, and he was looking at

it and forgot it when he left. The only thing is he never showed it to me."

"Isn't that peculiar?"

Max nodded. "A little." He handed his friend the chart. "Can you get to one of your technical people, the little elves, you know? They keep every chart in the world. Let's find out what company this is."

"I'll try.

"And . . ." Max hesitated, then went on. "Jimmy Singh says he doesn't remember plotting this chart, doesn't know anything about it. But he always did those charts for us."

"That's funny too," Berns said, surprised. "Get him in here and let me ask him some questions."

"Jimmy's out," Max said. "He's been sick a lot since everything happened. He's not here today."

"Wouldn't you know," Berns said.

On the trading floor of the Commodities Exchange, Brian Shamski watched the action with interest. Big money here, very large, very serious money. When first assigned to the Bannerman death he had ignored the partner's assertions of murder; now he was not so certain. There were elements that smelled. He was not a great believer in coincidence, and the package bomb was disturbing. Then there was all this money. Shamski had learned early in his career that most homicides were due to one of two factors—sex or money. As the veteran cops would ask about a suspect, "Is he a gambler or a lover?"

There were exceptions, of course, but it proved best to go by experience. Cy Bannerman's death suddenly held both possibilities.

He spotted Robinson quickly—not too difficult to do on the floor. The clerk was entering information on his clipboard when Shamski tapped him on the shoulder. Robinson wheeled around and, street-smart, knew instantly he was in trouble. He clutched the clipboard and waited.

"Are you Luther Robinson?"

The clerk nodded. Shamski identified himself quietly, but before he could go any further, Robinson said in an intense whisper, "Bannerman's partner sent you on me, right?"

"It's just questions," Shamski said calmly. "No one said you did anything wrong. Can we go someplace to talk?"

Robinson looked from side to side with quick, apprehensive glances. "Listen," he pleaded, "if I be seen going off with you, somebody's gonna know somethin's wrong. I'm askin' you to just let's talk quietly, here."

Shamski acquiesced. "Just tell me what Mr. Roy Herbert wanted you to do on the night Mr. Bannerman died."

"Nothin' special."

"Come on," Shamski warned, "stop dancing around or you'll finish up on the short end."

"He wanted some—grass—is all."

"Grass? Come on."

"What you want me to tell you, rock or somethin'? So you can bust me good?"

"What else did he want?" Shamski asked.

"That's it."

"That's not what you told Roberts."

"Maybe he didn' hear right."

Shamski tapped Robinson on the shoulder with a single finger. "Do yourself a favor—don't try being a badass."

"Roberts said he wouldn't say anything to you but he did," Robinson said bitterly.

"He had to," Shamski said.

"And what about me? I get called into a lawyer's office or into court—and I'm finished here."

"There's someone dead," Shamski said.

"I'm asking you to give me a break," Robinson pleaded.

Shamski sighed. "All right. You know what you're saying and I know what you're saying, so OK . . . for now."

Robinson sagged in relief, but as two brokers neared, he tightened again, looking worriedly at Shamski. The detective said loudly, "Buy low, sell high, that way we'll make some money."

"Right on," Robinson said fervently.

Shamski spent the next forty-eight hours digging into Roy Herbert. The more he dug, the more swamp he found. The man had something wrong with him. He brooked no interference and went to bizarre lengths to satisfy every whim. Shamski put Morrisey, a mousy-looking white shield, on Herbert. Four days into the investigation, Morrisey reported what he called "the damnedest thing.

130

"I tell you," he recounted, "this guy is slime. He goes into this loft building way downtown, near Spring. He goes up to the fourth floor. There is no name for the fourth floor. I decide to take a look. I go up the stairs and right there, on the landing, they're making a movie or something. But it's not regular. The girls are all naked, four of them. The rock music is going and a couple of guys are standing around laughing. I see Herbert in the corner and I think maybe I've gone too far—so I back down.

"I wait across the street for about two hours, then I see one of the girls I saw upstairs come out of the building. I go over and ask can I buy her a cup of coffee. She thinks I'm going to bust her for something, but I tell her if she's a good girl and talks on the QT, no sweat. She says OK. I ask her what's going on up there. She tells me this Herbert's making a kind of a videotape, paying for the whole thing; he's got the story and everything. What he's doing, this bum, he's got like a couple of favorite commercials—you know, stews in an airplane, girls in Levi's, women doing makeup stuff—he's making these commercial-type things—but get this—all the women are naked, yeah—they do and say these commercial things but with no clothes on. I really blinked at that one, believe me. The girl tells me Herbert's doing it because it's a gas, just for kicks. He'll show the cassettes to his friends and everyone will have a ball. You tell me this guy is a Wall Street big shot?"

"You get her phone number?" Shamski asked.

"Oh sure," Morrisey said, then he coughed nervously.

Herbert and Company operated out of five floors in an old conservative building on Pine Street. Before Shamski was finally sent to the fifth floor, he lost himself on the third, a warren of broker desks and cubicles, each bathed eerily green in computer glow, each occupied by intense men and women, phones in hot hands, lips moving rapidly, fingers punching keys, voices calling prices. Along the wall, a moving tape reported worldwide events moment by moment. Any snippet of news, any unverified item, even the fact of a kidney stone being passed by the chief of a Latin American country, might cause a run up or a run down in stock prices.

Exposed to the sight and sound, Shamski felt the pressure

like an electric current—and a lure. There were stories in the department of men who never rose above patrolmen, did their twenty years, turned in their papers, and then revealed they had made a fortune in IBM, in AT&T, in some godforsaken obscure stocks that no one had ever heard about, stocks that hit the jackpot, rose, doubled, doubled again, rose again, merged, split, all of it, all the beautiful things that could happen to a stock, all the beautiful things that the market could do for a man. But if it went against you—

The fifth floor held the calm of the admiral's cabin. The battle was below. Here, gentlemanly quiet reigned in the executive offices. Here, even in the glass-walled dining room, only muted voices were heard and the dessert cart rolled noiselessly over thick carpeting. But it was all made possible by the tension and tumult two flights down.

Roy Herbert was in. Shamski, ushered into a smaller-than-he-expected office with startling red-leather furniture, was greeted by the VP with a quizzical look and a comic, "Well, detective, what did I do now?"

"Just checking around," Shamski said, "with people who knew Cy Bannerman."

"Ohhh," Herbert mock-groaned, "did I know him. Sit down, we'll talk about fakes and liars. Would you like something? I've got anything you want—Coke"—he grinned—"the drinking kind, Pepsi, Chateau Petrus fifty-two."

"No thanks," Shamski said. "I get the idea that you and Bannerman weren't exactly best buddies."

"Ha." Herbert tilted back in his tall executive chair. "The guy was an asshole. He hated me because I was here when he came, you understand, because my father founded this firm, because he was one of those snots who come into the game with ten cents and try to take the jackpot. He pretended to be Mr. Niceguy but he'd slit your throat given half a chance. He was just one of those Johnny-come-lately shits."

"I heard some stories," Shamski said, "that you and he had a fight over a girl? Anything to that?"

Herbert grinned but his eyes showed flashes of working wheels within. "Over a girl? I don't fight over girls. The world is full of girls." He tilted back. "It's that partner, right? It's that jerk bad-mouthing me. Ha—he couldn't get himself arrested down here without Bannerman to lead him around like a blind man." He raised his hands in dramatic frustration. "Why do people do this to me? He isn't the only one. Jealousy is a horrible thing, detective, really horrible."

"On the night Bannerman died . . ." Shamski started, but Herbert interrupted.

"Are you joking? Are you going to ask me where I was, like some street criminal, right here in my own office? Hey," he laughed, "give me a break, detective." His laughter subsided. "I was at Space from eleven to three. You know the spot? They had a great environment—a shuttle launch pad, so help me—it was terrific. Space suits, space music, space light—the whole thing. I was with a girl whose name I'll give you if you really want to know. And I saw a whole raft of people there, and they saw me. And Bannerman died at about ten-thirty, didn't he? That's what the paper said, anyway, so—?"

"Do you play a lot of practical jokes?" Shamski asked abruptly.

"Me?" Herbert hesitated. "Sometimes—maybe, on special friends."

"How about on Bannerman?"

"No way. I never went near him socially."

"Never?"

The laughter vanished from Herbert's eyes. "Never. Don't listen to stories."

"But you do know where he lived?"

"Why would I know where he lived?"

Shamski held up. The implied promise he had made to Robinson stuck in his throat. He changed tack.

"I'm told you get involved in the movie business time to time, is that so?"

Herbert shrugged. "People come around for financing, you know how it is."

"Got anything going now?"

"Here and there." Herbert studied the detective's face. "You interested in . . . the business?"

Now girls, Shamski speculated. Herbert leaned back. "It's a funny business," he said, "so many girls trying to break in."

"I'll bet."

"Hey, if you want some laughs, I'll introduce you to a few."

Bingo.

"I'll take a raincheck." Shamski rose. "Well, we cops still have to work for a living."

"Well, there are all kinds of ways to make money." Herbert winked, "if you know the right people." He came around from behind his desk and slapped Shamski on the back jocularly. "I've helped a few of your buddies with that. Call me. We'll get together on a few numbers."

In the elevator, Shamski felt he had just seen a man so calculating, so sure of himself, and with such good moves that anything might be expected of him. More and more, he felt this case was not as simple as he had first thought.

Max arranged for repair of the bomb damage and spent useless hours, with Martha, gawking at bicycle messengers whom the police had dredged up from some netherworld. To no avail; Martha was right—they all looked alike. Meanwhile, his West Side apartment painters reported a delay. In the dining room, as they hacked away at peeling plaster, they had inadvertently broken through a wall and found a badly shattered water pipe that now had to be replaced by the plumbers—but a license to do that must first be obtained, which required that a plumbing plan of the entire floor be submitted. Since no one had seen such a plan for the last thirty years, things were at a standstill. Max called a plumbing contractor, trucked some more clothes to Cy's, and tried to shrug it all off. Julian Berns, pacing the floor, however, stoked the fire with his worry.

"If we really believe that that bomb was sent deliberately, and it's known that you're living here, what's to say something wouldn't be tried right in this apartment?"

There was no answer.

Carol called twice more and Max finally called her back. She suggested dinner, and, with some vague misgivings, Max agreed. They went to a new Columbus Avenue restaurant. There, they waited forty minutes to be seated, finally being granted a table so close to the open kitchen grill that smoke and steam constantly assailed them. Throughout the dinner, Carol looked at Max with troubled eyes. Touched by her concern, he assured her that he was all right.

"What have the police said?" Carol wanted to know.

"Finally," Max said, "finally, this detective Shamski be-

134

lieves me, I think, that everything's connected to Cy's murder. He's now going to check into every single detail of that night."

Carol stabbed at her swordfish. "I wish we had known each other before that night." She looked up at him, eyes shining with sympathy. "I keep thinking how awful it is. You two were so close. At the Exchange, some of them thought you were brothers."

He knew that.

"I wish," she said, "that I could take back that night for you."

In her apartment, Max became aware of a certain fragility in Carol that he had not discerned before. This discomfited him, and compounding the unease was his desire not to stay over, and he ascribed it to a strange sense of guilt—he could only identify it as that—about Sonya.

Seated near Max, Carol said, "It's really very strange. Meeting you and all this going on. I really like you a lot, if that's all right to say."

"I like you too," Max said, rising, "but I think I'd better go. I've got a million things to do early."

Carol studied him for a moment in silence, then said, with surprising emotion, "I'd really like you to stay."

"Listen," Max said, "my head is all screwed up. You can appreciate that."

"I know. I feel awful for you."

"I'll be in touch—really." He leaned over, pecked her on the cheek, feeling like a fool, and went out the door swiftly.

On the street, Max took a deep breath. He had, he felt, escaped something—what he was not sure. Carol was sweet but the sudden depth of her feelings was upsetting.

At Cy's building, Janos the night doorman stopped Max and grinned. "We have good market today or bad market?"

"I'll watch the news and let you know."

"Ho," Janos said, "you the pipple who make the news."

Max was about to pass him when the doorman reminded himself. "Oh—is funny guy comes to see you before. I tell you not home. He leave package for you. I have here." Janos reached back behind the elaborate front desk to pull a brown-paper-wrapped bundle from a compartment and extend it. Instantly Max stepped back, calling, "Don't do that."

"Ho," Janos said. "What . . . ?"

"Put it down on the desk." Max stared at the twine-bound oblong in the doorman's hand. "Do it slow, very slow."

"But is for you," Janos said, stepping toward Max.

"No," Max shouted, "put it down. Down."

Puzzled, the doorman lifted the package by its slack string and dangled it in midair.

"Don't do that!" Max cried out.

Startled, the doorman let go. The bundle fell to the floor. Max dived into a corner of the lobby, cradling his head in his hands. At that, Janos jumped back. There was a splat as the clumsy package came undone and a heavy sheaf of paper burst loose to rest on the polished marble flooring.

In the silence, Max uncoiled and looked up. Janos was staring at the paper as though it had actually exploded. "Mr. Roberts," he muttered, "Mr. Roberts—oh, oh." Max got to his feet and stepped slowly, gently, over to the burst package, fearing it might be booby-trapped. Careful not to touch even an edge, he bent over the bundle and looked down. Blue-printed lines and angles greeted his eyes, junctions, valves. Gingerly, he picked up the first bulky page. A note was attached.

Got the layout from the Housing Department. Give it to the plumbers first chance you get.

Max looked up at Janos's anxious face, then down again at the note from the man he had hired. His knees were weak, his hands not too steady, and he felt like an idiot.

"What?" Janos whispered.

"It's OK. I'm sorry, Janos. It was a mistake." Max swept the papers up. "I thought it was . . . something else," he finished lamely. "I'm sorry. Goodnight."

At midnight, Max lay in Cy's bed, eyes wide open, the nerves twitching in his calf. He twisted about to stop them, twisted back, sat up, lay back again, then pounded the bed in frustration. "Goddammit, Cy," he cursed. He switched on the lamp and stared at the blank-screened computer. From somewhere across the street, Barbra Streisand sang, her taped tones soaring across the canyon. Restless, fighting his impulses, Max went to the IBM, turned it on, reached into a drawer for the game disks. He pulled a few out, reached in again, and saw an envelope beyond, pushed to the rear. He extracted it and saw that it contained a crumpled letter. Quickly he took it out. It was handwritten, undated.

Cy:

My word for you is despicable. My despair is enormous and the guilt is yours, all yours, for the way this has ended, and the way I am now. You will, of course, rationalize, as you always do, but the fact is that you are to blame and that blame will come back like a boomerang. What you have done is to transform the deep love I had for you into a deep hate. But you know that, of course. What you may not, in your male arrogance, know, is that destruction can work two ways. An eye for an eye. Somehow.

Before he reached the scrawled signature Max knew Elizabeth Evers had written it. He looked away from the letter, all of his nerves jumping. What was the guilt, what had Cy done? Ended the affair? But it had been mutual—hadn't it? He examined the words again—an eye for an eye? Was it possible to conceive that Liz Evers had something to do with Cy's death or anything that followed? His head buzzed and throbbed. He tried to think of other things, beaches and woods, smoky green hills. Inevitably, the path led to the phone number he had already tucked into his memory. It took five long rings before Sonya answered sleepily.

"Hello?"

"Sonya, it's Max. I'm sorry if I got you up. I'm getting bugged around here and I wondered if it would be all right if I came up tomorrow."

"You sound terrible."

"I am. That's why I want to come up."

"Come, Max—of course come."

Hearing her sleepy tones, Max could see her eyes, her shoulders under the billowy nightgown. He could see the warm glowing wood in the room, the solemn trees dipping over the cabin, hear the quiet.

"Goodnight," Sonya said. "See you tomorrow."

His head no longer buzzed and the Streisand music sounded sweet and welcome. He slept.

In the morning, he checked on how the office repairs were going. He called Julian and gave him a rundown on Elizabeth's letter. Did that tie in, somehow, with this medical business?

"You don't think Cy gave her a dose of herpes or something, do you?" Julian queried. Max thought he was out of his mind. Cy never had herpes or anything else.

"You never know," Julian said. "The way things are today. Cy was a stud."

"I'd have known," Max retorted. "Guaranteed."

"What about Singh?" Berns asked abruptly. "Is he in today?"

"No."

"Umm." Berns hung up.

That was another thing he would have to deal with, Max thought. What was really happening with Singh?

The flight was choppy. "Little ol' turbulence here," the captain chuckled amiably over the speakers. The "little ol' " continued on and off the whole time, the aircraft thumping and bumping, rattling trays, inducing tight smiles on the faces of the two stewardesses and sweaty palms on their passengers.

As the plane touched down and wheeled in to the building, he wondered how he would be greeted, what Sonya really felt. Why had he called her, anyway? But he knew.

She was there in the terminal, waiting in her boots and jeans and purple cotton top that seemed to flow about her. Seeing Max, she waved and smiled. He felt the warmth ten paces away and walked them quickly.

"Hi," Sonya said, and all of Max's confusion faded. He was simply happy to be here looking at her face, close to her.

"Wow," he said, "you look great."

Her smile broadened; she leaned over and kissed him on the cheek. It seemed to Max that she might have hesitated close to his lips but it didn't matter.

In the familiar VW, as they wound about the countryside, he told Sonya about the bombing. She was horrified. There were other things, he said. Since Cy's death a lot was unraveling; he needed some space. He had called her on instinct.

"You're a lot like Cy," she said gravely.

"No way," he said, genuinely astonished.

"Oh yes," she said. "He was always doing a balancing act. I think that's what you do too."

At the cabin, Sonya busied herself making tea. She went

138

out to the garden for fresh mint and Max, jacket off, sat in the old rocker, eyes closed, breathing in the country. When she came back in, he said, "What a life you live here, what a wonderful life."

By the time they had finished tea, Max felt he had never been away from here. The ache departed from his bones, the miasma from his head.

"Let's go for a walk. I'll show you something."

She took him out, around the maple stand, and along the river, where the reeds sprouted high. They passed huge piles of granite and a grove of blasted, blackened oak trees.

"Lightning," Sonya said. "Only last year."

She took him along an unmarked path where the tree canopy was so thick the sky barely penetrated. Suddenly they emerged into the open. In front of them was a clear, sparkling lake, shimmering with reflection of the orange sun. Around the lake were half a dozen giant willow trees, their trunks reaching high and their branches sweeping down to the ground in a graceful, spectacular display.

"Wow," Max breathed, "just . . . beautiful. Nothing like this in Bronx Park."

"These trees and this pond," Sonya said, "show every change in season. I come here often. Whenever Cy came, he'd want to walk here."

They were almost silent on the way back. By the time they were in the cabin, the full glory of the sunset was at the gate.

"Dinner at the local Ritz?" Max asked.

"That's here—the best food in town," Sonya said. "In the cabinet over there is the hard cider; would you, please?"

Max fetched the bottle, poured. The fermented apples were thick and alcohol aromatic.

"This is a treat."

He watched in wonder as she whipped up a combination of cheese, eggs, tomatoes, and basil from her garden. Accompanied by her home-baked bread, it set his mouth aglow.

"This is," he stuttered, "I mean—this is . . ."

"Country simple." Sonya smiled.

She washed and he dried. Afterward they sat outside on the little wooden bench in the wonderful evening chill.

"Thank you for letting me come," Max said.

"I'm glad you did."

Max looked up to the sky, stars everywhere. "This is such

a good-feeling place, out of it all, safe. I suppose," he said, "Cy felt the same way."

"Yes," she said.

"I am so angry," Max said, "at who hurt him."

"Yes," she said, "I understand."

"It's hard to explain, what he did for me."

"He said you did things for him."

Had Cy actually said that?

"Can we go in?" With a simple, natural gesture, she took Max by the hand and led him inside. The door closed behind them. Sonya threw the iron bolt. "Sometimes the raccoons try to come in for the leftovers." She put the dishes away in the cabinet, folded some towels, checked some glasses. Max watched her with a growing feeling that she was doing things that needed no doing, that she was waiting for some movement from him. Uncertain, unbelieving, he asked, "Am I on the couch again?"

"If you like," she answered, her back still to him.

"I'd like . . ." he said and stopped.

Sonya turned to him then, laughing in her throaty way, and Max felt the stir to his toes. "Isn't this silly," she said and held out her hand. "Come on."

Max took her hand gratefully. As she had led him into the cabin, Sonya led him into her bedroom. There, feeling full to bursting, Max put his arms about her. Sonya's went about him and, in moments, they both swayed and fell, entwined, to the bed. He heard Sonya gasp, "Ohhh. . . ." and as he touched the white-linen coverlet, a quick, flashing thought of Cy stabbed at him, but he buried himself in Sonya's body and forced it to fade away.

8

Feet up on his desk at the precinct, Brian Shamski thought about the Bannerman case. The two victims of the bombing next door were still on the critical list. A thorough rundown of the diamond-importing company had revealed nothing that might have caused such violence. Every bike messenger in town, not unexpectedly, had a severe case of "Hey—not me, man." Had the bombing been a mistake? His phone buzzed. "Guy to see you, name of Borland."

"What does he want?"

"He won't say, some kind of official business."

"From where—the water-and-sewer department?" Shamski grumbled. "All right, send him in."

He buried himself in hated paperwork until a voice at his desk asked, "Mr. Shamski?"

Shamski looked up at his visitor with resignation, which changed, almost instantly, to interest. There was something familiar about the man, about the way he looked, dressed, brushed his hair back. When the man put his attaché case on the desk and said, "There are some things we have to talk about," a click went off in the detective's head and he reached for Max Roberts's phone number.

In his dream, Max and Cy were swimming together against a strong tide. On the shore, Adeline stood waving and shouting for them to be careful. With no warning, a cramp gripped Max's legs. Movement became impossible. Panicked, he floundered, thrashed about, called to Cy, and started sinking. His head went down; his mouth sucked water. Cy reached out quickly, gripping him around the neck, keeping him afloat. He started to black out. . . . At that point, Max struggled awake, feeling the beat of fear in his chest and the taste of salt in his throat. For half a minute he did not know where he was, and he lay there quietly until the terror faded. Then he remembered.

Sonya. But she was not in the rumpled bed, not in the room, nor could he see her beyond.

"Good morning," he called. There was no response, though outside the goat made a grating noise. As he lay there, the night flooded back to him. The lovemaking had flowed naturally, simply. Afterward, Sonya had held him close, his back to her belly, so that he had felt warm and safe.

Warmly, satisfyingly half awake at three in the morning, with the feel and smell of Sonya next to him in the shadowed room, Max had found himself talking softly of Adeline, of his childhood, of the money game that he and Cy had been playing—how, five years ago, when it began, it all seemed so urgent but now—

"Because your bank account is so fat," Sonya had murmured.

She had a disdain for money, a disregard of it; it was handy for survival, she agreed, but the systems one had to enter to make it were distorting to the spirit. What had she found in Cy then? he thought, and, witchlike, she had answered the unspoken question.

"He had this . . . radiation, this powerful Kirlian aura. It fascinated me, that power. It's odd, I admit. All my life I disliked the commercial world, with its power games. And here was Cy—right at its center—and I was . . . drawn to him. It was a real discovery for me."

142

THE THIRD FRIDAY

"Sonya—!" Where was she?

He left the bed and dressed. From the front room he peered outside. She was nowhere to be seen. He tried the small porch and walked around behind the cabin to the tool house. Only the donkey was there, languidly grazing. Returning to the front, Max realized the VW was gone. He was starting back into the cabin when he heard an engine and turned back again, expecting to see the small beetle shape come around the turn, but it was not the VW, it was some other car. He was about to continue on in when, with a sense of déjà vu, he recognized the sedan as the same blue one he noticed last time creeping, once again, along the road, tinted windows closed, as before. As he watched, it stopped, semiobscured by a large oak.

Max stared at it. A window started to come down in the rear and then went up again, as though someone had changed his mind. Apprehensive but angered, Max started toward the car with a determined stride. The sedan remained immobile until he was twenty yards away, then, frustratingly, as before, it started moving away slowly. Max increased his pace, breaking out into a run after five yards, but the car picked up speed and soon, as he chased it, disappeared down the road and around the bend, leaving him standing in the dust.

"Son of a bitch!"

The buzzing sound of the approaching VW turned him around. Sonya whipped the machine onto the worn grass she used for a parking space and emerged carrying a bag of groceries.

"Needed butter and stuff," she explained, then noting his tension, asked, "What's wrong?"

"I saw that blue car again," Max said. "The same one that came down the road the last time I was here. Twice is too much."

"Please," Sonya laughed, "spare me the big-city paranoia."

There were biscuits for breakfast and eggs snatched from under the hens. There was the herb tea that Max had learned to like. And the jam. But at one point, when Max rose from the table to fetch a cup, he passed the window and a flash of reflected light struck his eye from down the road. He looked hard at where it came from and it seemed to him like the reflection off a mirror, or a lens—a binocular lens, maybe. He thought of saying something to Sonya but resisted; why frighten her?

On the ride back to the airport, Max scarcely took his eyes from Sonya. When she kissed him good-bye, it was not with untoward passion but neither was it the chaste kiss she had bestowed before. When she turned and left this time, Max felt a wild elation.

Back in the city, there were calls to attend to. He returned Julie's and told him where he had gone. Berns was surprised and instantly a little suspicious of Sonya.

"No," Max said, "she was Cy's safety valve." Berns remained dubious.

"You better call that detective," Martha told him. "He said to get to him as soon as possible." When he was connected with Shamski, the detective said tersely, "Get down here, quick."

Max wanted to know what had happened but Shamski simply repeated, "Down here—quick."

At the precinct, he was directed toward an empty interrogation room. He opened the door, started in, and stopped in his tracks, staring at Shamski's visitor in open-mouthed shock.

"Close the door," Shamski said.

In his excitement, Max stammered and sputtered, "That's . . . him. . . . That's the guy . . . the guy . . ."

Shamski closed the door himself. "His name's Bill Borland. He's an investigator for the Securities and Exchange Commission."

"SEC?" Max said. "It's . . . Billy . . . that Billy guy."

Borland shrugged.

"What are you following me for?" Max demanded. "What's going on?"

"Mr. Roberts." Borland's voice was not what it had been; it was firm and sure. "The commission, in the light of certain information we have, has been investigating some of the trading activities of your company. Specifically we've been interested in Cy Bannerman. Now, that was before his demise. At this point, we've lost a little focus."

Max looked at Shamski angrily. "Did you know about this?"

"Not till forty-five minutes ago," Shamski said. "Mr. Borland came in here and when I looked at him, with the blond hair and the seersucker suit, I thought of your description right away."

"And what am I supposed to know," Max demanded. "What were you trying to sell me? What's all the playacting about?"

"When I came up to you," Borland explained calmly, "I was checking, testing you—seeing if you'd bite."

"And you were lucky," Shamski added, "that he turned

144

up when you were getting beaten on. Now sit down and listen to the man."

"I can hear standing up," Max said defiantly.

"Here's the point." Borland was unruffled. "We have reason to believe that the principal in Whizkids, Cy Bannerman, was trading for some company, dealing in commodities and options on a large scale for them."

"So?" Max was puzzled. "That's our business."

"Is it your business to act for a sham company, a front for elements of the organized drug trade?"

"Drug trade?" Max froze.

"That's what the man says," Shamski interjected.

"We believe," Borland went on, "that this company acts as a focal point, collects millions in cash from their dealers, and sends it abroad illegally. It comes back, laundered as supposedly clean money, and is then invested in one enterprise or another."

"A drug-money scam," Shamski simplified. "These wise guys take the dirty, make it clean, and have legit bank accounts to do whatever they like."

"On the street, the cash flow has been lessening. The drug people want to get into more and more legitimate businesses. But the funds have to be clean before they can do that," Borland explicated pedantically. "One way is to use the markets. The money works for them meanwhile, cleans it even further, and makes it hard to trace back. Cy Bannerman did that for them, through your firm."

"Never," Max exploded. "You're crazy."

Borland was unfazed. "We thought, frankly, that you were part of the operation, but at the commission we think now that Bannerman operated solo, knowing very well that it was a laundry operation and trying to keep it as quiet as possible."

Max jumped to his feet. "You're telling me Cy *knew* this account was drug money?"

Borland nodded. "We, at the commission, feel . . ."

"You at the commission," Max raged, "can take a flying leap to the moon! Never. Cy would never get involved in that."

"Easy," Shamski counseled. "These guys have been at it for a year, he tells me. They know a lot."

"They don't know Cy." Max glared at Borland. "What's the name of this company?"

"Well—" Borland hesitated, "there's a problem with that. We don't know the name under which they traded but we assume you have records in your files somewhere, though it may be full of concealment."

"How do you know all of this?" Max demanded.

"There's a front man they've been watching," Shamski chimed in, "a smart, clean guy. He's done stock-market deals at other places. Your partner was observed with him."

"So what?" Max protested. "Cy met with a lot of people."

"There has been a legal wiretap on your phone lines for six months, Mr. Roberts—and on Mr. Bannerman's home. The tapes show knowledge of the situation."

"What do you mean *knowledge*?" Max leaned forward intently. "Was anything said about drugs or laundering?"

"Not openly, but we know—"

"You don't know anything," Max flared. "We're traders. We traded, Cy traded, that's all you know."

Borland smoothed back his unruly lock. "Mr. Roberts, this isn't a penny-ante operation. We've tracked millions going in and out, many millions. In illegal securities operations."

"And you don't even know the name of the company?"

"It's been obscured and covered up," Borland admitted. "That's one of the problems."

"Problems?" Max was derisive. "Your problem is you don't even have any real proof Cy did anything!"

"We know."

"Where's your proof? Show it to me."

"The Securities and Exchange Commission," Borland said stiffly, "has sources that we're not about to endanger."

"You're endangering the reputation of a man who's dead, who can't protect himself," Max said.

"He was well aware it was laundered drug money he was handling." Borland stood firm.

"I don't believe you. I just damn don't believe you. I think you need a fall guy somewhere and you're making Cy into one."

"Easy," Shamski muttered.

"And what about this front man?" Max kept on. "Why don't you grab him and then you'll have it all?"

Borland threw a quick look at Shamski. "We have plans in that direction, but not quite yet." His lips tightened. "My auditors will be at your office at three this afternoon." He nodded briskly to Shamski, picked up his attaché case, and left. Instantly Max whirled on the detective.

"This is crazy: lies, a mistake."

"Listen," Shamski said thoughtfully, "the guy may look like a nerd but he's federal, OK? Independent. They don't even tell us what they're doing. Remember when you told me you thought somebody went through Bannerman's place? It was him. Playing private eye."

"Damn fool," Max said. "All he had to do was come to me."

"He thought then that you were part of the deal."

"There was no deal," Max flared. "Cy hated dealers."

"He used coke," Shamski reminded him.

"Like how many others? But he knew what dealers are."

"Listen," Shamski lectured, pacing, "Borland couldn't care less that Bannerman is dead. All he's interested in is securities violations. I don't give two farts in the wind for that but now we're into a badass drug scene, which *is* something, and I'm getting to think that maybe your partner was whacked as part of it."

Max sat back, stunned.

"Even if he didn't know what he was into," Shamski said, "he could have been hit to keep him quiet for their own protection. I'm telling you, it makes sense."

"Maybe," Max said grudgingly, "but Cy couldn't have known about the drugs, never. The nerd is wrong."

"We'll see," Shamski said. "You'll see."

The cab couldn't get back to the office fast enough. There was a huge traffic jam that extended for three blocks. Total gridlock. Horns blared. Drivers cursed and spat from their opened doors. Bikers, weaving in and out, gave everyone the finger, provoking more uproar. Half an hour later, wrung out with sweaty anxiety, Max reached the office. Martha told him there was an urgent call from Henry Bloomkind at the bank.

Calling "Later," Max rushed into the records room, where he called up the "trading accounts" file on the computer. There were not many and never had been—Whizkids traded mostly for themselves. He perused the list. This was foreign territory; he had rarely been involved in the minutiae. Trying for more information, he crashed the computer. Indecipherable letters and numbers appeared, blinking madly. He shut the machine off, cursing, and yelled, "Get Jimmy!" Martha came to the door questioningly. "Get him," Max repeated.

When Martha made the connection, Mrs. Singh came on the line. Apology in every syllable of her reedy voice, she regretted that Jeemy was unable to answer the phone. Misery attended his every move. Prayers were being said for him at the local temple.

"I want him here," Max gritted out. "Tell him I don't give a hoot in hell how he feels, but if he doesn't get here in an hour, the police may come looking for him."

He heard the terrified gasp with satisfaction and hung up. Six minutes short of the hour, a tense Jimmy Singh appeared. His tie was knotted well below his collar. Cigarette ashes decorated his jacket lapels. His eyes were set in a mournful glaze and a delicate cough kept repeating, like a hiccup. "I know that I do not look so bad," he said, "but I am feeling very bad. My whole family, you see, is like that . . ."

Max cut him off. "I've crashed this damn machine. Bring it back and check this client list. Every transaction."

Singh seated himself before the computer. "What is this about police? My wife is very distressed."

"Auditors are coming from the SEC," Max said sharply.

Singh blanched, touched keys. The trading list magically appeared. "Ah—most likely you misspelled the password. See, now the file opens."

"Run this screen down."

Singh put the cursor at the top of the list. "That is Mr. Cy's cousin from Milwaukee, the sanitation man." Garbage collector, Max vaguely remembered.

"Mr. Cy traded silver for him and he left his wife afterward. Ah—that is the actor. He plays the part of the handsome lover on the television, but it is gossiped that he likes only men. Oh yes—that is the millionaire who never pays taxes. Very clever man." Retailing tidbits, Singh keyed down. "Heifer Inc. That is the commune in Iowa that Mr. Cy makes a trade for—with his own money. All children with bad skin there, dancing round the holy man who comes from Larchmont in New York."

"Get on with it!"

Singh tapped on. The computer scrolled. "This is . . . this is . . ." He read the screen. "Dig. Trade." I do not remember a trade for a firm called Dig." He turned to Max questioningly.

"Where's the rest of the entry?" Max leaned over. There was nothing more. "Efficiency," Max groaned. "Keep going."

148

Singh poked away, watching the screen through the cigarette haze. At the last entry, he called out, "Here is one also I
do not know. Morey's Inc." He frowned. "Familiar but—"

"Morey's," Max said. "I never heard of it either." He examined the screen, searching for its secrets. "There's no address,
just a telephone number. Get the trading records." Singh's fingers worked. A new screen jumped up, holding one line of type.
ACCOUNT DISCONTINUED. Max stared at the empty expanse
uneasily. "Where are the records of the trades we made for
them? Or the other outfit?"

Singh puffed and tugged at his tie. "They should be in this
file. I do not know why they are not."

"You're in charge of the files," Max said.

"Yes," Singh said, "but Mr. Cy would come in always, to
pull this up or that. You know this is true, Mr. Max."

"Are you saying Mr. Bannerman junked the records, erased
them?"

"I did not say that," Singh objected, "but Mr. Cy was
sometimes a very impetuous man, you know. He could hit the
wrong key and crash the data by mistake."

"What about backup—don't we always have a backup file?"

Singh wiped a trickle of sweat from his forehead with a
finger and keyed in the backup code. There was a whirring on
the drive and the message BDOS ERROR appeared.

"What does that mean?" Max demanded.

Singh took a nervous puff. "We don't have the backup in
the system."

"Where is it?"

Singh shrugged helplessly. "Get the list back," Max ordered. When Singh had punched the original list back up, Max
dialed the Morey's telephone number with trepidation.

The voice came in with mechanical clarity: "That number
has been disconnected."

Singh looked down at the floor. "My head is pounding
and my bowels are like water, Mr. Max."

Max looked away from him unhappily. Morey's Inc. had
a disconnected phone. In itself that was a "so what?" But cou-
pled with the nerd's statements . . . and what had happened to
the backup? Still, even if the account had been the drug money,
there was absolutely no reason to believe that Cy had known
that, none at all. Here, on the street, often there were shell

149

companies—often people protected themselves for tax reasons with attempts at anonymity. It was not at all unusual for a client to appear with fifty or two hundred and fifty thousand in cash to invest. How many houses on the street asked questions about where the money came from? The rule was if you could net it then forget the rest. No, *if* Morey's was dirty money, the odds were that Cy never knew it. Still, as Shamski said, if something had not gone down right and they had to protect themselves, these were hard people. At the terrible instant, Max wondered, when Cy was pushed through the railing, did he have even a clue as to what it was about? For one fear-filled moment Max heard the steps, felt the shove that hurled him into the first terrifying second of that free fall, and he shuddered.

"I would like to go home now, please," Singh said. "My wife worries for me, you see. It is no good when a woman worries; she cannot do her work properly."

"All right," Max said grimly, "go home—for now. But we both know that backups can't disappear by themselves."

Singh rose, brushed the ashes from his jacket, and made for the door. There, he turned and looked at Max with sympathy. "Terrible times," he said. "Terrible."

After Singh left, Max wandered about in a haze. "Bloom-kind," Martha scolded, but Max waved her away. He took a call from Julie Berns, who had information on the stock chart Max had given him. Max told him other things had come to the forefront. Berns insisted on lunch. Over gravlax, Max filled him in. When Berns heard the words "drug money," he was horrified.

"Dealers? Max, those guys play for keeps. Jesus, it's un-believable." In his astonishment, he tried to butter a roll but the small frozen square slipped off. "Shit," he spat out through clenched teeth, "how could Cy get sucked into something like that?"

"It was just an account."

"And the SEC," Berns said grimly. "Once they get after you, they go back into everything you ever did. Forget the big players, they're going after everybody's ass. Look at that janitor at Drexel who picked up some scribbles about the Benzinger merger and bought in advance—remember? They got him for insider trading. The janitor, for chrissake."

"The auditors are coming up later. They'll take away every scrap they can find."

150

Berns pushed aside his half-eaten eggs Benedict. "They're out for blood. How about the records—are they all straight?"

"No, funny stuff." As Julie stared at him, amazed, Max went on. "Clients I never heard of, with no records of trades. Backup files missing . . ."

"What do you mean *missing*?"

"What I said. And Singh doesn't know anything about anything, he claims."

"And you believe him? Something's going on with that guy, Max."

"What would he have to gain by hiding records?"

Julian didn't answer. Instead he said, "You know, that package bomb might have been sent in order to destroy those records."

"Which don't exist."

"They don't know that, for some reason. Listen, you're lucky." Max looked at him questioningly. "I mean that they were only dealing with Cy; otherwise they might have been after you too."

"How do I know," Max said slowly, "that they don't think I know anyway?"

"Jesus." Berns slumped in his seat.

Max took a deep breath. "What about that chart Cy left?"

"The guy I gave it to recognized it almost instantly. It's the price moves of the McIver Corporation, reflecting about six weeks back."

"McIver?" Max was at a loss.

"Remember, Simon Nakian was trying a takeover move on McIver about then?"

Nakian. He had come from being the owner of a small junk-processing company to a major threatening presence on the American corporate scene. Backed by the R. J. Herbert brokerage firm, he had moved shrewdly and boldly on half a dozen great companies, bringing them to the table under threat of gaining control and trashing the management. Often, the threat kicked the price of the stock, which Nakian, with Herbert's help, had accumulated, to a much higher level. In four cases out of six, the directors had cut a deal with the raider, allowing him to tender the company his stock at an even higher price if he would only go away and bother someone else. Nakian had graciously agreed, thus splitting tens of millions in booty with his backers. In the process, the company's value decreased as the debt contracted to pay off the pirate grew, hurting only the stockholders. But that was stock biz.

Nakian had moved last on the McIver Corporation, which manufactured heavy road-building equipment.

"That deal went sour, didn't it?"

"Oh yes," Julian responded. "A little while ago. Those babies were too big for Nakian to digest; they gave him heartburn."

Max's mind raced. Why had Cy been interested enough in McIver to study its stock movement? He had never even mentioned the company, of that Max was certain. Had he ever mentioned it to Julie?

"No, never."

"At least now we know we've been in the wrong pew; Cy's death wasn't personal," Max said bitterly. "It was strictly business."

"I'm still going to get to the bottom of that Liz Evers business," Berns said stubbornly, "especially after that letter you found."

It was a depressing lunch. Afterward, Max went back to the office. Julian went back to his office and looked up Jimmy Singh's address.

At three P.M. promptly, Borland appeared with two blue-suited accountants. Martha gave them access to all the record disks and printouts available.

"Has Detective Shamski spoken to you yet?" Borland asked Max.

"About what?"

"I guess he's holding up, then," the SEC man said mysteriously.

Some other nerdlike business, Max concluded impatiently. "If you're through . . ."

"Your partner had some swinging reputation downtown." Borland smoothed his forelock, a gesture Max had come to despise.

"What's the point?"

"The point is a question. What happened to this company's funds?"

Max stared at the man. What kind of ploy now? Borland cracked open his attaché case and pulled out a small notebook. "As of opening time this morning when your bank statement was sent out, your company trading account had a negative balance of exactly one thousand, six hundred and forty-two dollars and eight cents." He looked up. "That's eight cents."

Max's eyes opened wide. "That's crazy. The trading account has over two and a half million in it."

Borland shook his head slowly side to side.

"Get Bloomkind at the bank," Max called.

"Where did it all go?" Borland demanded. "Bannerman milked it but where did he stash it? His private accounts only have about ten cents, net."

"Wait a minute, just wait a minute." Confused, Max went out to Martha's desk. She had Bloomkind, the bank man. He had been trying to get Max all day. The figures had come in only yesterday and the trading account was negative. Plus a twenty-six-thousand-dollar pay order had just come in from a brokerage house on an options contract. They were not, of course, going to honor that. And the business account, the day-to-day operating account, was also overdrawn. What did Roberts intend to do?

"I'll get back to you," Max replied weakly, "later." Hanging up, he felt his brain floating in air. Cy, he cursed angrily, you crazy bastard, what did you do? What is happening? Everything's falling apart. He returned to face Borland.

"I don't understand it. I'll have to speak to the accountant."

"Don't bother." Borland was smug. He flipped pages in his notebook. "Mr. Rothstein says his accounts are in order and they indicate a large outflow into presumed trading losses. I emphasize 'presumed.' What do you know about them?"

"I . . . I'm not aware of those kinds of losses," Max said. He felt a nausea in the pit of his stomach.

"I believe you," Borland said promptly. "Your friend made millions from these drug people and buried them someplace."

"No," Max said stubbornly, "that can't be."

Borland closed his notebook with a thwack. "We've just started on this. There's going to be a lot more to explain. What's important here, Mr. Roberts, is not that your partner got killed, but that the integrity of the markets was under attack."

"What?" Max stared at him incredulously.

"You heard me." Borland slapped the attaché case cover down. "We have a free marketplace in this country and if the

153

integrity of that institution is attacked, that ends us as a nation."

"You are an asshole," Max said slowly. "A man has been murdered and you don't give a damn about that."

"Where's the money?" Borland demanded.

"I don't know," Max said harshly, "but if you've finished, get out of here." Martha had come to the doorway, alarmed by the loudness of his voice. "It's OK," Max told her. "This man is leaving now."

When Martha retreated, Borland said, "One more thing. As of right now, you are not to speak to anyone, anyone at all, of this investigation or any aspect of it." He snapped shut the lock on his attaché case and walked out stiffly.

Alone, Max walked the floor, trying to face the implications. Whizkids had not yet made their annual profit distributions. This would have been done next week. Max's share was to have been a hundred and fifty thousand dollars. That was gone. And there was no money to even operate the office. Where was it all? It was impossible for Borland to have it right—Cy would not have milked the company secretly; as angry as he was, Max rejected that totally. But what had happened to the money? And what was Shamski to speak to him about?

Later, he stood in the center of Cy's living room, eyes half closed, feeling there were clues here to the truth, if he could only find them. In front of the open terrace doors he squeezed his fists together and tried to think, to backtrack. In the past twelve months had Cy said anything cryptic, anything that could be interpreted in hindsight as indicating some irregular involvement? He looked out at the terrace, where the sparrows balanced on the rosebushes, and he yearned for the peace of Sonya's yard, for the comforting quiet of the cabin and the silent glory of the pond. The phone beeped, startling him out of his reverie. It was Julie Berns.

"Did they come up?"

"Yes."

"What did they say?"

"They said . . ." Max held up, remembering Borland's injunction to keep silent. The urge to disregard the order was strong, but he decided to heed it—for the time being. "They said some things, you know."

"New things?"

"Some." Max squirmed. "It's all a little confusing."

"What do you mean?"

154

"Julie, it'll have to wait."

"You don't want to tell me." Berns was hurt.

"I can't right now. And I've gotta go, Julie."

When he hung up, he felt he was betraying a friend and didn't know what he could do about it.

Still thinking of McIver, he called Phil Carmody and asked whether Cy had ever discussed the McIver takeover maneuver with him.

"I recall he did," Carmody told him. "I suggested he stay away."

So Cy had been interested in McIver. But to what end?

Getting nowhere, he decided to go out to the new Woody Allen movie. In the theater, one of four small, uncomfortable auditoriums carved from a once-grand antediluvian movie palace, Max found a seat in the rear.

Before meeting Cy, Max had not seen too many Woody Allen films. Cy, however, was a committed fan. Woody's sensibilities were close to his own. Woody's humor, his humanistic sentiments sometimes slopping over into sentimentality, struck harmonious chords. Max had become converted.

He waited for the lights to go down and examined the crowd. A Woody bunch, definitely, even a Woody lookalike in the center, with a female Woody at his side. Max's eyes roamed the seats . . . and stopped three rows in front of him at the back of a head that seemed familiar. Startled, he realized it was Carol's head. Or was it? The head turned then, and Max saw that he was right; it was Carol. She was turning to say something to a man in the next seat. Max slumped down. The movie was wrecked for him. His eyes kept wandering from Woody, to Carol, to the man she was with. From time to time he thought of leaving but became, momentarily, caught up in what was happening on the screen. When the lights came up, Max headed promptly for the exit. He walked quickly down the street and stopped for an ice cream, brain bent, almost unable to choose from the forty-two-flavor repertory.

He finally chose, paid for the cone, swung about to leave, and blinked; Carol was in the doorway.

"Oh hi," she said amiably. "I thought I saw you in the movies."

"Right," Max said, recovering. "Woody Allen. Right." He realized, with surprise, that she was alone. "You having ice cream?"

"I'm deciding against." She hesitated awkwardly. "Well . . ." Max pushed the door open and they walked out to the still-warm pavement. For half a block neither of them spoke, then Carol broke the silence. "I've been concerned about you."

"I've been fine, OK." Max worked at his cone.

Carol said quietly, "And I've . . . missed you."

Max almost dropped the ice cream.

"Does that threaten you?"

"No," Max said hastily, "I don't think."

"Would you like to come up for a coffee?" She laughed. "We can discuss the movie."

Max took a deep breath, and threw the ice cream away. "Why not?"

At her apartment, Carol made espresso and produced some chocolate cookies. Max sat on the couch a bit stiffly, uncertain of how to feel. "Tell me," he said finally, "weren't you with somebody tonight?"

"Yes, a friend. I sent him on home."

"Oh."

"Yes," Carol said very directly. "I had been thinking about you and there you were. So I sent him home."

"And you came into the ice cream place—"

"No—that was accidental."

Max exhaled a deep sigh. "I don't know, I just don't know. Listen, it's just about the worst time of my life. I'm in the middle of a terrible situation. If you think I'm strange, I'm sorry."

"No." Carol leaned toward him. "It's all right. I can imagine what you're going through."

"It's not your problem."

"I know that," Carol said warmly, "but I feel bad because I don't know how to help you and I'd really like to."

Touched, Max took her hand. "It's complicated."

"Yes," she said, "I'm sure." She looked at him with a surprising intensity and Max felt a rush. He reached over and kissed her. Carol began to tremble and he stroked her head gently. When he did, her arms came around him with force. Her chin pressed fiercely into his shoulder. He patted her hair, kissed her face, feeling his own intensity that he was, yet, detached enough to wonder at. But as she clung to him, he found all thought of Cy, Shamski, and the rest vanishing in his need to push himself into her, to lose himself totally in the softness

156

of her breasts, in the roundness of her belly, and the springy mound below.

In bed, the two A.M. air-conditioner city sounds the only noises, Max lay watching Carol sleep, confusion nettling him. How could he do this? What about Sonya? Earlier, lying beside him, legs touching, Carol had asked gently what was happening. He had replied only vaguely but found it easy to talk to her; there seemed to be some common frame of reference. Still, he had retreated again into "It's not your problem." She replied that she felt part of it, in a way, simply by knowing him.

Max rose stealthily, and was putting on his shirt when Carol awoke and lay there, quietly contemplating him. "Shh," he said, reaching for his jacket. "Go back to sleep."

Carol sat up. Her eyes were indecisive and Max, worried that she would ask him to stay, said, "I've got an early appointment." He bent over, touched her face awkwardly, and mumbled, "You helped me."

"Yes," she said sardonically, "that's my woman's function, isn't it?" She watched him out with troubled eyes.

For the next two days, Max desperately tried every avenue in an attempt to discover where the funds had gone. Bank statements, invoices, payment demands, all the back office material, had been taken by Borland's blue suits, and the trail was impossible to follow. Going through his own records, he found unpleasant surprises as well. Many of his assets, the CDs, the mutual-fund shares, and some of the municipal bonds, his accumulation of the Whizkids bounty over the years, had been signed over to the company's trading account as collateral, and under normal conditions this was a secure enough operating manner; Cy had done the same. But suddenly there was no trading account—and when he checked it out, almost all of his personal funds had vanished, factored into the Whizkids' nonexistent balance. His checking account held some few thousands, and a CD coming due, unassigned, was good for ten thousand more. Shocked, Max faced the fact that almost everything had gone up in smoke. Adeline called one night and he confessed to her what had happened. She was unperturbed.

"Sonny boy, listen to me. It was blood money, taken from the pockets of the working class."

"Adeline, please," he groaned. "You don't know what you're talking about. It's all trading, a game, like Monopoly."

"I've seen it on television," Adeline said grimly. "Someplace there's a famine, no? Someplace, people don't have what to eat. The boll weevil is destroying the wheat."

"The boll weevil eats cotton, not wheat."

"So—cotton, wheat, what's the difference? From this they make millions."

"Forget it, just forget it."

"Tell me something." Adeline's voice softened. "Just one thing. Did Cy know? Did he do something to you, knowing?"

"No," Max declared, "I'm sure not. No."

"The police are still investigating?"

"Yes."

"Max," Adeline admonished, "be careful. Don't get into trouble. Let it be."

His first impulse was to argue with her. How could he let it be? But then he said, as always, "How's the heart?"

"Why should I complain?" she responded automatically. "When are you coming down? The condo dramatic group is going to do an original musical; they call it *Social Insecurity*. You don't want to miss that, do you?" She cackled at the prospect.

Mysteriously, there was no contact from the Borland people, and equally mysteriously, Brian Shamski was unavailable every time Max tried him. Midweek, Max was called down to the Exchange to discuss Whizkids' deficits. Already Phil Carmody had come to the rescue, agreeing to stand for them and whatever might emerge in the future. He took Max to lunch and suggested he simply sell the Exchange seat. It was mortgaged, Max reminded him. No matter; Carmody would find a place for Max in his firm, if he wished. "I don't know," Max said, "what I want to do when this is all over with, I'm not sure anymore."

On the way out they ran into Marcus Rich, who cornered Max as Carmody left. The Bannerman investigation, he said, was heating up, wasn't it? Max gave him nothing but the columnist persisted.

"I know it is, and I know what the focus is too."

"So if you know, why ask me?"

Rich smiled. "Because you're affected—in the pocketbook, at least."

The weasel had a pipeline.

158

THE THIRD FRIDAY

Max was living in a fishbowl, but he knew, unlike Cy, he was not equipped to swim in that water. On the street, walking past yet another white-faced mime doing an imaginary rope climb, he wondered for a bare moment whether it was possible that Cy had actually looted Whizkids, had knowingly taken Max's money for himself. Impossible, he concluded, never—and yet—

On Thursday, to his delight, Sonya came to town on her selling trip. Hearing her voice on the phone threw him into action. For a long moment he thought of Carol, but managed to bury the thought at the sight of Sonya, swathed in a colorful long cotton skirt and boots, tank top covered with a Mexican *rebozo*, her cascade of hair catching the sun.

It was a splendid fall day, otherworldly in the city. She wanted nothing to do with his usual life, nor movies or the theater. She wanted a small café in Soho and the smoky, mettlesome ambience of an artists' bar near the loft of a friend who painted on compressed plastic-encased garbage. That night the friend took them to a party that emitted such a decibel level that Sonya, hands over her ears, said to Max, "Isn't this terrible? Can we get out?"

They were gone in minutes to find peace at Cy's, where Sonya had never been. She looked about her, eyes wide, and wondered how Cy could have lived here; everything was metal or synthetic, lifeless. There was nothing organic, nothing *real*. She spent minutes with the photo of Cy and Julian Berns, both long-haired children with mischievous eyes, defiant in colorful rags.

"God, he had such a baby face. He told me a little about those days, funny stories."

"Julian knows them all."

"What happened?"

"I guess," Max said uneasily, "the times changed."

In the bedroom he felt inhibited, however. His lovemaking was fumbling and halfhearted. Everything here, he found himself thinking, was Cy's. He greeted that thought with only half-submerged feelings of resentment.

Sonya seemed to understand, though nothing was said. She smiled, finally, and said goodnight. They awoke early, Sonya concerned about chores she had left undone. She departed at seven in the Beetle, Max watching from the terrace as the car chugged away. He was about to boil water for coffee when the phone rang. It was Brian Shamski. He was sorry to call so early but Max was to come over as soon as possible.

"Wait a minute," Max complained. "I've been trying to get hold of you for days, now you call at seven o'clock in the morning and . . ."

"I've been laying groundwork." Shamski was brusque. "We're ready now."

"Groundwork for what?"

But Shamski had already gone off the line.

9

"You want coffee?" Shamski asked. "It's cop coffee, but it's here." Max looked over resentfully at Borland, who fiddled with a plastic cup, the inevitable attaché case at his feet, and said no.

Shamski began. "OK, for openers, it looks to me right now that you called it from the beginning; your partner was definitely pushed off that balcony."

"Finally," Max grunted.

"Sometimes it takes a while," Shamski admitted, "but we have kind of an idea who ordered the contract."

"You do?" Max was stunned.

Borland put his cup down. "Bannerman's stock deals with Morey's—"

"I don't give a damn about his stock deals," Max interrupted. "I want to know about who killed him."

"It's all part of it," Shamski said, "so be cool. This Morey's is key. We got information now that it's a front for the Brigado outfit. They bring in two hundred, maybe three hundred million a year in smack, coke, angel dust, all of it. Brigado himself, we don't even know where he is, but he's insulated, believe me."

Borland opened the attaché case, withdrawing a sheaf of papers. "There was Offshore Trading Associates, there was Benton Resources, there was Clarion Commerce—all Brigado's companies, all organized under different names originally, and changed a dozen times since."

"These wise guys get top professional advice," Shamski said.

"It's almost impossible to go after everybody." Borland was defensive. "We have limited resources and the paper trail twists and turns every which way." He flipped a page. "Your company wasn't the only one trading for them. We can't prove it but we think even a firm like R. J. Herbert handled some transactions."

Max sat up in surprise. Did the connection mean anything? "Why didn't you go after them?"

"There's nothing definite," Borland mumbled.

"The money goes everywhere," Shamski said, "and you can't trace it. Some city investigators believe that wise guys are behind Catalfo, the real estate guy. I'll give you a laugh," he continued, "these bums are very patriotic, you know. They love this country. They support the government. They put millions into buying treasury certificates. They sit back and collect the interest. They're part of the national debt. You and me, we owe them. You laughing?"

Borland stiffened. "That's a problem that we don't get into. There are other agencies involved, the IRS, the IAF, the FTC."

Max restrained an impulse to hurl a coffee cup. He turned to Shamski instead. "Why did you call me? So I could listen to this creep? He doesn't care about real people. He doesn't care about my partner. He cares about numbers and letters, that's all."

"No." Shamski was sharp. "It's background that you need if you're going to help."

Max absorbed that. "How am I going to help?"

"We know this outfit, Morey's, was operative," Shamski explained. "They fed your partner a lot of cleaned-up money, but the deal went sour somehow and so they whacked him."

"What went sour?"

"We think," Borland said, "that your partner told them he lost the money, but they discovered he was squirreling it away."

"You're pathetic," Max told him.

162

"Hold it," Shamski interceded. "Maybe he didn't tell them that, all right? Maybe they just got to thinking he was a danger to them."

"Bannerman skimmed from the top," Borland insisted. "That's the only way it makes sense."

"We don't know exactly," Shamski reproved the SEC man, "so let's not say. But for whatever reason, they got rid of Bannerman. Then they got worried about being traced, so they tried blowing your files away. It didn't work. I know, I know—there were zilch files on Morey's, but they don't know that. They don't know but that you're hip to what's been going down, and they're sitting there thinking about it—so there's this idea." He sipped from his cup. Max glared at Borland, who examined a scratch on the attaché case.

Shamski resumed. "There is a guy who does the deals for Morey's, a front man. He goes by the name of Lang, Dennis J. Lang. We can't get much of a handle on him but he seems to have worked downtown sometime or other. We know where he can be reached. The idea is that you contact him."

"Me?" Max was astonished. "If you know him, why don't you grab him?"

"He has no official connection with this Morey's," Borland said, "but we're convinced he acts for them."

"The thing is if we pull him in he just dummies up and we've tipped him," Shamski added. "Where does that get us? No, he'll be very interested in you. Particularly when you tell him you discovered what went down but kept it to yourself. But now you think maybe it would be worth their while to see that you made some money by continuing to trade for them."

"Trade for them?" Max was incredulous. "You think he'll believe me? It's a crazy idea."

"Don't jump," Shamski said. "We're sitting here wondering who these guys are and how to get them. They're sitting there wondering how much you know. You give them bait, they'll be cautious, but they think anybody'll do anything for money, and that's a pretty good assumption. If you can get them to believe you, at least for a little while, and we set it up right, we can find out a lot, maybe enough to get who pushed Bannerman. That's what you want, isn't it?"

Max tried to concentrate. "I don't know anything. He'll find that out right away."

"You might be general with them," Borland tried. "Vague,

as though you're not going to give away too much. As I did with you."

Max glared at this insane man. "You do it—you contact this man and be vague with him." He turned to Shamski. "If I admit knowing about them, why wouldn't they just want to get rid of me as well?"

"Yes," Shamski agreed, "they might, and we're going to give you as much protection as possible."

"Maybe"—Max thought of the blue sedan at Sonya's— "they've even been keeping track of me already."

"It could be."

"But they'll deal with you," Borland put in. "That's the point."

"And they're dumb," Max said sarcastically. "They don't know how to make sure they're not being sucked into some kind of trap."

"No," Shamski said, "they're not dumb. But we need some crack here, Max."

"If you could find out where Bannerman put the money—"

"You're a goddamned asshole," Max shouted at the obstinate Borland. "There is no money. Cy didn't steal any money. Don't keep saying that."

"Max," Shamski said, "calm down. If this is going to work, everybody's got to cooperate."

"It could never work, never," Max declared.

"It's a shot," Shamski persisted.

Max sat glumly silent.

He ate his breakfast at a coffee shop in angry confusion. How had Cy met the Morey's man in the first place? Whizkids would have been an unlikely candidate for a chance call by these bastards. And why had they killed him? That was central. Had Cy discovered who they really were and was threatening to blow the whistle? He felt his reasoning powers going.

Looking about him, he wished for a daily routine, for the comfort of familiar tasks done in a familiar way with familiar results. But even that was denied him. There were no tasks; Whizkids was finished, the clamor of the Exchange was stilled for him, and the option quotes on the screen meant absolutely nothing now.

He remained sunk in depression for the rest of the weekend. On Monday he roused himself and had a drink with Julie

Berns, who had been playing detective, it appeared, and had pursued his obsession with Liz Evers. "It turns out," he told Max excitedly, "that we both have the same dentist, Ralph Glantzman—on Fifty-seventh Street. He told me that about a year and a half ago, she had a lot of tooth problems that related to some physical condition they never discussed."

Max's mind was far away. "Umm."

"Listen to me." Julie rolled his eyes. "Glantzman thinks she might have been pregnant."

Max stared incredulously, then he broke into laughter. People said anything about Cy that came into their heads. "All right, where is this baby?"

"I don't know."

"They farm it out to Gypsies?"

"I know," Berns said hastily. "If Cy had a kid, he'd have rousted us in the middle of the night to tell us."

"He was crazy for kids."

"Yeah—way back then he used to talk about he couldn't wait to be a father, what being a father meant—stuff like that."

"Even if he had just gotten her pregnant, he'd have told us, true?"

Berns nodded.

"So where is it, then?"

"I'm telling you what I found out."

"From a dentist."

"If it was true, it could have some meaning here," Julie insisted.

"It could mean," Max said sarcastically, "that this dentist has a big mouth."

"Maybe," Julian said. "So what's happening with the investigation?"

"Not much," Max fibbed.

"I mean the SEC people," Berns persisted.

"It's all the same thing," Max said impatiently. "When there's something to tell you, I will." He changed the subject, but it was apparent that Julie was upset, and Max wished he could have opened up to him. That added to his malaise, which he relieved by calling Sonya. She was warm and, hearing her voice, he instantly conjured up the scene and felt a long-distance tingle. He asked if she had observed the blue sedan at any point. She giggled.

165

"No—no blue sedan. But I may be buying this beautiful old red Volvo because the bug is finally giving out. Come on up and I'll give you a ride."

He had an erotic dream later, in which he made love to someone in the red Volvo but the someone, to his surprise, looked like Carol. Shortly after dawn he was shocked awake by the house intercom. The night desk man apologetically said someone was downstairs insisting on speaking to him. "OK," Max said, apprehension mounting. He heard the phone being handed over and then sat up with anger as Borland's voice came through, whispering secretively.

"We've got to talk right away. My boys have uncovered something."

His boys! Borland's damned boys in blue suits!

"It's five o'clock in the morning."

"We've been working all night, Roberts."

He barely had time enough to splash cold water onto his face and throw on a robe before Borland was at the door. His suit was wilted, his cheeks beard-shadowed, his eyes red-rimmed.

"This had better be good," Max warned.

Borland clicked open the leather case and brought out six stapled sheets of paper. "Going over all the financial dealings of your company, this finally emerged." He shook the sheets. "These extracts are from bank records. Deposits into your trading account." He read, "February nineteenth of this year, one million, six hundred thousand, by wire from the Mercantile Bank of Lucerne, Switzerland. May, twenty-first, two million and one hundred thousand dollars from the same bank. April twenty-ninth, two million dollars, even, from the Bank of Davos, another Swiss institution." He looked up in triumph. "In the space of a few months, a total of five million and seven hundred thousand dollars has been deposited from untraceable Swiss accounts." He waved sheets of paper. "Are you aware of that?"

"I'm not," Max confessed, "but I didn't bother with that stuff. I left it to Mr. Rothstein and the bank."

"What this means to us," Borland said, becoming pedantic, "is that Brigado's syndicate somehow got this money out of this country and into numbered accounts in Lucerne and Davos banks, which are protected by law from giving out information. Then it was·transferred by wire to your trading account here, as though it belonged to you. But Bannerman knew exactly who it really

166

belonged to. When he made trades with that money, he, pre-
sumably, sent the profits to Morey's, but to where or what banks
we don't know, since those records don't exist. But these transactions tell part of the story."

"Money," Max said, "has come to us before from out of
the country."

"This kind of money—unidentified?"

"Not— to my knowledge," Max admitted. "But it doesn't
prove that Cy knew it was Mafia money, or that he stole any of
it, not to me."

Borland ignored that. "These transactions give you am-
munition if you call Lang. Because you can talk about them
intimately, as though you knew when they were being made—
dates and all, and it indicates that you know the rest."

"It's a bluff."

"Yes, but they have to be worried about you."

"That's just what I'm afraid of."

"I was under the impression," Borland said, "that you were
willing to take some risk to get the people who got rid of your
partner."

The son of a bitch thinks he's being so clever, Max thought.

"All right," he told Borland, feeling as though it were
someone else saying this, "I'll try. What do I do?"

At ten A.M., seated before the telephone in his office, at
once excited and detached, Max keyed in the number written
on the back of Shamski's card. It would be an answering service,
he had been informed, but there was no way of knowing whether
he would be connected through. After nine interminable rings,
a female voice responded.

"Dennis Lang, please," Max said as matter-of-factly as he
could.

"Please hold."

After that there was nothing but dead silence as Max waited,
the phone getting warm in his hand. A full minute later, he
turned questioningly to Shamski, but the flanking detective put
a warning finger over his lips. At that moment the woman came
back on the line.

"Who is calling Mr. Lang, please?"

"Max Roberts—Whizkids Trading."

"Please hold."

Once again, there was the frustrating lack of sound. Borland, at his shoulder, whispered, "Say it's urgent."

Shamski signaled for Max to ignore that. Another thirty seconds passed, then—

"I'm sorry, Mr. Lang isn't available right now."

"I'll leave you my numbers, home and office. He can call me at his convenience, any time—any time at all." Max gave her the numbers. She gave him no response except to click off immediately.

"He'll call," Shamski said.

"What if I'm not here?"

"He'll leave a message," Shamski said, "and the next time you call, he'll be there."

Max sat back as the tension drained away.

"It's just a matter of waiting." Borland tugged at his forelock. "Then what are you going to do," Max said belligerently, "come along in my pocket?"

He was exhausted for the rest of the morning. Sitting around the office in the quiet, he could hear Martha outside, phoning first her sister in Brooklyn, with hot family gossip, then her mother in Co-op City, to report on the conversation. Finally, he heard her call her friend Rose, wherever she was, to complain about both her sister and her mother. This was followed by more irritating silence as he tried to concentrate on the *Journal*. A half hour later, Martha knocked on his door and came in. "Look," she said, holding open a months' old glossy magazine, "the picture in the middle." It was Cy, leaving a taxi, a silly grin on his face. To his left in jumpsuit and cape was a frizz-haired Barbara.

Max stared at the face, the familiar grin, the body in action. In the concentration on Cy's death, he had almost forgotten the live Cy. "Whatever happened to that woman?" Martha asked. As she did, the telephone rang loudly, demandingly, at her desk and Max dropped the magazine. "I'll get it." Martha flew back. Max braced himself.

"Whizkids Trading."

Max waited, gripping the desk hard. Martha called, "It's for you—a Carol?" All the air came out of him. He picked up the phone.

"Hello."

"Hi." She was calling from the Exchange, he thought, because he could hear the noise in the background. "How have you been?"

"OK," he lied.

"I'd like to see you." Carol's voice held a serious undercurrent. "It's really important to me." Important, Max thought uneasily, he was getting to be important to her.

"Sure," he said. "Maybe later today sometime. I'll check my book and get back to you."

"Don't forget."

"I'll call you," he repeated. After that, he waited in the office for another hour, then, ceasing the torture, he left.

He stepped out into the afternoon sun and started down the bustling street. As he walked, his shadow preceding, he became aware that there was another shadow somewhat behind, walking at his pace. Nerves alert, he slowed, turned to a junk jewelry store's window. The shadow behind hesitated, then stopped as well. Looking at the conglomeration of paste earrings, gilt chains, and steel charm bracelets, Max debated turning casually to his left. He decided to do so, but the shadow started away, and by the time Max completed the maneuver, all he saw was the back of a pale-blue jacket disappearing into a building. If he was being watched, Max thought gloomily, and if they knew the two men who had emerged from the building only an hour ago, then the enterprise was doomed from the start. As he well might be. Cheer up, he tried telling himself. He could actually be going paranoid, as Sonya suggested. The thought did not relieve him.

He went to a coffee shop, had an omelet, went back to Cy's. Somehow the hours passed. He played with the computer, sat on the terrace with the cordless telephone at his elbow, struggling with the feeling that he was in beyond his depth, that he had been maneuvered into this by the creep from the SEC. When, as the sun was still high, the electronic ring sounded, he was so sunk in introspection that it went past his ears. On the fourth ring, he grabbed the phone by its antenna, threw the talk switch hastily, and said, "Hello."

An unguarded, genial voice came in. "Good evening, Mr. Roberts. Dennis Lang here. You called me?"

"Yes," Max said, surprised by the geniality, "I did."

"Well, here I am." A hearty, puzzlingly open tone.

Max decided to adopt the same. "Great. Glad you got back to me. Could we get together?"

There was a perceptible pause. "What would it be about?"

"Well," Max said, fumbling, "mutual advantage, I guess."

Another pause. "Would you know where the Tunnel Tavern is?"

Max said he didn't but he'd find it.

"It's on Eleventh Avenue, near the Lincoln Tunnel. It's new, upscale." Lang laughed. "The old Hell's Kitchen is going fast. Let's have a drink there about seven—if that's all right with you."

"Fine, great. But how will we know each other?"

For the first time there was a flatness in Lang's voice. "That won't be a problem. See you at seven."

After Lang hung up, Max sat, mesmerized. Coming to, he looked at his watch; almost six. Still holding the phone, he called the number Shamski had instructed him to call the moment he was contacted, and reported. Then he paced and rehearsed till it was time to go.

The Tunnel Tavern was not a place for sandhogs. Newly sprung from the bricks and bones of an old hard-hat, boilermaker bar, the once bilious-green walls had been stripped down to the brick; the spattered floors were sanded and stained to muted elegance. The bar was zinc and mahogany, backed by etched glass. And everywhere were plants, tubbed trees, hanging tendrils, trailing vines; gentility had struck hard. The West Side hookers, walking their truck-laden beats in hot pants, had been banished. As Lang had said, Hell's Kitchen was fast going.

Max stepped inside and swept a look over the place. At one end of the bar two women held each other's eyes. Near them, two men were equally intense. At the other end, three movie folk in expensive jeans and designer shirts bemoaned the local changes. Max took a seat in the center, ordered a gin and tonic, and waited, hoping his face did not reflect the anxiety nibbling at him. Music started, soft rock. A young waiter in a string tie approached and, to Max's surprise, said, "Your party has already been seated, sir, over there." Picking up Max's drink, he motioned toward an area around the bar screened from the front, and started away. Max followed, alert.

The table was almost private, masked by a huge rubber tree, gleaming leaves menacingly huge. The man seated there was portly. Well-combed brown hair artfully concealed the fact that most of it had gone long ago. Round-faced and round-eyed, with gleaming teeth, he had a brush moustache going gray, wore a blue three-piece suit, and was altogether nondescript. "Hello, sit down," he invited. The waiter left. Max sat slowly, uncomfortably, mumbled something about this place being new, and drank to gain time; the man before him looked more like a small-time retailer than a drug dealer. He had barely felt the back of his chair when, abruptly, Lang said, "Well, let's hear about your notion, Mr. Roberts," and Max almost gagged. Only hours ago, on the terrace, he had practiced, but now the script fled from his mind. He struggled to drag it back as Lang watched him.

"Well," he commenced carefully, "Cy, my partner, did some trading for a firm named Morey's." Lang's expression did not change. Max stumbled on, "They do some—importing. Special merchandise. He invested the profits. Sometimes overseas financing. From Switzerland." He waited.

"Uh-huh." It was said blankly.

Max finished the drink, feeling the gin warm his blood. "So, he did this trading, see, but then he . . . had an accident."

"Too bad," Lang said solemnly, "but these things happen."

"The railing on his terrace broke. He went over."

"Bad workmanship probably."

"He didn't survive."

"I'm sorry," Lang said. "When your number's up . . ."

"So they say. Now the thing is, Mr. Lang, that my partner traded for Morey's kind of on his own, but he kept me in the picture."

"Did he?" Something flickered across Lang's face, Max thought.

"Yes. When the deposits came in from the banks in Lucerne and Davos, you know, I checked them through."

Lang's eyes reacted to that. No question. But the reaction created a sudden coldness in his features, a hardness that was intimidating.

"It was about five million, or so, all in all, I remember. From just the two banks."

"You can do a lot of trading with five million," Lang said.

"Whatever trading he did"—Max stepped carefully here, —"it was all confidential. I kept it that way." He paused again, but Lang said nothing. In the silence, the waiter approached. Max ordered another gin and tonic, and he saw that Lang's eyes never left him. He decided to plunge in. "I was thinking it could be that Morey's might like to keep on trading. There's still a lot of money to be made in the market without taking too much risk and I thought I could keep on trading for them." He tried a smile. "I could use the commissions right now."

"Could you," Lang said.

"Always." Max kept a weak smile going. Was it possible that they had thought everything out and when he left this place they would not let him cross the street alive? But Shamski knew where he was and would set up protection, would he not? Still, there had been so little time. His second drink came and he drank half of that in one gulp, then asked, "So, what do you think?"

Lang played with a straw. "Why would this be interesting to me?"

"Because," Max said, feeling his throat contract, "you're connected with Morey's. Cy told me."

Lang bent the straw in half. "Did he?"

"I was his partner, wasn't I? Oh, he told me on the QT, but he told me." Max lowered his voice. "One other thing. I want to let you know that I'm the only one he told about the account, and I've told no one anything, not a word. I figured it was nobody's business."

Lang put the straw bits into the ashtray carefully.

"Listen," Max said, talking too rapidly, "if you need some deals done, there's no reason why we can't keep on doing business. We can all make money."

Lang smiled now, teeth very white. "You think," he said, "we could trust you to make money for us—you really have that notion?"

"The more money you make, the more I make," Max said.

"Uh-huh." The smile vanished. "Listen," Lang's eyes bore into his. "I heard you; I understand you, but do you understand me?"

Max hesitated, then said, "I think so."

"Make sure." Lang rose. His face resumed its usual open expression. "I'll get back to you." Max saw the portliness melt into a large-framed six-foot-four body. Without another word, Lang walked away and disappeared around the bar.

Slumping back, stomach tight with strain, Max finished

his drink, waited an interminable ten minutes, called for the check, which had already been paid, and left the Tavern for the street. On the avenue he stopped, pretending to adjust his jacket. He saw a parked van without a driver, but thought he detected movement in the rear, behind the porthole windows. Down the block, a man and a woman haggled. Nearby, a drunk lounged against the wall, bagged bottle in hand. Max started off, warily, crosstown. As though on signal, the van produced a driver, buzzed into life, and swung around into the crosstown street. When the vehicle neared him, Max cringed, ducking involuntarily. As it passed, he heard two bleats of the horn and glanced up. The driver, jeaned and bearded, wearing a Mets baseball cap, threw him a reassuring look and continued on. Max expelled air happily; Shamski's people—he was being protected.

At the apartment, he called the number again. This time, Shamski answered. Max reported the details, was congratulated. "He'll get back," Shamski assured him, "and soon. They don't want any loose ends, believe me."

Max asked about further protection but Shamski thought not. "It's really for your benefit because we're not perfect." Max listened with incredulity—his benefit. "If one of the guys gets made, that breaks it. We could never know but it might get very hairy then for you."

"So I'm out there alone," Max protested. "Great."

"This isn't stocks and bonds," Shamski said. "I told you there'd be risk."

The full realization of what he had stepped into struck Max. Nothing in his life had equipped him for the tension, the role-playing, the need for vigilance, and the sudden rush of fear. Cy might have reveled in it, he thought. He looked over to the silver frame on the end table and beheld his partner smiling at the goodness of life.

It was nine o'clock before he remembered his promise to get back to Carol. He called and apologized for the delay. Carol still wanted to see him but he told her it would be impossible tonight. She was instantly concerned. "You sound so uptight. Is something bad happening? Max, please tell me. I want to know."

Once again, she overwhelmed him with her intensity. He told her she was mistaking his tone; they would get together.

"You don't really mean that," she said. "And maybe that's OK too, maybe that's the way it has to be."

"Hey," he said, "this is getting heavy."

"Forget it," she said. "Yeah—just forget it."

The conversation ended sharply, which set him on edge. He thought of leaving word for Shamski to forget the whole thing and rushing up to Sonya's the next day. That night, Carol entered his dreams and became confused with visions of Sonya undressing next to her. He roused himself in alarm, watched a movie on the tube, and faded back to sleep with a mental caution.

For the next few days, Max felt in limbo, suspended. He went through the motions but everything in him waited for the contact to be made, worrying if it would be. He called Jimmy Singh each day and received the same tale of unbearable illness. He had a conference over the appalling bank accounts and came away more depressed than ever. He managed, however, to borrow against his near-due CD. That would at least give some operating capital.

Friday afternoon, Max headed toward the Trade Center. Outside the building housing the Exchange, he saw a familiar back. "Jimmy!" he called.

Singh whirled about like a dervish, arms flapping. "Ah— Mr. Max. So—yes, how coincidental to meet, yes?" He was edgy and embarrassed. He hoped all was well. He had just now recovered fully but he did not think Mr. Max would be needing him, was that not so?

"Maybe. But why didn't you return my calls?"

Singh swiped at the ashes on his lapel. "Ah—I was going to call you today, you see, one hundred percent certainty. But here we are so it is a stroke of fortune."

"There are a lot of questions about the trading records."

"Oh, Mr. Max," Singh cried out indignantly, "why are they doing this to me?"

"Who," Max asked, "doing what?"

Singh's eyes and teeth flashed. "First comes a detective, you see. He pretends to be jovial. 'Hello, my name is Morrisey.' He shakes my hand. Then he asks about my entire life—from the day I land in this country. I must give him every name, every date. He tells me he will look into my resident status. My wife starts to cry. It is mortifying."

"He's just doing his job," Max muttered.

174

"Then Mr. Berns appears at my door."

"Julian?"

"Mr. Berns, yes. He asks me a hundred questions about those bloody records. As though I have something to gain by destroying them. He tries to trap me. Mr. Max, I do not deserve this treatment. I have been so loyal to Mr. Cy as a vassal to a great prince."

Julian had no right to do this, Max thought, no right to take things into his own hands. More craziness. "I'm sorry," he said. "He shouldn't have done that."

Singh looked at his watch. "You will have to excuse me, Mr. Max, I must leave you now."

"Another job."

"No, I have not yet located a satisfactory position, but I have an interview for one." He sighed. "It will not be like working for you and Mr. Cy, of course, but whatever Karma is sent"—he shrugged—"one must be content with it." In a moment he was gone, a nervous figure looking back over his shoulder to wave.

Max went up to the Exchange, finished his business with the back-office executive he had come to see, and, almost by habit, found himself drifting out to the trading floor. Here, the usual cries rent the air, the usual bodies stood on the rings, the usual hands moved forward and back. Amid the shirts and jackets, Max spotted Carol intent upon prices. Her face animated, fingers in motion, she offered ten cotton contracts and just as suddenly, she was bought. A sudden smile illuminated her features and Max was touched. As she stepped back to scribble out an order slip, he came up to her. When she saw him, the smile went and her eyes became grave. He spoke her name and she took a deep breath, saying with affected jocularity, "Buying or selling?"

"Just looking," he said.

"Lousy day; no good rumors." She leafed through her order book with a concentration that, Max knew, was camouflage. She wore gray slacks and an oversize white top in which she seemed very small and very fragile.

"The other night . . ." he began.

"Please," Carol said, "it's the nineteen-eighties' tensions we read about so much. Don't bother." She stole a look at the board. "Look at that last sale."

"Right, the tensions," Max said.

"I'm going to wait," Carol declared. "I think gold is headed south. What do you think?"

"Are you free tonight—little Tex-Mex maybe?"

She looked at him appraisingly. "I don't think so."

She was getting even with him; well, OK. "Another time."

"I don't know," Carol said. "I think maybe it's just . . . not a good idea." Max could see some sort of struggle taking place within her. "Oh, the hell with it," she finally said. "All right. Tex-Mex."

Throughout the dinner in the crowded, noisy downtown restaurant, Carol was uncommonly silent, stealing odd glances at him. Max had asked her because the idea of sitting around waiting anymore was driving him up the wall. He had thought she would be a diversion, but her silence was unnerving.

"Cy loved Tex-Mex," Max said, making conversation.

Carol didn't answer.

"I learned to like it. I never did when we met."

She kept eating the nachos.

"He would try anything."

"Right." Carol looked up from the guacamole. "Cy would eat anything, do anything, go anywhere. He had great taste, great talent, great ideas. He was the best and the brightest. I know it's that way because you keep telling me it is."

"I don't think I keep telling you anything," Max said, surprised at her hostile tone.

"I'm sorry," Carol said. "You don't, no, but whenever you do talk about him, it's as though he was so incredibly special."

"He was in a lot of ways. Whatever we did."

She interrupted. "See, it's always 'we.' What about you, Max—by yourself, alone?"

She was harassing him. For what reason? "This is all wrong," Max said strongly. "There are enough things happening to me right now. I don't need this."

"Right," Carol said firmly. "Neither of us do."

"You don't understand," Max relented. "There could be a break in this thing. I'm involved."

Carol looked up and her eyes were the widest he had ever seen. He had frightened her, he realized, and was both sorry and a little gratified. She held the look for long seconds, then said, "I see."

He took her home and, downstairs, tried to check the mood.

The tremulous moments had passed; Carol was cool and assured. "See you," she said, and went inside.

On the next day, there was no call from Lang, nor was there one on the day after or the day after that. The calls were from Borland. His people were still following leads; Bannerman had to have stashed away the millions, absolutely; this was a real paper chase. Max hung up. He saw Shamski and, nerves already frazzled, said he thought nothing would happen; he would like to just stop this whole business. Shamski asked him to give it a few more days.

"Get this damned SEC guy off my back," Max fumed. Shamski promised to take care of it, but Borland called again, wanting more information about the record keeping, about Martha, about Rothstein, the accountant, about Jimmy Singh.

"Forget it," Max shouted at him. "They just worked for us. They don't deserve to be hassled by an asshole like you." It made no impression.

On Tuesday Max pondered a reply to Adeline. She had written:

> . . . Bakunin says that bourgeois society holds out the promise that every man can get rich. This makes people work and slave for the system, to gain more private property. For every one who does, there are millions who suffer for it. No matter what you tell me, I know that Cy and you, my dear son, must have changed in these years. Private property makes a person change. Mrs. Alexander here, in the apartment around the block, won fifty thousand dollars in the lottery. Before, she always talked about what a robbery the lottery was, fixed, you know. Now, she bought new furniture, a new car, a new refrigerator, double-door, and all she talks about is how great America is! All because of a lottery! Have you decided what to do yet?

Had he changed? From what to what? Had the access to so many possibilities altered him? But what had he been before meeting Cy? Unformed. Cy had, yes, formed him. Was that a bad thing? And, tempering his bewilderment and anger over the accounts, he knew that Cy's instincts had always been humanitarian, compassionate. He could recall a hundred instances of that. No, he concluded, Cy had not changed, not in what was essential. Nor had he. He was tolerant of Adeline's old-time, thirties dreams, but they were not relevant to reality—if they had ever been. She . . .

The phone startled him out of his polemic.

"Hello."

"Morning. Like to take a little walk?" It was Lang.

"A walk?" Max felt his throat going dry. "Sure."

"Well, how about you meet me on Fifth and Sixty-eighth in about half an hour?"

"Fifth and Sixty-eighth—OK."

"Nice day for the park," Lang said.

Max hung up, took two deep breaths, and called Shamski. "I got the call. We're going for a walk. A walk—can you imagine that? I'm meeting him at Sixty-eighth and Fifth."

"Hey, he's biting," Shamski said. "Keep it simple. You're open to do business, that's the point. Let's see what he has in mind. And try not to show any worry."

"I am worried," Max declared.

"I know," Shamski said, "but hide it."

Hide it. How was he to hide it? Max slammed out of the apartment resentfully. He escaped the desk man, who had yet another question to ask about T-bills, managed to find a cab and go west.

It was a day of unexpected heat—a temperature inversion, the weatherman called it. A humid haze hung over the city like a fine silken screen. The women on Fifth, dressed for fall, had arms, cleavage, faces covered with a film of moisture that eroded their perfume and ruined the ringleted hair. The men, waiting for buses, stood slumped over in their dark suits, feeling the underarm ooze. Joggers, ever determined, gasped in and out of the park.

Alighting from the cab, Max, already tense, felt his nerves tighten even more as the heat engulfed him. He peered across the street toward the park and saw Lang clearly, a tall figure seated on a bench, dressed in navy blue, a gray felt hat decorating his head, eating an ice cream bar. About to cross over, Max recoiled in horror. Seated three benches away from Lang was another figure he knew. Unbelieving, Max peered to make certain. It was Borland, attaché case between his feet, looking innocently skyward, fanning himself with a folded-over newspaper. Max retreated hastily and huddled behind a parked car, fuming. It was insane. Suppose Lang knew who he was? Surely Lang was being protected here and now. Max cringed behind the car and cursed the entire SEC. After a minute, he peeked out from behind the hood. He saw Lang finish the ice cream, rise, and walk toward a trash can on the corner, putting his back to Borland. Deciding to chance it, Max darted out from behind his cover, faced toward the benches, and waved frantically. Borland, he could tell, saw him. He waved once again and then fell back, retreating around the corner, out of the bench sight line.

He waited here, heart pounding, not knowing what might happen next. Suddenly Borland was before him, paper in hand. Max grabbed him by the lapels feverishly. "You crazy bastard. Are you trying to get me killed?"

Borland twisted away. "Keep your hands to yourself. I wanted to see him. It's important that I see the man."

"And suppose he knows right now it's a setup?" Max shook with anger. "What do you think he'll do to me?"

"He doesn't know who I am."

"How do you know that?"

"I know."

A passing man stared at them. Max looked away. They were attracting attention. "I'm not going over to him," he said.

"That's up to you," Borland replied.

"No," Max said, "you're the one responsible for this."

"I'm here doing my job," Borland insisted, "but now that I've seen him, I can go."

He adjusted his jacket and walked stiffly away. Max watched him go with loathing, then he advanced toward the building edge again and took another look. Lang had returned to the bench but was now looking at his wristwatch. Swallowing hard, Max darted out into the traffic, avoided a bus, and reached the sidewalk. Puffing some, he neared the tall man and said, "Good morning." At the same time, his eyes searched frantically for who might be guarding Lang. There were other bench seaters here and it might be any one of them.

"Good morning." Lang shifted over on the bench. Max sat and said, "It's a real summer day."

"Oh yes," Lang said in his genial mode. "You like some ice cream?"

"No thanks."

"Let's take a stroll then." Lang rose and headed slowly into the park. Max kept to his side. They walked past the dog walkers and the homeless napping. Max tried to see if they were being followed. It didn't appear so, but how could he really tell? Three squirrels charged down from a thick oak. Two of them scampered away. The third came over to inspect. "All the squirrels," Lang commented, "asking for a handout." He chuckled. "Just like the rest of the world." He talked away from Max, not looking at him. "Your partner was an interesting man."

"Yes." Max stepped carefully. "He was."

"He got rich quick."

"He knew the market."

"We all know the market but Bannerman was smart, no doubt about it, maybe too smart." He swung an appraising look at Max, who dared not respond. A child on a bicycle zoomed directly at them and only darted away at the last moment. They continued walking, Lang not speaking, Max waiting. Finally, Lang said, "My investors like people who will do exactly what they're asked."

"It's their money."

"And you'd like to get hold of a piece of it." The tall man stopped walking.

"I would just like to . . . do some business," Max finally got out. Lang waited. Max vamped, "There are some fine opportunities right now, in certain highly leveraged situations."

Lang smiled. "You sound like a mutual-fund report." He started off again. Max struggled to keep up. After three more minutes of heavy silence in the thick air and with no preface, Lang asked, "Ever been to Aspen?"

"No," Max said, "never."

"Beautiful this time of year." Lang pulled the hat from his head and smoothed out his hair. "You ought to go."

"To Aspen?"

"Aspen, Aspen in Colorado." Lang seemed suddenly annoyed. "That's what I said."

"Oh." Every brain cell alert, every synapse working overtime, Max asked, "When do you think is a good time to go there?"

Lang replaced his hat. "Maybe Monday."

"Monday." Max felt the sweat dribbling down his back, soaking his shirt. "Well, I'll sure check my calendar and . . ."

"Monday," Lang repeated, "and a good place to stay is the Aspen Hills Lodge."

"Aspen Hills Lodge."

180

"Yes, they'll take care of you real well there."

Max waited for more but none came. They walked around another two concrete curves. A begging squirrel came up to them, stood on its hind legs, balancing on its bushy tail.

"Sorry, there's no free lunch," Lang said. "Nice walk," he told Max. "You want to do business, you go to Aspen." Saying nothing more, he walked away deceptively fast for a big man. The squirrel kept looking at Max, hoping.

10

"Aspen?" Borland was so excited, the veins in his fair skin pulsed. "Lang's sending you to meet somebody in Aspen?"

Shamski, pleased, said, "You played it great."

"It's a breakthrough," Borland said excitedly, scribbling on a yellow pad. "I'll notify somebody from the western district that you're coming."

"Like hell you will," Shamski objected. "I don't want a million people brought in."

Borland froze. "The federal government . . ."

"Dammit," Shamski said, "the more people get involved the more chance there is to blow this thing."

"My office has a responsibility here," Borland replied.

Max watched the quarrel with a semidazed detachment, then said simply, "I'm not going to Aspen." There was a moment of shocked silence, then Shamski turned to him. "What do you mean?"

"Just that," Max said, hoping his voice was firm.

"You've got to go," Borland insisted, "got to."

"You go," Max said with anger. "You go and say you're me—how will they know?"

"That's ludicrous."

"And you're ridiculous. I don't know what I'm doing as it is; how would I know what to do away from here?"

"You do what you do," Shamski said quietly. "You're a businessman, a commodity trader—you behave like one, that's all, to anyone you meet."

He makes it sound so simple, Max thought, A-B-C. But these people kill. "How about I'm a little worried about what they might do?"

Shamski nodded. "That's real."

Borland was silent. At least the fool was quiet, Max thought. Perhaps he should not have taken even step one.

"I tell you," Shamski said thoughtfully, "like I said, I appreciate your feelings, OK? The only thing is if we don't take this shot, we're out of the game. They get away with murder. And we never know what really went on with your partner."

"Where he put the money," Borland chimed in.

"You creep," Max grated at the SEC man, "you say that again and I walk out of here."

"Shut up for a change," Shamski said to Borland. And then to Max, "There are questions I know you want answered."

"I don't have questions," Max said defiantly. "I know who my partner was."

"Right," Shamski said, "but maybe you don't know everything."

No, Max thought, maybe not, maybe goddamn not. He fell silent. Borland kept making his inane notes. Shamski drank more coffee. In the quiet, Max could hear the precinct phones ringing outside the office. He heard the rumble of voices, the whacking of ancient typewriter keys accompanied by the ancient curses. There was no option, of course. Shamski had known that all along. Max sighed helplessly. "OK, I'll go."

"Good," Shamski said. "That's good."

"Can I call you from there?"

"Twice a day," Shamski said, "if you want to, but use a public phone, and if you think things are getting too hot, just get on a plane."

"I have a private number." Borland came back to life.

"Shove it," Max suggested.

Once on the street, he regretted his decision but decided

it was too late to back off. He made the arrangements reluctantly, hoping that there would be no room at the Aspen Hills Lodge or that the pilots' union would declare a strike or that he might be stricken with some instant but curable disease. He pecked away at a computer game, poked, for the hundredth time, among Cy's papers, and felt suspended in time. By late afternoon the walls were closing in.

He fled to the street, walked aimlessly, and, passing a Chinese restaurant, felt a sudden hunger. Pure tension, he knew, but he went inside, took an empty booth, and ordered dumplings. Another need asserted itself. More tension, he knew. He was in the washroom for only a few minutes, but swinging back through the door, he saw that his booth had been occupied by two men. He hurried forward, but ten feet away, jerked to a halt in fear. Bobby Catalfo and his thick-bodied driver were in the booth and watching him carefully. Max made a move to whirl around. Catalfo called out raspily, "Hey—nobody's going to hurt you."

Max stayed where he was. Catalfo called again, "I'm being nice. You better be nice too." He motioned unmistakably for Max to sit. The driver rustled in his seat. Slowly Max approached and, trying to keep his voice firm, said, "I'm going out the door. If you try and stop me, you'll regret it."

"Don't be a wiseass," Catalfo growled almost amiably. "If I don't want you to go, he'll make sure you don't. Sit down."

Max sat slowly. The driver stared at him from across the table impassively. "First of all," Catalfo said, his pig eyes narrowing, "who was that guy who came along when I was trying to speak to you—the guy who gave me a shot in the head?"

Speak to him? That was Catalfo's version of a conversation, Max thought—and why was he changing tactics? "I don't know who he is," Max said tensely. "I never saw him before or since."

"Yeah?"

"Yes," Max said, choking a little.

"You scared? You got a right to be scared." Catalfo shook his head. "What you're doing . . ."

Max was startled. Catalfo saw the look. "Yeah."

"I'm not doing anything," Max bluffed.

"You're an asshole," Catalfo guffawed, "and your partner was an asshole. He got what he deserved."

Max studied the real estate man. "What does that mean?"

"What I said." Catalfo shook his head. "What sticks me is

185

that she boffs a dumb jerk like you and runs away from me. Feature that."

Barbara again.

"But I don't give a shit about you," Catalfo burst out. "It was him. I could buy him and sell him but that wasn't good enough for her. All right, all right." He calmed himself down. "I know she . . . like . . . confided in you, right?" Catalfo pasted a forced, lopsided smile on his lips. "I told you I can be nice. So, listen to me. We can do business together. I can put you in touch with people maybe you want to see, people who can do you some good. I know she told you where she was going, I know she did. All you have to do is tell me where she is. That's all you have to do."

Catalfo's eyes had become moist, almost pleading.

"I . . ." Max began and hesitated. Catalfo would never accept the truth. He *wanted* Max to know where Barbara had gone—Max had to know. Max looked from the obsessed eyes of the real estate man to the bored driver whose wrestler's body was bursting through his brown suit. Something was called for—some possibility. Max reached for one. "I was told she left the country, went to Rio."

Catalfo leaped on that. "Who told you?"

"Some friend of hers, I don't know her name. And look, I'm not interested in Barbara Stratton. That was Cy's affair. But . . . I'm willing to do business."

Catalfo laughed, a hoarse cackle coming up from his throat. "I'll bet you are. But I don't do business before I find her. Where'd you say?"

"Rio." Why not, Max thought; it was Barbara's kind of place.

"Rio." Catalfo mulled that over, and as he thought his face darkened in anger. "Rio. She ran to Rio, huh? With somebody?"

"Alone, I was told," Max elaborated.

Catalfo ground his teeth. "She think I can't find her? Wherever she goes, I'll find her. And when I get my hands on that bitch . . ." He stared hard at Max and rose up so suddenly that the banquette creaked. The driver jumped up with him.

Max stood up. "What you were saying . . ."

"When I get back from Rio, we'll talk," Catalfo rasped, "but if she's not there, if you're shittin' me . . ." He walked away. The driver hurried after him. The waiter came with the dumplings but Max's hunger had fled.

186

THE THIRD FRIDAY

* * *

Angered and worried, Max called Shamski. "When he finds out I've lied about Barbara, he'll go right for my throat."

"That's not going to happen." Shamski was reassuring. "He'll be put on notice."

"That's what you said last time."

"Well, look how he came on, soft and sweet."

"He wanted something from me."

"Well, you gave it to him."

"And he seemed to know I was involved in something."

"No way. It's a bluff." Shamski chuckled. "Imagine that goon going bananas for the girl. Tender—very tender."

He was still stewing over Shamski's attitude when Julian called excitedly. He had discovered something.

"Max, Julie. Listen, I've found out—"

"Wait a minute," Max said, annoyed. "I found out you went over to Jimmy Singh's place and badgered him. You had no right to do that."

"I'm sorry," Julie said, plaintively contrite. "I felt he wasn't telling you the whole truth, that's all. I was just trying to help."

"Don't help me so much," Max sighed. "Things are complicated enough as it is."

"OK, all right. But this is different. That Liz Evers business, remember?"

"What about it?"

"It's almost certain that she was pregnant . . . and had the baby."

Max yawned elaborately. "This is your dentist again?"

"No, this is from where Marcus Rich got his information, that crazy neurotic girl who used to work for her."

Max was incredulous. "You believe her?"

"Liz was pregnant, Max, why else would her doctor refuse to discuss it?"

"Because doctors don't discuss their patients."

"No." Julie was adamant. "I had an insurance guy call him and he gave Evers a clean bill of health but when it came to childbearing, he suddenly turned cold. What else could that mean?"

"Where would this kid be?" Max was skeptical.

"Farmed out with a relative maybe, given up for adoption—"

"Never, never with Cy."

"I know, but—I called Liz."

"You *what*?"

"Called her; she said come up."

"She did?" Surprised, Max fell silent.

"Cy's kid?" Berns's voice was passionate. "We have to know."

"I don't believe it," Max said.

"We have to find out. This would be the child Cy always talked about, Max. Carrying on his blood, his genes. Jesus, it's like our godchild. And"—his voice turned portentous—"it would be his legal heir."

To what, Max thought—the debts?

Liz Evers occupied the forty-ninth floor of a newly built East Side building that appeared to be constructed solely of mirror-polished brass and Italian marble—huge slabs of both, strips of both, circles of both. The concierge desk had been hewn out of one single block of travertine topped by bronze. The elevator doors were miniatures of the great Ghiberti doors of Florence. The elevators themselves, rosewood-paneled, lifted, in majestic silence, from lobby to penthouse in twelve seconds.

Liz Evers was not conventionally pretty. Her features were too asymmetrical for that, but the planes of her cheeks, the straight run of her regal nose, and the determined mouth held an attraction of their own. Her great gray eyes, made larger by the oversize red-framed glasses, surveyed the world from high ground. Her hair, no longer quite the girlish golden mass, was cropped and chic. She wore black trousers with a huge green overblouse and, as usual, her fingers held a cigarette. She exuded an air of sharp intelligence tinged now with great wariness. "Sit down."

The men sat on a beige floral couch.

"Thanks for agreeing to see us," Julian began. "We know how busy you are."

"I'm seeing you because . . ." Liz said and hesitated, looking away. "Actually, I'm not sure why."

"Things going good for you?" Max asked politely. She nodded.

"Good," Julian said briskly, "good. We know," he continued, "that you and Cy broke up some time ago but there is something we'd like to discuss with you."

Liz puffed, her eyes holding Julian's hypnotically. Max

188

sank back into the couch. Julian coughed and went on. "We heard—Max and I—from—reliable sources, that . . ." He hesitated, coughed again. "We've been told by trustworthy people that secretly you and Cy had . . . a baby together."

She blinked, just blinked. Berns continued uncomfortably. "As friends, almost like brothers to Cy, we felt we wanted to ask you—"

"Your people are not trustworthy," Liz said, detached.

Julian took a moment for that to sink in. "Oh, you mean . . ."

"I said what I mean."

"I see," Julian said. "But you certainly could see why we feel we had to find out the truth."

"And what would you do with—the truth?" She said it ironically. It was a quality, Max knew, that had appealed to Cy—it had reminded him of the girl who had come out of Wellesley at twenty-one, tall, awkward, intense, with deep-set eyes and a barely combed mass of yellow hair, the campus years imbuing her with a love of literature and a feeling for the oppressed.

Julian turned aggressive. "It would be Cy's child. That's important to us."

"Yes," Liz said icily, "wouldn't it—a little Cy."

"The man's dead." Julian leaned forward. "You had an important relationship."

"You could say that." She drew in smoke, blew it out, and looked away. The two men waited, but for her they had vanished. What she saw reflected in her lenses was herself on the bed that night, the clock reading four A.M.

"Can we talk about it tomorrow?"

"No," Cy had said, "we can't."

"I have a breakfast meeting."

"Eat lightly."

"Damn you," she had burst out. "We're over, finished, you can't come in here and give me orders."

"This is the most important thing in your life."

"Don't tell me what's important!"

Cy had tried to sit near her, his voice gentle. "Can we find some center in this?"

She had recoiled. "It won't work. You won't get into my skin this time. The tricks don't have magic anymore."

She always referred to his "magic," the elusive quality that

189

had existed for her ever since they had met at some party or other. Through the tricks of intimacy that he possessed, she had, after such a short time, let him into her inner life, allowed him to see the girl who had taken a job in advertising as a lark. "It was so ridiculous—so comic-book, you know, to write these ads. How could anyone with half a brain take dancing vegetables seriously?" But she discovered she could write the dumb stuff, she confided ruefully, and was soon moving up the ladder, changing agencies, orchestrating campaigns. "It seemed like a game—just a big game, but I discovered that success is addictive—very." In a short time her career had become her life. But while to most everyone she was a woman driven to move up, self-contained and wary, a hard diamond with a cutting edge, still, far away from ads, from TV monitors and demanding clients, was a portion of her time, stolen for reading, learning, questioning. That had fascinated Cy Bannerman, she knew. He loved the idea of a woman of power and achievement who had retained this other sensibility.

"OK," he had said, "but you know I'm right. You have a brain that loves to analyze—and you know I'm right."

"I know," she had said, holding on to her control, "what I want, what I need."

"But I can't supply it," he had riposted, "and if we do what you say, it will all end in hate."

"You're despicable."

"Only because I won't do what you want me to?"

"You know," she told him, "you come on as everything to everybody but we both know that you've simply found clever modes to get people to do what *you* want."

Abruptly, Liz propelled herself back from their last meeting. To the men before her, she said, "I think I was wrong in seeing you. Could you go now, please?"

Max saw the blaze in her eyes and rose. Julian kept his seat defiantly. "Hold it, we'd like to ask you . . ."

"You've asked. Now please leave."

Julian stood up reluctantly. "All right, but I know you loved him and . . ."

"I hated him," Liz burst out, "and I hate him now. Is that good enough for you?" She turned her back on them. Julian was about to say something but Max pulled him by the arm and started toward the door. As he opened it, he looked back. Liz was staring at them stonily.

In the elevator Julian said, "Jesus Christ, she does hate him—what happened between them?"

"I don't have a clue," Max said.

"About the baby—do you think she was telling us straight goods?"

"Does she look like a mother to you?"

"Hey—" Julian looked up excitedly. "She had a miscarriage. She's no kid, is she? She *was* pregnant but miscarried. So what she said was true—but . . ."

"A miscarriage . . . could be, yes." It was logical and sad. Julian felt it as well and was silent the rest of the way down and out to the street. There, Max told him he was going away for a few days. Julian was interested. "With anybody?"

"No."

"Where are you going?"

"Oh," Max said airily, "just a hotel—to get away from things." Julian wanted to know what the latest was with the SEC. Max told him all was quiet at the moment. Before they parted, Julian said, "If you hadn't told me about that . . . dope business, I'd be thinking again about Liz."

But Max's mind was already in Aspen.

11

What struck Max first upon landing at the small Aspen airport was how much sky there was. The mountains rose up, peak after peak, breathtakingly grand yet puny-appearing against such a vast azure expanse. The sky dominated, encompassing all, encasing the slopes, where, here and there, broad swaths of green ribboned down the hillsides from crown to base, curving in and out in *S* patterns. The sun blessed the hills with a bone-healing dry warmth. Daisies and marigolds dotted their slopes with color. The now-silent ski lifts lofted over them, chairs and seats dangling idly, waiting for the invaluable snow, marking time until ski madness returned, as it inevitably would. Then, the snow bunnies and the schussers, the powder burners and the hot dogs, the lodge loungers and the stern, accented instructors, would people this landscape. The lift machinery would clank and hiss. Calls and cries would echo. The Aspen Chamber of Commerce would be happy once again.

Max picked up the small Mercedes that had been arranged for, asked the way to town, and started down the highway.

The Aspen Hills Lodge was not one of the imitation Alpine

ski chalets that were strung, all wooden beams and balconies, along the streets of the picturesque village. It was a deluxe hotel, lording it over the town atop a slope of its own, staring down at the beer joints and pizza parlors.

In the lobby, as the polo-shirted desk clerk said, "Oh yes, Mr. Roberts, here we are," Max signed the register and glanced around to see if anyone seemed even casually interested in his arrival. A man in a chair nearby held a newspaper resolutely up over his face—perhaps too resolutely, Max thought. A hard-faced athlete in a jogging suit tying his Adidas glanced up at him and then quickly away. Before he had time to see any more, the bellhop had his bag and he was in the elevator going up.

His balconied suite was on the fourth floor overlooking the tennis courts, which were built on a man-made plateau that overlooked Aspen itself. After tipping the bellboy, he took a step out to the balcony and held up abruptly. From the balcony to his right, an undershirted, heavyset man stared directly at him. Max pretended not to notice and eased back into his room, the familiar flicker of fear licking at him. It took minutes to convince himself that fear was the wrong reaction. Just be cool, he told himself.

He unpacked the carry-on and went down to lunch. The terrace restaurant was well populated, and as he waited to be led to his table, despite his resolution, he scanned the faces. Whoever *they* were knew he was here. He would now have to wait till he was contacted and hope that everything turned out well.

The meal was uneventful. The rest of the day was the same. Max spent most of it on his balcony waiting for another glimpse of the T-shirted neighbor, who never showed, for the phone to ring, for someone to whisper key words to him in the corridor, for a significant knock on the door. Late in the day, when he went down to the lobby, he thought the desk clerk looked at him peculiarly, but he wasn't sure. He had a drink at the Mogul Bar, sitting in a conspicuous spot. When a rotund, blue-sports-shirted man with a slight limp sat down beside him, he became instantly alert. The man ordered a Campari and when it came, sipped, and said to Max, "Quite a place, isn't it?"

Max agreed it was, yes, quite a place. The man wanted to know if Max came here often.

"First time," Max responded.

"I guess it's not business," the man laughed. "Nobody comes here for business."

"Kind of—business," Max said, deciding to leave an opening.

"I've got business too," the man winked. "Here she comes now." He gestured to a willowy blond girl in a tightly zipped white velvet jumpsuit who had just entered. He slid off the stool and walked toward her. Max turned away, frustrated.

Past midnight, unable to sleep, he watched television, twisting the dials aimlessly. At one point he sat up in surprise as a big closeup of what seemed to be a piece of machinery, a piston pumping in and out of its socket, was revealed, as the camera pulled back, to be a penis thrusting into a vagina. They were both owned by naked actors on a bed, moaning and groaning to climax. Checking the dial, he saw that he had invited the X channel to share his lonely vigil. As the woman's too-theatrical moans reached a super-decibel level, the phone rang shrilly, competing. Max froze momentarily, then shut the television sound off. Hovering over the white phone, he let it ring again. On the third ring, he answered tensely, "Hello."

There was silence. He repeated, "Hello?"

A thick, phlegm-filled voice asked, "Who is this?"

"Max Roberts."

There was an immediate disconnect. Max stared at the phone. Could this be a test of some sort . . . or simply a wrong number? He hung up and waited. He waited for half an hour but nothing else happened.

Weary, but fighting sleep, he went out to the balcony, where he became intrigued by the number of stars that spattered the night sky. In great profusion they spread over the vaulted velvet, manufacturing a light of their own he had never seen before. He projected a jumble of images against the backdrop: Sonya's face, Carol's, Cy, grim and unsmiling. He heard Adeline's voice in his ears but what she said was as jumbled as the images. Finally, exhaustion overwhelming him, he stumbled toward the bedroom, not bothering to turn the TV set off. On the screen the silent lovers still pounded away, belly to belly.

In the piercingly clear morning, he forced himself down to breakfast, thinking he would make himself as available as possible. Nothing happened. After that he bought a newspaper, seated himself prominently in the lobby, and turned to the stock-market page out of sheer habit. Another takeover bid, another guess on interest rates, all the usual garbage. And where was the T-shirted neighbor? He went down the mountain and walked the village streets, looking in the shop windows still exhibiting the summer line of Aspen T-shirts and surfer trunks (where was the surf?). Nothing happened. At one point an open-top Jag drew to a halt near him and the driver, swarthy and gold-chained, stared. Max thought he was the object but it was a boy some distance away, pouting. The boy walked off and the Jag soon followed. When, Max asked himself, when was something going to occur? Or had they become suspicious and nothing ever would?

He returned to the hotel and asked for his key and any messages. Only a key was proffered. With it he opened the door to his room, hoping a note would be there on the beige carpeting. There was none. He hurled the key to a tabletop, missing, and wondered: Was it possible that no one knew he was here, after all? Was all this anxiety for absolutely nothing?

The afternoon spun itself out. Listening for footsteps approaching his door, waiting for the phone to ring, a rap on the wall, a whisper, anything, any sign his presence was acknowledged, was alternately exhausting and lethargy-inducing. By five o'clock the suite had become a jail. He slammed out and retreated to the bar downstairs. Sparsely inhabited, soft music purring from the loudspeakers, the room was shadowed and cool. Max seated himself at a banquette and ordered a gin and tonic. To his right, a short, button-nosed woman with a copper-colored hair mane was having trouble soothing a very young man with the sulky good looks of a frustrated teenager. Max averted his eyes from the intimate scene. A moment after the mesh-stockinged waitress brought Max's drink, a scuffling sound and a yelp erupted from the couple's table. Max turned, startled. The woman was being hauled to her feet by her companion. "Ray—" she squealed. He pulled her up by the shoulders until her feet were off the ground, then let go. She dropped back like a sack of potatoes. Her purse flipped from the table, scattering the contents.

"What an old bitch," the man said in slurred tones, and strode away. The woman, looking up, caught Max's eyes. She shook her head in mock despair, fluffed up her hair, and shrugged.

"You all right?" Max asked.

"Oh," she said airily, "impetuous youth, that's what it's

all about." She bent down to retrieve her things. Max knelt to help her.

"Well," she said cheerfully, "what can you do? Lord, these movie stars are so used to being catered to. Oh, there's my American Express card." Max retrieved it from a corner. "Thank you," she said. She stuffed her belongings back into her bag, seated herself with another tug at the mane, and said, "Now, come over here, you're so nice."

"It's OK," Max said.

"Then I'll come over there." She shifted to the banquette smilingly. "I'm Daphne Kaiser. You're not from Aspen, I know that."

"No. I'm visiting."

"Wonderful," Daphne said. Her eyes sparkled. "Having a good time?"

Max shrugged. She laughed. "Oh my, we'll have to see to that."

Is she the one? Max wondered. Was all this a plant, somehow, a scene?

"What do I call you?"

"Max, Max Roberts."

"All right, Max, you have to be taken in hand, I can see that." She went back to the bag, located a scrap of paper and a silver pen, and proceeded to scribble. "Here, you come over to my place tonight sometime, and we will show you a real good time, a real Aspen good time." She handed Max the paper. "I want to see you there. I'm a big Aspen pusher, you see." She looked at her blank-faced watch. "Oh—got to go." She rose. "Be a lot of swell people there. I give the best parties in Colorado. Ask anybody." She winked at Max. "See you later. Bye, Michael." She waved at the barman, who waved back familiarly. In a moment she was gone. Max looked down at the address on the paper. When he looked up again, the cocktail waitress was grinning at him.

At ten-thirty Max found a cab, gave the driver the address, heard him whistle in admiration, and settled back, feeling both grim and foolish. Soon they were rising up into the hills, leaving the village lights far down below. After twenty minutes the cab made a turn off onto a dirt road and the driver called, "Just about there." He snaked the cab through the darkness and abruptly came out onto an asphalt road that led, a hundred yards ahead, to a huge house, blazingly lit, shining beaconlike on the side of the mountain. Max leaned forward as they approached. Heavy metal rent the night. A side veranda was crowded with people moving, jumping, and laughing. Through the windows, Max could see more people inside. In a field important cars were haphazardly parked.

The driver pulled to a halt. Max emerged uncertainly and paid. As the cab took off Max was tempted to recall him, but it was already too late. He started up the stairs, the music pounding at him from this distance. He slipped through the dancers and walked through an open door into a large room crowded with more dancers, talkers, walkers, loungers. The men were not all young, not all in the prime of their athletic lives; the women, for the most part, were. Flat stomachs, smooth tans, clad in everything from tailored sweats to beaded shimmying skirts, they rocked and rolled as they walked, swung through gymnastic arcs as they danced. The men examined them, touched them, muttered to them, called to each other in loud tones. There was a steady, hammering sound from all of this, rising and falling in some unexplained rhythm. As Max hesitated, he felt a tap on his back and, turning, saw it was that afternoon's Daphne, dressed now in a blue velvet little number too figure-hugging for her birth date and cut too low for what she was revealing.

"Max," she cried, "you came." She leaned over, kissed him on the cheek, stopped a passing redhead with kohled eyes, and said, "This is Max."

"Hello, Max," the girl said unsteadily. "See you, Max. Gotta go reload, Daff." She slithered away.

Daphne said, "She's from Vegas—of course." She linked arms with Max. "Wouldn't you like a little refreshment? Come on." She marched him through the crowd in a proprietory fashion, pointing out the sights as they went—that little fat man was in Oklahoma crude, and making plenty despite problems in the oil patch, that smashing girl in red had just been awarded a fabulous divorce settlement. Did he recognize that great hunk in the corner? Looked different off the screen, didn't he, with his arm around that gorgeous blond young guy? The girl with the great legs to the left was one of Zoli's top models. The fun part was that she wasn't really a "she"—the Argentinian, what's his name—had done the sex change for her . . . and zoom.

"Refreshments," Daphne announced, motioning beyond

198

an archway, then left him, calling affectionately to someone across the room. Dutifully, Max moved on. This place was crowded as well. Along two walls, long tables were attended by barmen and bargirls. The tables held enormous platters of caviar and paté, smoked pheasant and fish, cheeses and hams. The drink was champagne, corks continually popping. A clump of guests hovered over a huge silver bowl set on its own table decorated with Aspen boughs. From this group erupted loud laughter belling forth in crackling, hysterical peals. Max accepted a glass of offered champagne and drifted along. Reaching the massed bodies, Max saw that the silver bowl was filled with white powder. It puzzled him for the barest second, then he realized he was looking at a massive amount of cocaine and he drew in a sharp surprised breath.

"Hi! Would you hold this for me?"

He turned to see a silver-haired girl in tight black shorts holding out a hand mirror. He took it.

"More flat," the girl fussed busily. "I'm trying to get my act together." She poured a small stream of coke onto the mirror face from a clenched hand, licked her fingers, produced a tiny penknife, and proceeded to cut the powder into lines expertly, chattering away. "Isn't this a gas? Isn't Daff the best? Isn't she the greatest? Hold it steady. She's just too much." From somewhere she drew a straw and, as she pulled Max's hand toward her, steadying the mirror, she put the straw to her right nostril and sniffed in hungrily. One of the lines instantly disappeared. She tapped her nose and sniffed again. "Good shit, really good shit. Daff's stuff is always great." She raised her head, offering the straw to Max. "You ready for a hit?"

"Not right now," Max said, staring at the bowl, still stunned by the sheer profligacy, by the *audacity* of it all as the rooting crowd openly dipped in, scooped up the coke, dribbled it on small silver trays stacked to one side, cut lines, sniffed, and snorted. In another small alcove off this room, Max saw glasslike lumps being passed from hand to hand. Crack, he knew.

"Hey, you're cute," the girl said, taking the mirror from Max's hand. "Come on, let's get some champagne." She took him firmly by the arm and led him away. Daphne passed them in the little hall and grinned.

A door opened, exposing a glimpse of hibiscus-flowered wallpaper and golden faucets. Someone emerged and Max's eyes opened wide. He pulled up.

"Are you coming?" the girl in the shorts chided.

"Wait a minute," Max said to her, and called to the woman who had just come out. "Barbara?" Then, realizing he could not be heard over the din, he made it stronger. "BARBARA . . . IT'S MAX!" When she swung around, Max saw, with a rush, that it indeed *was* Barbara Stratton. She had cropped her hair and it was on the green side but the incredible figure was the same and the huge eyes.

"Max," she called back, "what are you doing here?"

"I was invited," Max grinned as she neared him.

"No—I mean what are you doing in Aspen?"

"Getting a tan."

"Oh Max . . ." She hugged him affectionately. Max put his arms about her and felt good. When they separated, he realized the girl in the shorts had disappeared.

"I wish there was someplace to sit down," he said.

"Come on." Barbara clutched him and pulled him along, working her way through the human thicket to a mahagony staircase. She led him almost to the top and plopped down. He flopped beside her here, above the crowd and minimally beyond the din.

"So this is where you went," Max said.

"I had to get away." She hesitated. "Did you ever find out anything about . . . you know, Cy?"

"No," Max said quickly, "nothing yet."

"I think about him sometimes, you know. And you too."

Max wondered if he ought to tell her about Catalfo; he decided not to.

Down below, Daphne was a blur of somewhat awkward motion as she danced furiously, shimmying, stomping, flinging her arms out. "Her," Max asked, "who is she? I mean what is she?"

"Daphne?" Barbara leaned back. "She's got more money than anyone I ever knew, that's who she is. Divorced from some big cattle guy, they say. Max bucks. She knows everybody, loves to give parties."

"She furnishes all that coke in there, then?"

"Oh sure," Barbara laughed. "Anything you want, Daphne has. Nothing's too good for her guests, she always says."

"It's pretty out in the open."

"It's no problem here."

"Really?"

"Why should it be? This whole place, I mean Aspen, the big houses, all the stuff around, it all came from drug money."

Max looked at her questioningly.

"It's true. Way back. Drug guys came here, built big places, put their money into big developments, real estate stuff. I wish," Barbara said wistfully, "that I did drugs. Everybody thinks I'm freaky."

"Wait a minute. Aspen—skiing, mountains, all that, came from drug money?"

"That's what they say."

Not so crazy after all, that he had been sent here, then, Max considered. "You coming back east soon?"

"I don't know." A momentary shadow passed across Barbara's face. "It's complicated." She hesitated. "I keep thinking about what Cy said once. We were drinking a lot of champagne that night and he was going on about his time in San Francisco . . . boring stuff about Golden Gate Park and feeding people . . . him and his friend, what's his name . . ."

"Julie Berns."

"Whenever he mellowed out a little, he always talked about those days and stuff . . . himself this and Julie that, what they did for each other. He talked about you too, but different. Anyway, he said this once that people set their own traps for themselves and he didn't want me to do that. I didn't know what he was talking about, but I have an idea now." She was looking down below and Max, following the direction of her eyes, saw someone familiar staring up at them from the foot of the staircase. It was Roy Herbert, in a safari jacket with the sleeves rolled up. For a split second Max didn't recognize him. When he did, he looked quickly at Barbara, who smiled wanly.

Herbert mounted the stairs rapidly, his eyes shooting energy. "Well, well, look what we have here." Max rose to his feet.

Barbara raised up, saying, "Roy, you're bombed."

"Absolutely," Herbert laughed, "totally." He put his face so close that Max could smell the caviar. "But hey—this is play time here, Roberts. Everything's on hold. Got the picture?" He fondled Barbara's shoulder possessively.

"Will you stop that?" Barbara asked.

"Lighten up, it's a party."

"Roy—please."

His hand dropped away. The laugh became suspicion. His eyes challenged Max. "I found her, see. No one hides from me."

"Oh Christ." Barbara turned away, upset.

"You just came here for the scenery, eh?" Herbert said to Max.

"The air, actually. I had to get away from pollution."

"You can get polluted if you don't watch your step, though, believe me." He turned to Barbara. "Come on down. I want to dance."

"I don't feel like dancing right now."

"Well, I do." His hand rose once more, fingers digging into Barbara's upper arm. She winced, pulled her arm free, and said, "Stop being such a jerk. I'll be right down."

Herbert peered at Max. "You come here on business for your partner?"

"What?" Max was astonished.

Herbert threw a harsh look at Barbara and went back down the stairs. "He's bad news," Max said.

"Oh—I handle him."

"But why?"

"I got into some money troubles. He did some things for me." She wanted an end to it. "Where are you staying?"

"The Aspen Hills Lodge. Where are you?"

Barbara smiled. "Not with him. I have a house on Hillside Road." She found a pen in her tiny beaded bag and scribbled on a paper scrap. "Call me—tomorrow we'll have lunch."

She kissed him on the cheek and went downstairs. He watched her melt into the crowd and thought about Herbert's question. Was it a shot in the dark? Hadn't Borland mentioned his firm? Max descended slowly. He decided he didn't want to be here anymore. As he wondered what to do about a cab, he saw Daphne coming toward him.

"Where's your girl?"

"Gave her away."

"You're too generous."

"You're the one. Some party."

Daphne was pleased. "I love to see people having a good time." She leaned in against Max and he could feel the rolls of her flesh beneath the tight dress. "You going to be around for a while?"

"I'm not sure." He yawned elaborately. "I've got a little jet lag; I think I'd better get back."

"I'll give you a raincheck."

"Call me a cab," Max said, "before I fall down."

"Poor baby." Daphne patted his face. "Daphne will take care of you."

All the way back down the mountain, the question bothered Max: What was Roy Herbert doing in Aspen? After Barbara? Maybe—he'd go a long way for what he wanted. At the lodge, no message, no note. What if, Max worried, there had been some switch, they had called him at Cy's, had left some message? After all, that was the number Lang knew. He pulled his bag out and rummaged through it, looking for the phone-machine activating beeper. It was not to be found. He had neglected to pack it. He cursed himself for ten kinds of idiot and searched for a way out. Who could he trust to go to the apartment, get the messages, and ring him back?

When Max called Julie, he heard Streisand's voice soaring in the background and knew his friend was yet again watching *The Way We Were* on his VCR. Max said quickly, "Julie, I'm glad I didn't get you up."

"These days I'm not sleeping too much," Julie grumbled. Max announced that he was in Aspen, adding lamely that it was the holiday he had mentioned—albeit a confidential one. Instantly Berns wanted to know if it had anything to do with the SEC business. Panicked, Max told him to stop asking so many questions. Berns persisted. "It does, doesn't it?"

"Julie, are you crazy?" Max's voice rose. "That's old business."

"Who's there with you?"

"Somebody gorgeous."

"With you? Impossible."

"Julie, I need to know if there have been any calls for me at Cy's, but I forgot the beeper."

"Jesus," Julie grumbled, "how do I get in?"

Max told him there was a key at the office. He could get it in the morning and to call back instantly.

"OK, OK."

Max relaxed. "Guess who I met here?"

"How the hell should I know?"

"Barbara Stratton."

"You're joking."

"Uh-uh. She has a house here."

"I'll be damned. She say anything interesting?"

"We talked a little about Cy—what you did for him—what he did for you."

"What does she know about any of that?"

"Cy told her."

There was silence for a moment, then Berns said, "I'm missing this whole damn movie. All right, I'll check the machine and call you back."

"Julie, first thing."

"First thing, all right. Goodnight."

He had not expected to sleep but he did. When he opened his eyes, he felt oddly at peace—floating. Then he remembered where he was and the feeling fled. He ordered room-service breakfast, read the local paper, watched two duffers hack away at each other on the tennis court below, and managed somehow to get to ten A.M. without losing his mind completely. The phone sounded then. He jumped to it. It was Julie reporting.

"Who's Carol?"

"Just someone I know."

"I'll bet. She called twice."

"Dammit, Julie, were there any other messages?"

"Two calls trying to sell you stuff—one is for wholesale underwear, if you need any. A call for Cy from a Kathleen 'from two years ago'—she's a little late and obviously doesn't read."

"What else?"

"That's it."

Max slumped back. "OK. Thanks."

"Anytime," Julian said.

No call from Lang. All his anxiety flooded up. Where were they, where the hell were they? He called Shamski from the lobby; if there was no contact within twenty-four hours, he was out of there—gone, the hell with it.

Shamski agreed, "Absolutely."

"And Roy Herbert's here."

"Well, well."

"Now he knows I'm here."

"That might not change anything."

204

"Whether it does or not, I'm going if nothing happens."

"Fine."

Why was Shamski being so accommodating?

"I was at a party last night. I saw a pile of coke worth more money than you make in a year."

Shamski laughed. "That's not a tough figure to beat."

In bed later, he put the TV on, aimlessly pumping the remote. He passed the X-rated channel, where, this time, two ultra-high-decibled moaning, groaning girls groped each other, and found an old *Honeymooners* episode. He fell asleep as Gleason threatened to send Audrey Meadows to the moon once again. That, at least, was familiar and comforting.

In the morning, Max roused himself, certain that nothing was going to happen. Never. He would pack immediately and go. Convinced of this, his itchy nerves disappeared. Eating his breakfast grapefruit, he relented. He would give it till noon, he decided, and then take an afternoon plane out. Over and finished. The decision had relaxed him so that he went for a forty-five-minute mountain walk, actually enjoying the birdsongs and the dappled hills.

Upon his return, he called Barbara, who was happy to hear from him and giggled, "What a surprise to see you at Daphne's, my God."

"For me too."

"Listen, about lunch, though, today's no good, maybe tomorrow."

"I don't think I'll be here tomorrow," Max said. "As a matter of fact I'm sure of it."

"Oh—really?" Barbara sounded disappointed. "Today is . . . it's kind of tricky, but I did want to talk to you . . . about a lot of things but . . ." She trailed off inconclusively.

"Are you OK?"

"I'm fine," Barbara said, but Max read her voice differently. "It's just that it's a little complicated, that's all. Listen, maybe we can have a drink later, all right?"

"Sure."

"Max," Barbara said hurriedly, "things have to work themselves out, that's all. Cy used to say that if you give things enough time, that's what happens. I'll call you."

There was fear in her voice, Max concluded. Herbert was cracking the whip. He loved to be the ringmaster and she had, in some way, fallen into his ring.

Beeep. The phone, chirping again, caught him by surprise. He reached for it with anticipation and apprehension.

"Hello."

"Max, it's Daphne Kaiser. Good morning. What a lovely morning. Isn't it a lovely morning? Did you sleep well? Did you have a swim, play any tennis? You look in very good shape. Do you do Nautilus . . . or whatever they call it?"

"Morning," Max mumbled, deflated.

"I want you to come to lunch today."

"Thank you, but I don't think I can make it, Daphne."

"Oh you must, absolutely."

"Daphne, I can't." He decided to lie. "I may be leaving any minute."

"Oh no, you mustn't, not before lunch."

"Daphne—"

"It's not a big lunch, just an intimate thing. You have to come. You're the guest of honor."

"What makes me the guest of honor?"

"Because you are—that's all. There's . . . there's someone you should really . . . meet. I would just love to get you two together. You know how much I love getting people together, Max."

"Daphne," Max said, "you don't know anything about me."

"I don't have to know. Max, just come. Please. About one o'clock. Please, Max. Pretty please? I'll see you later, Max."

Before he could say anything else, she cut him off. Max stared at the phone. Why would he be the guest of honor? Who was she getting him together with? His stomach started roiling up again.

He took the rented car this time, getting instructions from the desk clerk. Driving up the mountain created its own serenity, and by the time he reached Daphne's he had almost convinced himself he had been mistaken. Daphne waved to him from the veranda as he pulled up. She wore a flaming red pajama outfit, dangling sapphire earrings, and pearls the size of small grapes. "Hello, sweet man," she called as he walked up, "you're looking good."

"You too," Max said. In response, she kissed him full on the lips, put her arm through his, and drew him into the house, which was very different now. Quiet, sun angling in, reflecting off the polished floors and stainless-steel legs of the leather couches, the room looked serene. Max looked over to where the silver bowl had been worshiped. The bowl was still in place but now held masses of flowers spilling over the sides.

"Come on." Daphne moved ahead, taking Max with her. She pushed a swinging door aside and they were in a glass-roofed breezeway leading toward a terrace. "You," she said coyly, pressing very close again, "must be a very important person."

Max laughed. "To my mother, maybe."

They were outdoors now and the terrace proved to be an extensive marbled area laid out at the edge of the mountain, surrounded by low plantings of exquisite jonquils, roses, and tulips, which created an intoxicating border of color against the sky. Below there was a picture-book view of the valley, with the town nestled in the center and mist-covered mountains beyond. At the terrace lip, a giant hot tub bubbled away. Here and there, lounge chairs were scattered about and, shaded by a vine-draped bower, a round table had been laid with blindingly white napery and heavy silver. From hidden loudspeakers, a beautifully modulated Frank Sinatra sang the "September Song." Max saw no one but himself and Daphne and said, "Your other guests are late."

"No, no, we're all here."

From the far end of the hot tub, almost hidden in the wisps of steam, a male figure rose up and stepped out onto the patio. He picked up a yellow terry robe lying nearby, donned it, covering the blue bikini trunks that had revealed a short, powerful torso, ran his hands through close-cropped jet-black hair, and called out, "Hi."

Max stared at this vision, then cautiously said, "Hello."

Daphne laughed. "He loves my hot tub. He says his never gets as good as mine. Donald," she warbled, "come meet Max Roberts."

Max saw gleaming white teeth set in a wide, dimpled smile. The face holding the smile was broad with high cheekbones, straight-nosed, and conventionally handsome. The dark eyes were amused right now but there was a piercing, commanding quality there.

"This is Don Brady. He's done so many things for Aspen, I can't begin to tell you."

207

Brady extended a still moist hand. "Good to meet you."

Max shook the hand and regarded Daphne questioningly. "Just the three of us?"

Daphne giggled. "I thought it would be nice."

Brady said, "I don't like big lunches. Too many people to talk to."

"Let's sit." Daphne snapped her fingers. Seemingly from out of nowhere, two white-clad servants appeared, pushing a cart. "Here and here, one on either side of me. I love it."

Max seated himself, looking at Brady from the corner of his eye. Brady said, "I was coming here today and Daphne said she met someone from New York last night and I said, Sure— invite him too."

The blank-eyed serving girl unwrapped a bottle of Pol Roger Brut, holding it at the ready. Daphne said, "Would you like a drink? Donald doesn't drink anything that comes from a grape. Calistoga water is all."

"I respect my body," Brady said, "but other people can do what they want."

Max declined. He felt discordant notes ringing everywhere. The manservant, delicate hands operating swiftly, set out crab-meat salad, hot rolls, three sauces. Brady started in hungrily. "How's New York?"

"The same," Max said, sampling the salad. It was superb.

"What do you do there?"

Max looked up warily.

"I'm in the stock and commodities market."

"Oh my," Daphne said. "I could use some investment advice."

"That's a risky business." Brady buttered a roll. "Where do you get these rolls, Daphne?"

"We bake them here."

"Everything's risky," Max said.

"You're right," Brady agreed. He seemed to be concentrating on the food.

Max ate quietly for a moment, then asked boldly, "And what do you do here?"

Brady looked up at him, smiling. "Little of this, a little of that."

"Donald does so many things," Daphne gushed. "You should see his estate, twelve acres, his own ski lift, his own runs. How many staff do you have now, Donald, twelve—fifteen?"

"No hot tub like yours, Daphne."

The next course was a perfectly poached salmon. Brady attacked that with the same interest he had shown the crab. Daphne chattered on. Brady bantered with her. Max chewed his underdone okra and decided he had simply been trapped into a Daphne Kaiser dipsy-doodle lunch. By the time the kiwi and crème fraîche arrived to accompany the espresso in little golden cups, Max had shut off, going inside himself, railing at the nonsense of it all. But suddenly Daphne excused herself. She had a couple of important phone calls to make; she was giving a big bash tomorrow night and arrangements had to be made; she knew they'd understand. And she was gone.

Brady sipped his espresso. Max sipped his, burning his lips. Brady toyed with the kiwi. Max sat still. Brady pushed the plate away. Max did the same. "I don't love this stuff either."

"So," Brady said in a quiet, conversational tone, "you're here to do business."

"Oh . . ." Max shrugged. "Sure—I'll work for anybody who needs a commodity broker."

"Your partner didn't do so good."

It had been said so simply that Max almost missed it. "What?"

"I said your partner didn't do so good."

Max stared at Brady, whose eyes held his in a gaze like a vise, then said tentatively, "My partner—" Phlegm caught in his throat. "My partner," Max began again, trying to control the fear-based excitement that gripped him, a drum in his head beating out the unbelievable message that *this was the man, this was the man.*

"What about your partner?"

Max swallowed hard. "My partner made mistakes, I guess."

Brady's eyes became like scalpels. They roved over Max's face, probed. "And you think you can do better."

"Yes." Max got bolder. "Sometimes Cy took too many chances."

"And you're smarter?"

"No. Just different."

Brady buttered another roll. "How many times did the police speak to you?"

"A couple."

"And what did you tell them?"

"That I don't know anything."

Brady bit into the roll. "What *do* you know?"

"A few things."

Brady's eyes reacted. Max took a deep breath. "I know some names of Swiss banks, and some numbers, and Lang."

Brady kept eating. "And you told them nothing, eh?"

Max plunged in. "I tell them anything and what chance do I have of doing any business? I've got to make some money, serious money. I'm in a bind here. I've got a mother in Miami who's almost an invalid. She drains me."

That seemed to catch Brady. "Your mother." He nodded. "Uh-huh."

Max drove on. "And my personal bank account is zero—that's something I can thank Cy for. I'm not a kid—I'm used to living a certain way; what am I supposed to do, become a clerk on the floor?"

This seemed to amuse Brady. "You're used to the good life in America, eh?"

"I'm not going to go backward," Max said emphatically. "You think I'd come here otherwise? I need the action; I have negative income. I have a girlfriend with problems." He wondered if he was pushing too hard.

"How do you know the Stratton woman?" Brady suddenly asked.

Max thought quickly. They *had* been watching him. "She went with my partner," he said.

"Is that so?" Brady paused. "You know other women he was with?"

"Women? There were a hundred women," Max said desperately. "Women always ran after him. In London, Hong Kong, Paris, always lots of women; who could keep track?"

"A man has to be careful with women." Brady was solemn. "Too many men tell women their business."

"Too many," Max agreed.

Brady fell silent. Max looked at the sky. Minutes passed in this silence, time that stretched each second into uncertain torture. Finally Brady broke it. "Your partner had this accident, you understand. We don't want any more accidents. We like things to go down nice and smooth. This is business. In business you have to trust people. When you can't trust them is when all the accidents happen, you follow?"

"Absolutely. And I know this is a . . . big business."

Brady said assertively, "You give people what they want, what they're willing to pay for, that's a good business. They tell me that fifty percent of the stuff the drugstores sell over the counter doesn't do a damn thing. But people want it, OK? They pay good money for it. That's a good business. That's the kind of companies to buy . . . where people shove money at you. That's the marketplace; that's what business is all about."

Max decided to sound professional. "I understand," he said carefully, "that lately a lot of people are trying to—interfere—with your business. What's that going to do to the cash flow?"

"Nothing. It's just politics. Our business is protected all around." Brady smiled and settled back in his chair. "Everybody takes—even those who don't want to take. You show them a number and if that don't work, you show them a bigger number and a bigger one after that. It's too much for people, see, all those numbers. Most people can't even imagine those numbers so when there it is, right in their faces . . ." He shrugged. "I'm a Catholic; I was brought up to believe we're all weak. It's true."

Max nodded. "Yeah."

Brady frowned. "It's not easy to build a business. Some people don't understand it's a different world today. Some of the older generation can't handle that. Vegas was enough for them in the old days. You talk to them about shopping malls or AT and T and they shake their heads. Cash flow isn't the problem. Turning it white is something different. That's where we need the help." He looked across at the hills, deep in thought.

Max ventured, "Yes, I can see that."

Brady looked back, frowning still. "Then we got some cowboys down there—they like to show who they are, big macho men, big ranches, big airplanes, big action, big trouble. They don't understand this country."

Abruptly, he stood up. As though it were a signal, Daphne started toward them from the house. "Now, she's a nice lady. All she does is good for people. Keeps her nose clean, gets her kicks out of doing favors—like having us here nice and quiet."

Nice and quiet, Max thought; he had arranged it this way, this man who drank only Calistoga water, this man who, most likely, would never go near the product that produced his cash flow. Schoolyard kids were snorting their lunch money, brokers

211

were burning out their nasal membranes, but it was just business here and it was, indeed, nice and quiet.

As Daphne approached, Max boldly asked, "Are you going to give me a chance to work with you?"

Brady didn't answer. Daphne, nearly upon them, said with delight, "There's a whole movie crew in town, and they're coming here tomorrow night—stars and all, won't that be fun?"

"What would this town do without you?" Brady asked.

"Isn't he something?" Daphne demanded of Max.

Something else, Max thought.

12

Swinging the car around in front of the Aspen Hills Lodge, Max tried to exit calmly, but his hands still shook. He had left Daphne's table, heart firing on overcharge, uncertain of what might happen. Once behind the wheel, he had charged down the mountain road at a breakneck clip, waiting to be intercepted at every curve. Halfway down, unimpeded, he began to have some hope. By the time he reached the village, pulse racing only a little slower, he realized that it had happened, he had been face to face with the power—or someone who represented that power—and they had believed him . . . maybe. Had he really sold himself to this man, who must have heard every story in the world, who must see through every supplicant, who must be suspicious of every approach? There was no way of knowing, but the best thing to do was to get away from this place as soon as possible.

Inside the hotel, he affected a casual stride toward the desk and inquired about the next plane out. The clerk checked his watch. "Oh-oh—it's after three-thirty—the afternoon plane just left. The next one's the night bird. Goes at six-thirty." He smiled, showing a gorgeous set of capped teeth. "Lot of champagne on that flight."

Max asked for a seat on the night bird, went up to the room, threw his few belongings into the carry-on, and waited anxiously for a confirming call. None came. He phoned downstairs to ask about his booking. The clerk was on another line. Max crunched the phone down, wandered the room in frustration, and turned on the TV. Aerobics. A dozen female thighs flashed in the studio lights. A dozen breasts jounced to the music. The phone brilled. Max grabbed it. It was the desk clerk. He was sorry but the night-bird flight was all booked up, not a seat to be had.

Totally unexpected. "I've got to leave on that plane, I absolutely have to."

"It's fully booked, they said."

"Put me on wait list," Max said desperately.

"They're not taking any more wait list, Mr. Roberts." Laughter came over the line. "For some reason a whole lot of people are leaving town tonight. Do you think they know something we don't know?"

There was nothing to be done. The first plane out, Max learned, was at noon the next day and he'd have to take that, but the prospect of another night here spooked him. He roamed out to the balcony, watched the shadows on the hills for a few minutes, came back in, sprawled on the couch, and tried to concentrate rationally. The job was to cool out, sit tight. But had Brady bought it? He recalled his remark about Adeline being a drain on him and Brady's sympathetic reaction; that was good. Had he shown enough greed? But Brady had to be used to greed. That man was not, Max thought, what he had expected, not at all.

Hours to go, worried hours. First, Max read the local paper, including the ads, and discovered he could buy a tractor and snowplow for only thirty-seven hundred dollars. Then came *The New York Times*, western edition. He read every line, including the fillers and obituaries. He dozed fitfully, he paced. At six o'clock he was pouring himself a gin and tonic courtesy of the minifrig, when the telephone ring startled him. Indecisive, he let it sound three times, then answered carefully. "Hello?"

"Max—well, hello there, how you doing?"

Despite his unfamiliarity with the voice, Max recognized Daphne's inflections. "Hello, Daphne."

214

"Just fine. Max, I'm right downstairs in the bar. Come on down and have a drink with me. I'm lonely."

What did she want, Max wondered—what was *this* all about? He answered with caution. "Gee, Daphne, I'm waiting for a phone call. I better hang in here."

"You can transfer it to the bar. Now come on, be sociable." She tinkled. "A fantastic girl is joining me later and you would both hit it off, I know you would."

"I really have to take it here—lots of paperwork and stuff." He gave her an opening. "Hey, thanks for the lunch again."

"My pleasure." The slightest of hesitations. "Isn't Donald a doll? He told me you may be doing some business together?"

"He did?" Max jumped alert.

"Uh-huh. He says you're real smart. Well, I knew that the moment I saw you." She giggled girlishly. "He says you'll be hearing from him most likely."

Max's mental gears whirled. "Did he? Well, that's good. Listen, when I come back, I'll stay a lot longer."

"I'll give you a bang-up party. Take care, Max."

"Sure will." Max hung up and replayed the conversation. It must be a signal, he decided, had to be. Brady had used her again. He gulped half the gin and tonic down in one nervous swallow. Amazingly enough, it had worked, he had pulled it off. He grinned at himself in the mirror and wondered if he might take up acting. And Daphne? Did she know what the business she had arranged was? It probably didn't matter. Being in the midst of the scene, intimate with the famous movers and shakers, was the function she had assumed. To her, Don Brady was simply an Aspen asset. But he had done it and felt triumphant.

Halfway through the second gin and the room-service lamb chops, the elation vanished. A wave of loneliness and resentment swept, surflike, over him. If Cy had not gotten both of them into this mess, he wouldn't be here now. He placed a call to Sonya. There was no answer. His annoyance was tempered with reason. Why would she sit in that cozy house and wait for his calls? He thought of calling Carol, but decided against it. He went to bed depressed. His dreams this night took him to a strange planet where everyone had shaven heads and cloven feet. Adeline was making some sort of speech to them and she, too, had her head shaven. It was such a startling vision that Max awoke with a jerk. He went

215

back to sleep in minutes, however, and the rest of the night was dreamless.

He awoke to an overcast day. The mountains that had appeared so close before now appeared to be a thousand miles away. By nine o'clock he had finished breakfast, and since there was no point in getting to the airport early, he had heavy time on his hands. He managed till ten, checking his watch every ten minutes, then decided to say good-bye to Barbara Stratton. He called but her line was busy. He tried again a few minutes later, found it was still busy, and gave up.

Fifteen minutes later he was on his way to the airport. The overcast was burning off and the sun began to burrow through. Searching for the turn that would take him out of town, a red light halted him momentarily, and he peered at the street sign to his left, which read HILLSIDE ROAD. That was where Barbara lived, he recalled. He checked his watch. Ten-thirty. He had an hour and a half before departure and the airport was only twenty minutes away. He retrieved her jotting and saw the house number, eleven eighty-eight. The light changed, and telling himself what the hell, Max turned left up the drive. He gave himself five minutes to find Barbara's house for a surprise good-bye in person; if not, he would turn around. But what if Herbert was there? he asked himself. Well then, up his, he answered defiantly, and drove on.

Hillside was a well-paved road along which impressive houses could be seen back behind clever garden walls and natural wood fencing. Max drove slowly, looking for numbers. He saw something in the six hundreds and then nothing more for a quarter of a mile. The next one he came upon was nine hundred and six. They skipped a lot here, he decided. He went on for another quarter of a mile, finding houses but no numbers. For all he knew, he'd already passed it by. After fifteen minutes, growing anxious, he curved around a sweeping tree, vowing to give it only till the end of this oncoming straight stretch. There was no house that he could see along the straightaway but as he neared the next curve, a hundred yards down the road, he spotted a wooden fence. The gate was open and two cars were parked nearby. He drove up and the cars resolved themselves into county police cruisers. He slowed, driving cautiously, and

216

as he passed the gate, peered in. Fifty yards back, surrounded by trees, there was a large, modern, angular house. Parked close to its wraparound deck there were two more county police cruisers and an ambulance with its red lights still spinning, jarring the harmony of green hills and sweetly chirping birds. Max was almost past the open gate when he caught sight of a barely visible number burned into the wooden gate, eleven eighty-eight.

He pulled up sharply, feeling instant apprehension. He backed, turned, and drove in through the gate, over to the house. He jerked to a halt, opened the door, and a tall uniformed man with a deputy sheriff's patch on his shoulder was suddenly there, leaning in to him.

"Hold it, please!"

A large hand touched Max's shoulder. Max came out of the car with it. The solemn-faced deputy said, "Could you tell me your business, sir?"

"I'm a friend of Barbara Stratton's," Max said quickly. "Am I in the right place? Does she live here?"

The deputy appraised him. "You're a friend of hers?"

"Yes, from New York."

"Oh—New York." The deputy hesitated. "You want to come with me a minute?" He indicated the house and waited for Max to walk first, then positioned himself behind him.

"What's going on here?" Max asked.

"Just walk along, please."

"Can't you tell me—?"

"Just walk along, please."

Disquieted, Max walked quickly toward the deck steps. He opened the carved-glass door and found himself inside a hallway lit by circular skylights. Three more sheriff's deputies clustered here in muted conversation. Seeing Max, they quieted in abrupt surprise.

"Friend of hers," the deputy accompanying Max said. He gestured to the staircase. "Let's go up, please."

Max walked up the steps with growing dread. At the top landing, a lean, sandy-haired older man also bore the logo DEPUTY on his unformed shirt. He seemed to be in charge, as he spoke to two more uniformed men and two medics who smoked and lounged. Once again, Max's deputy said, "Sergeant, this man says he's a friend of hers."

"I *am* a friend of hers," Max said. "What's happened here?"

217

The sergeant turned calculating eyes on Max. "I'm Sergeant Byers, sir—the county sheriff's department. Could you tell me who you are?"

"My name's Max Roberts."

"And what's your business here, Mr. Roberts?"

"I just told you. I'm a friend of Miss Stratton's. I came here on business. Now I'm going back to New York and I just dropped in to say good-bye. Would you tell me what this is all about?"

Wordlessly, the sergeant took Max by the arm and stepped him past two closed doors. He stopped at a third, which was open, gesturing inside. Max moved around the sergeant and looked into the room. It was a pink bedroom, Max saw, and directly in his line of vision was a massive four-poster bed. Lying motionless on the bed in a blue nightgown, her arms at her sides, was Barbara. Max stared, looked at the sergeant in questioning shock, and then back to Barbara.

"I'm afraid the lady died last night," the sergeant said quietly.

Max continued to stare. In her blue nightgown, Barbara looked peacefully asleep.

"I'm sorry it comes at you this way, Mr. Roberts."

Max pulled his eyes away. "How did it happen?"

"We're not sure. The cleaning lady found her in bed this morning and it looks like . . . well . . . like natural causes, heart attack or something."

"What?" Max swung his eyes back to the figure on the bed.

"The medical examiner hasn't had a chance to examine her real good yet. She was from New York too, wasn't she?"

"Yes," Max said, keeping his voice calm with effort. "What makes you think it was a heart attack?"

"The ME just said he thought it might be."

"She never said anything about heart trouble."

"Well," Sergeant Byers said, "sometimes people don't like to talk about those things, do they? The ME'll find out, that's for sure."

"Do you know," Max asked boldly, "if she was disturbed by something last night, any particular thing happen?"

"What have you got in mind?"

"How about someone who—" Max hesitated. "—who might have been with her last night, some friend?"

"No one we know about." The sheriff was becoming irritated. "This woman just died peacefully in bed, so far as we know right now. They'll be coming in soon to take her away, so you'd best just leave, I think. You making the twelve o'clock plane?"

"Yes, I am."

"Well, have a real good trip," the sergeant said. He patted Max on the shoulder kindly. "These things happen, Mr. Roberts. Hard on the loved ones but the Lord has His ways."

Max looked once more in through the doorway, to the bed, to Barbara. A heart attack. A heart attack? It seemed to him even the sergeant didn't exactly believe it.

He drove to the airport deep in shock. Barbara had come to Aspen to escape, but something had followed her. The more he thought about it, the more improbable a heart attack appeared, and the possibility that her death had something to do with his being in Aspen haunted him.

In the air, staring out the window at the snow-topped peaks below, Max's depression lingered. When the meal came, he had no stomach for it. With the cabin lights low, he tried to read one of the ten business magazines the airlines furnished. After a page of merger hallelujahs, he dropped it and went forward to where the plane's newest gimmick, the in-flight telephone, resided. He did his credit-card thing and took the actual wireless instrument, gripping it hard, into a lavatory, where he locked the door and waited for the connection to be made. When he reached Shamski, Max said, "I'm calling from the airplane, so it's got to be secure. I'm coming back."

"Are you all right?" Shamski asked quickly.

"Yes. I made the contact. It looks good."

"Great. Terrific."

"But, listen, something's happened here, just this morning." Quickly, he told the detective about Barbara, about her connection to Herbert, about her death. Shamski wanted to know what she was doing in Aspen. Max said he didn't know, she was just there. "But this heart-attack thing sounds made up. There's more to it, I know there is. And I can't shake the feeling that it had something to do with me, with my being there, I don't know—"

"Take it easy." Shamski was forceful. "I understand how you feel, but you're not responsible, you hear me?"

"How do I know I'm not? She said she wanted to talk to me."

"Stop whipping yourself. I'll get some people on it right away and we'll get the story, whatever it is. Your job is to get back here now in one piece. You're calling from the plane—really?"

"I'm in the can, sitting on the seat."

"Fantastic," Shamski said.

As Max sat, everything buzzing, all the plastic bits and pieces of the room vibrating in a shimmy that danced right through his tired body, he felt the absurdity of it all. What a—dumb thing—to be here, in a toilet on an airplane, holding a radio-telephone, speaking about a young woman whose life had just ended. But why Barbara—what was the sense in that? Unless she had known something she hadn't told him, something that Cy had told her. He sighed and whispered, "I could murder you myself, Bannerman."

The plane landed in a driving summer rain to the applause of the passengers. Dark clouds swept over the city and the lights of Long Island were shrouded in mist.

The apartment, when he reached it, looked comfortingly familiar. It was only as he unpacked that Max realized he had automatically given the taxi driver Cy's address and not his own. As his suit went into Cy's closet, he reasoned that until this ended it *was* his address. He checked the phone-answering machine and found no surprises. He tried Julian and got his tape announcing that he was out of town on a quick business trip and to "have a good market day."

At nine the next morning, Max was debriefed. To his annoyance, Borland was present and made notes in a spiral notebook, nodding at every sentence. When Max had finished his recital, Shamski considered a moment, then said, "This Daphne introduced him as Donald Brady."

"Brady, yes."

Borland picked a sheaf of typescript from his case and thumbed through it. "This is a listing of some known people. I don't read his name here."

"Describe him again," Shamski requested. Halfway through the repeat, his eyes lit up. "I will bet that you met Don Brigado." He clutched Max's shoulder. "That had to be Brigado. He was involved with the old Gambetta people but we lost track of him. We thought maybe he was out of the country, but he must have taken over when Gambetta had the heart attack. You met the top guy, Max. In Aspen. And he calls himself Brady." He laughed.

"D.B. It's always the same initials, somehow, I don't know why that is."

"Brigado is a Colombian," Borland said. "Did this man look Latin?"

"Do I look Polish?" Shamski said. "This guy has been out of sight for four years, and there he was all the time, pulling the strings, cool, calm. From what you say he didn't even have somebody watching his ass; that's how sure he is. Strictly business."

"Did your partner ever go to Aspen?" Borland suddenly demanded. Max ignored him. "I'm asking you," Borland repeated, "whether there's any record of Bannerman going to Aspen to meet this Brady?"

"No," Max said, "never."

"Doesn't it stand to reason that he had to be checked out, the same way you were?"

"You're a broken record," Max said heatedly.

"I'm being logical."

"Cy never met him."

"Are you sure?" Shamski was skeptical.

"Yes."

"A woman like that . . ." Borland started, but Max swung toward him.

"Shut up. You never knew her."

"The report says there was a pile of barbs on her night table," Shamski said.

"I don't care what there was. She never took them by herself."

Shamski was still skeptical. "Not even if she and Herbert were having a party?"

No, Max thought, she never took them with Cy and if she didn't then—"I think," he said somberly, "that someone did something to her."

Shamski considered that and Max repeated stubbornly, "She never did drugs."

"You mean someone killed her," Shamski said flatly. He thought a moment. "They're calling it an OD and they don't even want to do that because it gives the place a bad name. I talk about murder with them and they could stonewall. Well, we'll try for more details. Your job now is to concentrate on Lang."

Deeper and deeper, Max groaned to himself. He had nursed

the delusion that the trip to Aspen might provide an end to it all. Wrong. Now he fantasized a quiet beach somewhere, no sound but surf and someone on the sand beside him.

Borland punctured the daydream. "We are tracking what we can of the records, apart from the Morey's deal. There are a lot of gaps in the Whizkid records, trades that are unaccountable, like one called Dig Trade. What do you know about that?"

"Nothing. That was Cy's own shorthand." Max thought again of Barbara and felt a headache starting.

Shamski saw the look on his face and said, "OK, we know a lot more than we did before. Just knowing Brigado heads the organization is something we can give the Federal Drug Task Force."

"Brady told me," Max said, "that you couldn't stop his organization. He could throw around too much money. Nobody could resist, cops, lawyers . . ."

". . . And certain people on the Street," Borland interpolated.

"He could get anything done he wanted," Max concluded.

"Mostly true," Shamski sighed. Which could, Max thought, include getting anyone killed he wanted to. The detective read his mind. "Look, he may not have bought you a hundred percent but if he calls, and he will, it's fifty percent, seventy-five. OK? And he's still got to watch his step a little. He makes too much heat and guys who want *him* gone make a move. All right," he finished briskly, "you go about your business. Lang'll call."

"What are you going to do about Herbert?" Max demanded. "I saw him with Barbara and she's dead."

Shamski tried to cool him down. "We have to go easy from here. We don't want to get the Aspen people p.o.'d at us."

"Oh Jesus."

"Hey." Shamski turned stern. "I want to find out who killed your partner as much as you do. Not to mention the bomb next door and the people who won't ever walk again. And this Stratton woman. But there are ways and ways. Now just try not to miss Lang's call."

Keeping up a semblance of ordinary life, Max went down to the Exchange, caught a wave, and closed out two cotton contracts, which netted fifteen thousand dollars and provided some breathing space with the bank. He saw Carol there, thought about saying hello, but decided against it. Later he checked in with Adeline, returned a call from Phil Carmody, who just wanted

222

to know the latest, and talked to Julie Berns, who had returned from his trip. Soberly, Max told him of Barbara Stratton's death. Berns was stunned and angered. "What the hell did she have to do with this business?"

"No one knows what she had to do with," Max said gloomily, "except that bastard, Herbert—and the Aspen police are going to handle him with kid gloves."

"Jesus," Berns lamented, "do you think maybe she knew something about who pushed Cy after all?" He shuddered. "That's grisly. I mean he was in bed with her. They did the thing together. And she might have set him up somehow?"

Max didn't think so. Berns asked what the SEC was up to.

"Nothing much," Max said guiltily.

Unable to face the office again, Max went to the movies, seeing an action film in which there were four car crashes, two fires, a yacht explosion, and an underwater duel with spearguns. Afterward, he inspected his own apartment. Newly painted, bare-walled, with furniture piled in the center of all the rooms, it felt less his than ever. Disconcerted, he left quickly and walked across the park to Cy's. He hurried into the lobby and over to the elevator bank, where a middle-aged, creased-faced man in a wrinkled blue suit waited for a car. He glanced at Max only for a moment before looking away, but the look was so encompassing that Max felt instant alarm, and when the car arrived five seconds later, he hesitated before getting in. But he did, pressed the right button, and stood with his back to the car wall, alert. Two floors up, the man reached suddenly to the control panel, hitting the "stop" button. Max shouted, "Hey," and grabbed at his arm.

The man pulled away, countering, "Hold it, hold it, I'm from Shamski, from Shamski." He produced a worn leather case holding a silver police badge. "My name's Morrisey."

"Why didn't you say so first?" Max said angrily.

"You didn't give me a chance. I was hanging around waiting for you. The message from Shamski is this guy Herbert left Aspen Friday morning."

Max could hardly believe it. "Friday? When I left?"

"Yeah."

"Barbara was killed just the night before."

"I know that." Morrisey replaced his ID. "I'm the one been in touch with the Aspen department. They don't like the whole thing so much they don't even want to talk about ODs."

223

"Barbara did not OD," Max insisted.

"They claim yes. So they're not going to be too much help, you follow?"

"Herbert left—Friday?" Max was still incredulous.

"We checked the airlines and he didn't go out that way. Shamski wants to know if you have any idea where he could be."

Max thought a moment. If Herbert didn't fly out, he had driven. Los Angeles suggested itself instantly. Herbert loved that town; he was right in tune with it. "Try L.A.," he said.

Morrisey looked dubious. "L.A? Well, we'll try. But maybe we'll wait till he gets back here to question him."

"Gets back?" Max was incensed. "Suppose it's months from now. What about the L.A. police?"

Morrisey's worn face broke into an ironic laugh. "You got another pipe dream, Mr. Roberts?"

In the apartment, Max switched on the telephone-answering machine and went to the john. Pants unzipped, he came running out as Sonya's voice bubbled off the tape. "Hi, Max, it's Sonya. I'm in your terrible, wonderful city for the day. You can call me at this number." Max scrambled for a pen, and managed to get the number down before the message ended. Delighted, he called instantly. Sonya was there. He arranged to pick her up later and sat back savoring the idea.

When Max saw Sonya, when he heard the throaty voice, he felt the same flutterings in his chest as when he had first -seen her. "I've been calling you. You've been busy, I guess."

"Doing this and that. Lots to do in the country, you know."

They went to a Greek restaurant in the village that Sonya knew and drank retsina, which she loved. Max had less of a love affair with the resined wine, but managed his half of the bottle. There was a bouzouki player and a powerfully built woman singer with a mournful voice. For no reason at all, she sang "New York, New York" in Greek, the bouzouki wailing away. "It's so wonderfully insane," Sonya said, applauding enthusiastically, "it could only happen here." Cy had introduced her to this place; she was surprised that Max didn't know it, but now he did. Yes, Max thought, now he did.

They walked the angled, narrow streets arms about each other's waists. Walking this way, a sliver of new moon overhead, retsina working, was rhapsodic. The lights shimmered. Time had no meaning. There was no past. Every so often, Sonya would smile beatifically and pat his face. Little was said, even in the bed later. Afterward, Max held her and stroked her unbound hair. As he dropped off to sleep, he had the illusion that Cy, floating somewhere above the bed, was watching them.

The telephone wrenched him awake. He groped for it, simultaneously turning to Sonya. She slept.

"Yes," he mumbled into the phone, steeling himself, "hello." He knew it was going to be a hospital in Florida. Adeline. He saw the tubes and the wires, the oxygen, he saw her labored breathing.

"Roberts, this is Lang."

Disoriented, Max said, "Who?" Then he remembered, sat fully up. "Lang? What time is it?"

"Time to work. The Tunnel. Nine A.M. Breakfast." Before Max could collect himself, Lang rang off. Wide awake, Max stared nervously into the darkness. Beside him, Sonya stirred. She turned, moved closer, and he felt the roundness and warmth of her buttocks against him. All he could think of was Brigado.

13

From the corner of his eye, Max watched Lang devour two bull's-eye eggs and worked hard to control his gagging. The man had been there waiting for him. Little had been said. They sat at the same rear table as before. There were a dozen people, half at tables eating breakfast, half at the bar, drinking theirs. Max had ordered eggs sunnyside up but found it difficult to swallow more than a few bites. Lang reached for his coffee and asked, "You like Aspen?"

"I didn't see much of it."

Lang put his fork down. "Meet any people you know?"

Was this to see if he would lie? "I ran into a girl at a party," Max said. He reached for the toast and had the feeling that Lang was waiting. "And a man I know slightly."

"Yes," Lang said. He reached into his inside jacket pocket and produced a small notebook. He tore several sheets out, placing them before him. "Listen to me now, carefully. It is arranged that your company has a new credit line at the Bank for Commerce in the Cayman Islands in the Caribbean. Your officer there is Franklin DeVoe. It's all down here." He pushed one sheet forward. Max took it. "DeVoe at the Bank for Commerce. Got it?"

"Got it."

"The account you'll trade for is the EPB Associates. Here's what we want. Two angles. Profits and accumulation. You make the buys, discretionary. You decide to sell, the gains go into an account for EPB that already exists at the Second Mercantile here in New York." He pushed forward another sheet. "That's down here."

"OK."

"If you decide to hold, you transfer security ownership to this company in Switzerland care of the Bank Suisse Generale in Geneva with this numbered account. Got it?" A third sheet of paper came forward for Max. The company name was Euro-Partners of Brazil. The account number was lettered neatly beside it.

"I guess"—Max sipped his coffee and tried to be offhand—"I'm not the only broker you're dealing with."

Lang stared at him coldly. "That's none of your business."

"I didn't mean it that way." Max covered himself by asking boldly, "What's my end?"

"Two percent over standard commissions on trades plus a possible percentage of profit bonus for 'investment advice.' " Lang smiled mirthlessly. "That make you happy?"

"Fine," Max said, feigning enthusiasm, "very good."

"We didn't work this way with your partner." Lang's eyes bored in on him. "He told us he could make heavy deals, give us big percentages."

"Cy was very smart," Max defended weakly.

"He went off the rails. That's when accidents happen. You don't want to go off the rails."

"No," Max said hastily.

Lang leaned closer. "I don't have to tell you that my principals are careful people. They take precautions. They watch everything. They do what they have to do to protect their investments." Max felt his right leg start to twitch and tensed to control it. "And they have long arms," Lang concluded. He let that sink in, then asked, "You're all clear?"

"Absolutely." Max tried to be vigorous.

"Then that's it." Lang rose to his feet, looking down at Max from his full height. "Only one thing. Using you wasn't my idea. I'm not sure you're reliable, but someone else made the decision. So far as I'm concerned, you'll have to prove your-self." He dropped a twenty on the table and walked away. Max sat, papers in hand, the cold eggs sticking in his throat. He watched Lang go through the greenery and noticed he stopped momentarily near the bar to exchange swift glances with some-one hunched over a platter. Then he resumed his stride. Minutes later, when the waiter came by, Max roused himself, remem-bered Sonya, and phoned. She had a ten-thirty appointment, she told him. It would take an hour—did he want to meet her? If not, she would be on her way back to the green hills. Hearing her voice brought a degree of normalcy.

"Don't go back yet," Max said. "I need more of you." Even as he talked, however, he watched the back of the man Lang had spoken to, and when Sonya said good-bye, he walked slowly to the door with studied casualness, hesitated, and snatched a look at him. He seemed ordinary enough, thin, with a narrow face and plastic-rimmed eyeglasses. As Max watched, he pushed his breakfast plate aside and lit a cigarette. Max moved past him and saw that the man turned toward him slightly.

Max left the Tunnel, certain he was being followed. He walked down Eleventh Avenue, not daring to turn around. Crossing the avenue to get away from a miniskirted hooker in a see-through blouse provoked a shouted, "Hey—'fraid a catchin' somethin'?" He took advantage of the call to turn and scan the street.

To his relief, he saw only the black girl, who shouted, "Change your mind?" Quickly, he walked east and then north on Tenth. A group of kids was hanging out on the steps of a school, and as Max passed, a small-framed boy in white unlaced hightops whispered loudly in a rhythmic chant, "Got what you want, whatever it is, crack and smack an' angel dust, best in school, keep you cool, buy my brand you ain't no fool." He waved a glassine bag at Max, fourteen-year-old eyes mockingly defiant. Max moved past him, almost on a run. It came from here, the Cayman account that he would now help swell. It wasn't trades in cotton or shorting IBM; it was smart kids rhym-ing drug sales. Adeline would say this was where it all led to, of course. He hurried away as fast as he could.

He called the secure phone number and reported on his meeting with Lang. Shamski was impressed. "They're not only laundering that money," he observed. "They're dry-cleaning it. Oh, by the way, the Aspen police told us that somebody might have been with the Stratton woman the night she died. They found a take-out carton from a rib place in her apartment. The delivery girl said she heard a man's voice when she brought the stuff but she never got a look at him."

"I knew she wasn't alone," Max said.

"You've got a double bingo," the detective said. "Herbert *is* in Los Angeles, it appears, at the Bel Air Hotel."

"And what are you doing about it?"

Shamski chuckled. "Getting reports on his hot-tub action."

The conversation prolonged Max's bleak mood. It didn't help when Sonya insisted she'd had enough of the city. "The pollution," she said, "the despair on the faces. After twenty-four hours here I feel I'm getting to be a zombie, like all the rest. Max, I've got to go." Her face brightened with a sudden idea. "Why don't you come up with me—right now?"

"I can't," Max mumbled. "I've got things I have to do."

"Oh Lord, the money business again. What blows my mind is that it's so—worthless, such a waste of your life."

"Trading is as old as civilization," Max said weakly. "Spices, salt, myrrh. The Old Testament talks about myrrh and spices."

Sonya put the key into the VW ignition. "Max, doing that was the worst part of Cy. It's a shame to see it happening to you." She leaned over and kissed him gently. "Bye, Max."

At the office a packet had been delivered from the Second Mercantile Bank with a request for his file signature. Already there was a notice of letter-of-credit from the Cayman bank. Slumped behind his desk, Max realized he had to act, he had to have some picks. He thought of Carmody, who was pleased to hear from him.

"I've been thinking about you—how are things?"

"Moving along," Max said briskly. "I'm trying to pick up the pieces, you know."

"How's your mother?" Carmody asked, chuckling. "She still political?"

Max said that Adeline would never change, that he had a new, important client he needed some help with—was that possible? Carmody gave Max twenty minutes and a dozen suggestions. "Anytime," Carmody said. "Let me help anytime. You know what I thought about Cy. Anything I can do for anyone connected to him is just fine with me." He paused. "I miss him. We had some wonderful conversations."

Max plunged in. Within a week he had recklessly committed half a million of the new funds, within the next, an equal amount. Before the end of the month, to his surprise, he had made EPB two hundred thousand dollars, held rising stocks for them, and felt both elated and wretched. Lang called him twice for progress reports. The conversation at first was brisk and businesslike; Lang did not want trading profits to build up in the Mercantile account. He wanted more stock transferred to Switzerland and he wanted an accounting of the cash transactions. Then he said, "I have been informed that you saw a young woman last week. Who is she?"

"Just a girl," Max replied, unnerved. "Just a friend. I have a private life, you understand."

"Not when you work for us." Lang's tone was curt. "Not when we pay you. Just be careful, that's all."

Max hung up, chilled.

From then on, Max sensed a constant presence behind him even when it seemed impossible, even when there was no one on a street but himself. He stopped walking, taking cabs wherever he went, even for a few blocks. He left the office as little as possible. His lunch came in, pizza, sandwiches, unidentifiable dishes that Martha ordered from a local Hungarian restaurant. His dinners were take-out. He found it hard to get to sleep. Through it all, he feverishly bought and sold, bought and sold. It was like a disease. Unnerving him further, Borland came up to learn exactly what the activity was. They were on his tail, Max shouted. Suppose they knew who the SEC man was? He was endangering everything—including him. Borland insisted he was unknown and had to have details. Max gave him all the trade and shipment records. When he offhandedly remarked that Lang constantly monitored the cash account at the Mercantile Bank, the SEC man sniffed, "That should convince you that Bannerman manipulated the last cash account and skimmed it. They're not about to let that happen again."

"Cy never stole a nickel from anyone," Max retorted.

"The evidence is in front of your eyes."

"In front of my eyes is a jerk."

It ended with Max ordering Borland out. He was never to come here again, never—or all bets were off. When Borland left, Max sat hunched in his chair. It was enough. He met with Shamski at a secure out-of-the-way diner, taking two cabs to get there.

"It's getting to me," Max said, "everything."

Shamski was solicitous. "I understand. I really do."

"I'm making those bastards money," Max raged. "That's insane."

Shamski laughed. "Listen, if I give you a thousand bucks, what can you do for me?"

"I'm serious."

"Hell—so am I." Shamski's blue eyes were very steady. "I'd love to make some money but I'm a lousy gambler." He grinned. "It's all that Catholic-school training. I need a sure thing." Max sipped the iced tea unhappily. Shamski made—what?—perhaps forty thousand a year? For that, he did what he did—all of it, including taking the risks, while the Whizkids income had been stratospheric by comparison. Sitting here, he felt ashamed of those numbers. He knew all the rationalizations—the value of labor, the possibilities created by the free marketplace—yet he felt ashamed. Adeline, he said to himself angrily, she put stuff into me when I was too young to understand and some of the garbage stuck.

"Can you hang in just a little while longer?" Shamski asked. "We're checking some things out and it would be bad if the boat was going to be rocked now, but if it's really too tough. . . ."

He could walk away from Shamski, Max suddenly realized, but could he walk away from Brigado? Would they let him?

Later that night he paced the floor of the apartment, feeling enmeshed in a web that he was powerless to break. Getting away from himself, he called Adeline.

"I'm just checking on you, Addie. Do you need anything?"

"I would like to read to a grandchild."

"What?"

"Are you doing anything in that department? Max, we are the good people of the world; we need continuity."

"Adeline, give me a break."

Her tone changed abruptly, as she asked, "Max, are you in trouble?"

Max was startled. "No."

"You don't sound right to me."

"It's the connection," he said weakly.

"I read a piece in the paper here about the Wall Street robbers—what do they call them—the insiders."

"That's got nothing to do with me."

"Are you still doing that business?"

"Not much," he lied.

"Leave it," Adeline urged. "Somehow it hurt Cy, I know it did."

"Adeline, Cy had an accident," he faltered.

"Somehow it hurt him. I don't want it to hurt you."

"I'm not hurting," Max protested.

"Listen to what I say," Adeline concluded, "and think about continuity."

She was a witch, and would there be any continuity, any at all? Max wondered bitterly. He resumed his pacing through Cy's apartment, past Cy's furniture, Cy's pictures, Cy's walls, the spring inside his chest winding to the breaking point. "I am getting to hate you, Cy," he whispered and instantly felt a deep pang of disloyalty.

After another sleepless night, the next morning brought another round of tape watching and phone juggling. At eleven o'clock, Martha came in to announce that Marcus Rich was outside and wanted to see him. "He's got some suit on," she whispered. "It's Italian silk. I know these things."

Max's first reaction was panic. The columnist had heard something, was sniffing out EPB. Martha saw the look on her boss's face and was alerted. "You want me to say you're busy —in conference, an important client?"

"No." Max composed his features. "I'll handle it." He went to the door himself, swung it open, and said with vivacity, "Well, Marcus—you slumming?"

Rich, resplendent in off-white, smiled automatically, came in, and said, "I just wanted to touch base with you about a few things." He nodded toward the figures moving along the monitor. "Things are humming along, I understand—without Bannerman."

"Oh—a few odds and ends things here and there." Max bustled about nervously. "Would you like some coffee?"

No, Rich would not like coffee. He settled himself into a chair, fingered the knot in his Sulka tie, and said he had heard some things and wanted to check them out. For instance, had Cy Bannerman done any trading for a company called Morey's?

Max felt the question in the pit of his stomach and coughed to disguise the wince. The weasel had dug up paydirt and was now pawing around for more. He screwed on a thoughtful expression. "It sounds familiar but you know we had that explosion next door and a lot of our records were damaged."

Rich glanced at the still unrepaired wall. "That was an interesting explosion."

"That's some word—*interesting*," Max parried.

Rich nodded. "There are lots of interesting things about . . . Whizkids. I'm not out to get the dead, but I have an obligation to my readers."

Oh no, Max thought bitterly, you're not out to get Cy. You hated his guts for being someone you could never understand. And he made no secret of his contempt for what you did. Now that he's dead you can really get back at him. "I don't recall hearing about a Morey's," came out of him.

Rich leaned forward. "Roberts, you're a trader—let's trade. I happen to know something that you might like to know. Can I get something from you in exchange?"

What was he up to? Max wondered. Cautiously, he said, "I don't know what you're talking about."

"I'll take a chance," the columnist said, his eyes gleaming like a hunting cat, "on your sense of fair play. Can we trade?"

What did he have, what did the bastard have? "What do you think I'd like to know?"

"Ah—" Rich leaned back, savoring the moment. "Well, your partner, Bannerman, was a little profligate with his seed, wasn't he?"

Max made no reply and Rich went on. "As a result, Liz Evers became preggers."

"Really," Max said quietly.

"Oh yes, really."

"And what happened?"

"What do you think happened?"

"You're the one who's telling me things."

"Yes," Rich agreed. He hesitated for maximum effect. "The fact is that Liz Evers had an abortion."

"Not true," Max said sharply. "Never. Cy would never agree to that."

"It was aborted," Rich said flatly. "It was done at Cedars and the doctor's name is Richard Maneta. He's on the OB-GYN staff there."

"I don't care what his name is. I don't believe it."

"Believe it," Rich said with relish, "because it came right

234

from Maneta's office. And, if you remember, just about that time she and Bannerman broke up. She went out of circulation completely."

No, Max thought—something was out of kilter.

"The story was that she was recovering from a serious kidney infection. Some kidney—" Rich chuckled mirthlessly. "It was in her brain. She had a breakdown, a serious one. Her therapist is a Dr. Robin and his report has a lot of guilt stuff in it—and rage, lots of rage." He waited for Max's response but there was none. "You agree that I'm giving you information you want to know?"

Max nodded. "If it's true."

"It is true, one hundred percent."

"Are you telling me," Max asked slowly, deliberately, "that Cy agreed to abort their baby?"

"I'm telling you facts," Rich snorted. "You can interpret them any way you want. Now," he said, changing tack, "it's your turn. How tight was your partner in with Morey's?"

How could it be? Max thought. It couldn't. It didn't mesh.

"I'm waiting."

Max stalled. "What is it about this Morey's that's important?"

"Funny business." Rich smiled saturninely.

Max considered. How dangerous was it to admit dealing with Morey's? In itself, it was a dead end—but Rich had sources that might go further. Still, it might be less dangerous to be vaguely open than to deny what he obviously already knew. "Let me see." Max opened a file drawer and rummaged through as Rich watched him with amusement. Finally, Max closed the drawer. "You're right. There are some notes here in Cy's writing about a Morey's Inc. He handled some commodities and options for them."

"See," Rich said, "you are helpful. Who ι as the principal?"

Max wrinkled his brow. "That I don't know."

A green morocco-bound notebook sprang into Rich's hand. He made notes with his silver pen. "That's interesting, very." He rose, adjusting his jacket, and said, with cheer, "Well, that wasn't a bad trade, was it?" He started out, calling back, "Maybe we'll deal again?"

After Rich had departed, Max tried to order his thoughts. When Martha came in and asked tentatively if everything was all right, he told her to get Jimmy Singh instantly. Jimmy was not at home but his wife gave Max his office number. When he finally got Jimmy, Max warned that Marcus Rich might try to contact him for information about Cy's business. Under no circumstances was he to give him any. Singh was apprehensive.

"What is happening? Oh my!"

"Jimmy, take it easy. Nothing is going to happen. He's just snooping around."

"But he is a very powerful person, you see."

"All you've got to do is say you don't know anything."

He hung up on a frightened Singh and called Shamski to report Rich's dangerous interest in Morey's. Shamski said someone would call Rich off should he persist. Max replied that he should be watched anyway; he was a slimy son of a bitch. Even as he said that, his mind was not on Morey's, but on what the columnist had reported. He called Julian. They met, and Julian, incensed, was all for confronting Liz Evers.

"She aborted Cy's child? With his knowledge? No, never in a million years. No."

"He had all the names," Max said bleakly. "The OB-GYN, the analyst."

"She lied to us, then. She stone lied. Why?"

"Rich said she had a breakdown."

"It's fishy."

"Could it not have been his baby?" Max wondered.

"We deserve to know," Julian said strongly. "She won't want to see us again, but we ought to find some way to convince her."

At seven-thirty that night, as Liz Evers was entering the lobby of her building, Max and Julian were waiting for her. She looked at them coldly. "If you want the doormen to throw you out—"

"Nobody wants a scene," Julian said. "Let's be civilized. But if you insist . . ."

"You're contemptible."

Max saw the man at the concierge's desk eyeing them and pleaded, "Ten minutes, please—just ten minutes."

Liz Evers hesitated, glaring at Julian, who said, "There was no one closer to Cy than us. We're talking about his blood— you know what I mean. You have an obligation."

Grim-lipped, Liz Evers walked into the waiting elevator and made no further protest as the men followed her. No word

236

was spoken as the car rose, stopped, and they emerged to walk down the hall. No word was spoken as they stopped at her apartment door. No word was spoken as the three of them passed through the portal into the foyer. Finally, in the living room, Liz exploded, almost quivering as she said, "You bastards. Three men, but you're all Cy Bannerman, aren't you? You only lived through him, didn't you? You disgust me."

"We were his friends." Julian's tones were emotional. "We were his brothers. You always keep faith with your brothers. You never break that, never."

"We need to know," Max said unhappily. "We need to know about the baby. It's not a secret. Other people know."

Liz's hands made tight fists. "There is no baby. There might have been a baby, but there's nothing now, nothing at all."

"It was aborted?" Max's voice was very soft.

"I told you, there is no baby."

Julian stood rigidly. "If you tell me he agreed to abort his child then you're lying again."

"Ah," Liz said, "he was so thoughtful of humanity, so concerned, so loving, so giving. . . ." She turned away from them.

"You haven't answered me," Julian said.

"I know," Max said softly, "that you wanted his child."

"You don't know very much." Liz found a cigarette in the onyx box and hesitated before lighting it. The night she had told Cy the rabbit's results, she had reached toward the same box and he had stopped her hand with a kiss.

Hold it—you'll give the kid a habit!

Oh my. You're right. Only health food from now on and clean living. I can have champagne, though.

Cy had grinned, taken her in his arms, put his hand on her belly.

I feel it. I can feel the life.

You cannot.

But she had loved his saying it.

Oh yes, I can feel it go right through me. What a wonderful feeling.

She lit the cigarette and pulled the smoke deep into her lungs. Max looked at Julian uneasily. Julian scowled.

"Oh God," she said and turned away.

"You haven't given us any direct answers," Julian said.

She whirled on them. "Direct? I wanted that baby. Is that direct enough for you? I wanted a baby—*and he deprived me of it!*"

It was a wild cry, springing from some pounding heart chamber.

"He *what*?" Julian's eyes opened wide.

"It was his fault."

Julian was stunned. "He deprived you? How did he deprive you?" There was a grating buzz from the intercom. Liz went to it. Julian whispered to Max, "She's crazy."

"Rich told me she had this breakdown . . ." Max watched Liz with a deepening sorrow. A slight nausea attacked him. "I'll be right back," he told Julie and started to the bathroom. He heard Liz speak to the suspicious desk man downstairs. ". . . no, no, it's all right. These men are . . . I know them."

The bathroom was pink marble and had petaled wallpaper. He stared at himself in the mirror and saw that he was pale. A bubble of air came rising up and he burped. Spittle dribbled from his lips. He looked about for a tissue but saw none. Gingerly, he opened a drawer below the mirror and poked about. There was a box of tissues to the left and he pulled one up. It was recalcitrant and he pulled harder to release it. The box moved as he did and a small bulletlike object, half-hidden behind it, caught his eye. He reached over and picked it up. It seemed familiar, and with a shock of recognition he saw the name SLICK-ERS on the tube. He looked again. The letters came up at him. He twisted the top, revealing the creamy lip gloss. The nausea vanished. Liz Evers had told Shamski she never used Slickers. Puzzled, worried, suspicion flailing at him, he quickly closed the top and dropped the lip gloss into his jacket pocket. Then he went back out.

14

In the elevator, on the way down, though the tube of Slickers burned a hole in his pocket, Max hesitated in telling Julian of the discovery. He gave himself no reason for holding off but he knew that the sight of Liz Evers so distraught, so destroyed, stirred great pity in him. Julian had none.

"She's lying somewhere," Berns pronounced grimly. "How could Cy have deprived her of a baby? On the other hand, if she's crazy enough to say that, she's crazy enough to have been the woman with him that night and shoved him over."

"It's a possibility," Max replied guiltily, fingering the tube.

He kept the discovery from Shamski also, rationalizing the withholding as temporary. Liz Evers could well have been in the apartment, as Julian suggested, and pushed Cy over in a fit of rage, but there was so much mystery in what she had said, such contradiction about Cy, that Max longed to talk to her openly about it. He searched his mind for ways to make that happen and had the notion that the tube of Slickers might provide a wedge. When he reported to Shamski he simply omitted the find, telling himself he would not keep it from him for long.

As they left the diner, which by now had become their safe house, the detective said, almost casually, "Oh, we found out another funny thing, a couple of days ago."

"About what?"

"Your buddy Catalfo. One of Morrisey's guys has been keeping track of him and he was supposed to be out of town, in St. Louis, on a big real estate deal, while you were in Colorado. But where do you think he really was?"

Max stared at Shamski. "Are you telling me—?"

"Yup. He was in Aspen. We got it from a switch in airline tickets. For twenty-four hours. He left the same day you did. I'm surprised you weren't on the same plane." He grinned. "That Stratton woman must have had something special."

"What are you doing about it?" Max demanded.

"Trying to get the Aspen police to cooperate. There were some partial prints on the rib cartons, it turns out, but they say they're blurred. We say, Send us pictures anyway. They say, 'Uh-huh,' but so far nothing's come."

The rest of the day was equally frustrating. Two stocks he had bought went sour and the loss was substantial. Lang chose that afternoon to call, and when Max reported the fiasco, Lang was curt. The bad streak went on for days, and the prospect of reporting further losses was unnerving. Julian kept calling, wanting to know what the police were doing about Liz. Workmen came in, finally, to repair the office, and Max's refuge became a hell of dust and noise. He stayed in the apartment, working from there, feeling claustrophobic, trapped and desperate. His dreams became images of Lang's face alternating with quivering female breasts, of Brigado's cold eyes and heaving female buttocks. He called Sonya and said he would like to come up for a weekend, but it turned out she was going north. Still, if he wanted to use her house— He thanked her, miserable, and said another time, maybe. The next night, sitting in the half-darkened living room, his pulse quickening, he called Carol.

"Hi, it's Max Roberts. I was just sitting here wondering how things were with you after all this time."

"I'm good. You good?" Carol's voice was flat.

"Me? Fine, really fine."

"Good."

"You . . . busy?"

"You mean right now? It's almost midnight."

"I know." He fumbled for the words. "I just thought . . .

I just thought you might . . . like some company for the late show."

"The late show?"

"Or something." He hung over the phone, aware there was a pleading quality in his voice. Carol hesitated. "Oh well," she finally said, "sure . . . come on over."

In the cab, turning constantly to the rear window to check for a tail, Max told himself this was wrong, ridiculous, bad. But his excitement and need were undeniable. He came into Carol's apartment tingling. She was wearing a long red caftan, bare toes peeking out. Her eyes were guarded. She fetched a bottle of white wine. They bantered about the late show, about television, about the SEC's latest crackdown on insider trading. It was hollow talk and they were both aware of it, both waiting, both feeling the strain. It broke with a rush as Max took her in his arms. In minutes they were on the floor.

It was an hour of urgency, of animal thrusts, no speech, no gentleness. Max was over her body, moving, probing, breath rasping in his throat. Carol was more passive. Her eyes watched him, her pelvis responded, but almost in sympathy. Her hands smoothed his hair and her lips pressed close to his temple. After the hour, he lay at her side, on his back, drained, disgusted with himself.

"Listen," he finally brought himself to say, "I know how it seems." She said nothing and he went on, apologetically, "I'm a little shook up these days."

Carol sat up on the floor. "And I'm fine, I'm just fine." She seemed almost ready to cry.

Max sat up quickly. "I'm sorry, honestly."

Carol pulled her hands across her eyes determinedly and rose to her feet, pulling the caftan down. "It's all right. I'm just securing my reputation. Easy—very."

"No," Max said, "it's not like that."

"All right, talk to me, then—say something meaningful."

There was nothing he could say. "Then I won't either," Carol flashed. "I damn well won't. If the late show is over, you can go now." She left the room. Max waited fifteen minutes, confused and unhappy, then pulled himself together and slunk out of the apartment.

The following day, at four in the afternoon, still thinking of the previous night, Max left the office. The moment he stepped out onto the still glaring pavement a chill swept across his skin.

Behind a bus-stop enclosure he caught a glimpse of an unmistakable face. It was the thin-faced man who had been at the Tunnel restaurant. Half screened by the billboard, he was unquestionably looking in Max's direction.

Instantly, Max decided to go to a bar across the street and sit there. If the man followed, he would wait him out. Setting his face in what he thought was a relaxed expression, he ambled off in the downtown direction. Ten yards away was a jewelry shop. He stopped there and shopped the window. The angle of reflection allowed him to look back, and he was able to see that the man had moved out from behind the bus stop's protection and was now halted at a shoe store. Max walked farther down the avenue and halted again at a haberdasher's. When he snatched a glance to his left, his tail was at the jewelry shop. Max moved again, and from the corner of his eye was able to see his pursuer step out as well. Max started to cross the street, but a taxi cut in front of him, slowing to the curb. Max edged back onto the sidewalk and decided to walk on farther. He had taken only a few steps, when, from behind him, a loud, staccato chattering erupted. Startled, Max turned back toward the sound. As he did, he saw shop-window glass shattering, spewing out daggerlike shards. The air swished violently over his head, and Max realized with astonishment that bullets were zinging by. Instinctively, he dived to the pavement. All around him terrified screams and shouts rose up.

Up and down the length of the street, people ran, flung themselves prone, sought refuge in doorways, as the ripping sounds continued and ejected shells pinged to the concrete. Max scrambled away frantically. They had decided to eliminate him. Like Cy. Creeping, twisting, crawling, Max managed to reach a telephone pole and, crouching behind it, raised his head. From there, he saw that two wild-eyed men had emerged from the taxi, both holding small machine pistols, but they were not looking in his direction. One of them, wearing a somehow incongruous Panama hat, had been hit by someone else's fire, and, under Max's eyes, he collapsed, his pistol falling from his hands. The other assassin jumped back into the taxi and it sped off crazily. Only then did Max see that the thin-faced man who had been following him was lying on the ground, blood pumping from his chest, an automatic still clutched in his lifeless hand.

By now, a police cruiser, siren blaring, lights whirling, was coming up the one-way avenue the wrong way, dodging cars.

Before it stopped, two uniformed police, guns in hand, leaped from it, running to the fallen men. Two other police cars were behind them. In minutes, uniforms and detectives filled the street. Max rose, staring in horrified fascination. An ambulance came charging over to add more sound and confusion. The men in plain clothes fanned out to question the shaken pedestrians rising to their feet. One woman slumped hysterically and the medics gave her an injection. Before the police could get to him, Max backed away.

By six P.M., Shamski had gotten preliminary reports of the gunning, coroner's estimations, and identifications of the dead men.

"They weren't after you," he told Max. "It's a mob hit."

"I guess I'm lucky," Max said sourly.

Morrisey laughed. "Lucky you didn't get your keester into the crossfire. Those guys were using nineteen-shot pieces."

"The good news about this," Shamski said, "is your identification of the guy who was tailing you. He's a bozo named Mendito and he's worked in the past with the Medellín group. Those are Colombian combine people and we had no idea they were connecting with Brigado. The other guy . . . well," he shrugged, "we don't have a make on him yet but it looks like a typical takeover try."

Max hardly listened. The afternoon had drained him. "All I want to know," he said wearily, "is when is this going to end?"

"Hang in just a little while longer," Shamski cajoled.

"And if I want to get out," Max asked, "they let me, don't they? I just walk away from everything and you give me twenty-four-hour protection for the rest of my life, right?"

That night there was no sleep. He was trapped. Cy had trapped him. Could Borland, that putz, been halfway right? Could Cy have suspected that Morey's was not what it appeared to be? Tossing and turning, he held a dialogue with the shadows.

What the hell did you think you were doing—Jesus, Cy!

Max—Max, things got out of hand, that's all. It happens.

But dope? Cy—dope? Did you know?

He finally fell asleep as first light was creeping through the blinds, but woke again less than an hour later, brain numbed. He showered himself to some semblance of consciousness and was desultorily getting dressed when the phone rang. He answered it and was greeted by the hushed tones of Juli Singh, Jimmy's wife. She was in such fear she could hardly speak.

"Please, sir, please. Help him, please."

Max became instantly alert. "Help who?"

"Husband. He is so sick. He does things, he . . . he makes a promise, he does not say."

"What—what doesn't he say?"

"Oh—" she ended in a groan, "never we should have come here."

"Tell me what he doesn't say—tell me."

Her voice became even lower, a low moan in her throat. "You must not tell him I speak to you, sir—oh—oh." The phone clicked off.

The borough of Queens is another country. Once across the river from Manhattan, the vast richness of the world's populations is displayed. They are all here, and there is no melting in this Queens pot. Each nation occupies its own neighborhood, is neatly sealed off by common consent from the next.

The Indians occupy a corner of the borough only thirty-five minutes by subway from Manhattan's golden towers, but the smell of Calcutta and Delhi is in the autumn air. Here, the women on the street wear their glossy black hair in the long braids of their native villages and the diamond in their nostril fold. Juli Singh, huge-eyed, birdlike, was that way. She wore something that resembled a sari, but underneath it the faded legs of her blue jeans stuck out incongruously. She stared at Max worriedly as he stood in the doorway and all she could say was "You have come, oh—oh." Max asked if he could come in and she held the door open wordlessly. When he was inside, she hissed, "He is here," and gestured down the hallway.

Uncertainly, Max walked down the hall, which held three cheaply framed prints of Indian dancers. There was a closed door to his right and the sound of a toilet flushing came from behind it. Softly, Max called, "Jimmy?"

There was no answer and no further sound. "Jimmy," Max called again, "are you there?" He waited but there was no response. He rapped on the door. "Jimmy?"

Silence.

Tentatively, Max turned the doorknob and pushed the door open. It was a small bathroom with a closed window facing another building across the street. Singh was not in sight. Puz-

244

zled, Max paused. He went to the window. It was locked in place. Turning back, he saw that the shower curtain, drawn completely around the tub, was fluttering slightly. He reached out a hand and drew the purple plastic aside. Standing in the tub in blue undershorts, arms crossed over a hairless chest, his face screwed up in fright, was Jimmy Singh. At the sight of Max, he recoiled.

"Jimmy," Max said, "take it easy. No one's going to hurt you."

Singh tugged at his shorts. "Why are you here, Mr. Max, surprising me like this? I am not well, not at all well." He did not move from the tub.

"Jimmy," Singh was obviously terrified and Max tried to keep his voice gentle. "Come on out of there. I just want to talk to you."

"My doctor says to take baths, you see, many baths."

"With your shorts on?"

Singh blinked, swallowed hard, and said in a choked voice, "It is so bad—so bad, I cannot go on like this, you see."

"Come on out." Max extended his hand. Singh grasped it and came out of the tub, shivering. Max handed him a green towel, which he put around his shoulders. Singh groaned, misery plain.

"I am falling apart. I am not made to do this."

"Do what? Just tell me."

"Mr. Cy makes me swear I keep everything secret."

"From me?"

"Yes, from you."

Max held himself tight. "Tell me."

Singh shook his head. "Cannot."

"You have to."

Singh wiped his face with the towel. "It—it is like this. The business was losing much money."

"That's crazy," Max said, astonished. "I know the books weren't up to date but—"

"Yes," Singh said emphatically, "a string of bad luck. And then the Morey's account comes along. Mr. Cy asks me to set up separate from the partnership, a personal matter."

Max listened with growing hurt. Had Cy set this up for his own gain—or to insulate Max from the dealings?

"Now, let me explain, sir." Singh, becoming more reassured as he spoke, became pedantic. "Mr. Cy was using money from this account to pay for the large-margin calls we were getting."

"I had no idea," Max said, bewildered, "no idea at all."

"Then one day, Mr. Cy comes and tells me he has this confidential word, from the inside." Singh shrugged. "Who does not have inside tips? He tells me that Simon Nakian is planning to take over the McIver Corporation."

McIver; the name hit Max like a blow. It was the McIver company's stock chart that Cy had left at Sonya's.

"Nakian has been secretly accumulating the stock," Singh ground on, "and owns almost three percent. So, we are now to buy, for the Morey's account, call options on McIver. The McIver stock was twenty-seven when we started buying the calls. Each call would give us the option to buy a hundred shares, of course, at that price, if and when the stock hit thirty. The calls were cheap, only half a dollar each, because the strike date, the expiration date, was only nineteen days away. So, if we held and the stock hit the thirty before expiration date, we would make twenty-five hundred for each ten calls. Of course, if the stock started to go up, the calls would be worth more too."

Max was mystified. "It's good leverage. But it's a cash operation. A thousand dollars for twenty calls? Even if he buys a thousand calls, we're putting up fifty thousand . . ."

"No, no." Singh was emphatic. "Over the nineteen days, he buys half a million dollars' worth of options."

Max was astounded. "That's impossible."

"No, he does it. It is almost all of the money in the Morey's account, you see. He does it very cleverly, through other brokers, through California, Chicago, St. Louis. He manages to do this without calling attention to the volume. He was convinced, you see, that when Nakian's offer is announced, McIver becomes a thirty-six-dollar stock and the call price goes through the roof. We make millions." Singh's eyes glowed like coals as he continued. "The question was when Nakian would make the offer. Mr. Cy's information said within six days, well within the nineteen-day expiration date. It did not happen then, but Mr. Cy is still convinced. We are to buy more. At the end of every day, I would go home shaking. It was not my money, but I felt this bad Karma over my head. I could not even have intercourse with my wife, and I obey all the religious laws in this regard."

"Why didn't you come to me," Max demanded angrily. "You should have come to me."

"Please," Singh pleaded, "I knew it was not regular. You know how I cannot abide things that are not regular, but Mr. Cy said I was to keep it all secret; it was most important to keep it all secret. Life or death, he said, life or death." He wiped away the sweat that was beginning to stand out on his dark temples. "I became constipated. I always felt unclean. My children brought home good report cards and I said nothing. Nothing," he repeated bitterly. "Then suddenly, nine days before expiration, the McIver stock went up, it went up to twenty-eight, then twenty-nine and thirty. Rumors are all around. So the options went to one and a quarter—then to one and a half when the stock goes higher. Now Nakian makes the buyout offer and we have a triple, three times what we paid. Fantastic. Get out, I say to him—Mr. Cy, I said, all is treachery on the Street, we know that. One must snatch what one can. He says wait. It is now only four days before the call options expire, but we are in the black, you see. I am delirious. Then . . ."

"Jesus," Max said, remembering.

"Miserable. Miserable." Singh, wiping, mopping, relived it. "I begged Mr. Cy. I told him, but he was resolute—like the Himalayas—unyielding. It was painful. It would go to thirty-five and over, he said, in twenty-four hours. The call would zoom and he would have not only a triple—not only a fantastic triple—he would have an eight or a nine or a ten. I went near to madness. Those numbers. Even on a calculator, they look unreal. I could not eat my Juli's cooking. Even her special vindaloo was nothing to me. I cried in the toilet. She told me I had another woman and wanted to know the color of her skin. I struck her. Then it was two-thirty, on the Wednesday before," Singh mourned, "and the tape reported the offer withdrawn because of no agreement. Withdrawn. Ay. The stock went like a stone, Mr. Max, like a shark pulling a man under—swift, down. From thirty-two to thirty-one to thirty, to twenty-nine and a half by the bell. I was nauseated. I threw up in the gents'." He discarded the soaked tissue and snatched up another. " 'Go out,' " I pleaded, " 'your option stands an eighth lower than the buy. Run.' " His slight body sagged against the washbasin. "He said it was a ploy. It would come zooming back the next day."

But it had not, of course, Max remembered. The impersonal sellers, the dealers, the arbitrage people sold out. By three o'clock of that crazed Friday, the stock had gone down to twenty-six, the option had become worthless; Cy's investment, Morey's money.

"That afternoon," Singh's voice quavered, "I make a telephone call but Martha puts me on Mr. Cy's line by mistake. I hear him telling somebody about the loss, arguing with them, saying he will make it back for them. The other man is very angry. He says too much money has disappeared, something must be wrong, he cannot get away with this. He hangs up. When Mr. Cy comes out of his office, he looks sick."

Lang, Max knew; Lang, of course. And later that night, men in Panama hats had come to balance the books. Singh sat down on the toilet seat. "I am having cramps again." His wife appeared in the doorway, looking in. "Go away," Singh shouted. She fled. "That woman called you, did she not?" Max nodded. "Miserable woman." Singh sighed. "The trading records. I have them, you know."

Max was surprised. "But they're not in the computer."

"No," Singh admitted. "I took the backup disks after we deleted the records from the hard disk. He told me to do that," he added quickly, "Mr. Cy."

Would they, Max wondered, reveal anything on the laundry network, who securities might be assigned to, what banks, what companies? Did it matter? Shamski would want them, Max thought grudgingly, and he asked Singh to get them. "Yes," Singh agreed, "but I do not have them in the house here. To keep them safe I bring them to my cousin Anand. He is a dentist in Ferndale—that is up in the state, very pretty there. He has a good practice. I ask him to hold them for me."

"Well, get them as soon as you can."

"Yes, Mr. Max, yes. Oh—my stomach," Singh moaned, "I am being punished."

"Me too," Max said in sympathy. "Take it easy. When he left, Singh in his blue shorts and green towel, grimacing, waved a doleful good-bye and closed the bathroom door.

Max rushed back to the office to call Shamski, who wasn't in. Restless, he wandered the office, aimlessly watching the Quotron, and waited for the detective's call. Singh had put a final piece of the puzzle in place. Poor, damned Cy, Max groaned, imagining how he must have felt when the takeover failed and the deal collapsed.

The phone rang. Max called, "I'll take it," but Martha was already on it. In moments, she clicked to announce a call from a Mr. Lang.

Max panicked. "Lang?" His first impulse was to have Martha say he was out. Instantly he knew it was futile—and dangerous. He took the call.

Lang's voice was very tight. "I want to see you at ten o'clock tomorrow morning. At the Tunnel."

"Oh? Well, I'm looking at my calendar," Max said desperately, "and I have a meeting at ten."

"You be there." Lang bit his words off. "Ten o'clock sharp.' The connection broke, leaving Max upright in his chair. Where could he go? Russia? China?

15

The diner's fluorescent beer sign buzzed like an angry, electrified bee. Some of the truckers were just finishing a late lunch and the smell of meat loaf in the air, plus the overburdened air-conditioner thumping and rasping, added to the strain as Max sat sullenly listening to Shamski reason things out. "Singh's dope tells me that Brigado was p.o.'d at Bannerman. Dealers always have rip-offs on their mind. My hunch is that after they made an example of your partner, they tried to blow up your office with that package bomb and destroy the trading records, get rid of everything."

Borland, looking out of place in the diner, salivated at the prospect of recovering the records. The idea of looking at data, solid numbers, solid names, was orgasmic. "But this Singh has committed a serious crime," he said severely, "by removing those records. He is not to be trusted. I want someone with him when he goes to get them. He might tamper."

"He'll bring them back," Max said. "Let him alone. The man's a wreck. Any more trouble and he'll go off the deep end."

"Those records are all important," Borland persisted. "They are not to be put at risk."

"How about me?" Max asked. "You damn well aren't interested in that, are you? You weren't there on the street with those guns. Or in the office when the bomb went off. Now let me tell you what I'm going to do about Lang's call—nothing. I'm out of it, as of now. The thing for you to do is go there and arrest him."

"Thanks for telling me my business." Shamski was sharp. "I do that and I get nowhere. Now, here's what I think—"

Max was defiant. "It's too much, it's just too much."

"I thought," Borland said, transparently oversolicitous, "that you wanted to find your partner's killers."

"You know who it is," Max exclaimed. "Brady, Brigado—Lang."

"There's very little," Shamski said calmly, "very little hard. We need the connections. We go to the D.A. with you and you talk about Brady, that's only talk—unverified. If Lang clams up, and he will, it's zilch."

"I can't help that." Max was adamant. "Dammit, I have a life to live."

"Listen to me," Shamski said. "Lang's calling you like this has something to do with what happened, the street shooting, I know it does."

Max had no idea what he was talking about.

"I told you once we needed a break. Maybe we can get it here." Shamski looked at Max peculiarly. "What I'd like you to do is go see Lang tomorrow morning, and—"

"No."

"Hear me out. You go to that meeting with Lang and—"

"And what?"

"And," Shamski concluded, "you wear a wire on you."

"Wear a what?"

"A wire," Borland explained, "a miniature transmitter."

"Whatever is said, we record on tape," Shamski added.

Max stared at him, amazed.

Shamski went on. "So we can get whatever he says on record, something solid, not just what you say he said but his own words. And maybe you can even get him to talk about Brigado. You call him Brady, though . . ."

"You're crazy." Max started to get up. "You're both gone."

Shamski put out a restraining hand. "Let me finish."

Borland echoed, "Yes—let him finish."

"Believe me," Shamski said, "the odds are he doesn't think you'd do this."

"No? Maybe he knows what I've been doing and the meeting is to get me there and then . . ."

"No," Shamski interrupted. "Because if he knows we're hooked up, he also knows we'd protect you at any meet he called, so it's not that."

There was some kind of logic there, Max agreed, but he had drawn a line. What Shamski was suggesting was so far beyond that . . .

"We'll be in a truck outside, monitoring everything," Shamski explained. "If there's the slightest problem, we'll move in and bust him. But if there's none—and we get anything on tape, you could break it wide open, Roberts. Otherwise, you tell me." He sipped his pale coffee. Borland sipped his lemonade anxiously and both men watched Max carefully.

As astonished as Max was, he considered. If his doing this would break it open, as Shamski said, end the insanity. . . . He tried to work his way through the possibilities, the danger.

"Could Lang tell I was wearing this . . . thing?"

"No way," Shamski said. "Not unless he took off your shirt."

It seemed so far out, but the notion of trapping Lang and the others this way held a curious attraction. "How does it work?" Max asked hesitantly. "What do I have to do?"

That night, just in case, Max called Adeline. She reported a heat wave in Miami. Senior citizens were advised to stay indoors, close to the air-conditioners. "So all they have to do is talk about the stock market, about CDs and mutual funds and the big crooks. It drives me crazy. Thank God I never told anybody what you do. Are you all right?"

He told her he was fine but thought *her* breath came in gasps.

"I just came off my bicycle," she explained. "The dial says I went thirty miles in thirty minutes, but I think there must be something wrong with it; I couldn't go so fast. I could be seeing you soon," she added, surprising him."

"How come?"

"I got a letter in the mail, Max, about a reunion—some of

the old group in the Bronx coops, the Kropotkin Bund. I'm maybe going to go."

That would be a reunion, Max thought. Old arguments, old dreams, old promises. "Let me know."

"You're still at Cy's?"

"For the time being, yes."

Adeline's voice grew softer. "You miss him?"

"In a way, and in another way I . . ." He broke off, uncomfortable with the direct question.

"His house is not your house, Max."

"Adeline, my place has been painted—it's not back together yet."

The conversation induced a mood of melancholy. Standing on the terrace later, the sky dark and autumnal, Max stared at the repaired railing and tried not to think about the next day. For a swift second he thought of Carol, but banished her quickly from his mind. Instead, he switched on Cy's computer to ramble through some games, and ended up staring hard at a piece of a letter entry from Cy to Liz Evers that he had seen once before. It held new meaning now.

> . . . the confusing thing is that what one believes in the abstract sometimes comes face to face with an operating reality. And then one sees how the belief is totally abstract, and the reality is the actual . . . With us now, that's the case—

Max shut the machine off, sat in front of the blank screen pensively, and, feeling remarkably calm, went to bed.

At seven-thirty the next morning, as instructed, Max appeared at a seedy office building in the west Twenties. There, he took an elevator to the twelfth floor, where the offices of "Millikin Factors Inc." were located. Standing before the office door, Max had the urge to turn around and run down the staircase. Instead, he rang the buzzer. The door opened almost instantly, and Max saw what appeared to be an ordinary windowless office. He also saw Detective Morrisey, who greeted him with a big smile. "Morning. Hey, don't we all work early? This here's Larry Kovoni." He indicated a serious-looking middle-aged man with bad teeth and a receding hairline who was in shirtsleeves and held a number of small boxes. "Kov's the expert." Kovoni nodded and proceeded to stow the boxes away into a filing cabinet. Morrisey closed the door, which clicked shut with a double lock.

"I thought Shamski would be here," Max said uncertainly.

"He's going to be at the stakeout on Eleventh," Morrisey explained and nodded to the expert. "Wire him up."

Kovoni opened the filing cabinet and withdrew a small oblong box. "The jacket and shirt come off," he said in a professional tone. Max removed his jacket and pulled the tennis shirt off over his head. Kovoni frowned. "I like long sleeves."

"You're going to come inside the jacket anyway, aren't you?" Morrisey declared. "So what's the dif?"

"Yeah. I just like long sleeves, that's all." He held up the small black box for Max's inspection. "This is the transmitter. It's like a miniature radio, OK? Two inches by two inches by a quarter of an inch. See how light it is." He placed it in Max's hand. "Model-C-four-seven-two," Kovoni intoned. "Three and a half ounces. It's got a quarter-mile range, though, with a strong signal. You hold it here." He placed the transmitter in the center of Max's bare chest. Max pressed it to him. Under Morrisey's watchful eye, Kovoni proceeded to secure the box with one-inch surgical tape, the winding encircling Max, chest to back. "Too tight?"

"No." Max felt oddly disembodied, as though all this were happening to someone else. Kovoni touched a tiny button on the transmitter he had left exposed. "This powers it up. You get into your shirt and press it, like fifteen minutes before the meet. It's automatic from then on." He plugged a tiny wire into a miniature port. "This is for the mike. Now let's see." He scrutinized his handiwork.

"Just go up his shoulder," Morrisey suggested, "through the short sleeve, and into the inside pocket on his coat—what's the big deal?"

"That's what I'm doing," Kovoni said. He told Max to put his shirt back on. Max did, then checked his chest area. The transmitter made a surprisingly small bulge.

"And when your jacket goes on top," Morrisey reassured him, "it can't get made, believe me."

"I hope you're right," Max said grimly.

Kovoni threaded the microphone wire up Max's left sleeve and out. Next, from the filing cabinet, he produced a tiny, perforated disk, half an inch in diameter and almost perfectly flat.

"This is your mike, a beauty, all-directional, high sensitivity." He snapped it on to the wire. "Now, put your jacket on." Max obeyed. Kovoni secured the mike wire to Max's sleeve with a safety pin and, pulling it down toward Max's inside jacket pocket, placed the microphone into the pocket itself. "Button the jacket now." He took a step back to contemplate his handiwork. Max buttoned his jacket and patted the pocket region. He could hardly feel the microphone.

"Look in the mirror," Morrisey said. "You're beautiful." He swung open a closet door and Max saw a full-length glass on the inside. He looked at himself and saw nothing unusual. He unbuttoned the jacket.

"Sit down." Kovoni put a chair under him and Max sat, still staring at his image. Nothing bulged; nothing looked strange.

"Let's test out," Kovoni said, opening a filing-cabinet drawer.

"Press the start button," Morrisey told Max. Max reached inside his shirt, feeling first the tight band and then the tiny button. He pressed it, expecting some sound, but there was nothing. Morrisey stood over him. "So, like I was saying," he whispered, "this is one of the best wires ever made. Don't you think so? Say something."

Feeling foolish, Max said, "Yes, it's one of the best wires ever made."

Kovoni poked about in the filing cabinet and Max heard first Morrisey's voice and then his own in a perfect tape reproduction.

"Shut it down." Morrisey smiled broadly. "You're wired."

Max reached in once again and pressed the button, then he rose from the chair. "What do I do now?"

"Get him to talk," Morrisey said. "The more he says, the more we'll have."

A flicker of nausea attacked Max as the reality began to assert itself. He looked at his watch. A quarter of nine. He had over an hour. He would wait at his office. Morrisey patted him on the shoulder. "Hey, it's going to be all right. We'll be in a green van with the name 'Lindy Movers' on it."

"I'll just get going," Max said.

"Excuse me, Mr. Roberts," Kovoni called to him. Max turned. "I understand you're in the market. Got any suggestions?"

Max looked at Morrisey, who grinned. "Hey, cops have mortgages to pay too."

"Buy U.S. treasury bonds," Max said. "The Japanese do."

THE THIRD FRIDAY

Downstairs, the lobby held a dozen people waiting for elevators. Max threaded his way through, the weightless transmitter a hundred-pound burden on his chest, the hidden microphone shining out through his jacket pocket like an incriminating beacon. He had the feeling that everyone knew what he carried and he tried to shut out of his mind what would happen an hour from now.

In the office, Max tested. He lifted his left arm and felt the slight rustle of wire. He studied himself in the shaded window reflection. His inside pocket, it seemed to him now, bulged out. He called Martha in. When she faced him, he stood before her and raised his hands. "I haven't worn this jacket for a long time. How do you think it looks on me?"

Taken by surprise, Martha said, "Looks fine."

Max waved his hands in the air. "Doesn't bulge out any-place?"

"No more than usual," Martha said, mystified. "Is it a special jacket or something?"

"No," Max said quickly. "I have this appointment and I want to look good for it, that's all."

He's going a little off the deep end, Martha thought, and ascribed it to strain. The phone rang and she skipped back to her desk to answer it. Max, concerned still with the jacket, only half heard her.

"Oh—I see. . . . I'll tell him, yes."

Martha came back in. "That was your Mr. Lang."

Max came instantly alert.

"Your ten o'clock is changed to half past one."

"What?" It was a cry of dismay.

"Gee, he didn't even want to talk to you—just wanted to leave the message."

Max contained himself until Martha went back to her desk, then, closing the door behind her, he sat, shaken. A delay. What had gone wrong? He took a minute to collect himself, then called Shamski to report the change. The detective heard the tension in his voice and said, "It may not mean a damn thing. It may just be more convenient for him, that's all. Listen, it's dangerous to let your imagination run away with you." He talked soothingly for five minutes, but Max felt no better at the end of the conversation than before. Hours to go—hours, and all wired up.

He battled the funk engulfing him. He made busywork. At eleven the mail came in. A note from the bank on his overdrafts, trade confirmations, invitations to buy insurance, an expensive handout from the Brokers' Association announcing their annual bash at the Space disco. The headline read COME AND PICK UP YOUR SEXY STOCKS. It all seemed relievingly normal. When Julian called just to touch base, Max suggested an early lunch. Julian was agreeable, and at a quarter to twelve Max left for the restaurant. Soon, trying to ignore the restraining wires and tape, he was seated opposite Berns, amused by one of his Alloway stories.

"—so Alloway says to me that the stock market keeps America strong. Like Russia has no stock market so it'll never get anywhere, would you believe?" He speared a shrimp. "I've been thinking about Cy lately—and Liz Evers."

"Julie, Cy was involved in something . . . complicated," Max said. The shrimp stopped a centimeter from Julian's mouth.

"Where'd you get that—the SEC?"

"Singh," Max said. "Singh has Cy's trading records."

Julian's eyes opened wide. "You said there weren't any."

"He has them," Max repeated. "He's getting them. Some of them involve McIver Corporation. Remember the chart I gave you?"

"Yes. So what else do they have?" Excited by the development, Julian reached over to the shrimp sauce, but his hand pushed the dish, toppling it. A stream of yellow gushed out, and despite Max's quick push backward, a spray of viscous liquid settled on his jacket and shirt front. He looked down, shocked.

"Gee, I'm sorry," Julie said.

He lifted his napkin toward Max, who jerked back even more, loudly saying, "No!"

"Put some water on it—cold water," Julie said, chagrined.

"Dammit," Max snapped, standing up. He threw his napkin down and walked rapidly to the men's room.

The washroom was small with two stalls. Luckily, no one was in the place. Max examined the damage in the mirror. There were definite, conspicuous yellow spots on the jacket and shirt. How could he meet Lang this way? Perhaps they would come out with cold water. If not, he would have to race back to Cy's and change. But how could he, wired up as he was? Telling himself to keep calm, he ripped a long span of hand-drying paper from the dispenser, wet it thoroughly, and went into a stall, locking it. There, he carefully removed the microphone and tucked it into his belt. Without disturbing anything else, he

258

managed to extract his right hand from the jacket sleeve and, with it, proceeded to soak the soiled spots in a stroking motion. He worked feverishly, vigorously rubbing and soaking for the next few minutes until the yellow disappeared and was replaced by water stains. At least, he thought, it's less conspicuous. As he was balling up the paper, he heard the outside door open and froze. Quickly, he flushed the paper down the toilet, slipped the jacket back on, smoothed it, and came out of the stall. Julian was there, about to go into the other one. "Did you do any good with the stains?"

"Somewhat," Max said, and then saw that Julian was staring at him, perplexed. Max looked down at the already drying water stains, looked back up at the quizzical Julian, and became conscious of something dangling at his waist below his jacket. With an icy rush, he realized it was the forgotten button microphone, which had come loose from his belt and was now swinging by its umbilical. At this moment, the door opened again. Julian looked back to it as a whistling young man came in. Max reached down swiftly, grabbed the mike, and shoved it into his pants' pocket, making certain the wire didn't show. When the young man went into the stall, Max went past Julian and out. Hand in his pocket, he walked purposefully to the table and sat. After a few minutes, Julian returned, and Max swiftly asked, "What were we talking about?"

"Jimmy Singh," Julian said, his eyes asking questions.

"That's right, Jimmy—well, we'll see." Max brushed fingers nervously against the damp spots. "You know something, Julie, I'm not hungry. But you go ahead."

"I'm not hungry either," Julie said, his eyes still holding Max's. "Not at all."

In the cab, making certain he wasn't observed, Max took the microphone from his pants' pocket and, carefully pulling the wire up, replaced it in his inside jacket pocket. He pressed the start button and waited. As in the office, there was no sound. But, anxiously, it occurred to him that he might have hurt the system by taking it down. And if that had happened, this was all for nothing. Worse, he had no way of knowing. He bent his head down to his chest and muttered, as close to his breast pocket as he could get, "Testing, testing, Roberts, testing, damn you all." He sat back, closed his eyes, and took deep breaths. Julian had seen the mike but had not asked questions, though he had obviously wanted to. Max was grateful. He had enough

259

to deal with as it was. He looked down at the damp spots and saw with relief that they were drying; at least that.

He left the cab two blocks from the Tunnel restaurant. The air was thick with humidity, making it hard to breathe. He checked his watch—one twenty-five. A Latin hooker, white hot pants showing off long, shapely legs, waggled her shoulders at him and called provocatively, "Hey, honey, you wanna make chic-achica-boom-boom?" Not until Max passed her did he realize, from the shadow on her cheeks, that she was a transvestite. He kept walking, his eyes darting, searching for Shamski's people in the Lindy Movers van. It wasn't on the avenue and as he approached the Tunnel, he grew more and more apprehensive. Coming up to the entrance, he hesitated, looked around the corner, across the street, down the street, but it was not to be seen. "Where the hell are you?" he muttered and loitered for a minute more, hoping against hope that the van would swing around and park, but it did not.

Throat scratchy, body taut, the band around his chest, which before had been almost unfelt, now constricting the air from his lungs, Max could not delay any longer. In he went. The restaurant was half filled with diners, their chatter mingling with the throb of light pop from ceiling speakers. He walked directly to the table behind the plants and, as he knew he would be, Lang was there. He wore a severe expression and Max's constrictions worsened. Lang pointed to a chair and said, "Sit down, we're on a schedule." Max sat. Lang studied him for a full minute and Max felt his eyes boring in on the still-visible water stains and prayed nothing else showed. The minute stretched to two, stretching Max's nerves as well.

He decided to be bold. "Listen, I know I've lost out on some trades, but over all—"

"We need you to do something else for us," Lang interrupted. "Today. In exactly half an hour. Are you listening?"

Max nodded. Lang leaned forward, lowering his voice. "When you leave here, you go directly to the Second Mercantile Bank, where you have our company trading account. You go in and ask to see Mr. Carl Clemmons. You have a perfect right to see him because he's your account executive there. He's a vice-president of the bank and has an office behind the cages. He will be expecting you. Is that clear so far?"

"Yes," Max said, "but why am I—"

"Just listen to me," Lang hissed sharply, his own strain

evident. "Under the table, there is a large Gladstone bag." Instinctively, Max's eyes went down. Lang's voice rose. "Don't look down." Max looked back up. "When you leave here, you just reach under and take the bag with you. It's not light; it has some weight to it. You take this to the bank. When Clemmons comes out to see you, you tell him you're on your way to the airport but you wanted to discuss the account. He will ask you to follow him to his office. In his office he'll take the bag from you for a few minutes and then give it back. You'll leave then, and that's it."

A delivery, Max thought, stunned. He was to make some kind of a delivery. Lang saw the hesitancy in his eyes and said, "There's nothing to worry about. Someone else was supposed to do this but there's been a . . . change of circumstance. And it's perfectly natural for you to go to the bank. You'll be compensated for the errand, if that's what's on your mind."

Was Shamski hearing this, Max wondered? What was he supposed to do about it? He tried to think clearly; they had said to get Lang to talk. "I'm sure you'll take care of me," he said awkwardly. "Mr. Brady knows I'm not in it for fun and games."

Lang looked away. Max tried again. "But when we talked about things in Aspen, Mr. Brady never mentioned this kind of a job."

Lang swung back. "You should leave in a few minutes."

"OK." Max reached out a tentative foot and felt the solid outlines of a suitcase under the draped tablecloth. "By the way, did my partner go to see Mr. Brady the way I did?"

Lang was annoyed. "That's a dumb question."

"I'm just curious, that's all."

"You are, yes." Lang's eyes were cold. "It's time to get going."

Disappointed, Max reached down. His hand touched butter-smooth leather and found a handle. He rose and pulled at the same time. The bag came up with him, but it took surprising effort. It was tan, oversized. The sides puffed out and the brass lock was clipped shut. Lang's eyes narrowed at Max. "You go right to the bank, no detours, understand?"

"I'm on my way." Holding the bag tightly, Max headed for the door. At the bar were two men who inspected him casually as he passed. Or was it so casual? he wondered. Why did Lang need him to do this? Because he was not known to anyone else?

Outside, he hesitated for a moment, searching once again for Shamski's van. Once again, it was not in sight. But did it have to be in sight? Morrisey said the range was a quarter of a mile. But what was he supposed to do now? The bag burned a hole in his hand. He walked across the avenue, stalling, pretending to look for a taxi. Was he supposed to actually deliver this bag? He lingered on a corner but felt conspicuous and had to move. A taxi came by and reflexively Max hailed him. As he opened the door he realized he had no option; if he did not follow Lang's orders, the game was blown.

"Second Mercantile Bank," he told the cabbie. The driver swung around, and in moments Max was heading east, the Gladstone bag on the seat beside him.

16

During the ride, Max felt the case all over, finding it stuffed to the corners. He fiddled with the sliding brass catch but it wouldn't give, and forcing it might be dangerous. There was nothing to do but sit back, try to be alert, and wait. Fifteen minutes later, he walked into the imposing Second Mercantile. Toting the Gladstone and trying hard to appear casual, he approached the service desk and asked to see Mr. Clemmons. In minutes, an open-faced, brown-haired man in a bankers' gray suit and striped tie approached with outstretched hand. "Mr. Roberts," he said easily, "nice to see you."

"Nice to see you," Max said. The desk girl was two feet away and Max continued loudly, "I'm on my way to Kennedy but I wanted to check on the account with you before I went."

"No problem," Clemmons said, earnestness oozing. "Come on into my office and I'll get the report up on the screen." He led the way past the desk, opened a door with a key, ushering Max through to a small corridor that led to a number of offices.

"Here we are." Clemmons pushed open a door bearing his

name. Max preceded him and the bank man closed the door behind him. He clicked the lock and turned to Max quickly. "Let's have it." Max handed him the suitcase. Clemmons set it on the floor, produced a small key from a vest pocket, bent down, unlocked the catch, snapped open the brass fitting, and as Max waited, pulse racing, the banker pulled apart the leather jaws, scrutinizing the contents. Max stepped over, the better to see, craned his neck, and controlled his eyes with effort. The suitcase was filled with packages of U.S. currency, thick, rubber-banded stacks of green, bundles of paper pressed together like so many invoices. Underneath the band on each parcel was a number, and Max realized it was the denomination. He saw stacks of twenty-dollar bills, stacks of fifties, of hundreds. He saw a packet marked thousands. There was no way of telling how many packages there were. They had been packed so tightly that when the bag opened they rose up like a green tide. Max was staggered; he had half expected envelopes of white powder, but this was the income, not the product

Clemmons pulled a few bundles from the top to check farther down inside. "Looks in order," he said calmly. He then hauled the Gladstone to a closet, and under Max's astonished eyes, transferred the contents to a canvas duffel bag, handling the bills as though they were so much scrap paper. He tossed the green mass in roughly, package after package. When bills dropped to the floor, he hurled them back with annoyance. "This is some load," he huffed. Finally he was done and tightened the cord on the neck of the duffel. "That's that." Kicking the duffel into a corner, he closed the closet door and handed the Gladstone back to Max. "I'll take care of it later, after hours." He smiled wryly. "I'm sure he knows to the penny how much there is. It'll be credited as coming from the Caymans." He escorted Max back out to the lobby. There, with another hearty handshake and a "Have a nice trip," the banker left him.

Stunned by what he had seen, Max left the bank. On the street, directly in front of the Second Mercantile, he saw a beat-up van with a scrawled LINDY MOVERS on the side. Max walked past it still dazed. That was coke money, crack money, pill money. Had Cy ever seen that? Lang had not answered the question. But had Cy seen that—ever? His knees weakened and he stopped walking. He leaned against a lamppost, feeling as empty as the Gladstone.

264

THE THIRD FRIDAY

* * *

Half an hour later, at the Millikin Factors office, Kovoni untaped Max's chest. "We got it all," he said, "no problem."

"Great." Shamski was enthusiastic. "He directed you to the bank loud and clear."

"He didn't answer me about Brady, though," Max reminded him.

"No, but if we squeeze him hard, he could bend. How much was there in the bag, do you think?"

"I don't know." Max tried to judge. "Half a million—a million, maybe more."

Borland, constantly making notes, said, "He's going to wait for his chance and put it into the cash vault. Then he'll fake a deposit wire from the Cayman Island bank and file it. That's brazen." He was amazed and respectful.

"They probably take the cash out of the country by plane or boat," Shamski said, "but there was a switch in plans; something happened . . . the killing on the street? Could be." He turned to Borland. "You think this Clemmons is in on it alone?"

"It's doubtful. He could have orders not to ask questions about cash deposits for that account. We're talking about a lot of transfers over a year. The bank makes interest on the overnight float on the cash. And charges commission on every transaction as well. That's profitable business. Banks need good bottom lines. Clemmons gets a nice bonus for being a productive VP. If they get caught, they claim there was a mixup in instructions, in transfers, in the paperwork."

"So what now?" Max asked quietly. "What do I do now?"

Shamski didn't hesitate. "You did what he asked. That gives him confidence you're right in there, so you keep up business as usual. We'll put someone into the bank and set up a surveillance on Clemmons. When Lang calls you for a meet, we'll take them both, and Clemmons will sing to save his neck. They always do."

"It's got to be soon," Max declared. He rubbed his chest where the removed tape had ripped out some hair. "Or I just walk away. . . ." But he knew it was a hollow threat. No one would let him.

Three days went by before Max heard from Lang again. There was no reference to what Max had done. "On balance, things seem to be going along well. Just keep on doing business." That was it, short and to the point.

Shamski was disappointed. "What we need is for him to make a meet." But he hadn't and more waiting was in order.

"I'm not going to stay on this hook much longer," Max warned.

"It won't be that long," Shamski said. "Just make sure you don't miss his call." Max hung up on him.

Meanwhile, Max traded recklessly. To his amazement, he could not make a bad buy. It all turned into profit, a good market, a bad market—it didn't matter; it was black ink all the way. The accountant laughed. "You've inherited Cy's touch," he said.

Toward the end of the week, Max saw Carol at the Exchange and ripples of guilt assailed him. He asked if they could talk for a moment.

"About what?"

"I just want to . . . apologize, I guess. The last time we saw each other . . ."

"It's not necessary. Honestly. Let's just leave things as they are." She looked beyond him to the monitors. "Those are very depressed prices." She looked back to Max. "It's better this way, believe me." She walked away briskly.

That night Max called Julian for dinner. Berns was testy, wound up over the show, he explained, but he wanted to know what was happening at Max's end.

"Nothing much," Max responded.

"What do you mean—nothing much? Something's got to be going on. Don't you think you owe it to me—or to Cy, to tell me?"

"Honest, Julie," Max squirmed, "no one's told me anything new."

"I see," Berns said. "OK."

"So—what about dinner—we can talk more then."

"I can't. I've got an Alloway crisis. I'll catch you later."

Now I've hurt Julie, Max reflected morosely. There's no end to it. He went to a Chinese restaurant alone. When he returned, he checked the telephone-answering machine and found a hang-up with no message. His first thought was Lang—and he had missed him. What was he supposed to do, he thought angrily, lock himself in day and night and wait? He was looking hard at Cy's beach picture when the phone rang. He leaped for it expectantly.

THE THIRD FRIDAY

"Hello."

"Mr. Roberts, it is Juli Singh, please."

That meant Jimmy with the records. "Hello. Put Jimmy on, will you—and don't tell me he's sick again."

"No, he is not here, Mr. Roberts—that is why I call you." Her nasal soprano was even higher-pitched with anxiety. "He goes to see his cousin who is the dentist yesterday, but he does not come back even today, you see."

That was surprising. "Did you call his cousin?"

"He says . . ." She faltered. "He says that he left him last night, but he is not here. Do you know where he could be, Mr. Roberts?"

"He didn't call you—he just didn't come back?"

"No—he says nothing. He never stays away a night."

"Just stay there. I'll get back to you." Max called Shamski instantly.

"Goddamn," Shamski said, "something's giving."

Within an hour, Shamski, Borland, and Morrisey joined Max at the house in Queens. Juli Singh, her eyes wide and worried, sat kneading her hands. "He only says to me that it is important he goes to his cousin Anand. Then he goes. Where —where can he be?" She looked at Shamski imploringly.

The cousin confirmed, by phone, that Jimmy had come, taken a small package from the basement, and left within an hour of arriving.

"How did he get to you?" Shamski asked.

"How? In his automobile, sir."

"And what was in that package?"

"I have no idea, sir. It was in brown paper and he left it here weeks ago, you see . . . in the basement. It is very dry down there because we have dehumidifier."

"He never told you why he was leaving it with you?"

"Just to store, he said. It was nothing bad, I hope."

"And you never opened it to see."

"No, oh no." The cousin was aghast. "I forget all about it, sir."

When Shamski concluded, he turned to Morrisey. "He says he knows nothing from nothing. Get someone up to see the guy."

"You want an all-points on the car?"

"Right away."

"It doesn't smell right," Borland said darkly. "The man

came up there, took the records, and left for parts unknown. Why did he do that? He told us what was on the disks. What is on there he didn't tell us, though?"

As Max was leaving with the others, Juli Singh clutched him by the hand and, controlling tears, asked, "He comes back, Mr. Roberts, yes?"

"Yes," Max said, patting her thin-boned shoulder, "of course he will."

But after forty-eight hours of an all-points for a blue 1985 Toyota hatchback, there was no word. Warned by Shamski to say nothing to anyone, Max refrained from mentioning it even to Martha. He called Juli Singh to ask if there was anything he could do for her in the interim. She said there was not. She had told the children that their father had gone on a business trip and would be back soon. That was right to do, was it not? "Sure," Max said. He hung up, distressed, and as the hours went by, was filled with more and more foreboding. To increase his anxiety, there was no call from Lang.

"But keep doing business as usual," Shamski ordered. "We don't know what his channels are and we don't want to give him any signals at all."

Four days after Jimmy Singh was reported missing, a state trooper's Harley broke down on a little-used back road near the Hudson River fifty miles upstate. When he dismounted, cursing, he radioed in for help and went behind a thick row of trees to relieve himself. As he unzipped, he saw some distance away the back end of a car that had crashed its way through the brush and was halted, engine off, almost totally screened from view. Hand on the butt of his revolver, the trooper moved slowly toward the car, came around it carefully, and calling "Police!" emerged from the trees. There was no response. The trooper, one hand still on the butt of his gun, edged closer and closer until, pushing aside a huge vine outcropping, he came smack up against the driver's closed window. He pressed his nose against the glass, looked in, and saw the driver, still belted up, chin down against his chest, arms at his sides, eyes shut.

The trooper tried the door. It was unlocked. He pulled and was greeted by the acrid smell of decomposing flesh. He twitched his nose and tried pulling the driver's head back, but the neck had already stiffened, and he gave up. He searched the man as quickly as he could, having trouble with the resistant body, wrestling with it to reach the pants' pocket, where he found a wallet. He extracted the driver's license, shoved the body back into the car, slammed the door, and stood for a moment breathing in the fresh air. Then he scrambled back to his motorcycle, where he called in.

"Unit three forty-six. I'm still nonoperative about eight miles outside Studville on C-nine-oh-seven. I just investigated a blue Toyota parked way off the road. It has license number UG seven-oh-four-three and that's the Toyota hatchback on the all-points bulletin. The driver is a male—dark Caucasian—and he's dead. Over."

His radio hummed back, "Wow. Base to three forty-six. Stay at the scene. Assistance on the way. Ten four."

Six hours later Morrisey called Max with the news of Trooper Hollings's find. "Singh was way in the bushes, the windows were all closed, the air vents were shut tight, the gas gauge was empty, and the ignition was still on."

Max was numbed. "I don't understand."

"Exhaust," Morrisey said. "Comes right in."

"He killed himself?" The numbness changed to shock.

"I didn't say that. I said he's dead from the carbon monoxide. But there's a big bump with blood on the right side of the Indian's head. He could have hurt himself crashing through the trees and stuff but he also could have been hit hard by somebody and knocked out. It don't take long for carbon monoxide to put you to sleep, you follow me?"

"You mean somebody killed him?"

"We'll know more when the ME gets the body. Oh yeah —the guys took the car apart, but there's no package in brown paper. If there was one, somebody took it."

Max stared into space. Jimmy Singh was dead—like Cy. What could possibly have been in those records that was not already known? And what about Juli Singh? What would she do now? What about himself, for that matter; why hadn't Lang called? He felt hollow.

By noon the next day the medical examiner had determined that Singh's bruise had been caused not by any protuberance in the car since there was no blood on any interior surface. The wound, however, was consistent with a possible sharp blow delivered by a blunt instrument. Shamski went back to Juli Singh.

"Did you notice anybody in the neighborhood you didn't know—kind of keeping an eye on you?"

The new widow tried to concentrate on what the detective

was asking but she was far away, it was apparent, and her voice was dull and low. "I . . . cannot say."

"How would anybody know where your husband was going and when he was going there?"

"Just you," Juli Singh said softly.

Shamski was puzzled. "What do you mean me?"

She sighed and pulled at the skirt of her dark sari. "Your . . . policeman. When he called and asked me where my husband was . . ."

"Wait a minute," Shamski interrupted. "You say someone from my office called?" He shot a look at Borland. "Did you call?"

"No." Borland was surprised as well. "I never called."

"When did this man call?" Shamski asked.

The widow thought a moment and said, "The day my husband leaves, your policeman calls to speak to him. I told him he had gone to see his cousin. He asks me where Anand lives and I told him. Then he asked me when he left. I told him that also." A cloud came over her face. "Did I . . . do something wrong?"

"No," Shamski said unhappily, "it's all right. How would you know?"

There was a religious service for Jimmy Singh, but Max couldn't bring himself to attend. He sent Juli a check for five thousand dollars and huddled in Cy's apartment, clouds thickening about his head. He muttered at Cy's photo, "He was so loyal . . . so loyal. . . ." There was still no call from Lang and Max was convinced that somehow he had been discovered.

Shamski argued against that. "You have all the bank-account authority, the transfer knowledge. You made a cash delivery. They're not going to walk away from all that."

"Then why hasn't he contacted me?"

"We have to wait it out."

"They've just killed another man, for God's sake."

"I realize that," Shamski said soberly, "and believe me, I'm not taking any chances. The moment he calls to meet you, it's over. I'm trying to find the guy right now, but you don't get talk on the street about someone like him."

Max was silent.

"Just be careful," Shamski said. "Talk to nobody about anything. Keep your eyes open. It's a time clock."

The clock ran. Every hour without a call from Lang was an hour of worry and speculation. Max hung over the phone as though tethered, checked the tone often to make sure it was working, called in constantly when he was out, but Lang was silent. Meanwhile, Borland sent one of his people to the Second Mercantile as a bank examiner and found that there were many wire transfers to and from the Cayman bank. It was impossible to ascertain which were real and which had been faked to cover cash, but the bottom line was that millions were moving back and forth, being cleaned; this was a big operation. At the same time, following instructions, Max kept trading haphazardly and scored much of the time. Still, there was no call. What should he do? Max asked. Profits were building up, there was a large cash account that Borland insisted should not be sent to the Swiss numbered account for fear it would be lost forever. "But if I don't do that," Max said, "he'll know and think I'm ripping him off."

"Your partner didn't do it that way," Borland said.

"My partner didn't do it any way!"

"Let's just take the chance," Shamski interposed.

"Moreover," Borland said, "we've been tracking down all the printouts we have. Your partner did some other funny-money trades. We can't pin down the specifics on some of them—but it looks very much like insider stuff."

"File a suit," Max said wearily, "against someone—anyone."

A week after Singh's death, despite Shamski's attempts to keep it quiet, the *Journal* ran a small story calling him a "close colleague of the late Cy Bannerman." This drew a complaining call from Julian Berns. "It's a hell of a note when I have to learn a thing like this from the paper. Why didn't you tell me?"

It was a minute of tortuous fumbling and lame excuses. On that same day Max saw Carol at the Exchange. She had a new hairstyle, he noticed, one that softened her face and made her eyes more luminous than ever. She was kibitzing with one of the more lecherous traders and saw him, he thought, but turned away deliberately. It depressed him even more.

At six the next morning, rain hitting the terrace like falling shot, the phone rang, and, even submerged in restless sleep as he was, Max knew it was Lang. He reached wildly for the phone and croaked out, "Hello."

"Good morning," Lang said. "How is everything?"

"OK. . . . Good." Max cleared his throat. "I've been waiting to hear from you. I'd like to see you and talk some ideas over."

"You are the trader."

"Yes," Max said, trying to hide his anxiety, "but I would appreciate your input."

"It will have to wait."

"But there are some things—"

Lang broke in, his voice impatient. "There's an urgent situation and we're short-handed again. Another emergency delivery has to be made."

Max's first reaction was an inward groan. He fought to clear his brain and realized that it didn't matter; there would be no need to go through with the delivery. When Lang turned it over to him, Shamski would sweep in. "Well," he said cautiously, "I guess I can do it."

"I realize it's not your area." Lang was conciliatory. "But you've been doing very well for yourself, haven't you?"

"Yes, no complaints."

"Good."

"So, where do I meet you?"

"For a variety of reasons, it's a little different this time."

"Whatever you say."

"Yes, well—here is what you will do today." Lang turned brisk again. "A messenger will deliver an envelope to you this morning. In it there will be a key to a locker in Penn Station. You go there, open the locker, and you will find a suitcase . . ."

Oh—I am not going to see him, Max thought despairingly, all the plans—

". . . take the case to Clemmons at the Second Mercantile. He'll be waiting for you. Is that clear?"

"Yes," Max said urgently, "but I think we have to meet and talk about the account."

"I know what's happening. I have my sources."

"Right," Max said, half-frantic, "but there are some situations we should check out."

Lang was implacable. "Right now this delivery is most important. The funds have to be transferred this morning. We'll meet another time."

THE THIRD FRIDAY

"I see." Max tried to keep his voice calm, but he pounded a fist down on the bed in frustration.

"Good, good. I'll call you again."

Lang clicked off. Dazedly, Max wandered about the bedroom, muttering, "Cy—Jesus . . . Jesus. It's not going to end. What now?" He woke Shamski up and said grimly, "He wants me to do it again—but he didn't make a meeting. I'm not going. I mean it this time."

Shamski was patient, as usual. "I understand, I really do, and I wouldn't blame you if you walked away . . . but we're so close. Just do this, Max . . . just this. Because if you don't, it's all blown."

"Suppose he's setting me up? Suppose there's no money at all, but . . . something else?"

"I don't think he'd do it this way."

"What way would he do it—pills?" Shamski stayed silent. "I hate it," Max shouted, "and Cy never did this—never—no matter what the nerd says."

"I agree with you," Shamski said quietly.

The messenger arrived at nine o'clock. Max checked the envelope cautiously. It contained only a key to locker number F-sixty-two at Penn Station. In the cab, Max felt the possibility of diarrhea coming on but he controlled it. Once at Penn, he lost himself in the high-ceilinged station amidst the litter, human and otherwise, nauseated by the rancid smells of fast food coming at him from every corner. Finally he reached the locker bank and found F-sixty-two. He hesitated in front of it for fully five minutes before inserting the key carefully and opening the door. The end of a large gray suitcase butted out. He reached in and, gingerly feeling for the handle, found it and pulled.

The suitcase slid out easily enough, but when Max had it in hand, his shoulder sagged. It was heavy—heavier than the Gladstone had been. He carried it around the corner to where there was less traffic, set it down, and examined it. The case looked reassuringly ordinary enough. It had two straps and a snap lock. He put his ear close to the vinyl side, pretending to fuss with the buckles, but listening for a possible time-clock tick. He heard nothing except the echo of his own rapidly beating pulse. He rose up and hefted the suitcase. Nothing rattled.

Case held rigidly in hand, Max walked back through the smells, through the discarded paper cups and straws, through the clumps of bewildered tourists. As he passed a bench, a muscular young black man in hightops, a flowered Hawaiian shirt, and green shorts jumped up, ran toward him, and reached for the suitcase. "Hey, man—let me help you."

"No, no," Max called, "I'm all right."

"Let me," the man insisted. His hand grabbed at the handle.

Max swung sideways. "I don't want any help. Get away from me." He fought the hustler's grip but the man held on.

"I'm doin' you a service, man—you owe me a dollar."

Max pulled hard. "I said get away."

"Hey!" With a practiced movement, the hustler jerked at the handle and pulled the bag free. In control, he suddenly pointed behind Max. "Hey, Jim—your wife's lookin' for you." He whirled, and suitcase in hand, dodged to his right, feinted to his left, then spun back to his right like a basketball forward. Surprised, Max froze for a moment, then, as the thief whirled once more, grinning, Max lunged after him in despairing anger and smashed at his back with a fist. It landed, but had little effect. The man raced away, zigzagging across the concrete floor, the bag dangling from his thick hand. Max started after him as fast as he could, his legs pumping, his arms swinging, his heart pounding. I don't believe this, he said to himself, frantic. I don't believe it.

Nearing a wall, the hustler misjudged a stanchion and the suitcase hit it with a loud thwack as he went by. "No!" Max cried out, terrified that the bag might break open and scatter its contents over the station floor. For a moment the thief staggered as the bag's momentum swung him partially around, but he recovered quickly and sprinted to his left, to the subway exit. Max plunged after him. This isn't happening, he thought as he ran. It can't be, it just can't be. He looked for uniforms, saw none. He looked at the passing crowd. They were either frozen or intent on their own errands. His breath was coming in gasps and liquid swam before his eyes.

Up ahead, the hustler was about to plunge through to the subway when two women in flowered dresses, coming into the station, collided with him. Squealing with the shock, they reeled back. The thief tried to get around them but in their panic they kept blocking his path. He swung at them with the suitcase and they separated, screaming. As they did, Max came up, puffing hard. Seeing him, and with a quick flip that belied the bag's weight, the hustler tossed the bag into the air. Magically, a young, leather-jacketed white kid appeared from nowhere, caught the suitcase, and as the black youth danced away, dashed toward a hot-dog stand.

Momentarily confused, Max whirled from one attacker to the other, then, surprising himself with speed, he took off after the leather-jacket, grabbed for it, caught it, and yanked with all his remaining strength. The boy's head bounced back. He dropped the case and it skittered away. Max let the jacket go and scrambled to the bag. The boy karate-kicked at him and Max felt a hot poker in his side. He staggered, flailed back behind him, and caught the boy in the face. The boy screamed, "You mother—" and was about to dive at him when two uniforms appeared, changing his course. He dived for the hot-dog stand instead, emerged on the other side away from the police, and in seconds was lost to sight. His chest heaving, Max moved quickly to the suitcase and crouched to examine it. The vinyl was slightly scuffed, and one end was bashed in. Max tried the lock. It hadn't budged, and the straps were still secure. The policemen came up as he was lifting the case and one asked, "You all right?"

"I'm OK," Max assured them. "I'm fine."

"These goddamn kids, they're all over. They try a hustle first and then, sometimes, a grab. You gotta be very careful here."

It would have been some grab, Max thought, some grab. He brushed himself off. What would have happened if he had nothing to deliver? In the day, in the night, when he least expected it, in a way he least expected it, they would respond. He squelched a shudder, pulled himself together, and, clutching the bag tightly, went outside to find a taxi. He still had the delivery to make.

17

As he entered the cool halls of the Second Mercantile again, Max firmed his face into what he conceived to be a businesslike expression and marched over to the reception desk. He made the same request he had before and in moments Clemmons was before him, a genial, professional smile on his face, hand stuck out like a railroad signal. "Another trip, eh? You people surely do have all the fun. Come on in."

Once again Max followed the bank man into his office. Clemmons was relaxed and chatty. "What rotten weather—I tell you. The damn moles love it, though. My wife has roses and those little buggers are chomping on the roots." He approached the case Max had placed on the floor. "Let's see what we have here."

He kneeled to the suitcase whistling, as though this were an everyday routine, a legal requirement for a banking license. Max watched him worriedly as he noticed the damage.

"What happened here—try to open it and sample the stock?" Clemmons laughed. "Wouldn't be a good thing to do."

"It . . . fell," Max said.

"Big delivery today, very big. And hurry-up." Clemmons produced a brass key and with practiced motions opened the lock. He unsnapped the buckles and pulled the straps away. He unzipped the cover and bent it back. Max had expected bundles of currency packed tightly together, as before, and they were there—dense, rubber-banded packets lying neatly stacked this time, edge to edge, layers deep, spreading out like printing samples. What he had not expected was the denomination. Sweeping his eye along quickly, Max saw, with amazement, that the entire load he had been carrying consisted of five-hundred-dollar bills. He did a swift calculation. If each neatly pressed bundle held one hundred bills, if each stack held ten bundles, then in that space, two and a half by six inches, there was half a million dollars. Fascinated, he tried to count the stacks—four lengthwise, and six along the fifteen-inch depth of the case, twenty-four in all. He was staring at twelve million dollars.

Clemmons ran a hand over the money matter-of-factly. "They shouldn't do so much at one time," he complained, "but they're in a hurry for the buy, I suppose." He went to the closet for the burlap bag. What buy? Max wondered—what was this cash to buy?

"These cash deals," Max ventured. "They can be tricky."

Clemmons started transferring the packages. "Give me a hand, would you?" Startled, Max found himself scooping up the bundles and dropping them into the sack. Clemmons said, "If you were selling your company to . . . our friends . . . you'd want all cash too. This gets transferred right to the rest of the Cayman money. I understand the deal has to be closed by next week."

"Right," Max said. "I heard that too." He dropped the final bundle into the bag. "Must be a profitable company."

"Profitability may be beside the point," Clemmons said wryly. He kicked the twelve-million-dollar bag into the closet and closed the door. He looked at his soiled hands with distaste. "These bills are always so dirty—"

Max decided to take a chance. "Lang told me the name of that company but it's escaped me."

Clemmons looked up in surprise. "Really? He never told me."

Max covered himself by looking at his watch and exclaiming, "I'd better get going." He closed the empty suitcase and

278

tried one more desperate ploy. "Oh . . . I'm supposed to call Lang when I leave . . . to get the suitcase back, but I don't have his number with me . . ."

Clemmons's face visibly tightened. "I don't have any numbers. He always contacts me."

Max said weakly, "I'll hear from him, I guess." He jerked the suitcase up. Clemmons, saying nothing more, led the way from his office and out to the front of the bank, where he shook hands with Max and turned back. Before he left, however, he turned to look at Max speculatively.

Within an hour, Max met Shamski and Borland at the diner. He told them of the twelve-million-dollar delivery and the cash buy.

Shamski was impressed. "They moved twelve million? That's a real risk. They're in a hurry. Whatever they're buying must be special." He turned to Borland. "What do you think?"

"We need more information. Trying to find out what they're buying," Borland said morosely, "is like looking for a needle in the haystack. Companies don't have to list themselves as up for sale."

"The bank man gave me this funny look," Max said grimly, "when I tried to get Lang's number. If he tells Lang about that, they'll all know in a second I was lying." He faced Shamski directly. "I did what you wanted—I made this delivery—so that's it."

"Max." Shamski used patient tones. "We can move in on Clemmons now and stop that channel. But who knows how many others there are."

"I don't give a damn about channels," Max said flatly. "I got into this because of Cy, that's all."

"Your partner was involved with these channels," Borland said.

"So you keep saying," Max countered.

"Lang is key," Shamski said, "to everything. We need you to get his call for a meeting and go. Then we smash it all."

"I'll give it a couple of days," Max agreed angrily. "After that, I'm leaving the city . . . if I'm still in one piece."

He went back to the office, where Martha had tax forms for him to sign. There had been no call from Lang. At six o'clock he went back to Cy's, moving very warily. The answering machine had no messages, none at all.

Lang—call, call, call—the litany kept repeating in Max's

head like a looped tape. He escaped by ordering Chinese food in. While eating the soggy dumplings, Max suddenly put the fork down and stared dismally at the oily dough. His life had changed so much it was unrecognizable. He looked at the picture of Cy on the beach. "God, you crazy son of a bitch," he muttered. "What's going to happen to me?"

The phone rang. He let it ring again with tingling antici-pation, then jumped for it. "Hello."

"Max?"

With a twinge of disappointment, he heard Adeline's voice. "Oh, hi . . . how are things?"

"It's cool here," Adeline announced. "I didn't bring the right clothes."

"It's cool here too."

"No," Adeline said. "It's the same cool. I'm here."

"You're here?"

"No," Adeline said caustically, "I'm in Moscow, throwing stones at Stalin's tomb. I told you I might come in for the get-together. I'm at the airport."

Max pulled at the phone wire in helpless annoyance. She wouldn't give him any warning, would she? He didn't need his mother here now; it was exactly the wrong time. "Adeline," he asked plaintively, "why didn't you tell me you were definitely coming?"

"It is not in our contract that I have to discuss everything with you. I have been in contact with my friend Agnes, the Catholic church activist—she used to be an anarchist in the old days but she switched—she asked me to stay with her."

"You don't have to do that. You can stay at my apartment while I'm here at Cy's."

"And how long will that be? It's enough already, Max. Cy is not coming back."

"I'll meet you at the apartment," Max said.

Within the hour, Adeline bustled in, her old blue suitcase corseted in the middle by a leather belt. Max stowed it in the bedroom. "Isn't it time you got a new suitcase?"

"For what? The one trip I make every three years? How is Julie?"

"I haven't seen too much of him lately."

Adeline fixed him with shrewd eyes. "So, see him."

He called Julian to have dinner with them, but the evening produced no relief. Julie was very subdued and Adeline tired after her trip. Max noticed lines in her face he hadn't seen before and was aware, with a start, of her aging. When she went to the ladies' room, Max confided to Julian that she had not come at the most convenient time.

"Why not? I thought things were quiet now."

"All kinds of problems at the office," Max said lamely.

"That SEC investigation is still going on, isn't it?"

"Uh-uh—that's over."

Julian looked at him quizzically and Max was sure his friend knew he was lying still—but what else could he do?

He took Adeline to his apartment, fussing over her to such an extent that she finally said, "Go home, sonny boy—I live fifteen hundred miles from you and I take care of myself every day—so goodnight." At the door she stopped him, though. "Lately I have been thinking to myself about how it was years ago, after your father died."

"We didn't have a bad time, the two of us," Max said.

"No, but I never became interested in someone else . . . someone serious."

Max laughed. "Your friends were serious about politics, not life, Adeline."

"Still," she said insistently, "I never even tried to give you another father."

"I never wanted one." He kissed her on the cheek. "So goodnight."

"Max," his mother said quietly, "take care."

He tossed in his sleep that night, woke up at three, sweat-soaked, could not remember the nightmare that had shot him awake except that Lang's face had dominated. It took him half an hour to calm down.

Shamski called early the next morning just to see how he was.

"Tight, very tight," Max reported.

"Lang'll make some move soon," Shamski assured him. "Even if he's copped to something, he's not just going to fade away, believe me."

"Is that supposed to reassure me?"

At the office, Martha sensed her boss's grimness and kept her distance except for the moment that she came in with word that January cocoa, which Max had offhandedly bought for Euro-

Partners, was going to the limit; there would be a big profit. Max heard the news with mixed emotions. Why couldn't Cy have had a run of luck like this? he thought bitterly.

By noon, there was still no call from Lang. Max fled the office for a breath of the sweet fall day. He had barely emerged from the building when he saw Catalfo's stretch limo at the curb, its dark windows up. No, Max thought desperately—Rio! He scrambled to duck back inside, but a front door of the car opened and the brute driver came running out swiftly and caught up, calling, "Hey!"

Max put his back against the wall and covered his face. The driver raised his empty hands and mooed plaintively, "Take it easy . . . hey . . . he just wants to talk to you is all . . . I swear, just talk."

Max peered back at the limo. A rear window was down now, and Catalfo's puffy face was there, head nodding vigorously.

"What does he want to talk about," Max asked, "the state of my ribs?"

"That was, like, a mistake," the driver fumbled nervously. "You know . . ."

"I'm being watched," Max said. "I'm warning you."

"Got it," the driver said. "Yeah." His eyes were like an entreating spaniel's and he seemed more foolish than threatening. Curious now, Max decided to chance it. He walked out to the limo. The back door opened and he stepped inside. Catalfo was huddled there in the leather, an outsize cigar clutched in his hand.

"You . . . want one?" Catalfo proffered a cigar case.

Max shook his head, puzzled. Catalfo snapped the case closed. He licked his thick lips. "You conned me about Rio." Max tensed but Catalfo went on. "I'll pass that by because there are other things."

A real surprise. Max stayed silent.

Catalfo said, "I got to ask you something."

"About what?"

"About Barbara." Catalfo's eyes misted over and his voice shook. "I know you were there . . . in Aspen when she died."

Max stared. There were genuine feelings being expressed here. "I happen to know you were there as well."

"I . . . can't get over her," Catalfo said, hanging his head.

"I went looking for her. I don't know what the hell it is. I never felt this way before. And she's gone."

The man was in love, Max thought, amazed; this thick-necked, brutal, iron-balled man was choking with tenderness. "Why do you want to talk to me?"

Catalfo looked up, his small red eyes hard again. "You been in with the cops on it, I know that."

"They just asked me a few questions," Max said defensively.

"Yeah? They told me she OD'd but I don't believe it. Do you?"

Max shrugged uncomfortably. Catalfo bore in on him. "You saw her."

"For a few minutes."

"Was Roy Herbert with her?"

Catalfo had a new enemy, Max saw. "He was around."

"Around?" Catalfo was anguished. "She could have come to me for anything. I would have given her anything she wanted. But that son of a bitch moved in on her. Did you take her home that night? You can level with me—I know you boffed her before, but OK."

"No," Max said quickly, "I left her at a party."

"Herbert go home with her?"

"I don't know."

Catalfo mashed the cigar out viciously. "He did it. He made her take the pills. He forced her. He's a pervert!"

Not impossible, Max thought, not at all. Catalfo looked at him through narrowed eyes. "I know you went there . . . on business."

What else did he know, who else—Lang?

"That ain't my affair, but you hear one more word about what happened in Aspen, you contact me, OK?"

"There's no reason for me to hear anything."

Catalfo ignored that. "I give you something up front." His eyes glittered. "Herbert's tied in."

Max felt a surge of excitement. "Tied in to what?"

"Speak to old Carmody. That's all I'm telling you now." Catalfo looked away. "They got her buried out there but I'm trying to get her back here. I got plots in a beautiful place on the Island. I'll put her in one. It's kept up nice with flowers and everything." He sighed. "I'll build her a stone vault—with a statue of her saint." He buried his face in his hands. The driver turned around and made motions for Max to go.

Max let himself out of the limo and watched it roll off smoothly with the bereaved Catalfo. Minutes later, he was on his way to Phil Carmody's, praying he hadn't gone to lunch yet.

Carmody wasn't eating lunch. His colon was acting up and his desk held a glass of hated buttermilk. He was happy to see Max. "Cy used to tell me," he said plaintively, "to get out into the country more. It would help my digestion. I dislike the country, though. The city on a weekend is just fine with me."

Seated opposite a Giacometti sculpture, Max asked, "Mr. Carmody, are you involved with Roy Herbert in a financing project?"

Carmody laughed. "I wouldn't call it 'involved.' There are some companies I know who want buyers. He came to me with some possibilities . . . the usual thing, you know." Carmody came out from behind the desk. "I once said to Cy he ought to get into the investment-banking end of things; there's a lot of money to be made there with no risk at all."

Max hid his impatience with the reminiscence. "What kind of companies?"

"Various." Carmody was surprised by the intensity of the question. "Forgive me, Max, but what's your interest?"

Max hesitated. He should really tell Phil Carmody the truth, he knew, enlist him. But the one truth might lead to all the others, and that wouldn't do. "It came up," he said, "a stock-buy thing."

"In what company?"

"I . . . don't remember the name," Max fudged. "It was a small one—in Florida . . . I think."

"Ah—that could be Southern Bird."

"Southern Bird?" Max played at recalling. "What is that?"

"It's a local air-transport outfit." Carmody grimaced. "I'd stay far away. It's lost three million last year and will lose another three this year. Are you surprised they're anxious to sell?"

"No, but who's Roy Herbert buying for?"

Carmody shrugged. "Max, it's all just in the talking stage. He says he has a few entities stupid enough to want to pay good money." He laughed again. "The bigger-fool theory again."

Max couldn't wait to tell Shamski and Borland. He called from a pay phone on the street and saw them in the now-familiar diner an hour later.

"Their own legit air-transport company, what a dream," Shamski explained. "They move anything they want when they want. They operate carefully enough, no one notices."

"This gives you what you want, doesn't it?" Max said to Borland. "You can find out who Herbert's fronting for now."

"It may not be the best tactic." The SEC man frowned. "We go to Southern Bird, and no matter how quiet we keep it, it leaks right out."

"It will," Shamski agreed. "We know that Herbert's acting for an unknown buyer, but on the face of it he's doing nothing illegal."

Max was exasperated. "But you know he's going to buy Southern Bird for Brigado to move drugs with."

"How do I prove that he knows that?" Shamski demanded irritably. "How do you know he knows that? You say your partner never knew what he was into. No, no, we've got to take it step by step here or everything could fly away."

"You're always going slow with Herbert," Max flashed.

Shamski's jaw tightened in response. "What does that mean?"

"It's just the fact."

"You hear me," Shamski said. "I build cases that stand up in court. Maybe you don't have to deal with that in your business. It's a hot tip, a scramble. Get that stock! Afterward—who cares? But I've got D.A.'s and judges and juries to worry about."

There was an uneasy silence after that until Borland said, "We wait till papers are filed for the sale. When they are, we'll know the name of the company—"

"When . . . when," Max said in anger. "When Lang calls, when the sale is made . . . meanwhile my partner is dead, I make all that money for his killers, I deliver all those millions, and you can't touch anybody."

"Believe me," Shamski said, "we move too soon, we blow it."

"You don't move soon enough," Max said, "and you blow me." He rose, seething, and left them in the half-haze of the frying burgers. He felt enmeshed, caught in a net from which no amount of thrashing about would relieve him. And inadequate—he felt inadequate. Herbert would get out of this.

He returned to the office still agitated. No call from Lang. He would never call again, Max felt—but something would happen, something terrible would suddenly happen. As he stared out the window, Martha came through on the intercom. "Mr. Roberts, there's a lady here to see you." Then, as though in a dream, Sonya's voice floated in on the speaker. "Max. Hello. It's me. . . ."

Half unbelieving, Max ran to the door and jerked it open. Sonya was there, laughing at his dumbfounded look. She wore a nubby tweed skirt of her own weaving and a Chinese brocade jacket. Her blond hair swung free. Martha was impressed. "I was seeing a buyer near here," Sonya said, "and I thought I'd surprise you. Is it bad? Are you busy?"

"No—no." Max took her hands. "You look great. Come inside, come on."

Sonya waved a large patchwork bag. "My swatches."

"Here, leave them with Martha. Martha, this is Sonya," Max burbled.

Martha smiled formally. Sonya said, "Hi."

Max dragged her into his office and closed the door. "Wow." He embraced her tightly. She laughed and patted his back. He pulled away to look at her. "How long are you staying?"

"Overnight." She laughed, her face lighting up. "If it's all right with you."

"All right?" Max hugged her again. "It's fantastic."

"I thought," Sonya said, perching herself on his desk, "we'd go downtown to that place for dinner, and then . . ."

Adeline. Max suddenly remembered Adeline. But what a great thing, he thought. What a remarkable opportunity to get them both together. They would love each other. "Sonya," he burst out, "you came at the perfect time."

Max had telephoned her, so Adeline was prepared for Max's friend. When she came in, striding freely and radiant, Adeline looked over to her son. Max grinned.

"Sit down." Adeline played hostess in her son's apartment. "Sit down."

Sonya plopped down on the couch, looking about her. "So—this is your real place. I like the clutter."

Adeline said, "You were a friend of Cy's."

"That's right."

Max groaned inwardly at Adeline's measuring eyes. "I met Sonya," he said clumsily, "through Cy—kind of."

"Cy told me a little about you," Sonya said. "He said you were a . . . special woman."

Adeline kept examining. "You have your own business, Max tells me."

"It's not a business," Sonya gently corrected. "I'm a craftsperson, a weaver."

"Ah," Adeline said, "a weaver."

"Look at that skirt, Addie," Max said proudly. "Is that fantastic? Sonya made it."

"You sell what you make, though," Adeline said, pursuing the economics. "It's your business."

"It's not a business," Sonya declared, unhappy with the word. "I sell what my loom makes. But the fact is I wish I didn't have to sell at all; I'd never leave where I am."

"She has a wonderful place in Vermont," Max said.

"There's almost no pollution there," Sonya added. "It's unchanging—mostly. The world doesn't touch it."

"Ha—" Adeline snorted, "the world touches everything."

"Yes," Sonya agreed, "but you've got to try to keep it out if you're going to have a soul, don't you think?"

"Some working people can't afford to have a soul," Adeline said wryly.

Sonya looked at Adeline uncomprehendingly. Adeline explained, "I mean to go off and live in the woods is a luxury, no?"

"Addie," Max said, hoping she wouldn't start, "not everyone is interested in political action."

"A person can't stay in a corner," Adeline expounded. "Even Bakunin said while social organizations become corrupt, the individual must still take responsibility."

It was clear that Sonya was not acquainted with Bakunin, nor did she agree with him—or Adeline. "A person takes responsibility for herself—to grow and be and develop."

With a growing sense that disaster was approaching, Max said, "Hey, it's time to go to dinner."

At the table in the Italian restaurant Max tried to understand what was happening, for something surely was. He had thought that Sonya's naturalness, her freshness, her free lifestyle, would fascinate Adeline, but it was growing rapidly and painfully clear that his mother was not impressed with the effort to reach one's human potential as a life's work.

"There is so much bad going in the world, so much exploitation, so much unfairness," she proclaimed, "a person has to take sides."

"Adeline," Max protested, "these are not the thirties."

"Just the same."

"But if you're creative, you can't spend your life doing that," Sonya asserted. "Your head has to be someplace else."

"Plenty big creative people were political—Paul Robeson, Picasso, Frank Sinatra."

Max blinked. "Sinatra?"

"At one time," Adeline amended swiftly. She speared a shrimp. "These are very good."

By the time dinner ended and Adeline returned to the apartment, a distinct coolness was evident between the women. Walking between them, Max felt the cold breeze. Upstairs, in the doorway, his mother said a formal good-bye to Sonya. Max said he'd call her tomorrow and hastily took Sonya downstairs. There, he said, "You have to understand she's a real creature of her times."

"Right," Sonya said. "Yes."

"When we get back to the apartment," Max said brightly, "we'll open a bottle of champagne and . . ."

"I don't think I'll stay over," Sonya interrupted soberly. "I've changed my mind. I'd like to drive back tonight."

Max was shocked. "This late?"

"It's no problem," Sonya said. "And it has nothing to do with your mother. I'm in a different mood, that's all." She patted his cheek. "Come on."

The VW was parked four blocks from Cy's, and while getting to it, Max tried, only once, to dissuade Sonya. "I like driving at night," she answered. "No traffic, the stars out, my tape deck going. I really feel free." She slung the patchwork bag into the back, put herself behind the wheel, and tried the ignition. The engine protested but caught. "Good girl," Sonya crowed. Max bent to kiss her clumsily through the open window. " 'Night Max," Sonya said, and put the car into clashing gear. Max pulled himself back unhappily.

"I'll call you tomorrow and . . ." He stopped in mid-sentence and stared across the street, where amidst half a dozen cars parked, one caught the tail end of a streetlamp's arc and reflected blue. Max peered intently over the Beetle.

THE THIRD FRIDAY

The VW pulled away with a squeal. Across the street, the blue car sprouted sudden smoke from its exhaust and, with lights out, moved away from the curb and disappeared into the night.

Max was riveted. The blue sedan?

18

Max slept little, lying in bed, anxiety eating at him and, at three in the morning, knowing Sonya could not make the drive by then, called anyway. He let the phone ring ten times and gave up. He did the same an hour later with the same results. He fell into a fitful doze and jerked awake at six as night dissolved. He called Vermont again and as the phone rang six times, seven, eight, nine, he tried to control his rising panic. By now she would have made it, certainly. He was about to hang up despairingly when a breathless Sonya came on the line.

"Hello? Yes? Who is this?"

Relieved, Max said, "Sonya, it's me, Max."

"Max, I was out doing chores and you dragged me back in."

"I'm sorry," Max said, taken aback by her obvious annoyance. "You got back OK, then?"

"Of course I did."

"I was worried, that's all."

"Max, I've got to get back now," Sonya said. "Good-bye."

Max hung up, relieved, and headed for the shower. He turned the control on cold and jumped under the spray, shivering. As he did so, the phone on the outside of the shower stall sounded. Max reached for it. Water splashed into his nose and he gurgled, "Hello."

"Roberts?"

Frantically, Max grabbed for the water control. His chilled skin tingled. His feet slipped on the tiles. It was Lang. "I'm here," Max said quickly. In his haste, he switched the control to "hot" and sudden, scalding water came down at him. He dodged away from the stream.

"What's that noise?"

"Nothing," Max said. He jabbed at the control from afar and it stopped the torture. He wiped the water from his eyes. "I want to see you. There are some very interesting situations coming and we ought to discuss them."

"Why?" Lang said sharply. "You're doing well. Keep it up."

"Yes, but a couple of these things have . . . big downside risk; I need input."

"You're the trader," Lang said. "That's what you get paid for."

"I know, but the kind of investment I'm thinking about—"

"It's impossible right now."

"We have to get together," Max said in desperation.

"Why do we have to?"

"Because . . ." Max floundered, "it's a great opportunity."

"That girl you saw last night," Lang said, and Max's stomach jumped.

"What?"

"That girl," Lang repeated deliberately, "she is someone your partner knew and it's not too smart to keep up that relationship."

It had been the blue car, the same blue car. He had been right. Max said quickly, "She has nothing to do with anything. I don't speak about my business to her. Cy didn't either."

"I'm suggesting you stay away from her," Lang said. "Do you understand me?"

Max hesitated. Defying Lang this way was stupid. As soon as he managed to meet him, it was over. He changed the subject. "I still say we should get together as soon as possible."

292

There was a pause, then Lang said, "I won't be available. I'm going out of town."

"Let's meet today." Max suppressed an urge to cry it out. "Anytime you say."

"Can't be done." Lang was brusque. "Keep working till you hear from me."

"Wait a minute!"

But the connection was already broken. Max stood in the shower, wet and dazed. Lang was gone. He had called and the chance was over now. "Son of a bitch," he shouted to the showerhead. Early as it was, he roused Shamski at home. "Now what?" he raged. "Herbert's all we have. Take him in at least."

"Damn it." Shamski was impatient with him. "There's nothing to gain that way. We don't have anything to even hold him on. Lang will come back to you, he has to. Just cool down—my wife can hear you yelling. Go back to sleep."

No way, Max thought over coffee. He'd had enough. He would take whatever his share was in Whizkids and go. To Vermont? Yes, maybe there—why not? He would settle his affairs, arrange for the apartment to be sold, lock, stock, and barrel. He would also, he thought with a twinge, send another check to Jimmy Singh's widow, and he'd be out of it. Cy's death would be . . . unfinished business. There was nothing more he could do.

Resolute, he called Adeline. She had slept well, she reported, and delicately asked how his friend was. "She went back last night," Max said shortly, "and you weren't all that nice to her."

"We disagreed politically," Adeline said.

Max went down to the Exchange for what he vowed would be the final time. He would close out everything outstanding, turn all the papers over to Shamski, and it would be his headache from then on. The floor was in full swing as he arrived. Silver was shooting up to the limit and no one knew why. He saw Carol some distance away, writing orders, and decided he could not leave things as they were. He walked to her quickly and when she looked up at him, he said, "Hi—got a few minutes?"

She hesitated and then answered, "Sure."

They left the noise and escaped to the comparative quiet of the administrative section, where the trading din receded. Seated on the circular bench against the wall, Carol eyed Max speculatively.

"I'm making some changes in my life," Max commenced, "and I don't want to make them feeling some things are . . . kind of up in the air."

Carol was startled. "What's up in the air?"

"I think," Max said, struggling, "that you think I've acted—not great," he finished lamely.

"Oh"—Carol seemed relieved—"that. Well, it's all right, honestly."

"I just wanted to tell you that. I mean you're a very special person."

By now, Carol's eyes held a glint of amusement. "I'm a real good old pal. OK, I accept."

Max laughed. "I'm clumsy at this."

"But sweet." Carol laughed as well. "What kind of changes are you talking about?"

"I'm not sure—getting out, getting away."

A shadow came over Carol's face. "Is it because of what happened?"

Max had the urge to tell her but settled for "Lots of things come into it."

"Oh, Max," Carol said, and Max was startled at the depth of feeling in her tone, but she pulled back quickly. "Well, whatever happens, I'm glad we spoke like this, like friends."

"Yes," Max said.

Carol rose. "Back to the salt mines." She leaned over, kissed Max on the cheek, and went swiftly back toward the roar. Max tingled where she had placed her lips and wished . . . Confused, he didn't know what he wished. He only knew that he could not live this way.

He told Martha he had new plans, called Julian and made a next-day lunch date. He was considering how to handle the Euro-Partners trading account when Martha buzzed in with a phone call for him—a woman who, coyly, wouldn't give her name—"It's a surprise," Martha said dourly.

Max picked up the phone. "Max Roberts. Hello."

"Hello, Max." The voice was high-pitched, excited, vaguely familiar.

"Who is this?" Max asked.

"Surprise, surprise, it's Daphne," she giggled.

"Daphne?"

"Daphne Kaiser, your old friend from Aspen. Oh, poo—you've forgotten her already."

"No, no," Max said, shrugging his shoulders helplessly at Martha, who went back out, "I remember you very well."

"I'm in your wonderful city to look over some fashion shows and have some fun. Come on over to the hotel and have some fun with me."

"I can't," Max said. "I'm all booked up today."

"Oh—you big New York businessmen. I called up Roy Herbert too, but he's busy making deals."

"Daphne," Max said with sudden inspiration, "tell me something about Barbara Stratton."

"Oh—that poor girl," Daphne said. "She just, you know, went too far."

"What was the scene?"

"Oh, Roy was . . . helping her out, you might say, financially."

That was surprising. "But she was always all right, that way."

"I heard," Daphne said, "that she went into something to make a real killing and it hurt her very badly, some stock thing. Roy was pulling her out of it. Oh, Max, come on over—we'll have a good gab session."

"I can't, Daphne, not today, but what was really going on between them—Roy and Barbara?"

Daphne rambled, then said, "Well—Barbara told a good friend of mine that it was getting to be too much for her, old Roy was making all these demands, you know." She giggled at the thought. "And she wanted to break away but didn't know how she could. Maybe that's why she did what she did. But she was sooo pretty and sexy, wasn't she, Max?"

"Yes," Max muttered automatically. She had wanted to get away from Herbert. And the next thing was she was dead.

"Max," Daphne said, "I'm going to be here for a couple of days. Let's have lunch tomorrow. It'll be fun."

Max sighed. "Can't do it, Daph."

"All work and no play," Daphne pouted. "I'm having lunch with someone I don't know and you could be an ice breaker because you know his friend."

What was she chattering about? "What friend, Daphne?"

"Well, I told Don Brady I was coming east and he asked me where I was staying and I told him and he told me that a friend of his would call and take me to lunch and we'd have a good old time, and he did call."

"Well, have a good lunch."

"Be more fun with you, Max, I'm certain sure. Mr. Lang's just taking me as a favor to Don but if you came along it'd liven things up."

It was a trip-hammer in Max's ear. He stammered, "Who . . . did you say?"

"Dennis Lang. Sounds very courtly on the phone. You know him?"

Max went blank for a horrifying moment. "No—I don't. . . ." Then his brain whirled, went into high gear. "Wait a minute. Listen, Daphne, maybe I can cancel tomorrow—and come along with you."

"Oh . . . we'll have a party." Daphne was pleased and excited. "You know what—this sweet young thing came through Aspen a month ago—I have her phone number and I'll give her a call."

"Terrific." Max pumped enthusiasm.

"I am not promising because she's sort of a well . . . a business girl, if you know what I mean." Daphne squealed with delight. "Won't that be a kick?"

"Where are you meeting—and what time?" Max waited, holding his breath.

"The Oak Room at the Plaza," Daphne replied. "One o'clock."

"Great," Max said. "I'll see you there."

"Max," Daphne said, laughing, "you've made my day."

"It's the other way around," Max said.

He hung up, euphoric, and called Shamski. "He'll be there, at the Plaza. It's what we've been waiting for."

Shamski caught the fever. "Bless that little lady's heart. You want to be there?"

"No," Max said, "I really don't."

"You don't even want to be outside and watch him come out in handcuffs?"

"You going to get handcuffs on Brady? He's really the one."

"That's another story," Shamski admitted. "First this one."

When Max hung up the full impact hit him. By tomorrow afternoon it would all be over—the months of worry and fear, the danger and the lies would be finished. He would have discharged his debt to Cy. But what if something went wrong? What if, somehow, Lang didn't show? After all, there was only the word of a ditzy Daphne to depend upon. And what if—he took a deep breath as he thought this—Brady had set this up for some reason—to test him? It could be that Lang was onto him and Brady was using Daphne, as before, for his own purposes. Then what would happen?

He tried to shrug off the cloud, but it stayed with him all afternoon. Exhausted but keyed up, he took Adeline to the Museum of Modern Art, an experience that left her cold. He called Sonya, aching to tell her that his life would change. To his surprise, a male voice answered pleasantly. "Hi."

Flustered, Max asked, "Is this . . . Sonya's?"

"Oh sure." In the background Max heard the click-clack of a loom.

"Could I speak to her, please," Max said cautiously.

"Sone," Max heard the man sing out. "For you."

Max's stomach tightened in resentment. The clicking ceased. Sonya's voice floated through. "Hello."

"It's Max," he said in low tones.

"Max?" She was puzzled. "Didn't we talk this morning?"

"Yes," he said, deflated.

The man's voice came through in the background calling intimately, "Sone hon, want some tea?"

"Love some," Sonya answered away from the phone.

"You've got . . . company," Max said, dismayed.

"Uh-huh."

"A . . . neighbor?"

Sonya laughed. "You might say that."

"It's not a good time to talk, I guess."

Max heard her say, "Oh—thanks." And then he heard a liquid popping sound and a giggle. He listened intently. The same sound—a kiss, unmistakable. "I'll call back another time," he said in confusion.

"Oh, Max—not for a few days. We're going up north for a little backpacking."

"Oh—" Max retreated. "I see. Right. Backpacking."

"Yes."

"When will you be back?" Max asked plaintively.

"Oh, two, three days—it's loose," Sonya said.

In the background he heard a deep chuckle and a muttered, "Very loose."

"I'll talk to you, Max. Bye."

Max sat in front of the phone, dazed. "We," she had said,

"we." Who was this man? Why had she said nothing about him? Had she given him even a clue that there was this . . . "neighbor"? Should she have? Only last night, he thought, dismayed, she had planned to stay over. Today—? He felt betrayed and foolish.

The introspection was gradually superseded by concern for the next day. Anything might go wrong, might *be* wrong even now. He double-locked the terrace door and chained the service entrance. Tiredness took its toll and at ten he fell asleep. He awoke at midnight, dazed, and fell asleep again. At eight in the morning he blinked awake, cramped, his right arm and leg devoid of circulation and needling pain into him.

Five more hours. He had breakfast, thought of calling Shamski one more time, but decided not to. Somehow the morning eked itself by. He went to the office. There had been no calls. Every fifteen minutes he tortured himself by checking the time. Twelve-thirty arrived—only a half hour more. He was sitting at his desk trying desperately to blank his mind, when Martha called out, "Mr. Berns is here."

Max sat up in consternation. What—? Then he realized he had forgotten their lunch date. The door opened and Julie waltzed in.

"I was nearby and thought we'd go over together. You ready?"

Max opened his mouth but nothing came out. Julie stared at him. "What's wrong?"

"Nothing," Max managed. "I guess I forgot."

"So, let's go."

Martha came through again. "A Mr. Morrisey on the line."

Max tried to control his face. "Morrisey? Can I call him back?" To Julian he said, "He's a . . . a bank guy." Julian plopped down into a chair.

Once again Martha rang through. "He says he has to speak to you."

"Damn." Max picked up the phone. "Mr. Morrisey, I'm a little busy right now and I can't—"

The detective overrode him. "Listen, Shamski wants you to be ready. As soon as we make the collar, you come on down."

"Oh. I see." Suddenly Max remembered what had been overlooked, what was absolutely essential. He glanced over to Julie, smiled wanly, and said carefully into the mouthpiece, "How are things going to be set up?"

"As soon as he comes in," Morrisey responded with enthusiasm, "he's gone. We've got guys in the lobby and guys in the restaurant and Shamski is—"

"No," Max interjected. "What I mean is . . ." He broke off, hesitated, and called to Julie, "I've got to check some papers, be right back." He left Julian alone, went out to the anteroom, picked up the phone there, sat himself down in a corner, to Martha's surprise, and continued the conversation in low tones. "Morrisey, how is anybody going to know who Lang is? I'm the only one who knows what he looks like."

Morrisey was reassuring. "The Fed guy, Borland, he saw Lang, remember? He's gonna sit with Shamski. And tomorrow there'll be two of our guys in the bank ready to grab Clemmons. Two more of Borland's crewcuts already have a court order to grab the records." Morrisey chuckled. "It's all comin' down, don't worry."

"I am worried," Max replied heatedly. "If it doesn't go off . . ." He heard his office door open and glanced up. A puzzled-looking Julian stood there. "Forget it," Max concluded to Morrisey and put the phone down. To his friend, he said apologetically, "I won't be able to make lunch, Julie." He longed to tell him that very soon Dennis Lang would walk into the Oak Room, there would be pandemonium . . .

"I see," Julian said stiffly. "Well, you've got a better offer, OK." He walked past Max without another word and was gone. Max returned to his office unhappily.

Brian Shamski had never been in the Plaza before. Sitting at a corner table in the staid Oak Room with a tweed-suited Borland, he looked little different from the other men drinking, chatting, relaxing in this once totally male haven. Morrisey, seated two tables away with another detective, was another matter. He had on his best blue suit and had shaved carefully that morning but there was something about him that suggested either an out-of-town millionaire or a plumber on vacation. A table away from him were two keen young cops in blue blazers and gray flannels. They had been chosen for their looks and seemed completely at home with their untouched martinis in front of them.

"You're sure you don't see him here now?" Shamski questioned Borland.

"Absolutely. He's not here yet." Borland brushed back his cowlick.

Shamski fretted. He hoped Borland would recognize Lang when the moment came. He regretted letting Roberts stay away. At least he knew them both, Lang and the woman. Shamski's eyes roamed the room. This case had come very far, he mused. And mostly through Roberts's obsession, he had to admit.

A single woman being escorted by the maître d' to a table at the end of the room caught his attention. He followed their progress, then muttered, "What do you think?"

Borland swiveled toward them. "That's a designer dress," he whispered, "in the two-thousand-dollar range."

"You go to fashion shows?" Shamski kept his eye on the woman. She sat, made herself comfortable, opened her purse, extracted a mirror, touched up her carefully blown hair. Shamski drummed lightly on his table with his fingers, a prearranged signal. Morrisey caught it and followed his boss's eyes. He nodded slightly and made his own signal to the two flanneled cops. Six pairs of eyes watched Daphne Kaiser intently.

Five minutes passed, then ten. Daphne looked at her watch and ordered a Daiquiri. Borland kept sipping nervously at his Perrier. Shamski began to tap his toe, caught himself, and stopped abruptly. Morrisey began to sweat in his heavy suit and yearned for an off-duty drink.

Ten minutes later Daphne was still alone. Shamski saw the uncertain frown on her face.

"What if he's been tipped?" Borland muttered.

Shamski wondered if the woman was some kind of plant. "It could be," he started to say, but Borland pulled at his arm and said, in a strangled voice, "There he is."

Shamski shot his eyes toward the entrance. The maître d' was leading a tall man directly toward the woman. Her frown disappeared and a welcoming smile took its place.

"It's Lang," Borland confirmed. "You think he has anybody outside?"

Shamski put his hand over his mouth, as though to cover a cough and murmured into his lapel microphone, "A tall guy . . . fifties . . . brown suit . . . just came in. Did you make him, and is he carrying anyone?"

In the lobby, where three of Shamski's people sat in club chairs, the pretty young woman reading *W* placed the paper so that it hid her face and responded, "Saw him. Seems alone."

THE THIRD FRIDAY

Borland looked at Shamski questioningly.

Shamski adjusted his ear piece. "He's clean," Shamski said. "We're going." He glanced over and saw Lang sitting stiffly formal, a fixed smile on his face. Daphne, meanwhile, was telling a story animatedly. "Thirty seconds," Shamski said and checked his watch.

As he did, Borland gripped him by the arm. "Look." Shamski lifted his head. Lang had risen and was leaving the table. "He made us," Borland whispered agitatedly. "He's going." Shamski was up and moving forward before Borland finished. On this cue the flanneled detectives leaped up, startling the diners next to them, and fanned out, one to the right, the other to the left. Morrisey and his companion were already up, following Shamski's lead. Only Borland held his seat, watching keenly as Lang threaded his way through the tables toward the rest rooms at the right. Halfway there, he looked back momentarily toward Daphne, and Borland saw his startled look as the five moving figures were, unmistakably, converging. Instantly, Lang reversed and headed toward the swinging doors of the service entrance, but Morrisey was already there. Seeing him, Lang swerved away and cut to his left toward the lobby, but one of the blue-jacketed detectives had planted himself in front of it. Lang cut back once more, trying desperately to avoid Shamski coming straight at him. This brought him on a path back to Daphne, who was staring in bewilderment. By now, the entire room was aware that something unusual was occurring and there was dead silence. In that silence Shamski called out, "Lang!"

Lang froze. He was only a step away from Daphne as he did and he gripped the back of her chair hard. She jerked up sideways, frightened. In two seconds the table had been surrounded. Shamski held up his gold shield in the leather wallet. "Police. You're under arrest."

Daphne squealed, "Oh my God!"

The blood drained from Lang's face. He stood stiffly and silently as Shamski recited Miranda. Daphne collapsed into the chair and sat, horrified, hands to her mouth. Every eye in the room was on the encircled table. Shamski said, "Let's go."

He nodded to Morrisey, who produced handcuffs and said to Lang, "Put 'em out." Lang's hands did not move from the chair. "Don't give me trouble," Morrisey said.

Lang faced Shamski. His voice was tight but controlled. "Do you have to do this?"

"I'm afraid so," Shamski said. Grim-faced, Lang held out his hands. Morrisey slipped the cuffs on his wrists. The locks clicked.

"Oh . . . ," Daphne breathed. Lang turned toward her swiftly, his eyes burning with accusation.

"No," Shamski said. "It wasn't her."

"Am I—arrested too?" Daphne was near tears.

Shamski said, "No, but we'd like to ask you some questions. Would you come along with us, please?"

They moved through the quiet room, Lang's face like stone, his manacled hands down, Morrisey hovering over him. Borland joined the party when they reached him. Lang looked at him and Borland said, with satisfaction, "SEC."

Outside, two unmarked police cars had pulled up and Lang was shoved into the back of the first. Daphne was placed in the second and the cars sped off downtown.

Within an hour Lang had been booked on six charges, including accessory to murder. "You've got it all wrong," he said.

"Lang," Shamski said amiably in the interrogation room, "you're in it up to your neck. We've got Clemmons at the bank. He'll give you up in two minutes—you know that."

"I am not involved in any murder," Lang insisted. "You're wrong."

"What's *involved?*" Shamski asked. "You didn't get your hands dirty, but you know who put the contracts out and who did the jobs."

"I am not involved in any murder," Lang repeated.

"Lang." Borland took an unctuous hand. "You're white collar. Save yourself."

Lang was firm. "I'm not answering any more questions until my attorney arrives."

"You're a fool," Shamski said. "We know who Brady really is—and you're going to take a fall for him while he sits on his hill in Aspen. You think he'd do the same for you?"

Lang looked away.

As Lang was being interrogated, Morrisey called Max and told him of the capture. Max yelped with delight and rushed downtown. He was put into a small office to wait and paced the floor anxiously. He was there for twenty minutes when the door opened without warning and he was looking at a haggard Clemmons, firmly in Morrisey's grasp. Clemmons's eyes opened wide as he saw Max. Morrisey grinned. "You two know each other, I see." He poked Clemmons into the room a bit farther. "Roberts, just for the record—this the man you turned over the money to?"

Max nodded wordlessly. Clemmons's voice trembled. "What's going to happen?" He suddenly broke. "My wife—could somebody call my wife? Please . . . please . . ." Max felt a wave of sympathy for him.

"Come on, sonny." Morrisey shooed Clemmons out, calling back to Max, "Lang's hanging tough. His lawyer's coming."

The lawyer was already there. Youthful but grave, he wore a three-piece suit with a fraternity key hanging from a gold chain across his vest. He was tall, with a brush moustache and gold-rimmed spectacles. His name was Walter P. Vinson and he came from a prestigious firm. These bastards always had guys like that, Shamski thought with some anger. After a short conference with Lang, Vinson said to Shamski, "If you want to ask my client some questions, go ahead, but I don't think he's disposed to answer your charges—and I'd advise him not to."

Shamski spoke privately to a detective, who left the room. Then he turned to Lang. "You're going over, believe me. We've got direct connection between you and Brigado." He saw a slight flicker in Lang's eyes.

The lawyer said, "If you can make a case, make it in court. I'm going to ask for reasonable bail and we'll all go about our business."

Shamski spoke directly to Lang. "He'll get you bail, Lang. But he won't do the time for you. And I guarantee that if you walk out now, your chance for a deal is gone. You'll do that time." He took a step back. "Look at you—you're soft, you're used to the good life. You'll never make it." He saw a swift, slight grimace. There was a knock on the door and he called, "Yeah."

The door opened then, and a detective urged Max into the room. Directly ahead of him Max saw Lang illuminated by a desk lamp. Lang saw him at the same time and an incredulous look swept over his face. Shamski nodded. "You took the bait, Lang. You swallowed it. And it's going to choke you now."

"Who is this man?" Vinson asked.

Shamski ignored him. "Remember when you gave him that load of cash? The tricky bastard was wearing a legal wire on you. And the tape talks loud." Now there was the first hint of fear in Lang's eyes. "I'm doing you a favor by telling you this," Shamski said. "Now it's up to you."

Max watched. He had been instructed to keep silent and he obeyed orders. Lang's mouth opened and closed without a sound. His stolid expression dissolved into a mass of creases. His shoulders sagged.

"Just a minute." Vinson turned to Lang. "Let's think this through."

"He's locked, and he knows it," Shamski said harshly. "There's nothing to think."

"I'm not involved in murder," Lang suddenly shouted. The dam had broken and the rush of his fear sluiced out. "There can't be a murder charge." The room was galvanized by the shout but Shamski spoke calmly, soothingly. "OK, all right, tell us why."

"Because someone else killed Bannerman; I know they did."

Shocked, Max surged forward. Morrisey put a restraining hand on his shoulder. Max said, "How the hell do you know that?"

Vinson tried to stop the flow. "Mr. Lang, please."

Shamski interposed quickly. "No—Lang, you tell us the whole story. Let's get it out on the table. If there's a deal there, you'll get it, I promise." He threw a glance at the tape recorder to make sure it had enough tape on the reel. Lang sat down, hunching his large frame, his hands locked together.

"I . . . have worked for Brady, OK. Whatever he does, he does."

"He runs a big drug ring, that's what he does," Shamski laughed. "And Morey's was just a front."

Lang looked away. "I don't inquire. I have no part of that; my life has been on the Street, investments. From time to time I have gotten shipments of . . . cash and it was my job to . . . send it to the right places."

"Clean it, you mean," Borland said.

Max glared at Lang. "What about Cy, what about my partner?"

"He traded for us—for Morey's—the same way you did."

"Then what?" Shamski asked.

"He was losing a lot of money. I was very concerned. We didn't know if he was skimming or not." As he spoke, Lang composed himself; his manner became professional. "He'd send

304

me statements I didn't like. The losses went very high. You can't have those kind of losses, in any business."

"Did he know it was drugs?" Max demanded. Lang shrugged. Max's voice rose. "DID HE KNOW IT WAS DRUGS?"

"We never used that . . . language," Lang replied. Max retreated in frustration.

"Go on," Shamski urged.

"I learned I was getting incorrect bank statements. I relayed that fact to the principals."

"Who were the principals in Morey's?"

"The Cayman bank was my contact. Morey's was an offshore company."

"A blind," Borland put in. "Morey's was Brady."

Lang continued evenly. "That week in July, I received a message. I was told that some people were going to see Bannerman and discuss the matter—on that Friday."

"Discuss? These guys went to have a high-level financial discussion with Bannerman, you're telling me?" Shamski glared at Lang. "They went to dump him, didn't they—to make an example?"

"Whatever they went for," Lang said firmly, "it didn't happen."

Max looked at him with mingled anger and disbelief. "My partner was killed."

"Yes, but it happened sometime before," Lang insisted. "These two men got into the apartment looking for him. He wasn't in any of the rooms. They saw the terrace door open and went out there. They found the railing crashed in and down below they saw—him. They went out and left down the stairway."

Shamski walked directly up to Lang. "How do you know that?"

"They told me . . . the next day."

"Who are these men?"

"I don't know," Lang said. "They came from out of town. They left right after we spoke. I never even knew their names."

"Did the orders come from Brady—Brigado?"

"I don't know. They came and they went. But they didn't kill Bannerman." He looked straight at Shamski. "That's the fact."

Shamski said, "And I'm supposed to believe that?"

Vinson said, "That's up to you. He's admitted a lot of things I wouldn't have advised him to."

Max, puzzled, studied Lang's face. Was he telling the truth? How was it possible? It couldn't be.

Shamski frowned. "Did you send the package bomb to Whiz kids?"

Lang paused nervously. "I—knew it was sent."

Vinson tried to salvage something. "But you, personally, had nothing to do with it."

"Let him answer," Shamski growled.

"I . . ." Lang swallowed hard. "I gave the address."

"Gave who the address?"

"Brady." It was a whisper.

"Jimmy Singh was killed too," Max said, "and Barbara Stratton."

"Not involved, not in murder, no." Lang's voice was strong and sure again.

A thread of uncertainty entangled Max. "You're lying," he said to Lang. "I know you are."

"That's what happened."

"No," Max grated through his teeth, "you're the ones, you're the only ones. It doesn't make any sense otherwise!"

Lang locked eyes with him. "He was dead when they got there."

"All right," Shamski said to Morrisey, "let's start to get this down on paper. Call the D.A's office; they're waiting."

Vinson said to Lang, "You're sure this is what you want?"

Lang looked at Shamski. "You'll keep your word about a deal?"

Shamski nodded. "If the D.A. goes along."

Lang looked at Borland. "I'll take securities manipulation." He swung back to Shamski. "But no capital charge. Because that did not happen."

"You son of a bitch," Max said.

Lang took no offense. His voice actually softened. "You fooled me, you know. I thought you were weak, but you fooled me."

When they took Lang out, Max turned to Shamski and asked bluntly, "Do you believe him?"

Shamski took a moment, then answered slowly, "He didn't have to tell us about the two men who were sent."

"But do you believe him?"

"He doesn't have anything to gain by lying now."

"Do you believe him?"

Shamski frowned and nodded.

Max was bewildered. "But who else—why?"

Shamski had no answer. He left Max alone in the gloom of the small room. Impossible, Max told himself over and over again. It was impossible. Brigado's hitmen had murdered Cy, and Jimmy too. Lang was lying. But a fear that he wasn't began to spread, like an evil, swift-running virus, through Max's brain.

A hundred questions followed.

19

Brought into the station house and questioned, Daphne Kaiser, it became clear to Shamski, had no notion that she had been a pawn in Lang's capture. The event itself, Shamski knew, could not be kept secret for long, but at least Max Roberts would be kept out of it. Daphne was sent on her way and later called Max excitedly to tell him what an adventure she had.

"I was so scared," she related. "It was thrilling. I still don't know why they arrested that Mr. Lang. They wouldn't tell me. I think maybe he's a Russian spy, though. I'm going to have some story to tell when I get back home."

Over the next forty-eight hours, Lang was interrogated almost to exhaustion by a team from Borland's office. His answers were checked and rechecked, the bank connections made, the flow of laundered money charted, the companies bought into by the Swiss entity listed. The outline sketched was of a businesslike international operation fueled by endless amounts of cash that was fed into the corporate world through a maze of holding companies, subsidiaries, and shell corporations. The result was a money trail almost impossible to follow—the desired end of it all—with Brigado and the others shielded. For no piece of paper showed them as any officer of any company anywhere.

Through all this, the word "drugs" was never spoken. Lang would talk only of his securities activities, his "cash disbursals," his Street and bank connections. He admitted knowing Brady and having telephone conversations, but never about anything illegal that might be proved. For his part, the bank officer, Clemmons, readily talked of accepting bags of cash and wiring transfers to the Caymans and other offshore banks. He had received cash bonuses to do that but insisted that at least two other vice-presidents at the bank knew what was transpiring. They, in turn, denied knowing anything. Clemmons was hung out to dry. Borland, interested only in the securities revelations, was in his element.

Brian Shamski was not. Where was drug dealing and homicide in this? They seemed to matter less, even to the D.A., than the glamorous millions and their conversion. Max was more angered.

"Cy is dead. Singh is dead. Barbara is dead. Lang is a son of a bitch whose hands are bloody but he's being treated like a spy who came in from the cold, just someone like Borland who happened to be on the wrong side."

"It's tough," Shamski agreed.

"But you believe him," Max pressed, "about the hitmen, for instance."

"His stories check out, almost everything. Listen to this." Shamski picked up a large sheaf of interrogation transcript and read from it. "Me: You know Brady tried to get rid of the Whiz-kids records with a bomb. Why wouldn't you try to get rid of Singh himself when he went for the records? Answer: I told you, I am not involved in violence and I wasn't aware he had them or where he hid them; how would I know?"

"Someone called Juli Singh," Max interrupted heatedly, "and claimed to be from the police, remember? She told him where Jimmy went."

"Right," Shamski agreed, "but we played her a tape of Lang's voice yesterday and she didn't think it was him."

"It could have been one of his people."

"I don't think he'd trust them to pull that off." He read further. "Me: You kept close tabs on Roberts, didn't you? Answer: You deal with people, you have to know something about them. He made a few trips to this woman in Vermont, for instance, and I had somebody keep an eye on him there, yes. And there's another woman as well, someone from the Exchange."

Shamski looked at Max with interest. Max deflected it. "What did he say about Roy Herbert?"

"Right out front. Here it is. Lang: I know Herbert from the Street—which is not illegal. Me: What about the Southern Bird Company? Answer: Herbert discovered that company. He was acting as a middleman. That's not illegal. Me: Shipping out millions in cash to the Caymans to buy that company, though, is. Answer: I've already gone into that with Mr. Borland."

"Right." Max was disgusted. "Him and the creep. If you dragged Herbert in . . ."

"My orders are," Shamski said apologetically, "to hold off. There's a tight cover on everything until every lead is pumped dry."

Max left, his head in a spin. If Lang was telling the truth . . . But it made no sense; it fragmented everything. He resolved to walk away from it all but it clung to him, wrapped him in uncertainty. He spent hours trying to work it through. Nothing cleared. When Adeline called, he only half listened, absorbed in his thoughts. If not Brady, then who—what?

He went to Cy's computer and poked through a stack of disks. He put one on and roamed through it. It was a collection of letters and there was a note to Julian:

> The old days are very vivid in my mind, the Digger days, the feeling of brotherhood and friendship. That's most important to me. I need that. You and Max are like out of those days to me, sturdy, dependable companions. It will be really interesting to see us grow old together.

Max broke off reading. That would never happen now. Cy would never grow old with them. Moved, he resolved to call Julian; they would get together; he would fill him in, despite Shamski. He would be isolated no longer. He went straight to the phone on the night table and his eyes fell on the slim orange tube of lip gloss, lying amidst his wallet and keys, the Slickers. It held him hypnotically, and he began to wonder why Liz Evers had lied about it. What did she have to hide? She had said peculiar things about Cy. What was the truth? He lifted the tube to his eyes and examined it carefully, as though he would find the answer in the fine print. If Lang was not lying, was it possible that somehow Liz had . . . ? He continued the meticulous examination and with each passing second, it became more and more urgent to see Cy's former lover and confront her. She would not see him willingly, he knew, but catching her off guard might work.

In the late morning Max went to the bustling building on Madison housing her offices. On the twenty-ninth floor he entered the half-moon reception area of Evers-Nagourney, nodding with faked familiarity to the blonde behind the reception desk. He waited till a messenger came out of the door to her right, caught it before it locked again, and went through.

The offices of Evers-Nagourney were a jumble of cubicles separated by snakelike corridors. In these enclaves of creativity labored the teams that brought the country its steady diet of snappy TV commercials, for which they ravaged every corner of classical and pop culture. They reveled in their beards and jeans and denim skirts, which signified their status as rebels. They reveled, as well, in the rewards a grateful agency bestowed upon them. Liz Evers understood them very well. Her partner, Milton Nagourney, a mysterious Romanian design visionary, provided the striking layouts for which the agency was noted.

Max walked through the corridors, which opened into an executive area. To his relief, no one gave him a second glance. Here there were no beards and jeans, but blue blazers, gray slacks, and penny loafers. Here were the people who dealt with the real world of the clients, out to sell more detergent and not win Clio awards for cleverness. He passed first one door, then another. To his left he saw a walled-off section and veered toward it. Within ten yards he came up to a desk at which a short-haired, severe-looking young man in a blue suit, purple shirt, and orange figured tie sat whispering into a telephone. Behind him was an unmarked, carved walnut door. Max hesitated and pretended to fumble with his briefcase. He heard the blue-suited guardian say a British-accented, "I'll get Miz. E. to call your man for a new lunch date, dear, never fear. Ta." He pressed a button on the console and spoke again. "Doll, catch my phone for the next few, will you, I'm off to the loo." He hung up and scooted away, waving to Max.

Alone, Max walked cautiously toward the walnut door. He heard some footsteps to his left and waited nervously till they faded away. Quickly, before someone might actually arrive, Max went up to the door, steadied himself, and knocked.

"Who's that?" It was Liz Evers's impatient voice.

Max opened the door, stepped inside, and swiftly closed it behind him. He found himself in a corner office, many-windowed and bright with plants. Liz Evers, seated behind a huge mahogany rolltop desk, stared at Max with disbelief. She rose and slammed down the layout she had been studying "How dare you?" She said, "Get out of here. Instantly." Her hand reached to the phone console.

"Please," Max said. "I'm sorry about this, but I knew you wouldn't talk to me."

"Exactly right."

"But you have to. For your own sake."

A questioning look came over Liz Evers's face. Her fingers trembled over the phone buttons. Max reached into his pocket and withdrew the tube of Slickers. "I found this in your bathroom when Julian and I were in your apartment."

She blanched. "You searched my bathroom? You invaded my personal things?"

"It wasn't like that," Max said quickly. "I was feeling sick looking for a tissue." He came closer to her. "This stuff was on the glasses in Cy's apartment. You said you never used it. You lied to the police."

"I did not," Liz flared. "I may have used it once—and forgotten. That's all."

"They don't know I found it," Max told her quietly.

She stared at him, surprised, questioning, suspicious.

"I've told no one. I wanted to speak to you first . . . not only about this."

"Oh," she said, "I see. You want to drown yourself in some more Cy. You want me to drown in it." She turned away

"It doesn't make sense," Max said softly. "It has to make sense to me. You said you wanted a child. He deprived you of it."

"Yes." It was said dully.

"Cy wanted a child."

"On his terms, only on his!" The words burst from her lips like water from a sac.

Max was startled. "What terms?"

"His, his!" Liz Evers started to tremble. "His way, only

his way." She sank down into a leather chair, dissolving, her tall frame almost visibly shriveling. "Nothing counted but what he wanted." Tears sprouted at the corners of her eyes. "I wanted that baby, oh God, I wanted it. But I wanted a father for it, a real father, the one he was supposed to become." She slumped deeper into the chair, huddled into herself, and looked at the ceiling almost vacantly. Max remembered her breakdown and felt a stab of guilt.

From the depths of the chair Liz Evers said, "It was that night, that terrible night. He told me he was dying to have a kid. He couldn't wait for it. But marriage, well, marriage now wasn't right for him and maybe not for me." She turned her face up to look at Max with accusation. "He always adored telling people what was right for them, didn't he? He said he was just being honest." Her voice became stronger. "I told him it was always honesty with him, every nasty act, every brutal thing is done in the name of honesty, freedom of choice, all the rest of the malarkey that he carried around with him from those old times." She sat up suddenly.

"I told him that we have made this baby, we have a responsibility to it. He gave me one of those patented patient smiles of his and said . . . I can hear him now . . . 'Yes, but what's marriage got to do with it?' "

She jumped straight up from the chair. "I screamed at him that it had everything to do because I wanted the life I want—not the secondhand life he wanted for me, because we talked about how every baby should have a full-time father. He said that he was the father but marriage, even living together, was something else." She went up to Max, her eyes blazing as though Max were Cy. " 'Oh,' I told him, 'you'll visit and bring toys. No! You knew I wanted marriage if I became pregnant.' We talked about it. Do you know what he said, what came out of him?"

Max shook his head.

"He said . . . he said that his mistake was in taking me seriously. *In taking me seriously.*" She shuddered. "I told him if that was the case I did not take his fatherhood seriously. I told him the baby was mine, not his, and that he'd never even get a look at it, ever, ever."

Astonished, Max said, "You told Cy that?"

"Yes. I said, 'You will never see this baby, count on it, and if you get lawyers, I'll get lawyers, and if you do other things, I'll do other things.' God, I hated him so. When he left, I wanted to . . ." She teetered, spent. Max made an unfinished gesture toward her but she moved away from him, walked to a window and looked out.

"He didn't call for weeks. I became blocked. I couldn't work. Nothing was important. My analyst said I was in a dangerous conflicted state, becoming unconnected. It was true." Her voice became dull again. "I . . . suffered stomach pains. I lost weight. The doctors became concerned. They said the baby wasn't getting enough food from me, wasn't growing right. I tried to eat more, to stuff myself, but I . . . couldn't keep it down. My analyst said I had to accept what had happened, but how could I? Every day the baby was hurting. I could feel it hurting. I was hurting it but it was really *his* fault. He was the one. So one day, rather than hurt it anymore . . ." She turned to look at Max. "He deprived me of my baby. He deserved whatever happened to him."

Max was stunned. "He walked away, just like that?"

Had Cy known what she was going through? Had he cared? Had he suspected, even a little, that she would abort this child? What had happened to him? A time frame meshed in his mind. Cy had met Sonya just about then. Had he seriously thought of marriage to *her*?

Liz Evers's eyes cleared. Her entire demeanor changed. "You got what you came for, so get out now."

"The Slickers . . ." Max started, but without warning Liz picked up a heavy blown-glass sculpture from the desk and hurled it at him with all her strength. Max saw it coming straight at his head and ducked. The sculpture smashed into the wall behind him and shattered like a bomb. Razor-edged slivers of blue glass caromed off the wall and exploded past his face. The door opened and the startled secretary was framed in the doorway, open-mouthed.

"Out," Liz Evers screamed at Max. "Out!"

Max fled, the Slickers still in his hand.

In the cab, still shaken by Liz's roaring anger, Max contemplated the orange tube. Out of control—she had been out of control. Had that sculpture hit him. . . . He flicked back the top of the tube, revealing the bullet-shaped tip, and detected a faint aroma. Gingerly, he touched the point to his tongue. It was greasy and he recognized the vague taste of canteloupe. Exactly what had been found on the champagne glasses. Why, really, had she lied about never using Slickers?

Adeline had settled into Max's apartment easily. She did that by ignoring it. She had never taken much interest in furnishings or the degree of dust on shelves or what was in the refrigerator. For better or worse, her concerns had always been elsewhere—the manifest inequities of society, the venality of the organized movements, Communist, Socialist, Republican— she lumped them all together. The fact was that she had not changed much from her firebrand days. The small-boned, gray-haired old lady with the sweet face of age and the cornflower-blue eyes was hardly what she appeared to be. But now the flame existed only in her mind.

She had never come to terms with what Max was up to, but the stories Cy had told her about the madness of it all made it seem less like capitalist big business than a poker game in an insane asylum. She had come to think of what Max did as a postadolescent rebellion against all the values she had tried to instill in him.

Cy's death changed that. Its overtones made her fearful. She had come north not only to see her old comrades but with a vague hope of getting her son to change course before complete corruption set in. She thought for a moment about the Vermont weaver girl. Pretty—oh yes, but not in the real world, she concluded, not someone who had the values she hoped would emerge in Max.

Today Adeline planned to see her oldest friend, Agnes, whose still-living husband she despised. In the past the quarrels between them had been monumental. He owned a small printing business and remained a firm believer in the greatness of "this country" and "where would you be if your folks had stayed in the old country?" He didn't understand, Adeline would complain bitterly to Agnes, that "that wasn't the political point."

She smiled as she sat in Max's big lounge chair near the window and dialed Agnes's number. It would be a very pleasant day. After a visit with Agnes, she would meet Max at his office for an early dinner and, maybe, a serious talk. Agnes's husband answered the phone. Hearing who it was, his voice took on a wary tone. Agnes, it appeared, was not home—but was expecting her old friend. She was to come up—oh, certainly. Adeline detected the reservation in his tone and thought, Things never change.

"I'll come up," Adeline said, "but maybe I'll just spend a little time at the zoo, it's so close."

"The zoo?" It was apparent to Adeline that Agnes's husband considered this freakish—adults didn't go to zoos; that was for kids. "You going to ride the elephant, Adeline?" A dumb laugh.

"Maybe."

What Agnes's ignorant husband didn't know was that Adeline had always loved Bronx Park and its zoo. Living only blocks away, it was where she had wheeled Max in his carriage many times. The great apes, particularly, she had always found fascinating and Max had absorbed that. Yes, she thought—a small visit there after all these years would be just fine; then she would go over to Agnes's. She was changing from her bed slippers to the molded plastic shoes she still wore, the only shoes that didn't bother her bunions, when the doorbell sounded. She padded over and called through the door, "Yes?"

A high-pitched male voice said, "Delivery for Mr. Roberts."

Cautiously, Adeline looked through the peephole and saw, through the fisheye lens, the distorted figure of a thin man in green trousers and a black windbreaker. He wore an outsize navy-blue cap with a bill that almost obscured his pinched cheeks. Mainly he seemed to be all restless eyes. He held up a small envelope and waved it. Adeline unlocked the door and opened it. In person, the messenger appeared to be in his twenties, had a beaked nose and thick red sideburns descending from the cap. Seeing Adeline, he blinked rapidly. "Max Roberts?"

"Max is my son," Adeline said pleasantly. "I'll take it for him."

"I'm supposed to give it right to him," the man said. "Ain't he here?"

"No—but I'm meeting him later. I'll get it to him."

"He ain't coming back?"

"No," Adeline said, "but I told you I'll be meeting him."

"Never mind." The messenger walked away rapidly. Adeline closed the door and thought no more about it.

She thought no more about it until she had taken the train to the zoo, until she spent a nostalgic twenty minutes in the primate house. Here, as always, the small monkeys flung them-

317

selves about to the children's delighted squeals while the great apes, her favorites, sat on their piles of artificial stones and brooded. There had been few changes in this house, she noted, since the time she had first come here as a shining-eyed young wife and mother pushing the stroller. Even these majestic animals, regarding their viewers with priestly solemnity, seemed unchanged. The changes, she thought with a fleeting sadness, had all taken place in her.

She left the monkey house, and it was then that she saw, or thought she saw, amidst the crowd, the navy-blue cap and the hawklike profile under it. It was someone who looked like that kid, she told herself, another underprivileged street urchin grown up into another messenger.

In the open air, she sat alone on a bench to rest her feet. She sat back, continuing to think of other days, and was not aware of someone sitting down near her, but when she finally turned in that direction she saw, with surprise, that it *was* the messenger. The pupils of his eyes were very large now and his tongue kept flicking at his lips. One hand was in his jacket pocket and the other clenched and unclenched like a mechanical fist. Adeline's heart pounded so she could almost hear it in her head. She felt dizzy and started to fall off the bench, but caught herself. The man said nothing, only watched for a minute, then he moved even closer.

20

Max went directly to Julian's office in the TV studio, bursting with what had just occurred, but Berns was elsewhere. He left word to be called immediately and returned to his own office, still stirred up. He glanced at *Time*, had no patience for it. He read the junk mail distractedly. Pleas for funds, letters from congressmen, another glossy announcement from the Space disco office about their "Wall Street, the Power Street" night.

He tossed everything into the wastebasket and thought of his resolve for a new life—and of Sonya. Perhaps, he decided, he had been too quick to draw conclusions. He wondered if she had returned from the backpacking trip. Cautiously, he dialed her number and felt his pulse quicken as she answered.

"Sonya, it's Max," he said tentatively. "How was your backpacking?"

"Max," Sonya's voice was warm. "It was really good."

"Sonya, a million things have happened here." Max was urgent. "Are still happening. I really need to talk to you."

"About Cy?"

"No, about me . . . about you."

319

"Oh."

Max sensed a dismaying reticence. "My mother is still in town so I might not be able to make it for a day or two, but after that . . ."

"Max," Sonya said, "I won't be here. We're taking off to visit my dad out west and sort of hang out with him for a while."

Max heard the *we're* with dismay. "Who's the we?"

"My friend."

"Your neighbor?"

"My friend, yes."

There it was, then. He had been right. Max felt disappointment.

"Sonya, I thought . . ."

"Max, sometimes we think what we want to think."

"It wasn't just thoughts between us, Sonya."

"Max, my life is my own." Sonya was only slightly impatient.

"I didn't mean that it wasn't," Max said helplessly.

"A person goes through different cycles; nature arranges it that way."

What was she saying?

"There are many stations on the road."

Talk to me, Sonya, Max begged silently.

"I really don't have to explain myself."

"No," Max said.

"Anyway, stay well," Sonya said, "and go well."

"You too," Max whispered. He sat back in his chair, unsettled. He closed his eyes, invoking Sonya, shocked at how much he had staked on her. He had planned all these changes, with her as the linchpin of his life, he realized. He had imagined that she was the answer to all his problems, that she was this perfect person, this wonderful essence of woman, this woodland creature of deep feelings who had responded to him. With her he would live out an uncomplicated idyllic existence in the enchanted forest. Had that fantasy been Cy's as well? It didn't matter. He let out a deep sigh. She would be only a memory from now on.

The phone in the outer office rang, breaking his reverie. Max didn't wait for Martha to answer. It was Adeline.

"Max—it's me."

Max slumped onto a corner of the desk in disappointment. "Hi—what's up?"

THE THIRD FRIDAY

"Max—I'm not feeling very well."

Max rose in alarm. "What's wrong?"

"My heart's not right, Max. . . . I don't want you to worry about it, but—but could you come and get me?"

"Addie, of course I'll come. Where are you?"

"Up in the Bronx."

Max heard the tension in his mother's voice and tried to keep his own from mounting. "Where in the Bronx—whose house?"

"I'm at the zoo, Max."

"Did you say the zoo?"

His mother's words came in a rush. "Yes—the zoo. I was going to Agnes's house. And I thought I'd like to see the monkeys. I'm at the telephone booth near the—you know—the old monkey house."

Max gulped in air. The monkey house; the woman was having a heart attack at the monkey house. "Addie, sit down on a bench—I'll get an ambulance."

"No—I don't need an ambulance." Her voice trembled and he felt fear spiral up in him. "Just come."

"All right. Sit down out of the sun."

"Hurry." His mother's voice almost faded out.

"Adeline!"

But the line was dead. With no word to Martha, Max raced from the office and out to the street. He jumped off the sidewalk and stopped a gypsy cab with his body. The black driver hit the brakes hard and shouted in a Caribbean tone, "Hey—wot you doin', crazy bugger?"

Max jerked at the rear door of the banged-in Pontiac. "Get me to the Bronx, please . . . to the zoo. It's an emergency."

The round-faced, near-hairless driver blinked. "You playin' a joke, mon—a zoo emergency?"

"Dammit," Max said, "my mother's in trouble there."

"Oh mon, I'm sorry." The driver threw the car into drive and they hurtled forward. The ancient sedan bumped and rattled as they headed east toward First. The driver jumped lights, sat on his horn, passed traffic on the right, pulling shouts and honks after him. In minutes he was on the bridge, thumping over the metal and hurling his cab in a wide arc to the Bronx. Max sat back, feet braced, not feeling the ride at all. His mind was on Adeline sitting on a bench in the park, controlling her own panic as her heart skipped beats trying to pump, as she felt the tightness across her chest and her breath come short. "Oh God," he whispered.

"You mum going to be all right, mon," the driver called behind him, swerving away from a limo. "You got to t'ink dot way. Don' give no bad vibrations. We makin' good time." He jerked at the wheel and escaped the exhaust of a huge truck. "Look at dot son of a bad ass whoremonger's git."

They were on Bruckner now and the driver pushed the pedal to the floor. The gypsy screamed along the asphalt, every weld protesting. A police cruiser came charging along the other way and slowed. The driver shouted, "Don' you stop me, you blue-suit po-lice bandits." The cruiser resumed its speed and in moments, the gypsy had swerved onto the Bronx River Parkway. Max watched the greenery fly by and looked at his watch. Twenty-five minutes had passed since his mother had called.

"Comin' up zoo. She's right here." The driver turned hard left at a sign and sped up to a gate and parking lot. An attendant waved toward the lot, but the gypsy quivered to a stop at the barrier. Max leaned out of the open window. "We've got to get to the primate house."

"Hey." The attendant was a young boy, pimples dotting his chin like beard stubble. "You can't drive beyond here."

"My mother's sick . . . a heart attack," Max said. "She's waiting on a bench."

"Gee—gee—" The boy was at a loss.

"Let's go," the driver shouted.

"You can't," the boy said desperately. "There's no car road."

The driver looked at Max questioningly. Max jumped from the cab. He tossed a bill at the driver, shouting, "Wait!" He hurdled the barrier and sprinted along the broad walk as fast as he could. He was not even in the zoo proper, he knew—just the walk leading to it. He struggled uphill to where the first directional signs were nailed to a tree. They told him how to get to the reptile house and the seal pond. He plunged on, passing enclosures in which red foxes and tiny deer stalked back and forth. He saw the seal pond, heard the barks and the splashes. Momentarily breathless, he halted near a glass-roofed aviary where dozens of large birds chattered and swooped. Two teen-aged girls in cutoff shorts came giggling up. He whirled on them. "Where are the monkeys? Where's the monkey house?"

The girls, struck silent, moved a step away.

"Please," Max repeated, "I have to get to the monkey house."

"It's that way," the taller of the two said, pointing vaguely straight ahead, "you creep." Both girls ran off, the giggling high-pitched and hysterical. Chancing it, Max continued straight on, walking swiftly. From behind him came a tinny honk. He turned to see a Toonerville trolley tooling along on its rubber wheels, carrying a load of visitors. The overalled motorman nodded his thanks and rolled on through. "The monkey house!" Max yelled. The motorman pointed to his left. Max changed direction and dashed off. He passed animals and enclosures and people and trees. They were all blurs. As he entered a small plaza, chest heaving, he stopped at a complex of signs. Antelopes, elephants, bears—no monkeys. He looked about him and tried desperately to induce memory. He had been taken here so much as a small boy. Then he realized there was no sign because he was here —there was the old primate house. But where was Adeline?

He checked for a phone booth and spotted one across the plaza. Heart leaping, he saw his mother seated on a bench. "Adeline," he shouted, and ran the twenty yards across to her. As he neared, Adeline looked up at him, and he saw worry in her eyes. He leaned over, reaching for her hand. "How do you feel? Is it any better? Just hang in, we'll get you downtown to a hospital in a jiffy. They'll know what to do."

"Max." Adeline's lips trembled. "Oh—Max—"

"Take it easy. Maybe we can get some sort of wheelchair in here." Max rose up to scan the area. As he did the man next to his mother spoke with quiet intensity.

"Sit down."

Not looking at the seated man, Max said, "No, we've got to get her to a—"

"Sit down," the man hissed.

"Max, listen to him," Adeline said in a small, choked voice.

Max looked now. What struck him was the large-billed cap and the eyes below. The pupils were shimmering wildly. Chilled, Max thought, This thin-faced man was very high. Slowly Max sat.

"Aw right," the man whispered. "Jus' sit."

Max pushed close to his mother, looking at her intently. She exchanged looks with him and he thought that she did not appear ill and he realized she wasn't. She was frightened—or was she? The skinny man, looking off in the distance, said in a soft, tense voice, "I got a piece here in my hand with a silencer, unnerstand? I can blow her away like that. So jus' sit till I tell you what to do."

Max looked at his mother, shocked. She nodded grimly. Max waited thirty seconds, then whispered, "What do you want?"

"Stay shut."

"Maxie, shh." Adeline pressed her son's arm. The three of them sat in silence till the flow of visitors ebbed, then the wild-eyed man said, "Stan' up now."

Max held on to his mother's hand and obeyed.

"C'mon." The man took the middle position, Adeline on his right, Max on his left. "Walk." He set out in the direction of the plaza perimeter.

Adeline whispered, "He made me call you."

"Shut."

Adeline bowed her head.

They walked for minutes away from the populated places, onto a small path that led through the woods. He was trying to get them away from everyone—completely isolated, Max realized. He looked at Adeline. She was ashen. He considered leaping on the thin-framed man, overpowering him. As though reading Max's mind, the man said, "Don' try nothin', not nothin'."

"Listen," Max said, "think a minute. We can make some kind of deal. Whatever you want?"

"Jus' shut."

"Think about it—whatever you want."

Their tormentor stopped walking. Max and Adeline stopped with him. Almost trembling, his eyes blinking rapidly, he said, "Like I say—you do like I say. Move in there." He pointed toward an opening in the woods. Max looked around in desperation. A couple wheeled a baby carriage ten feet away, quarreling in Spanish as they went. He thought about calling to them, but would they respond? And would this crazed cokehead shoot?

"G'head. Now."

If he and Adeline went into that patch of woods, Max knew, they would never emerge again. He looked at his mother. She was having trouble breathing and her left hand was on her chest. She saw his look and managed to say, "I'm all right, don't . . . get him excited."

"She's having a heart attack!" Max felt as though he were having one.

The gunman, face muscles twitching, took this as a breaking point. "I had enough outta you," he said at Adeline. "You screwed it all up fer me." Unaccountable rage swelled up. He pushed at his right pocket and Max saw the black snout of a gun barrel peek through a tear in the material.

"Let her go," Max pleaded. "You want me, not her. I'll be quiet, I'll do anything you want, but let her go."

The gunman pushed Adeline roughly to the opening. Max reached for him, but Adeline called, "No—Max." She stumbled toward the woods. Max followed her. "In there, in there," the gunman commanded. In seconds the trio were swallowed up by brush. He had to do something, Max told himself, anything, or within the next ten seconds the insane end of it all would take place . . . with Adeline punished for what he had done . . . or what Cy had done.

Suddenly, Adeline moaned and gasped. She fell to the pine-carpeted earth, her short legs collapsing. Her blue skirt flew up above her swollen knees and her arms struck the earth once and then were still.

"Addie!" Max shouted and bent toward her.

"Get away from her," the gunman shrilled. He pulled his weapon from concealment and waved it in panic. It was an automatic, and the screwed-on silencer had been cut down. Max ignored him and bent to his mother, whose eyes were closed and whose breath was coming in gasps.

"Addie," Max said in despair. "No, Addie. Please, Addie." He patted her face. Her cheeks were cold. He reached for her wrist to find a pulse. Her breathing slowed and she let out a deep soughing sound. "No, no—" Max called, feeling helpless.

"Get up." The gunman reached down and, putting the gun barrel at Max's head with one hand, pulled at him with the other. As he did, Adeline came to abrupt life. Her left foot kicked out at the gunman. Her ancient, heavy, molded plastic shoe caught him directly in the side, tumbling him back and expelling his breath into "You bitch . . ." Frozen, Max could only stare at his mother as she reached for his hand. He recovered, jerking her to her feet.

"Go," Adeline screamed, "go."

The gunman, only a yard away, was rising, cursing, and reaching for his weapon, which had dropped from his hand. Pulling at Adeline, Max lurched forward, bending low. From behind him, he heard a popping sound followed by a whine and a sharp thwack as the bullet cracked into a tree trunk. There was another pop and the swish of air as a second piece of lead slammed by him. Head down, he churned forward, dragging Adeline behind him. She stumbled, almost fell, but kept to her feet. The gunman thrashed after them, but in moments they were out of the glade and onto the road.

Max pulled up, feeling his mother slacken.

"Max, I can't go anymore. . . ." Adeline's voice was hoarse.

"You can, you can." Max tried to jerk her forward, but she staggered and rocked clumsily. From a corner of his eye, Max saw the gunman emerging from the woods opening. "Try . . . try." He put an arm about his mother's waist and moved her another few steps. Meanwhile, the gunman had come out openly to the middle of the road and was raising his automatic to fire.

"Down," Max shouted and fell heavily to the asphalt, taking Adeline with him. She hit hard, her breath streaming from her. Max covered her body with his own. The gunman, arm outstretched, pulled the trigger again. At the pop, Max buried his head in his hands. He heard the bullet skitter off the road somewhere, raised up, and saw, with terror, that the gunman was advancing toward them. Unable to tear his eyes away, unable to move, Max saw the large floppy cap come closer and closer. Then, in a jarring counterpoint, he saw, coming up behind the gunman, the almost-silent Toonerville train and heard the horn *toot-toot*. The gunman, hearing the beeps at his back, whirled in surprise and gaped at the oncoming train. Once again, the motorman sounded his horn, and again. At the sound, the gunman wavered, and as the train kept rolling toward him, broke and ran back into the brush.

Max raised up, lifting his mother. "It's all right, Addie. He's gone." Adeline, puffing, scrambled to her feet with some difficulty. Max helped her anxiously. "Are you hurt?"

Adeline shook her head. She brushed the dirt from her skirt and staggered. Max caught her. "I'm all right," she said, "but I banged my bad knee."

The trolley had reached them by now and the five passengers looked on, wide-eyed. The motorman, a seamed retiree park volunteer, jumped from his seat. "Did he try to mug you?"

"Yes," Max said. "Can we go back with you?"

"Hop in."

Max helped Adeline into a seat. The motorman returned to the controls and reassured his flock. "It's all right, folks— you get bad apples everywhere, you know . . . even in the park." He tooted once, releasing his brakes, and the train gently started forward. Max turned his eyes from one side of the road to the other, worried that the crazed gunman might follow and try another shot—the pace of the train was slow enough. Was he alone or were there others? And Adeline? He cringed at the thought of what might have happened.

"Are you really all right?" he asked his mother in low tones.

Adeline attempted to put her wrecked braid back in place. "I'll live."

Max brushed a leaf from his mother's blouse. "It was awful, terrible. I'm sorry to get you involved in this. It won't happen again. You'll go right back to Florida."

She did not respond, but looked ahead stonily.

"Your heart," Max said tentatively.

"It's working."

"When you collapsed back there, I thought—"

"I didn't know what else to do."

"It was terrific. Keeping your head that way."

She turned back with flashing eyes. "In the old days, when the fascist police were coming at us on horseback like Cossacks, we learned not to lose our heads, my son. Who was that man?"

Max hesitated. How much should he tell her? "I don't know him. But I suppose he was sent to—" He could not finish.

Adeline plucked at her gray silk blouse unhappily. "Why, Max—why is all this happening?"

"It's hard to explain."

"It has to do with the money business, though—I know it does."

"In a way," Max admitted. Then he added, "It has to do with Cy."

"Ah . . ." Adeline drew in her breath. "Again with Cy— always with Cy."

"It's . . . something I had to do."

"When will it be enough with Cy?"

"Ma, I have an obligation," Max said uncomfortably. "It's something I'm . . . working out."

"Working out. I see."

Max scanned the undergrowth on both sides of the road for any sign of the gunman but he had vanished. Max turned back to Adeline. "How did he get to you?"

Adeline bent to wipe some mud from her Murray Space Shoe. "He rang the doorbell."

"Didn't the desk downstairs ring you first?"

"I didn't think about that."

Max was astonished. "And you let him in?"

"He told me he had a delivery. Am I supposed to think you're involved with gangsters?" Adeline glared at him. "He said he could only give what he had to you. He was nervous, jumpy, but he's just trying to make a living in this city, I thought—so why shouldn't he be jumpy? I told him I'd be meeting you later."

"He followed you to the zoo—to get to me?" Max was astonished. "That's plain dumb. Drugged-out thinking."

"When I saw him, the gangster, I almost had a real heart attack. I realized that he followed me all the way up here to the Bronx Zoo. For what reason? He loves chimps? I tell him he's mistaken, I'm not meeting you here, but later. He gets angry right away. I could see his eyes rolling back in his head. He tells me he has a gun and will hurt me if I don't listen to him. I can hardly believe him, Max. But he shows me the gun! A little piece of it. My heart almost stopped then. I thought to myself, This is capitalist society, this is how they make gangsters out of half-starved exploited boys. I ask him what he wants. He tells me to call you. He takes me to the telephone and tells me if I don't call, he'll . . ." For the first time during her recital, Adeline's voice shook. Max clutched her hand.

"I saw he was a crazy," Adeline resumed. "I saw that he would do what he said he would, but how could I call you to come? I said to myself, Adeline, keep your head. Be smart. Somehow you'll let him know something's not kosher. I tried." She shook her head dolefully. "I didn't do it right."

"It doesn't matter," Max said, "and as soon as we get downtown, we'll get you a plane . . ."

"The reunion . . ." Adeline faltered. "I promised all the people I'd be there."

"No," Max said. "Adeline, it's too dangerous."

"I came all the way up here," Adeline said stubbornly.

The horn tootled. "Last stop," the motorman sang out. They were near the gate and the parking lot. With relief, Max saw that the taxi was still waiting for him.

"Come on." He helped his mother out of the train and hurried her over to the cab.

The driver looked her over. "How you doin', mum?"

"Let's get going—quickly," Max said.

"We off." As the driver slammed the door home, he winked at Adeline. "You got a good boy there."

"The best," Adeline said, "yes." She turned to her son and said, "I don't want to miss the reunion." Max saw the set of her face and knew she meant it.

"All right," he said grimly. "I don't think they'll try this again but we can't take any chances. We'll find some out-of-the-way hotel for you to stay at and you'll have police protection till you get on a plane going back."

Adeline's eyes opened wide. "Police? Never. I would never put myself in a position like that."

"Ma, be sensible," Max begged.

From the driver in front came, "We make a run up here like the wind, mum, he a good boy."

"No," Adeline said firmly. "It's only the day after tomorrow. I promised Agnes." Max sagged. She would never give in and he would worry every moment she was in his apartment, or Cy's. But where could she go, who was unconnected to him? An almost instant answer suggested itself—if she would do it. He said to Adeline, "All right, I'll go along with you. But you'll have to go along with me."

When Carol heard Max's urgent voice on the intercom, her initial reaction was surprise mingled with concern. When he appeared with his mother, it changed to shock. She stared at this small, gray-haired woman, who examined her as intently, and was at a loss. Max introduced them and went on urgently, "This is an emergency, Carol. I need your help."

"Max," Adeline demurred, "I'll be all right."

Max ignored her. "She'll be on a plane back to Florida in thirty-six hours, but can she stay here with you till then?"

Carol was wide-eyed. "What's wrong?"

"Can I wash someplace?" Adeline exhibited her smudged hands.

"Right around there," Carol directed, and turned to Max anxiously. "Are you all right?" She touched the streaks on his face with worry. "What happened?"

"It's just dirt," Max said grimly. "Somebody tried to . . ." He hesitated. "Some crazed-out kid with a gun in the park. He followed my mother."

"My God."

"I need her safe till she goes."

"Of course, Max . . . Oh . . ." Her voice trembled. Max

reached out to her and she moved toward him, clutched his hand.

"I have to get to the police right away," he said.

"Was it a . . . robbery thing?"

"No, that's why I want her here."

"What was it, then?"

"I . . . don't know," Max said. "I'm not sure."

Adeline returned, a limp evident. "I have to call Agnes and tell her why I'm not there."

"Please, Mrs. Roberts, use the phone."

Adeline marched to it. Max said, "Addie, I've got to go. I'll be back in a little while." Adeline nodded and tried to remember Agnes's phone number.

"Thanks," Max said to Carol, and before she could even answer, he was gone. From the telephone, surreptitiously, Adeline looked Carol over. Carol, in the middle of the floor, looked deep in thought.

"So," Adeline said, "this is a nice place; what do you do?"

Carol turned to her, eyes brimming with tears. "I'm so sorry," she said. "I'm so very sorry."

21

Shamski listened to Max's story with amazement. "He followed your mother—a cokehead? Sounds like amateur night, but what is it all about?" He took Max to Lang, who had been hidden away in a midtown hotel. Lang, sitting on the hotel bed uncomfortably, a beached whale, was adamant that none of his connections were responsible; it made no sense.

"What if Brady's learned you're turning state's evidence," Max demanded, "and if he eliminates me, I can't confirm what you say?"

"That doesn't fit," Shamski objected. "Right now you're irrelevant."

"It happened," Max said grimly. "He had a gun to my head, he shot at us. Somebody sent him."

"Look elsewhere," Lang said dryly.

"I think it's been a double-trailed situation all along," Shamski said soberly, "and we've been on the wrong one."

Yes, Max thought, but what was the other trail?

"The right one," Shamski mused, "could be something personal."

"Roy Herbert," Max said.

"I know you've got that bug," Shamski said, "but there's nothing hard to connect him. Where's your mother now?"

"With a friend," Max hedged.

"Would you like me to send some blue suits over?"

"I would," Max said, "but she thinks they come on horses, wear fur hats, and carry swords."

Shamski wrinkled his brow.

Max left, went to a pay phone, and eagerly called Julian Berns, who was surprised to hear from him and cold, which Max understood. He had been keeping away from Julie and there was resentment. But it was different now. "Julie, could we have a quick drink?"

Julian was vague. "I'm having trouble with the show, Max. I'm not sure."

"Julie," Max urged, "there are things I haven't told you but I can now. I've got to talk to you."

"What do you mean—things?"

"I just haven't been honest with you, Julie. That isn't the way friends should be."

"No," Julian said, "it isn't. All right."

They met at the bar of an old Italian restaurant not far from the TV studio. Julian seemed wary, but when Max launched into his undercover work with Brady and Lang, described the millions he had carried, and brought him up to date, Julie's eyes grew wide.

"I thought," Julian said, with evident relief, "that you were into something, but I had no idea what it could be." He put an arm about Max's shoulder emotionally. "Max, my God, what you went through . . . just today." He clutched his friend. "And Evers—that bitch aborted the baby because she convinced herself it was damaged? That's murder." He was very shaken by the revelation.

"But we still don't know who killed Cy," Max said.

"No," Julian said, "but I'm glad it's cleared up between us."

"So am I," Max said and asked Julian to have dinner with Carol, Adeline, and himself. "You'll like her, Julie, but I don't think Adeline does, and it'll take some of the heat off me." Julian couldn't make dinner, however, and Max met the two woman at a small West Side restaurant, convinced he was in for a duel.

332

"We've been talking about thirties and forties things," Carol said. "It's fascinating."

"This girl didn't know there was ever a time without Social Security," Adeline commented. Max braced himself for the attack, since Carol was also in the "money business," but it never materialized. Instead, Adeline admitted, "She knows a lot about the capitalist system, and not from books, either." To Max's great surprise, the two women seemed to have a healthy, if wary, respect for each other. The dinner was very pleasant and only at its conclusion, when Adeline's decaf came, did she ask her son, "What happened today—that was all because of Cy's business, wasn't it?"

Max could only answer with a sigh and say, "Addie, it's complicated."

After dinner he took them back to Carol's, where Adeline insisted she could sleep on the sofa but Carol, equally stubborn, insisted she have the bedroom. At the doorway, when Max said goodnight, Adeline asked, "Did Cy ever know this girl?" Max told her he hadn't. "You're lucky," Adeline said. "Goodnight."

Max lingered only minutes after that. "She's not as strong as she pretends," he told Carol. "She went through a lot today."

"I know. I'll take off and kind of stay with her tomorrow, if you like, till she goes to that reunion."

Max kissed her gratefully, gently, and went back to Cy's.

He spent the next day wary and watchful and worried about Adeline. He called five times. Everything was fine. At the last call, he caught Adeline just before she left for the get-together.

"Is Carol going with you?"

"She is not yet that politically developed," Adeline huffed. "I don't need a baby-sitter. Good-bye."

"Wait a minute—when will you get back?"

"When I get back!"

He checked the air schedules, found a late plane leaving at ten o'clock for Florida, booked Adeline a ticket on that, and prayed that she wouldn't resist. He and Carol went for a quick dinner at a pizza joint and she related that his mother was a remarkable woman. They had spent the day in almost nonstop conversation. "She did most of the nonstop, though, I'll bet," Max said.

"No." Carol surprised him. "It was me. She was very interested."

At eight o'clock, just when Max was getting edgy, a mordant Adeline returned. It had been a ridiculous affair, of course. Seventeen grayheads rehashing their lives, catching up, promising to keep in touch. It had nothing to do with politics any longer except that Agnes's husband was still a fool and a few others still had stars in their eyes about socialism. She had stirred them up, argued with all of her old opponents, and had a Manhattan cocktail. Max could tell she'd had a wonderful time. "I've got you on the ten o'clock plane back home," he told her, and we'd better get going."

"Tonight?" Adeline was clearly dismayed.

"Adeline," Max said, "you have to go."

It took her a moment but she nodded and went to pack her things. Carol asked Max if she could go to the airport with them but Max thought it better if she didn't. When Adeline returned with her suitcase, Max took it from her and Carol fell silent. At the doorway, Adeline turned. "Thanks for everything."

"Yes," Max echoed, "thank you."

Carol nodded. She seemed to want to say something but didn't.

"Good-bye." Adeline leaned over, and, as though she had done it a hundred times before, kissed Carol on the cheek. Carol's eyes opened wide in surprise. "So come," Adeline called to her son and bustled out.

All the way to the airport and into the terminal, Adeline was unusually quiet. It was only as her flight was called that she looked at her son and said, "Max, yesterday we were so close to something terrible, I don't even want to think about it. I only want to know it's not going to happen again to you."

What could he say to that? Max thought. How could he reassure her?

"I like that girl," Adeline said suddenly. "She's in the real world, she's not la-de-dah. She's got sense." She put her arms about her son. "Take care, Max. Remember, I want grandchildren."

Max hugged his mother and let her go. Without a look back, she entered the passageway for her flight and, watching her disappear, watching the short legs in the sturdy shoes vanish, Max had a sense of loss and displacement.

Shaking that, he walked slowly toward the street and decided he owed Carol the word that Adeline was safely on her way.

"That's good," she said, hearing Max on the phone. "She's really something."

"Yes, she is." Max hesitated and then said, "Listen, is it too late to come back for a cup of coffee? I'll tell you some Adeline stories."

"No," Carol answered quickly. "Come on."

When Max arrived, she had the coffee ready and a cheesecake from the freezer. He found himself happy to see her but she seemed tense, and he wondered why she had asked him to come. He told her some of the old anarchist co-op tales, but her response was strangely strained and he thought he had made a mistake in coming and decided to leave. "It's getting late," he said.

They were sitting on the beige couch and Carol, shoeless, her legs tucked under her, said tremulously, "Oh, Max," and turned away from him, obviously distressed.

Puzzled, Max reached over. "Carol?"

Carol turned back, half crying, her arms reaching out. Max enfolded her, patted her. She raised her head and he bent down, his lips on hers. She clung as they embraced and Max felt the kiss move into him and through him, inducing a whirl of feelings, not just need but a complex of desire and protective instincts, of rushing blood and tenderness. Carol's lips were smooth, open, moved against his.

Suddenly, he broke from her, frightening Carol by the suddenness of his move, and stared at her, touching his mouth.

"Max?"

Max reached over and drew his finger across Carol's lower lip, then licked his finger.

"Jesus," he said slowly, shocked.

Carol sat up, confused. "Max, please."

"It's canteloupe," Max said accusingly. "It's Slickers—Slickers are on your lips."

"What?"

"Slickers," Max repeated in disbelief.

Carol shrank back, her eyes wide. "Please—Max."

Max moved away from her, feeling numb. "Slickers was the stuff on one of Cy's champagne glasses; the police found it there."

335

Carol's eyes closed. Her breathing quickened as though in pain. "It's not just a coincidence, is it?" Max pleaded. "Tell me the truth."

"Max . . ." Carol repeated, choking, "please . . ." Her expression betrayed her and Max knew then with the certainty of death.

"You were the one. You were in Cy's place that night."

"Max." Carol gulped air, her hands clenched beseechingly. "I was going to tell you . . . tonight . . . other times, I was going to tell you about it."

"You were there." Max's voice rose. "You were there when he died."

"No," Carol cried out, "I wasn't there when anything happened, Max. No, God no."

"But you were in Cy's apartment that night."

"Yes." Carol hung her head.

"Then what—what?"

"Give me a chance."

"You just lied, all along."

"I know." Carol looked back up, her eyes pleading. "I couldn't bring myself to say anything . . . to anybody, especially you." She wiped her eyes with the back of her hand defiantly, like a small, unrepentant girl.

Max's voice turned softer. "What happened?"

Carol pulled herself together with effort. "That Friday, I was at the bar having a drink with some people. So was he. I saw him looking at me. I looked back. He came over. He seemed so burned out, the fabulous Cy Bannerman. We talked. I'd seen him on the floor and heard so much about him." She held up momentarily, a hint of embarrassment in her eyes. "I went to his place—your place—for a drink. I was fascinated, I guess. He was so bright, you know, and funny, and he had this— energy—it burned like a light. I'd always noticed him but he'd never . . ."

She paused again.

"He opened a bottle of champagne. It got on a little and he called this Chinese restaurant to send some dinner. We talked about a million things. I talked too; it wasn't one-sided; it was a meeting, real people. I was so shocked. I remember I asked him why he was so tense. He laughed, that's all. Then he tried to . . ." She stopped, set herself, and continued. ". . . to make

336

love with me, but he couldn't." She waited. Max said nothing.

"It was no big deal." Carol took a deep breath. "He was very quiet after that and I left just ten minutes later. The doorman was snoozing, I remember, and I just walked past him and that was that except . . ."

She reached out a hand for Max. He withheld his and demanded urgently, "What—except for what?"

"When I," Carol faltered, "when I went out of his apartment and while I waited for the elevator, I heard a little noise and thought he had opened the door. He hadn't but I saw someone scooting around the hallway there, a man."

"A man?" Max leaped at that. "One man or two? Did you see two?"

"I just saw one."

"You're sure?"

"Yes."

"Is it possible there was another one hiding there and you just didn't see him?"

Carol thought a moment. "I don't know. I just saw the one. And he saw me. Because he ducked away. The elevator came just then and I jumped into it. He frightened me."

"What did he look like?"

Carol tried to recall. "I didn't see him well. He was in the shadows."

"You had some impression," Max urged. "Tall, short?"

"On the taller side—maybe."

"Come on. It's very important. What color was his hair? You could see that."

"Dark . . . brown or black, I'm not sure." Distressed, she added, "Max, I'm sorry."

"When you read Cy was dead, why didn't you go to the police?"

"I don't know. I didn't want people to know I'd been there, maybe, I'm not sure. When we met, I couldn't say anything to you, I just couldn't. Can you understand that?"

"Maybe," Max said. Had she seen the two men, he wondered, that Lang said had been sent, or had she seen someone else, someone who had actually killed Cy? Or, and he held his breath at the idea, had she done it—for whatever reason, a quarrel, a fear—pushed him over? As though she read his mind, Carol said simply, "Max—I'm not making this up. I had nothing to do with it. I felt sorry for Cy, and when I left he was sitting on his couch brooding. You'll have to believe that."

Max searched her eyes. "About this man— Could you identify him, recognize him if you saw him again?"

"Maybe. I'm not sure. You think he might have gone in and . . ?"

Max nodded. She had been there, she had been with Cy. It was a painful idea, somehow—and yet . . . He regarded her face, sorrowed and haunted. She was telling the truth, he knew. He sat up rigidly. Who had she seen? Suddenly tired, he closed his eyes and leaned back against the couch. Wordlessly, Carol edged over and rested her head against his shoulder. Her eyes closed. They sat that way for a long time.

Shamski was more interested than surprised when Max brought Carol to him. Many witnesses to an actual crime held back for one reason or another. He queried Max about her, had discreet checks made on her background.

"Well," he told Max, "this girl is a swinger."

"It's not that way," Max flared. "People talk a lot."

"You like her?" It was a point-blank question.

Startled into considering that, Max said, "I believe what she says happened."

"That isn't what I asked you."

"All right—my mother likes her," Max responded.

Shamski laughed. He took Carol back to Cy's apartment and had her reenact the moves of that night. Max, powerless to intervene, felt for her as she went through the rooms, step by step, explaining in a tight voice to Morrisey and the others what had occurred, including Cy's failure.

"I felt so—demeaned," she told Max later. Shamski also interrogated Carol deeply, wanting any detail she might recall. Carol tried—she invoked the image of the man again as best she could. This time she remembered a light suit, and seeing her, he had definitely been startled. She remembered him jumping away. "But let's face it," Shamski observed, "the guy could have had nothing to do with this but was coming out of his married sweetheart's place on the same floor."

"He was right near Cy's door," Max protested.

After all of this, Shamski conceded, Carol was probably telling the truth. And though it was the longest shot of all, he left Carol alone with endless books of mug shots—known hoodlums for hire. Her eyes grew bloodshot and weary but she recognized none of them. He showed her Lang's photo, but it was no one like that.

"She's no help," Shamski confided in Max, "unless we find the guy and she identifies, but without that . . ."

Julie Berns, however, was shocked and angered when he learned about Carol. "Who the hell is she?" he fumed.

Max tried to stem the tide. "She's not what you think."

"No? How do you know she didn't push Cy over?"

"She didn't." Max was firm. "But the man she saw . . ."

"She saw somebody she can't remember." Julian was scornful. "Could have been a woman in drag, a guy coming home late, anybody."

"He tried to hide from her."

"That's her impression."

They were in Julian's office. The TV monitor revealed Alloway having a tantrum on the set. "That bastard," Berns muttered.

Max was neither watching nor listening. In the silence Julian asked, "Hear anything more from the SEC guy who started all this?"

"Bobby Catalfo," Max said. "He'd kill for Barbara."

"He wouldn't do such a thing himself. He knows all the capos in town. He'd put out a contract . . . if anything."

"Liz Evers," Max said. "She hated Cy enough."

Julian considered that.

"She's a bitch, but would she go that far?"

Max told him then what had been in his mind all along, what had burrowed into his brain and taken tenacious hold. "Roy Herbert would." Julian looked at Max with disbelief. "I'm telling you he would," Max insisted, "and if he went himself . . ."

"Come on, Max, you're losing perspective. . . ."

"No. I believe Lang. Because things happened after they picked him up. Why did someone try to get at me through Adeline?"

"You're going overboard."

"No," Max declared. "Herbert's twisted enough to do all that and to have had some kind of showdown with Cy and . . . done it."

"You mean actually been the man this girl says she saw," Julian said derisively.

"She has to get a look at his face," Max said, picking up speed. "If she could see him, she might be able to identify him."

"Might," Julian said acidly. "That'll convict him."

"No." Max was not to be swayed. "But if she did, Shamski would take it seriously. You have pictures of Wall Street people on file. Get some of Herbert."

"If you want." Julian was unenthusiastic but Max was determined. He asked Carol if she had ever seen Roy Herbert on the floor, at the Exchange.

"I may have," she replied, "but I don't remember him."

"My friend Berns is getting you a picture. Then we'll see."

Berns's search revealed half a dozen photos of William Roy Herbert, but they all had been taken a few years back when he had worn a moustache and small beard. Viewing them, Carol turned them this way and that, but declared it impossible to know. The man she'd seen was clean-shaven.

Max then thought there must be a current videotape of a Alloway show in which Roy Herbert appeared. But he hadn't, Julian reported, for some time.

It was frustrating. Even an anonymous approach to the Herbert company's public-relations department produced only a glamorous retouched headshot that made Herbert look totally unlike himself but much like Robert Redford.

Forsaking pictures, Max tried to think of other ways Carol might spot Herbert. She waited, one day, across the street from his town house, but the one time he was there he went so swiftly from his limo to the door that she caught no glimpse of his face. She and Max went to lunch at Herbert's favorite restaurant and kept watch at his table, but he did not arrive. When, finally, Max went to Shamski, the response was what he feared.

"The man has done nothing illegal. He tried to make a business deal. You want me to put him in a lineup?"

"It's the same story, isn't it?" Max said. "He can get away with murder because of who he is."

"Hold it. I need more than just a notion of yours to do anything about this." More gently, he said, "I know you feel your partner died and there's more noise about the money deals but we're trying. This guy in a hall . . ." He shook his head.

How, Max thought, was there any way to do this? It became an obsession. A new idea struck him. He went downtown to the Exchange and found Luther Robinson. Over coffee at a tiny falafel restaurant around the corner run by Israelis, Max asked his favor.

"It's not crazy and it doesn't hurt anybody."

"I'm listening."

"Can you contact Roy Herbert and arrange to meet him someplace?"

"Then what?"

"Just that."

Robinson's eyebrows raised. "Just . . . meet him?"

"Yes. But it would have to be someplace open, someplace where someone can get a look at him."

"And nothing else?"

"No," Max said, "nothing else."

Robinson stirred his cup. "Well, I owe you. I'll try to set it up."

"If you do," Max said, "I'd be the one to owe you."

He told Carol what he was attempting and, in the night, in her bed, they held each other like two children in a storm.

22

At one o'clock the Chock Full O'Nuts on Broadway has a full counter; every fast-food emporium in the Wall Street district has a full counter. The steam and smoke of the food vendors who line Broadway with their "ethnic" snacks rises up from the carts to hover over the narrow, twisty old streets. The avenue teems with cheap merchandise, radios, batteries, umbrellas. It is more like a Middle Eastern *souk* than the most powerful financial center in the world.

Carol sat nervously at one end of the U-shaped counter, a cup of hot chocolate in front of her. She tried hard to relive the moment in the hallway, and struggled to bring the man's face into focus. Down the counter, Luther Robinson munched a doughnut and waited. Roberts had not told him who was supposed to get this look at the guy or why, and he checked the faces. No way of knowing. He hoped Herbert wouldn't go bananas when he learned there was no powder and no rock. It was possible. He had seen the guy go right up against a dealer he had taken him to when he didn't like what was happening.

The dealer had pulled a piece and split. Herbert was always on the edge, you could never tell with him, particularly if he was using a lot and his brain was half fried. Robinson checked the big wall clock. After one. He chewed on the doughnut thoughtfully and waited.

Carol's eyes went to the same clock. She avoided looking over to Robinson, who had been pointed out to her by Max, gulped the chocolate down, and ordered another.

At a quarter past one, Robinson balled up his paper napkin and held it tight. Rarely in the past had the man been late for a score. Was something wrong? Was this some kind of a setup?

At one twenty-five, Carol grew increasingly tense. She had been shooting covert glances at Robinson and seen no one stop near him. How long would he wait? She sipped the rest of her chocolate, and when the waitress put her check down, ordered a nutted cheese sandwich.

As each minute passed, Robinson became more and more convinced that something was wrong. With Roberts? He didn't think so, but Roy Herbert might, for whatever crazy reason, be trying to turn him in. He would give it a few more and then get out. He looked at the people around the counter again. Were any of them cops?

At twenty minutes of two on the big wall clock, Carol saw Robinson rise abruptly from his stool and walk swiftly to the exit. She watched him right out to the street, where, alone still, he cut skillfully across the traffic and disappeared from sight. Confused, yet relieved that she had not been put to the test, Carol paid and followed him out. She hurried, as planned, to a bench behind Trinity Church, where Max would be waiting.

Seeing her coming toward him, Max rose and met her expectantly. She blurted out, "Max, he never came."

Max's face fell. "You're sure?"

"I was watching Robinson all the time. No one came near him. Then he just left."

"What could have happened? Luther told me he'd be there."

"I don't know."

"Damn," Max exploded. He considered the possibility that Robinson had lied to him, but rejected that. He sank to the bench, defeated.

Max told Julian what had happened and he thought it was an idiotic attempt. He was concerned more with what Liz Evers had done with Cy's child. He wanted a measure of revenge.

344

"But Cy wasn't a hero there," Max observed. "We have to face that. He made the baby with her and then drove her to the wall."

Julian was defensive. "All we're hearing is her story. If Cy were here, he'd tell us his side. And so far as this girl goes, who she saw"—he waved that away—"it's not going to help anything." He waved a finger at Max solicitously. "And you look terrible. Go away someplace. Relax."

"There has to be some way for her to get a look at him," Max said. "There must be."

"I give up on you," Julian said.

That night Max had two dreams he remembered. One was about Sonya and Cy. They were in the woods near the pond she had shown him, in a boat, floating tranquilly. In this dream Max was not jealous, but happy at the sight. She was Cy's. They belonged together. He had been an intruder. The other dream was a nightmare vision of himself falling in space, down, down, terror freezing his veins. He woke up in a sweat, realizing that he had played out Cy's last horrifying minutes.

He stumbled out of bed and into the living room, fumbled the desk lamp on, and sat near it, dazed still. Why had Herbert not kept his date with Robinson? Had something simply come up? Was he suspicious? Was he planning some new move? It seemed like such a simple thing to get Carol a look at Herbert, yet . . .

He was on the Exchange floor as soon as it opened, searching for Luther Robinson. The traders on the rings were just beginning to shout and gesticulate, the tapes had just started their endless journey. He caught sight of his quarry and Carol at the same time. Robinson was checking a handful of slips and Carol was on the telephone. She saw Max, smiled, and was about to come over, but he waved her away and headed straight for Luther, who looked up at him in surprise. "Hi—how you doing?"

"Did you hear from Herbert?" Max asked quietly.

"Do we got to talk here?" Robinson was uncomfortable.

"Just tell me."

Robinson pretended to be writing as he muttered, "I called him. He told me he had this emergency thing and couldn't meet."

"Emergency about what?"

Robinson was getting more and more distressed. "He's on

345

some damn committee about this disco blowout and they needed him. That's what he said."

"Did you arrange something else?"

"Listen, I don't want to get involved no more. I don't want to get myself messed up."

"I understand but—"

"It ain't going to work." Robinson tried to control his agitation. "That Wall Street disco thing is day after tomorrow and he's on that goddamn committee, I told you. He's working with them all day.

"Wall Street disco?" Then Max remembered: the Space disco "Power Street" affair.

"We got to cool it," Robinson muttered. "I got a lot of stuff to do." He walked away rapidly.

Max cursed the luck and then suddenly sucked in his breath as he realized it was the other way, it was the opportunity he had sought. Repressing his excitement, he went to Carol at the phone bank and said, "We have a chance. At the Wall Street thing on Sunday. He'll be there. So will we."

"Oh, Max." Carol leaned against the booth.

Max tried to put her at ease. "It's all right. He has no way of knowing who you are."

"Unless he saw me somehow," Carol said, her voice quavering.

"I don't think so," Max said. "It'll be OK. Honestly."

Carol grimaced. "How's your dancing?"

"We'll find out." He wanted to reach out and touch her reassuringly but thought better of it. He left the Exchange, the excitement returning, and tried to plan ahead. If any trouble was to occur, what would he do, how would he handle it? He would give Shamski one last damn chance, he decided. He sped to the precinct and barged in on him. Shamski was with Borland, who had questions of his own for Max.

Referring to a computerized list, he said, "We've just completed an investigation. Are you aware that certain trades your firm had executed have all the earmarks of insider involvement?"

"I don't know what you're talking about," Max said, "and I couldn't care less."

"We care," Borland said. "The department cares. We don't go to great effort to track sales and companies for our own amusement. Insider trading destroys confidence in markets, destroys our reputation. We'll prosecute every case we can prove."

"You go ahead and do that," Max said. He turned to Shamski. "I want to speak to you—alone."

Shamski took Max into another room. "OK, Max," he sighed, "let's have it."

Max told him of his intentions and then said, "Carol's worried that he saw her and will recognize *her* at the club. It could be."

"Your Roy Herbert thing again."

Max flared, "It's your job to give us some protection."

"It's not my job to believe every screwball thing people come up with. There's nothing on Herbert, Max."

"You didn't believe Cy was killed in the first place," Max hurled at him. But it was useless; Shamski was firm. Fuming, Max left and went to find Julian Berns.

He located him in the TV-studio control room. On the floor, technicians were adjusting cameras and lights. The guests were sweating their makeup away. Alloway was rehearsing his ad-lib jokes.

"I can't talk to you now," Julian said. "I have a hundred problems to work out." He suddenly shouted to a woman at the console, "No shots of nervous feet or shaking hands. I want confidence shots today."

"Julian," Max said, "all I'm asking is that you come to that dumb party. Carol is scared. I want to be able to tell her she's going to be protected."

"I've never even met her," Julian grumbled.

"You will," Max urged.

Berns shouted again, "Why can't I see faces? Is Con Ed out of business? Light the faces." He turned back to Max. "Max, what's the point? I still think Cy was killed by these mob people. What's the difference who she saw outside his door?"

"Julie, it could be connected somehow."

"All right," Berns agreed grudgingly, "I'll go along for the ride." He turned away to complain again and when Max left, threw him an exasperated look.

Saturday passed in nervous anticipation. Max and Carol tried the Met, but the featured fourteenth-century icon exhibition did little to calm them. Sunday's sun papered over their agitation somewhat, but the day seemed to last forever. At nine o'clock that night Max paced the floor at Cy's. He had arranged to pick up Carol at ten, and they would go on, together. Julian would go by himself and keep a sharp eye on everything.

For the fifth time, Max looked in the mirror and adjusted his crooked bow tie. For the fifth time, the catch stuck.

"Goddammit!"

Calm down, he told himself. It was all nerves. He rushed to Cy's clothes closet. Tucked into the breast pocket of the Adolfo dinner jacket was his tie, a broad and jaunty one. Max snatched it, strung it around his collar, and rushed back to the mirror. Perfect. "You've come through for me, Cy," he muttered.

In the cab, holding Carol's hand with its sweaty palm, Max tried to be soothing. "It's not going to be a big thing. I'll point him out to you and you'll get a good long look. That's all that's going to happen."

"Yes." Carol's voice came out tiny.

"You look terrific," Max said. She wore a figure-hugging dress of silver that shimmered even in the darkness of the taxi. Her earrings were elegant jade teardrops and around her neck was a gold-and-onyx choker.

"You too. I like your tie."

Max smiled ruefully.

348

23

This night, Space's designers had outdone themselves. The vast two-tiered area had been transformed into a satirical, surrealist impression of finance. The first floor was made into a mock trading pit, with dancing in the center. Each ring was labeled with legends: BREAK THE BANK; MILLIONAIRES MADE HERE; TRADE, AMERICA, TRADE. The walls were alive with twenty big screens strung side to side, showing videotapes of money being churned out by the presses, brokers screaming at each other, brokers crying, people waving from yachts, lemmings going over a cliff into the sea below. It was three hundred and sixty degrees of visual cacophony repeated endlessly. From speakers strategically placed came subliminal trading cries and snatches of Lawrence Alloway's program intermingled with the strains of "The Stars and Stripes Forever." Coming into it was nightmarish.

Upstairs, the balcony had been made into replicas of trading offices with tickers, banks of phones, desks manned by life-size papier-mâché figures. Each office had its own legend. One read ARBITRAGE SHALL MAKE YOU FREE! Another was JUNKBONDS

AIN'T GARBAGE. A third stated TAKEOVER—AMERICA'S BEST BUY. On the walls here, giant ticker tapes moved, looking authentic, but careful examination revealed the prices and companies were anything but. It was Wall Street askew. Overriding all the other sounds was the music emerging from ten gigantic boxes wired to the rafters and pouring down their aural torrent onto the whirling, leaping dancers below. It was controlled by the DJ high up in a tier by himself, in a glass cage labeled for the night SEC.

"It's perfect," Max said.

Carol looked about at the hundreds of revelers, some dressed in evening clothes, others in wild getups. "How are you going to find anybody here?"

A trader from the Exchange came rushing by. "Max, isn't this great!" He saw who Max was with and winked knowingly.

"Schmuck," Max muttered.

"I see a couple of people I know over there," Carol said.

A new mass of dancers stormed the floor. Max suggested they go upstairs, where the view might be better. They took the escalator, which for this night had been labeled UPWARDLY MO-BILE, and ascended to the mock traders' booths. Here, on lounge chairs, onlookers watched, sipped drinks, flirted, exchanged cards. Some danced in the walkway and some made repeated trips to the Art Deco bathrooms, returning with renewed energy and dry throats.

From a vantage point on the balcony, Max searched the edges of the floor, looking unsuccessfully for Julian.

"Let's try another angle." Guiding Carol, he took her around to the other side. They were passing a booth at the corner when Max saw a bulky figure in a dark-blue suit and stopped abruptly. It was Catalfo. He was smoking a cigar and talking to a red-haired woman in a gold lamé dress. Max pulled Carol back and whispered in her ear, "That man there, the heavy one—can you get a look at his face?"

Carol asked quietly, "Is that him?"

"No. Someone else. But get a look at him. Just walk near there."

Carol swallowed hard. "If it's not him . . ."

"How do we know? It could be. Please."

Carol nodded, took a deep breath, and stepped back toward Catalfo's booth. As she approached, she heard him say, ". . . when I go, you just sit here, no matter what happens, you

350

understand me?" The woman nodded and Catalfo said grimly, "Soon."

Carol stopped and, pretending to examine her nails, looked at Catalfo from under lowered lids. She looked as long as she dared, then she hurried back to Max, who moved her away quickly and asked, "What do you think?"

"I don't think so," Carol said. "The man I saw wasn't that heavy and he was taller."

Max nodded. "Just a shot. That's Bobby Catalfo, the real estate developer, and I wonder what he's doing here." He turned to look down below again and caught a glimpse of Julian on the edges of the trading rings talking to a woman. "I see Julie," Max called, "over there, in the midnight-blue tux. Let's go back down to him. Maybe he's found out where Herbert is."

They were on their way to the escalator when a voice from a booth called, "Max!"

Max looked through the open door and saw Phil Carmody sitting alone, motioning for him to come over. "Just for a minute," Max told Carol and took her with him to the old man. Carmody, courtly, rose. Max shook his hand and introduced Carol, who knew his name. "This is one place I wouldn't expect you to be," Max said.

Carmody laughed. "Me neither. It's a benefit for something or other and my wife is out of town so I thought I'd come and see what the younger generation is up to." He put an arm over the papier-mâché figure. "And this is it."

"Have you seen Roy Herbert around?" Max tried to make it as innocuous-sounding as possible.

"Downstairs someplace, cavorting—you know Roy."

"Then he's definitely here?"

"It's his show, Max, of course he's here."

Carol drifted over to the rail, fascinated by the scene below. Carmody asked Max, "How are things?"

"Fair."

"Good. I have a special interest in your company, of course." He sighed, "That Cy, it's hard to forget him."

"I know," Max mumbled. "You helped him a lot." He wondered how long he had to stay and talk.

"Well, I tried." Carmody was openly sentimental. "I tried. Whenever I could, gave him clients, you know that."

"You did, yes." Max's eyes opened wide in reflex. For, just as a distant, distorted landscape is suddenly resolved by a lens, Max saw the truth clearly and was only surprised that he hadn't seen it before. He looked directly at Carmody in wonder. Carmody's eyebrows raised in question and Max said softly, but with total assurance, "You gave us the Morey's account, didn't you?"

A barely perceptible look of surprise shaded Carmody's eyes for a second. "Morey's . . . ? Morey's? That name doesn't strike a bell."

"I'll remind you," Max said evenly. "You recommended Cy to a man named Lang. Does that strike a bell?"

Carmody shrugged. "In a lifetime in this business, Max, you hear ten thousand names."

Max held him with his eyes. "This one is special."

Carmody smiled ironically. "Every one is special." He started to rise. "Well, time to circulate."

Max put a hand gently on Carmody's arm, forcing him down. "You knew from the start that Lang was drug money, didn't you?"

Carmody was startled. "What did you say?"

"Drug money," Max repeated. "You knew all about it."

Carmody pursed his lips. "Be careful, Max."

"You knew all about it," Max repeated, "but it didn't matter to you, did it?"

Carmody sank back into the chair and said, almost contemplatively, "Max, I know you're young and rash but it would be wise to be very, very careful."

"Did Cy know?" Max pursued. "Did you tell him right off?"

Carmody's face muscles started to work. He rose up again. "You have more nerve than brains, my friend."

"You didn't answer me."

"I don't have to! Who do you think you are?"

Carmody was on his feet now and the affable look had changed into diamond hardness. "You're a stupid, undeveloped boy. Don't talk money to me."

He started forward, but again Max put a hand on his arm. Pleadingly, he asked, "Tell me, please, did he know it was dirty money?"

Carmody pushed his hand away. "For Cy's sake, I'll tell you this. You don't ask questions about money. Does that get through to you? Money is its own thing. There is no such thing as good money or bad money. It's all money—and all money makes money. Everyone in this place knows that. Now, excuse me." He walked past Max, who remained staring at the open door.

Carol asked, "What was that?"

"Cy's teacher," Max said bitterly, "giving lessons." He shook it off. "Let's go down."

As they stepped off the escalator into the gyrating life on the floor, Max headed them toward where he'd seen Julian, but he was already somewhere else. The music down here was louder than it had been upstairs and pounded away. Spotlights began traversing the crowd, picking up individuals, caressing them, making them stars. The light held a couple of men nearby in dinner jackets. Max stared, surprised. Carol felt him hold up. "Max, what?" The light moved on. Max peered through the sudden shadow.

"What?" Carol repeated.

"Just come," Max said and pulled her toward the two people. They managed to move within a few feet of them when one turned in their direction and Carol breathed, "Max, it's a woman."

"It's Liz Evers," Max muttered. "If Julian sees her . . ."

Carol now saw that the tuxedo was not exactly a man's; the shirt was beautiful lace and the high heels on Liz Evers's feet could not be mistaken. But her hair had been cut short, artfully, and she looked masculine enough from a distance. She saw Max and looked at him stonily before saying something to her companion, who took her arm, and in seconds they were swallowed up. Carol looked after them in fascination. There were other women wearing men's garb on the floor but there was something distinctive about her, something familiar.

"Who is she, Max?"

"She was a . . . friend of Cy's." He saw Carol's look of concentration. "What is it?"

"I don't know." Carol shook her head. "I feel like I've seen her before someplace."

"Where would you see her?"

"I don't know."

Max thought a moment. Liz Evers, in her business life, wore her own adaptations of men's clothing—pants, jackets, ties. It was chic, in tune with the new wave of female executives.

"You recognize her?"

"I didn't say that."

Max put his head close to Carol's. "All right, it's crazy—but could you have seen her outside Cy's door, in slacks, a jacket, she wears them. Could you have mistaken her for a man?"

Carol was startled. "But why would she—"

"Just tell me if it's possible," Max interrupted.

"I can't say." Carol was at a loss. "Just that . . . I've seen her before. Max, would she have done that to Cy?"

"Yes," Max said, "and more."

The DJ's voice came crashing down upon them. "Hey there, all you Street people, hol' tight. Here's a big honcho with some hot tips." A light hit the DJ booth. Roy Herbert's voice came booming down.

"Good evening, good evening. Welcome to the ball. Happy you're all here to celebrate our industry and what it means to America. Bankers, brokers, and fund managers, lend me your ears. I won't charge you more than prime rate interest." There was laughter from the floor. "All I want to say is . . . have a great time."

"That's him," Max said excitedly. "Can you see him?"

Carol looked up. "Not really."

"He'll be coming down. We'll catch him."

The music started again, a vocal screaming, drumbeats thumping. Herbert disappeared from the window. Max saw a door on the far side with a silver star stenciled on it. "Over there." Taking Carol's hand securely, he pushed his way through the pressing horde of dancers and onto the dance floor. "Dance through."

He made vague dancelike movements, edging, as best he could, toward the door. Carol stepped out, her arms and hips going, her head tossing. It took a full five minutes before they reached the other side and Max, breathless, hoped they hadn't missed Herbert's emergence. "Let's wait here."

They stopped in a comparatively open spot near the starred door and waited. More minutes passed. Carol pressed Max's hand hard in worried anticipation. Max thought they had been too late but the door opened and two women burst out laughing. They were very young, with miniskirted bouffant dresses and masses of hair. Behind them came Roy Herbert, all charged up. "What a night," he shouted and started to dance like a mechanical man. The girls surrounded him, prancing and mimicking.

354

"Look at him, take a good look," Max urged.

Carol half-looked in Herbert's direction.

"It *is* him, isn't it?" Max felt the music pounding in his blood and his rage at Herbert grew.

"I . . . I can't be sure," Carol said.

"Try, try," Max insisted. "Look at him. Look at those eyes, at his nose, his hair. You *can* remember."

Herbert jerked and shook like a puppet on a string. He scooted this way and that and came almost face to face with Max. His movements slowed and ceased, though the women kept on dancing. His eyes narrowed. "What the hell are you doing here?"

Carol fell back. Max said, "You want to see my invitation?"

"It was a mistake." Herbert glanced at Carol. "What are you doing with a loser like this?" Carol took a step behind Max. The women paid no attention, dancing away. A sneer on his face, Herbert said to Max, "You're a joke, do you know that? One hundred percent joke around here."

"As big a joke as Southern Bird," Max said, "or Dennis Lang?"

Herbert was obviously startled.

"Or the kind of ribs you fed Barbara Stratton?"

A deep, angry flush suffused Herbert's face. Max goaded him further. He touched Carol's shoulder. "Was it a big joke to hide in Cy's hallway when you heard her come out?"

Carol flinched. Max said, "She saw you—saw you clearly."

Herbert glared balefully at Carol. "In your dreams? What are you on?" He turned to Max contemptuously. "You don't belong here. I should have you thrown out, but you're not worth the trouble." He started after the girls. "Hey—let's really get down." He danced away violently.

Carol watched him go with relief. "He's a horror."

"Yes," Max said anxiously, "but did you see any resemblance, any at all?"

"Maybe." Carol tried hard to recall. "He was tall like that but I can't be sure. I'm sorry, Max, I really am. Maybe if I think about it and see him where he's not moving around, but . . ."

Max sagged. "I feel dumb," he admitted. "Let's go sit down."

They went back upstairs, where the sound was lower, and found an empty booth. Max dropped into a lounge chair dejectedly. "I thought absolutely you'd recognize something about him."

"All I had was a quick look. . . . Oh." Carol's eyes opened wide.

"What?"

"I just remembered where I saw that woman . . . in *Ms.* magazine. They did a piece on women executives; she was in it."

"Oh Christ." Max was deflated. There was a sudden commotion down below and he looked over the rail to see what was happening. Off to one side of the dance floor he saw one man pummeling another viciously as the crowd scattered. Max peered and his mouth opened in surprise. It was Bobby Catalfo. His face contorted with rage, he was smashing at Roy Herbert with practiced fists and kicks. Herbert tried to dodge away but was ineffectual. His bloodied lips were screaming but the cries were drowned out by the music.

"That's why he came," Max shouted. "Looking for Herbert."

Two security guards rushed to the floor and Catalfo allowed himself to be escorted away. Herbert, knees sagging, dripping blood, was helped to a banquette, where Max lost sight of him. The music cracked out louder than ever and in seconds the dancers returned with unflagging spirits.

"Max?" Julian Berns, resplendent in midnight blue, poked his head in the doorway. "I've been looking all over for you."

"The same here." Max introduced his friend to Carol, then asked, "Did you see what just happened?"

Julian grinned. "It couldn't happen to a better man."

"But it's been a useless exercise. Carol can't really say."

"Not really," Carol said with a sense of failure. "I'm sorry."

Julian grimaced. "To make it worse, Alloway thinks we should have had a crew here taping it for the show. So what now?"

"I don't know." Max looked over to Carol. "You feel like staying?"

"Not really."

Julian concurred. "Let's get out."

"Right," Max said. "I'll do the gents' and we'll go. Be right back."

Max left and Julian looked down at the scene. Carol pushed aside the papier-mâché trader, who was listing, and sat in his place.

"You've known Max a long time."

"And Cy," Julian said. "I knew him first. We were in the Haight together, in San Francisco. That was a time. You wouldn't know. Max came later, but Cy was special."

As Berns talked nostalgically, Carol looked away from him, hardly listening, wishing that she was away from here, that the whole evening had never happened. When Julian faded back into her consciousness, nostalgia was gone, replaced by sadness. "When Cy died, it was like a piece of me going. Everything changed, everything. Those bastards, those sons of bitches."

Startled, Carol stared in wonder as his teeth clenched and his eyes flashed angrily. Berns moved away in agitation, the papier-mâché trader obscuring him momentarily, and Carol felt her breath leave her. Her entire body went weak. That face, his face; but how could it be? She tried to keep her composure but her lips had become parched, her throat dry. Julian stared at her. "What's wrong?"

"Nothing," Carol said, trying to control the quavering in her voice. "I wish Max would come back." She avoided Berns's eyes, those wide-apart eyes, that jaw. It was the face she had seen in the hall. A scream came up inside her. She fought it down.

Julian regarded her, puzzled. Then he took a step forward and despite herself, Carol stood up quickly, trembling. She told herself that she must be mistaken, this was Max's best friend. But she knew with a terrible certainty that his was the face she saw, the nose, the hair, the eyes—the concerned eyes. He had been in the hall.

"There is something wrong," Julian said.

"No." She could hardly get the word out.

"There is." A shadowed look came into Julian's eyes.

"I want to go," Carol said. "I'll wait downstairs."

"Wait a minute!" Julian kicked the booth door closed. "I know what you're thinking, but you're making a mistake."

"Please," Carol begged, "open the door."

Julian took a step forward. "Listen to what I have to say."

"Max!" Carol cried out and tried to slip past, but Julian's foot came out, tripping her. She started to fall, but recovered. Berns reached for her. She swung at him wildly, falling back, hitting his face. "Listen to me, listen to me," he said. His hands reached her throat and went around it. She felt the air cut off abruptly and the pounding in her ears became unbearable. She thrashed about and Berns's grip became tighter.

357

He had lost control of himself completely and squeezed with all his strength. With the last vestige of her own, Carol threw herself at Berns, her head smashed into his face, and his hands dropped away. Hurt, Carol managed to stagger toward the door as Berns fell back. She flung it open and lurched out into the walkway, where she stopped, dazed. Revelers, dancing, looked at her, amused.

"Help me," Carol pleaded.

Someone snickered. "She's fried." They ignored her. Behind her, Julian appeared in the doorway, his cheek bleeding. Breathless and terrified, Carol ran as fast as she could toward the escalator. Berns came after her, shouting, "Listen to me. Wait!"

Someone called derisively, "That must be real good shit!"

Carol reached the down escalator, everything in her hurting, crying out for Max. She heard a heavy thump behind her and saw that Berns had leaped aboard and was clumping down toward her. Holding the rail, she stumbled down the steep incline, slipping and catching her feet. A yard away from the floor, she jumped off, falling and recovering. In front of her was a thick crowd, and she pushed into them as best she could, trying desperately to lose herself.

She came face to face with a couple gyrating smoothly and went between them, crying, "Please . . . please . . . help me." The man stared at her, open-mouthed; the woman glared and pulled her partner away. Berns, only steps from them, bumped them as he came on.

"No!" Carol screamed.

"Listen to me!" Berns called in answer. His arms reached out and one of his hands caught Carol by the shoulder. He swung her toward him in what was almost an erratic dance movement and flung her back. She pushed at him but he came at her with his superior strength and they were lost in the crush of dancers. At that moment, with a suddenness that startled everyone around them, two men and a woman in evening dress charged into the midst of the melee, hurling people aside in their efforts to reach Carol. When they did, the men grabbed Berns expertly and pulled him away. The woman, holding Carol, said, "It's all right—we're police officers. Take it easy, honey."

Carol was uncomprehending at first. When she understood, she drooped into the woman's arms and the tears came. The music had stopped and there was an eerie silence. In that silence Carol heard Max's terrified shout. "CAROL!"

She looked up. Max was on the balcony, gripping the rail, horrified and unbelieving.

24

In the large interrogation room there was total silence. Outside, daylight had long since arrived, but here the darkness was broken only by the rays of a powerful bullet lamp that fell directly upon Julian's white and frightened face. He sat on a straight-backed wooden chair encircled by Shamski, Borland, Morrisey, and three other detectives. Against a wall, in the shadows, Max and Carol stood, clutching hands. Carol's throat had a red blotch where Berns's fingers had pressed. Max looked at Berns, still feeling the shock. When he had run down the escalator like a madman, Shamski himself, who had been waiting in a car outside the disco, appeared. He had sent people there because he had believed Max—but was not about to tell him, lest he blow it in some way. It hadn't quite worked out as he thought—but close, Shamski told himself, too damn close.

Berns had become wildly hysterical when handcuffs were placed on him. His wracking sobs had continued and grown till he required sedation at Bellevue Emergency. He had passed out then and fallen into a deep, troubled sleep, thrashing about and jerking in the hospital bed as the uniformed guard watched him nervously. Max had returned to the precinct with the police and waited, red-eyed, heartsick, and mystified for Berns to awake and be brought over. He urged Carol to leave, to go home, but she would not. The rest of the night had passed in a confused welter of coffee, pacing, dozing in chairs. At seven in the morning, Julian Berns opened his eyes. His police guard approached the bed instantly and hung over him. Seeing the uniform, a primeval, anguished groan issued from Julian's mouth.

Now he sat on the chair, arms about himself, rocking slightly back and forth, back and forth. Shamski, near him, asked gently, "Julie, what happened—what was it?"

Berns's answering voice was like a keening mourner's. It came in waves, flowing and ebbing, flowing and ebbing.

"The whole thing was the money . . . the money. All around me I saw men becoming millionaires . . . dumb, stupid men. I wanted what they had. They all had it—why shouldn't I? I couldn't do it just by jumping into the market, I knew that! But Cy could help me. He could do it for me. Through a . . . contact, I got inside information that the Marshall Tool Company was going to buy back the company, go private. It was hush-hush because the offer was going to be way over what the stock was selling for. I asked Cy to get as much of it as he could. . . . He knew it was an inside thing; but he did it for me." His voice dropped. "In the end . . . I made almost three hundred thousand."

Borland consulted a notebook. "Was that the trade Bannerman listed as the 'Dig Trade'?"

"Yes."

"Why that name?"

Berns's voice became a whisper. "It was short for—Digger."

"What's a Digger?" Shamski asked.

"Back in the Haight-Ashbury days, there were some of us who would scrounge up day-old bread and week-old vegetables. We would go to Golden Gate Park and cook for all the people who were hungry. Cy and I were both Diggers."

"That's a long way back," Shamski said.

"A long . . . long way."

"So you made an insider trade with Bannerman's help—then what?"

Berns took a deep breath. "I knew Cy was in some kind of trouble, I didn't know what. I was worried that the trade might come out. He told me it wouldn't, but I wanted to talk about it. He said to come up to his apartment. I went up to see him." His face twitched. "It was that Friday night. The doorman was busy with someone, and I went right up. I was in the hall on Cy's floor when the door opened suddenly and a girl, she—rushed out. I was nervous already and I didn't expect this. We looked at each other for a few seconds. Then she took the elevator down and I waited a few minutes. The next thing I knew I heard a scream coming from Cy's direction and shouting of some kind and this terrible kind of . . . thud."

He had been there, Max thought, right there in the hall when it happened. He looked at Carol, pained. She clutched his hand, held it tight.

"Then what?" Shamski was matter-of-fact. The tape recorder whirred.

"I started over to the door but I . . . I froze. I was paralyzed. I waited there, in the hall, for I don't know how long . . . maybe five minutes. Then I heard some other noises."

"From the apartment?"

"Not at first. There's a window in the hallway on that floor. It was open. You can hear things from the other terrace sometimes. And I heard . . ."

He faltered and Shamski pushed. "What did you hear?"

"I heard"—Berns's voice emerged from him with effort—"people climbing, scrambling from the other terrace. Then I heard them on Cy's side. I heard doors slam and footsteps and their voices."

"Could you make out what they were saying?"

"Only one thing . . . this man . . . laughing . . . and something about a wasted trip."

Shamski turned to look at Max with a subtle nod.

"I didn't understand, then." Berns's head dropped to his chest. "But I knew something . . . something. I ran away."

Shamski asked, "This girl got a look at you. How come you allowed her to see you again?"

"I never thought she'd know me. I wouldn't know her."

"What happened after that, when you found out Bannerman was dead?"

"I panicked. And when I learned that the SEC was moving in, I almost lost my mind. I know how they are. I knew they'd get the records and follow it all out and I'd be caught. They would take all my money and put me away. Three years, five years. I knew they would. I worried about the records. I worried about who Cy might have told anything to. I was going crazy. When I found out where Barbara Stratton had gone and that Max was there too, I just . . . I had this feeling that Cy had confided in her and that she was pulling Max into something against me. I went there in the morning, found where she lived, and that night, I called her. She said to come over and I did. We talked, had some food sent in, and I asked her if Cy ever talked to her about confidential things. She said it was none of my business and wanted me to go. I said I would. While I was putting on my jacket, she opened the drawer and took out some sleeping pills and took one, very cool, very calm. I asked her again about Cy. She said she knew a lot but it was her affair. I lost my head. I jumped at her and held her down. Then I saw the open bottle of pills. I . . ." He found it difficult to go on and looked at Shamski pleadingly.

"Keep going."

"I managed to force half the bottle down her throat." Berns lowered his eyes. "It was awful." She gagged and swallowed and then just . . . collapsed. I took off her clothes and put her into the bed and smoothed everything out. I was horrified, but it was already done. So I got out of there, took the night plane out, and tried to forget about it."

Max felt the vomit come up in his throat. He turned away from the light. Carol put her arm about his waist.

"You knew she was dead." Shamski was as impersonal as ever.

Berns's voice was low. "I told you I tried not to think about it."

"But you did."

"Yes."

"What about Singh?"

Berns shifted his weight in the chair. "When Max told me at first that there were no records, I knew there had to be. I worried that Singh was playing some kind of game. Then, when Max told me there *were* records and Singh had stashed them away, I panicked. I called on the telephone, but his wife told me he was away. I told her I was from the police and she told me where he'd gone and that he was getting something there. I knew immediately what it was. I went up to the mountains. I just wanted to look at the records. I met his car on the road and . . . we quarreled. I lost control again and I hit him with a wrench. Then I felt I was really in it and I got his car off the road, closed the windows, and started his engine. I found the disks and destroyed them."

Max was hit by a new wave of grief. Poor Jimmy, poor damned Jimmy, being so loyal to Cy and Whizkids, protecting, protecting. He stared at Berns as though he had never seen him before.

Shamski asked, "You kill anybody else?" It was gallows humor. Berns did not smile. Max slipped Carol's arm from his waist and moved three paces forward into the circle of light. He stared hard at Berns.

"Did you send a man with a gun after my mother?"

"No!" Berns paused. "Those weren't his . . . instructions."

"Weren't *what*? You sent him," Max raged. "You shit, you murdering liar." He surged forward, but Morrisey restrained him.

"In the men's room, at the restaurant," Berns said defensively, "I saw what was on you once—a wire and a microphone. I thought you were in with them, you were taping me, hoping to get something on me. I thought you were betraying me, Max. That drove me crazier than anything. Then, when you ran from your office when you got a call so I shouldn't hear what you were saying, I was sure." He knotted his hands. "Max, I'm so sorry. Max, I love you."

"You are crazy," Max said. "You are gone."

"He was not supposed to hurt you—just scare you. Max. Please believe me."

"Who was this creep?" Shamski asked.

"I asked . . . someone I know . . . for help and they sent him to me. I gave him five hundred. It was a mistake—I knew it then when I saw him, but I went ahead anyway. He was just supposed to warn you off, Max, to tell you that he would . . . hurt your mother . . . if you didn't. That's all he was supposed to do. Max, I was so scared."

"He could have killed them both," Shamski said quietly.

"I never meant it that way, never, no." Berns pulled at his dangling bow tie. He looked at Max. "I thought if you could do that to me . . . after you and Cy and I . . . after Cy and I . . . after Cy . . . after . . ." He burst into agonized tears, his body rocking back and forth. "Oh God," he wailed, "oh God."

Max turned and walked back to Carol, drained. Shamski said to him, "You're not needed here anymore." He opened the door and took Max and Carol out into the small dun-painted corridor. "Take him home."

In the cab, Max asked, "Would you come with me to . . . the apartment? I want to get some things."

Carol nodded.

"You're sure it's all right."

"Yes."

They fell moodily silent then and the driver's omnipresent radio invaded. The newscaster was in a state of controlled excitement. ". . . panic right from the opening bell this morning in the world's markets. At this moment, the New York Stock Exchange reports a loss in the Dow Jones average of over a hundred and fifty points and falling. Hundreds of millions of dollars in equity have already been wiped out. The commodity markets, too, are reeling. Investors are shell-shocked. No one knows where it will end. . . ." Max's eyes opened wide. He turned to Carol, speechless. Her eyes were as wide as his.

"Jesus!" The cabbie slammed his steering wheel viciously. He turned and shouted at them. "It's crashing—it's crashing. Jesus."

At Cy's building, Connor, the day doorman, face wreathed in despair, called to them as they passed him, "What's happening? Mr. Roberts, please, tell me what's happening? It's two hundred points down. I can't even get my broker on the phone." He rushed inside to the radio on his desk.

Once in the apartment, Max went into Cy's bedroom to change his clothes. Carol stayed in the living room and switched on the TV's financial-news channel. The tapes at the bottom moved swiftly. The commentator, young, good-looking, and contained, analyzed events calmly, a pathologist at a dissection.

". . . there are no buyers here, only sellers and already this plunge is being called Black Monday. Whether the reeling markets can recover any time soon is a question. . . ."

Carol shut the sound off. Max came to the bedroom doorway. "A blowoff."

"Yes," Carol said. "Twenty-nine."

"All that useless paper." Max felt strangely removed from it, someplace else. "There's one person who'll love this," he said. "Adeline." Carol didn't answer and he asked, "Are you OK?"

"OK," she called back, which was a lie. It had nothing to do with the tumultuous events happening downtown from which she, like Max, felt a great distance. It was the fact that she felt, now, distinctly uncomfortable on the couch in this place. The walls seemed to be closing in and the terrace railing, visible from where she was, had a brooding light cast on it.

"Maybe," Max called from the bedroom, "we ought to go to my place—what do you think?"

"If you like," Carol called back.

Max buttoned his shirt, and was attracted by the red glow-ing eye of the computer. He had neglected to shut it off last time. He went to it, hesitated, and sat down. He booted up the letter disk, searching for the words he had read, the words about friendship that Cy had written to Julie. He scrolled through files and suddenly a file appeared he had not seen before. It was part of Cy's journal. Max stared at the amber letters with fascination.

. . . the thing of it is that, sitting here on this third Friday of the month, the day the options run out, I realize that my own options have run out. I also realize that I have gone back on whatever I might have become to other men, to women, to myself. But the other was too strong. Power is—well—powerful. The best time of my life, probably, was with the Diggers. The one thing I'm glad of is that I managed to keep Max out of all this . . .

Max hunched over till his nose almost touched the screen and read again, "The one thing I'm glad of is that I managed to keep Max out of all this." He moved back, his eyes burning. Cy had kept him away deliberately, knowing how dangerous it could become. He had protected him, sheltered him. It took a moment before he could continue reading.

I am sitting here trying, really trying to look down the road but the problem is that I don't see any road. It's not self-hate, maybe, for a ten-cent analysis, self-disappointment. And then there is this thing of nowhere to move, having performed so badly. So, if you look at the curve, as the pundits like to say, it has only one place to go . . .

It ended abruptly, nothing following, the rest of the screen blank, unfinished. ". . . only one place to go . . ." Max stared at the words. The screen gripped him, held his stomach in a vise. ". . . only one place to go . . ." Though he fought against

367

it, Max experienced Cy's emptiness. ". . . only one place to go . . ." His breath came fast with Cy's fear. ". . . only one place to go . . ." Stricken, he saw Cy hurl himself against the railing with desperate resolve, crashing through and out and down and . . . He tore his eyes away to erase the vision. When it was gone, he sat quietly and looked over to the small but real Picasso on the wall over the dresser, to the photograph of the vineyard in the south of France that Cy had bought into. Then he looked back at the screen with trepidation, but the words were just words and, as he peered intently, he seemed to go right into the screen and beyond it, piercing the walls, shattering space. He felt flowing through him a strange sensation, a letting go. Later he would describe it as—being set free.

"Good-bye, Cy," he whispered and closed the computer for the last time. He packed a small suitcase swiftly and came back out into the living room. Carol, hearing him, stood. "Ready?"

"I'm ready."

Carol went first. Max was about to leave when he noticed that the silent TV was still on. There was a shot of the trading pits on the screen and closeups of frantic tape watchers, half mesmerized, half anguished. The ticker tapes themselves ran, as always, at the bottom of the screen inexorably, remorselessly.

Max shut off the set, closed the door, and went home.